Books for Freemasons.

Tales of Masonic Life.

By ROB MORRIS,

AUTHOR OF "CODE OF MASONIC LAW," "HISTORY OF FREEMASONRY IN KENTUCKY," "LIGHTS AND SHADOWS OF FREEMASONRY," ETC., AND COMPILER OF "THE UNIVERSAL MASONIC LIBRARY."

LOUISVILLE, KY:
MORRIS & MONSARRAT,
PUBLISHERS OF MASONIC LITERATURE.
1860.

STEREOTYPED AT THE FRANKLIN TYPE FOUNDERY, CINCINNATI, O.

TO HIS GRACE

THE DUKE OF ATHOL,

GRAND MASTER MASON OF SCOTLAND,

This Volume,

As a feeble acknowledgment of his fraternal courtesy to a dear and valued Brother, is respectfully

Dedicated.

Preface.

BUT little will be demanded in the form of prefatory remarks to a volume like this. To delineate *the practice* of Masonry is an end that can scarcely fail to command the good wishes of all who love the *Craft* or the *cause*. To do it in language simple and easily understood secures a wider range of readers, and, consequently, of usefulness. To select illustrations of an every-day character, will be most likely to awaken a spirit of emulation in the minds of readers: and these three ideas form the key to this little volume.

That the literature of Freemasonry is deficient in that department that professes to teach *theory* by *example*, may be seen at a glance at Masonic Bibliography. There are rich treasures of lore in its History. Its Philosophy has authors in abundance. Its Poetry has not been neglected. Even its Jurisprudence lifts up its head through several works of more or less merit. But in Tales, and Sketches, and Practical Illustrations, of the influence of Masonic sentiments upon the characters of men, there is a lamentable deficiency. The avidity with which such works as "The Lights and Shadows of Freemasonry," "Life in the Triangle," and "The Two Saint Johns," have been welcomed, is the best evidence that the Craft have felt this want, and it is an earnest of the welcome fondly anticipated for the present volume.

Contents.

PAGE

THE Widowed Sister's Lodge.. 1
The Right Eye—The Right Hand.. 9
The Good Man, True Man.. 18

Chapter I.. 18
Chapter II.. 32
Chapter III.. 50
Chapter IV.. 65

The Broken Column Unbroken.. 81
The Five Orders of Architecture in Brentford Lodge.............. 88

Brother Lemuel Fairfax, of the Tuscan Order.................... 88
Brother Frank Ashdod, of the Doric Order........................ 96
Brother Joseph Concoran, of the Ionic Order......................105
Brother Henry Evans, of the Corinthian Order......................113
Brother Bowling Fant, of the Composite Order......................122

Bob White and his Lectures.. 131
The Leak in the Lodge.. 139
Three Episodes in the Masonic History of Loring Hahded....... 146
The Peace-Maker.. 165
Brother Bauer from Berlin.. 175
The Badgered Witness.. 197
The Duel.. 201
Staying the Hands.. 207
The Tongue too Silent.. 221

CONTENTS.

PAGE

The Great Dedication Day of King Solomon's Temple........... 228

Chapter I.. 228

Chapter II.. 241

Chapter III.. 257

Chapter IV.. 272

A Night in the Lodge-Room.. 286

The Timely Warning.. 292

The Three Brothers.. 296

The Conquest of a Lady.. 302

Charity No Humbug.. 314

The Haunted Lodge.. 324

The Master Elect.. 340

TALES OF MASONIC LIFE.

The Widowed Sister's Lodge.

A TALE OF WOMAN'S DEVOTION.

Inscribed to Bro. John Augustus Williams,
PRESIDENT DAUGHTERS' COLLEGE, HARRODSBURG, KY.

THERE is much in the nomenclature of Masonic Lodges worthy of record. We have gathered up many curious statistics under this head. Many a noble deed is hidden under some lodge name, that, conveying no meaning to the uninformed, is significant, to those cognizant of the christening, of charity, fortitude, or undying truth. When the disciples were "first called *Christians* at Antioch," the christening was not a matter of popular interest—to the mass, indeed, the name must have fallen dead upon the ear; but to the enlightened, to those who knew the story of the miracles, the supper, the agony, the crucifixion, the resurrection, and the ascension, the name *Christian* recalled incidents dear as the apple's eye to the persecuted band; pregnant, more than any other word that the language contained, with mournful, triumphant, deathless interest.

"Jacob called the name of the place PENIEL; for I have seen God face to face," says the sacred record, "and my life is preserved." "Therefore was the name of it called GALEED and MISPAH; for he said, the LORD watch between me and thee when we are absent one from another." "He was afraid, and said, How dreadful is this place! this is none other but the house of God, and this is the gate of heaven. And he called the name of that place BETHEL." "He called that place BEERSHEBA, because there they sware both of them." "Abraham called the name of that place JEHOVAH-JIREH; and as it is said to this day, In the mount of the Lord it shall be seen." "He called the name of the well EZEK, because they strove with him." "He called the name of it REHOBOTH; and he said, For now the LORD hath made room for us, and we shall be fruitful in the land."

These Scriptures, like all others, are for our instruction; and surely there is an eminent propriety in entitling our lodges by names significant of God's gracious dealings with us. If we adopt those of living or deceased benefactors of the Order, let us use those only whose worthiness will reflect credit upon the system we profess to cultivate. Names so often in men's mouths should be *good* words.

Widowed Sister's Lodge was worthily named, as the reader will acknowledge, when he is advised of the circumstances from which the cognomen was derived. Mrs. Page is the honored widow of an honored Mason of the ancient stock. She is of that class of widows whom Paul credits with the epithet, "widows indeed," and describes as "trusting in God, and continuing in supplications and prayers night and day," and concerning whom Timothy was exhorted to give special honor. She is not over-burdened with the riches of this world; yet, by prudent foresight and management, she is enabled to keep her little family upon their inheritance—rising early and retiring late to secure this object.

Of this estimable widow it shall be said, in her funeral eulogy, in the words of the wise man: "When the ear heard her, then it blessed her; and when the eye saw her, then it gave witness to her:

"Because she delivered the poor that cried, and the fatherless, and him that had none to help him.

"The blessing of him that was ready to perish came upon her, and she caused the widow's heart to sing for joy.

"She was eyes to the blind, and feet was she to the lame.

"She was a mother to the poor."

After the hurricane of political excitement which grew out of the disappearance of William Morgan had in part subsided, and men began to breathe again with freedom the same atmosphere with Masons, the Craft in and about the village of Spafford gathered together to inquire, Shall we revive the lodge or not? Their temple was indeed in ruins; the Chaldeans had "broken down the wall of Jerusalem, and burnt all the palaces thereof with fire, and destroyed all the goodly vessels thereof." Their furniture, books, charter, everything that could identify them as a lodge, were scattered broadcast and lost. They had forgotten the work, forgotten the lectures, alas! in two instances, forgotten the *principles* of the institution which once they had solemnly vowed to cherish. But they retained, some of them at least, *the love of Masonry*, and remembered, with a keen relish, the employments and enjoyments they had once experienced in its exercise. And when a voice, as the voice of King Cyrus, was heard proclaiming, "Who is there among you of all God's people? the Lord his God be with him, and let him go up to Jerusalem;" a response, feeble but sincere, was heard from them, "Here I am! I will go up!"

But a survey of the existing obstacles chilled the zeal of these few, and appalled the remainder of the brethren to whom the project of re-organizing the lodge had been broached. The *expense* was great—a house, a charter, jewels, furniture—it was very great. The *trouble* was more; to visit intelligent Masons abroad; to commence again the very rudiments of Masonic instruction. But *the opposition* to be encountered, this was the worst of all. Ridicule might be anticipated from all that generation which had sprung up since last a Masonic procession was seen in the streets of Spafford. Annoyances of various sorts would, undoubtedly, be thrown in the way. The trash of antimasonic literature was in every house; and, vile and mendacious as it was, there were many men, otherwise of good estimation, who believed in it, and were influenced by it. But what matters this long array of objections which was presented before the little meeting of the brothers assembled in the parlor of Sister Page! They were sufficient to justify the conclusions to which the party came, "that the reinstatement of Masonry at Spafford, under the present untoward circumstances, was impracticable, and was for the present postponed."

The brothers, however, would not disperse until they had announced their decision to the good sister herself, and a messenger was sent to the door of her sitting-room to announce it. She came at their summons, leading by either hand a stout boy, stalwart lads, once the pride of the father as they were now the hopes of the mother. She listened, with downcast eye, to their statement of the obstacles which had deterred them from pursuing their desire, and answered not a word until the catalogue was complete. But then a change came over her face; her eye kindled with meaning as she directed it toward them. She arose with a dignity they had never seen her exhibit before; and, placing her two boys before her, thus began: "This is not what I looked for from the companions of my deceased husband. On his death-bed he charged me to prize, as one of my highest privileges, *my claims as a Mason's widow*. He said that these boys would never want a father while there was a Mason in the land, and that a Mason's Lodge was the widow's home!" From this startling exordium, she went on to make known, what was clearly evident to her mind, that without the establishment of a lodge, it was useless for men to profess themselves Masons; that all the benefits of the Order flow out of the lodge as the fountain; and that as her husband was buried at the hands of the Brethren in lodge assembled, so she hoped some day to see her sons initiated by the same body. In short, she pursued to its legitimate conclusions the argument, "that every Brother ought to belong to a lodge," and "that without the lodge there is no Masonry;" and she pressed it so earnestly home upon each of her hearers, that he could not resist it.

Perceiving, with a woman's tact, that she had convinced them as to the expediency of the effort, she proposed to furnish a vacant chamber in her dwelling, and to see to it that all necessary furniture and clothing were supplied for the work of the lodge. She offered—we have a copy of her letter before us as we write this—she offered to furnish the lodge gratuitously with refreshments, at every meeting, until they could do better; and that the public might not be deceived as to the respectability of the institution, she would march with the lodge in its first public procession, and *protect* it.

Of course she triumphed—of course the petition was prepared and signed that very night; forwarded to the nearest lodge for recommendation that week; sent to the Grand Master for approval that month; and returned *accepted* ere the moon waned. At the organization of the lodge, the subject of a *name* was agitated; but all suggestions and debates ceased when a Brother proposed "Widowed Sister's Lodge;" it was too good to admit of a moment's hesitation. The aprons were ready, made of white silk, furnished from her own old-fashioned wedding-dress! Her family Bible made the first Great Light—could a better be desired? The gavels and other implements were provided at her charge. An ample supper was ready at the close of the meeting, and she presided at the head of the table, with her little boys at her side. Her own domestic wine made the beverage in which the regular toasts and her own name, the best of all, were duly honored.

But the occasion of her public appearance *as a Mason,* is the most interesting part of our tale. Father Lawson, the oldest member of the lodge, died suddenly, yet not so suddenly but that he had time to request a Masonic burial. The Brethren hesitated. They were not quite prepared to meet the public eye. They referred the matter to Sister Page. She, good soul, unhesitatingly told them they were *bound* to obey a dying Mason's request—much *she* knew of the matter!—and declared her determination to go with them! The procession formed at Bro. Lawson's—the whole population of Spafford gathering together in doubting whether to laugh or applaud—and, true to her word, the resolute woman marched at its head! It must have been a moving spectacle to see the dear lady, dressed in deepest mourning-weeds, leading her little sons one by each hand, and walking the whole of that weary two miles in front of the Tyler! Many was the proffer from the gentlemen of the village to lend her a conveyance; many was the door opened to invite her in to pause and rest; but she refused all entreaties; was the first as well as the last at the grave; and joined, by permission of the Master, in casting clods of earth upon the coffin!

That day's exercises settled the question for all this generation as to the popularity of Masonry in Spafford. After that, there was no room for ridicule; for the thought of that devoted woman's adherence to the institution in its hour of adversity, incontinently banished it, or gave it a favorable turn. Men, who knew nothing of Masonry, admitted that it must be a good thing to deserve the support of so estimable a lady as Mrs. Page. The first effect of her devotedness was to bring in the adherence of many of the demitted Masons of the vicinity, who, from timidity probably, had stood thus far aloof; and this gave great additional strength to the lodge. Its second effect was to allure a few outsiders, whose parents, long ago, had taught them the value of Masonry as a social tie, and thus the temple was still further enlarged. The next thing was to nerve the Fraternity to a public procession, an address, a public dinner, and all that sort of thing; and when that was over, they felt strong enough, as Bro. Rakkoone somewhat lightly remarked, "to out-mouth His Satanic Majesty himself." Was not "Widowed Sister's Lodge" rightly named?

The Right Eye—The Right Hand.

A TALE OF FRATERNAL SACRIFICE.

Inscribed to R. W. Bro. Col. S. B. Campbell,
TORONTO, CANADA WEST.

HOW shall I describe the consternation—by what language we Brethren know prudently to use, can I depicture the alarm apparent in Spondylus Lodge, No. 19, at Peckville—you understand, reader, the name is a fictitious one—when the discovery was made that that old Mason, Bro. Lewis Shipman, by many years the senior, in age, of the other members, and long the Master of the lodge, had committed a certain act which cast him at once beyond the pale of Masonic forgiveness! No such signs of distress were ever seen in that lodge before. In all their trials, in all the troubles of the antimasonic warfare through which the members of No. 19 had passed with clean aprons, though many a token of despondency remains upon the records of the lodge, there was nothing comparable with this.

When a friendship of ordinary character is severed by word or act, and transformed into the coldness of ordinary acquaintance; when love, which once seemed perfect, is lost in satiety or the craving for novelty; when a favorable opinion is turned to the opposite pole of my doubt; the change, to the lover of good fellowship and social confidence, is painful enough; but when, as now, perfect confidence, which has had its entrance into the innermost chambers of the soul, unreserved affection with what train of blessings accompanies it, and that love that knows no rival, are, in an instant, changed to abhorrence and disgust, the scene becomes the most painful that can overshadow the checkered pavement styled human life. These were the signs manifest in Spondylus Lodge, No. 19, at Peckville, upon the occasion to which I have alluded.

Bro. Lewis Shipman was, in the best sense of the word, *the Right Eye, the Right Hand* of his lodge. Its angles had all been drawn by his hand; the horizontals of its foundation lines and the perpendiculars of its walls derived all their merits from his skill. What are all the regulations of the Masonic Institution unless there is a good head to control the lodge! In No. 19, were all the tokens of the clear vision and the steady muscle. Bro. Shipman had organized the lodge; had been its Master while working under dispensation; had been its first elective head. Save one term—a certain event precluding his service that year—he had been an officer, by the friendly persuasion of his brethren, ever since that period; and not once had he been absent from the Grand Lodge as their representative. Among that brotherly and dignified band, No. 19 was best known as "Bro. Shipman's Lodge."

All which, the instruction communicated in Spondylus Lodge, through an entire generation of members, bore the stamp of this intelligent and zealous man. Its grips were *his* grips; *his* rituals were its rituals, whereby we knew its lectures were the old lectures known by every one Mason of "auld lang syne" as "the lectures of Preston and Webb." His peculiar views of Masonic law, history and philosophy—you may know them by asking the veteran, Salem Town, who yet lives—were a law to his brethren at Peckville and surrounding places, who desired not to know any other system but Shipman's. In the dark days of Morgan and Miller, the Craft had clustered around *him* as their central column, well-proportioned, well-planted, and whatever he counseled, had adopted without opposition, hesitation, or debate. As in those days of gloom, so now in the light and hopeful times that have followed, whatever he advised was adopted, without debate, opposition, or hesitation. The finances, that fruitful source of quibbles and squabbles in affiliated societies, were managed under his directions without a question. The records were not only signed, but, in truth, drafted by him, or what is the same thing, under his personal supervision; for his secretary was taught, as a first duty, "to observe the Worshipful Master's will and pleasure." The by-laws and rules of the lodge were drafted by him alone. His mind, in short, had stamped itself indelibly upon every action of the lodge.

Nor would we be understood to imply that tyranny,

duplicity, dishonesty, or mismanagement had manifested itself the least in this one-man power of Bro. Shipman. Not so. The Grand Lodge, through its committee, had declared the records and the proceedings of Spondylus Lodge, its rules and by-laws, and its current legislation, "models of excellence," and "worthy of general imitation." In all that district, the presiding deputy "found no lodge which, in every particular, came so nearly up to an enlarged view of the Masonic theory as Spondylus Lodge at Peckville." Surrounding lodges made it their pattern of work, lectures, and discipline, and were largely gainers by so doing. Visiting Brethren went away delighted with the courtesy of their reception (though following upon the strictest, the severest, the most unrelenting examination), and the beauty, grace, and perfection of all that they saw. They carried the fame thereof into other lands, until Spondylus Lodge attained an enviable notoriety in these particulars. And in all these things Bro. Shipman was *the Right Eye, the Right Hand* of his lodge.

And we must add something still more to his credit. In all deeds of benevolence, in all interpositions of brotherly love, in counsel, in rebuke, in fraternal commendation, this man Shipman, the Master of Spondylus Lodge, shone pre-eminently conspicuous. He sought glory, he sought fame, but he sought it only for his lodge, even as our imperial Brother, the poor exile of Helena, had sought these things, in his days of fortune, for his beloved France. None could accuse him of indolence in the performance of any duty appertaining to his post. Under his guidance, Spondylus Lodge became a perennial fountain of charity. Widows remembered it in their prayers, and dropped grateful tears when it was named; orphans revered it as a thing awfully mysterious and divinely good. Its gavels rang sweet music in the ears of indigent applicants; and well they might, for rarely was its senior warden's pillar elevated, and its Bible spread open, but various calls were made upon its charities—calls that were not often rejected. And in all these Bro. Shipman, whose purse was the first to open, whose donations were the nearest the purpose desired, was *the Right Eye, the Right Hand*.

Alas! had Bro. Shipman but died during this happiest, this most useful, this most honorable period of his existence, what a memory had he left behind! what tears had bedewed his coffin! what reminiscences had the records of Spondylus Lodge and the hearts of its members retained of his virtue, knowledge, and zeal! how had his character shone as a mark to those who should follow him! There is no gift our Father gives us so directly and so permanently available to all our highest purposes as the character of a good Mason, dead.

But in the wisdom of him "who doeth all things well," Bro. Shipman was spared for the public exposure of his villainy, for the scandal of his lodge and the institution, and for the heartfelt anguish of those who had so long loved, followed and reverenced him. His crime, providentially detected, was exposed in a manner which admitted of no denial or dispute, and three witnesses became cognizant of all the facts of the case.

These three witnesses were all members of Spondylus Lodge, and stunned and confounded as they were at the knowledge they had so providentially come in possession of, they had discretion enough to bear it only to the lodge, to the lodge called by the senior warden as to a case of the sorest emergency, for the purpose of taking the matter into immediate consideration. To the bosom of that lodge, opened with prayer and solemn exhortations, this secret was confided, and then the members present set themselves earnestly to work to devise a plan of action suited to the occasion.

We shall not fear to furnish a handle for accusation to our bitterest opponents, if we confess that voices were heard there that night, which suggested, only *suggested*, that perhaps, under the circumstances, considering Bro. Shipman's long and meritorious services, considering that only the members of the lodge were aware of his guilt, and the immense scandal to the Order that would grow out of it, and the dreadful shock Spondylus Lodge would experience from giving publicity to the affair—that perhaps, possibly, it might be better *to keep the matter still.* To the credit of Spondylus Lodge, however, the proposition, if it could fairly be styled a proposition, met so inhospitable a reception, that its movers, in confusion, protested against its being considered any opinion of theirs, and the idea was instantly dropped.

Turning from that, we give with honest pride the

sentiments which *did* pervade those assembled hearts, and which, originating with Bro. Crystal, were finally adopted by a rising, unanimous vote:

"It can not be denied, my sorrowing fellow-members, that Bro. Shipman has been, in all respects, to human observation at least, our *Right Eye*, our *Right Hand*. He has so identified himself with all our deeds of a Masonic character, that *to think* of Masonry as it has operated around us is to think of Bro. Shipman. His hand has been the first to strew the evergreen and the clods over the remains of all who have been carried from this lodge to the grave. His foot has been the first to tread the threshold of want, and his contributions the first to relieve it. He has been our Wisdom and our Strength—yea, our Beauty likewise, for there was no comeliness we desired beside him."—A pause, emphatic with sobs from the entire group.

"The loss to us appears quite irreparable. So much as we have boasted before other lodges of our intelligent and enlightened Master, so much does his loss now afflict us. For me, I can devise no method by which this immense breach in our temple wall can be repaired. To undertake the heavy cares of the lodge, rendered to us all the heavier by the remarkable perfection of system to which Bro. Shipman has reduced them, and the perfect facility with which he performed them, who is equal to it?

"But what then, my brethren? Admitting, as all of us do and must do, that Bro. Shipman is *the Right Eye* and *the Right Hand* of this lodge, and that his loss to us is irreparable, is *our duty* rendered any the less plain? Nay, is not our duty the plainer and the more perceptible? Does it not, in fact, loom upon our vision in a gigantic figure from this very acknowledgment that it is *a hard duty?* Open, Bro. Chaplain, to that blessed Sermon on the Mount, given, as it would appear, for the use of just such a distressed, unhappy band as this, and read the twenty-ninth and thirtieth verses.

"*And if thy right eye offend thee, pluck it out and cast it from thee; for it is profitable for thee that one of thy members should perish, and not that thy whole body should be cast into hell. And if thy right hand offend thee, cut it off and cast it from thee; for it is profitable for thee that one of thy members should perish, and not that thy whole body should be cast into hell.*

"There, my brethren, is a succinct statement of *our duty.* 'Pluck it out, cut it off, and cast it from us.' Better that one of our members, though the most valued and cherished of all, should perish, than that we should falsify every principle of the Masonic system by retaining in our ranks one who is so egregiously unworthy of us."

And so thought they all. In due time, and by the due course of law—for it is a tedious and an embarrassing case thus to dispose of a Master—*the Right Hand, the Right Eye* was cast away. Amid a flood of public scandal it was effected. It afforded every possible facility, for awhile, to the tale-bearer and the antimason, and Freemasonry in Spondylus

Lodge languished under it. There was but little work offered for a considerable period, and for a more considerable period there was but little spirit in the lodge to do work.

But gradually public prejudice wore off. The immense sacrifice the lodge had made upon the altar of truth and justice won for them, in due time, the favor of the just and true. Hope revived in their hearts. They were aroused to industry by the very necessity of their position. Every available means of acquiring information were put into requisition. The immense vacancy formed by the abstraction of their Wisdom, Strength and Beauty was filled, though slowly and with difficulty. Each officer and member took it upon himself to learn his part, and that, too, a large part of Masonry. Masonic books and papers took their proper place as *teachers.* The visits of authorized lecturers were encouraged, and in due time they reaped the reward of their devotion.

How many lodges, beside Spondylus, have found themselves suddenly deprived of *their Right Hand, their Right Eye!* How many have been suddenly bereft by death! What then? Shall the Temple of Masonry fall, like that of Dagon, because some Samson is prostrate? Nay, verily. The lodge is made up of *men.* No eunuchs, no women, no persons of ill report, none of feeble intellect. All its membership is men, mentally, morally and physically perfect. Let such, then, in a contingency like this, bestir themselves up to repair the breach, and their present loss shall be their future and lasting gain.

The Good Man, True Man.

Inscribed to R. W. Bro. James S. Reeves, M.D.

OF McCONNELLSVILLE, OHIO.

CHAPTER I.

THERE were various causes, in the melancholy months and years of Antimasonry, why the minds of the loving Brotherhood were disposed to a mournful cast. Brother of the present generation, you will follow us through this disclosure and read them for yourself. Under any state of circumstances, the initiate must lament "the casting-down of the dwelling of God's name" to the ground; the lodge-room, once consecrated, can never, in the heart of its former denizens, be divested of all the mystery and sanctity that once possessed it. Its wood, its stone, its metals are ever afterward sacred in the esteem of the faithful Craftsman. But there were special reasons to grieve over the ruins made among the temples of Masonic devotion, when the strong arm of the enemy was unloosed upon them, and made the words of David seem real—a man was famous according as he had lifted up axes upon the thick trees.

For example, there was the scoff of the enemy, keen as a serpent's tooth to the mind of a Mason. Then were the prophecies of the timid fulfilled, and the fears of the coward, "for the days of the Institution are numbered!"; and the accomplished threats of the rejected and the expelled, two classes whose reasons for wrath against Masonry are indisputable; and worst of all, the sharp rebukes of conscience, that told how these evils *might have been remedied* had the Craft but put shoulder to shoulder when first threatened, and interlocked their shields, forming bulwarks that no foe ever penetrated—shields, I rede you, "of faith, and patience, and prayer," forged in the armories of God.

Freemasonry gains nothing by concealing the truth; our fathers, previous to the period named, had committed one serious error which brought its own penalty after it: *they threw open the portals of the lodge too widely.* The loaded camel passes not the needle's eye. What then? why either the loaded camel should be turned away from the gate, which may God grant! or *the larger gate*, a passway for the caravan be thrown open, which may God avert! By some infatuation, the temple-builders, prior to 1826, had broken down the barriers of ages, opened *the larger gate* and admitted the multitude. The story we give you, reader, shall carry nothing along with it but truth, though sometimes possibly offensive and unpalatable. Our fathers opened *the greater portals* as well as the *needle's eye*, and lo! the results will never be forgotten by those conversant with the history of that day. The evils remain in too many a lodge, the city gates *remain open* and the loaded camel continues to enter.

In such places Masonry fails to fulfill its mission as an exclusive, eclectic circle, surrounded by defensive armor; it becomes rather a moral hospital, into which men come expecting to be healed. It needs, oh! how it needs the Divine Visitor, with scourge of small cords, to enter the lodge as He once entered it, to cast out them that sell and buy therein, to overthrow the tables of the money-changers, and to remove all who make "the Father's House" a place of merchandise!

They who, by negligence and ignorance, sowed the wind, in the days of which we are writing, reaped the whirlwind. At the period mentioned, there began to be exhibited before the eye of the observer, a moral phenomenon—observe it with me now, kind reader—as difficult of satisfactory explanation with the lights then possessed, as the phenomena of the great pestilence which followed it, six years later. It has been well styled, *The Antimasonic Warfare*, and secondly, *The Sweep of Political Antimasonry*. That reckless politicians should grasp with avidity anything that promises them aggrandizement, is not the matter of surprise; it is that a large portion, or even a respectable portion of the community should have sustained them in efforts whose success could be achieved only in the ruin of the best Institution in the land—this it is which forms the standing wonder in American history. It is as if the Craftsmen at the building of King Solomon's Temple should have given in their adhesion in considerable numbers to an attempt of two or three ambitious spirits, there to build themselves up at the cost of whatever was venerable and truthful in the society whose affiliation they all enjoyed. Yet the evil may have been permitted, we suggest it in all reverence, by the Divine Master, that Masons be taught to put more trust in God. The plague was assuaged in Jerusalem ere the race of the faithful perished, and so not all the strength of the Craft was consumed ere "He arose to judgment to save the weak of the earth, Selah!"

It was during the fourth year of political Antimasonry, and the cloud had extended from the east of New York and New England to enshroud the skies of the more southern and western States. Those who have heard the sound of ax, hammer, or any tool of iron crashing against the ancient walls, can imagine the distress of those who apprehended, in its spread, the moral evils that had followed upon its first issuance. Brother Luther Otranto had started, one fair morning in February, from his residence in the vicinity of Lowbridge, to attend the Grand Lodge of the State as the representative of his lodge. The saddening influences to which we have referred were pressing upon his mind as he journeyed. His own lodge had yielded among the earliest, to the opposition of evil men, and one by one its members had fallen away until there was but a constitutional handful remaining. The blood had left the extremities to gather around the heart,—a heart yet sound, but beating faintly.

Not treason alone, but misfortune and cruel ingratitude had borne heavily upon the lodge. Their evils were an iliad. Two of the world's orphans, whom the Brethren had befriended and adopted and in good time enlightened by the light of Masonry, had betrayed them, joined the ranks of denunciation, and become foremost in opposition. Their treasurer, a man of years, of high standing in society, and of good worldly substance, had followed in the same path, had diverted the funds of the lodge from their legitimate channel, and refused to render an account for the act. By this blow the lodge was rendered bankrupt.* Its patriarch, Judge Lowers, than whom there was no one in the county who was abler to turn the current of opposition, was called suddenly from labor to refreshment, and as he went up for his reward, his Brethren were disconsolate indeed. How could a building stand thus assailed by storm, lightning and earthquake all together!

Bro. Otranto, the then present Master of "United Voice Lodge," and the subject of our tale, was scarcely the man for such stupendous opposition as this. His *zeal* truly was an abounding one; his *discretion* was that of the wise; but his *knowledge*, the link that unites zeal with discretion, and renders them subservient to the highest interests of Freemasonry, was unequal to the magnitude of the demand. His character was fashioned, not for the stormy age in which he lived, but for a quiet and prosperous day. Being one of those who value the adage of the an-

* When called upon by disinterested friends to explain his conduct, he said, "the Masons will only spend it for an evil purpose; they shall not have the opportunity."

cients, KNOW THYSELF, he had long sought to know his own defects, and had striven mightily to repair them. A liberal portion of his leisure he had given to Masonic studies, since the day his foot first trod the checkered pavement; but in his plan there proved to be a radical error, which rendered much of his labor nugatory. He studied to commit the work and lectures simply, unmindful of the lessons they taught, to the mind. Pursuing this method with all the zeal of an amateur and the perseverance of a devotee, he was notoriously proficient in that department. The *work*, erected by his hands, was well-constructed, well-polished; the *lectures* upon his tongue were smooth, eloquent, legitimate. United Voice Lodge was proud of her Master, and gave him such wages for his service as Brethren can give and Brethren can receive. Yet, in his hands, Masonry languished; the Brethren ceased, one by one, their connection, and remained without the door; the treasurer embezzled the funds; and, with little aid of fancy, one could have read upon the architrave MENE, MENE, TEKEL, UPHARSIN, engraven not with some iron tool, but with the finger of fate.

For why? Because the *spirit* of the whole was wanting. The work and lectures of Masonry are but its letters, its ceremonial law, which, like that of Moses, served as a casket to inclose the jewel of God's more precious promises. Its spirit lies in an exposition of its principles, its sublime tenets. Without these, Masonic teachings were dead as stones; without these, the system were as sounding brass or a tinkling cymbal; a tree without fruit; a specious deceit, all captivating, but sand-based and ready to be destroyed.

This, then, was the character, rough-hewed, of Luther Otranto, whom we find journeying, on the last day of winter, to seek, in the communion of the Grand Lodge, for that consolation which the circumstances surrounding the Craft at home failed to impart. It is a squared privilege of those dignified bodies, yclept Grand Lodges, to give such cheerful refreshment to worthy seekers.

The first three days of the journey passed with little incident. Called by sunset's dimness to a halt, it was at the first cabin by the roadside at which the request for a night's lodging was made, and most promptly was the call answered: "Alight, stranger, and come in." The fatigues of the many-numbered miles disposed the body to prompt slumber in the rustic bed to which it was consigned; a bountiful breakfast fortified it for another day; and so the traveler went on. About one hour past high twelve, he paused nigh some sweet stream flowing from nature's quarries hard by; and, unsaddling his horse, gave to both the shade and rest; whence they were seen to emerge, an hour later, recruited for the afternoon's task.

It was on the fourth day, as Brother Otranto was passing round the head of a deep ravine, where the road described a sharp curve, he was surprised to hear, a little distance in advance, a voice, raised to a loud key, singing some Masonic verses very popular at that period, and with a gusto as if the tall timbers around were a group of applauding hearers. The ode referred to the merits and virtues of that majestic column — felled, alas! by death — known among men as George Washington. The sentiments of the song, the correctness with which each technical word was enunciated, and the hearty manner with which the vocal organs co-operated with the prepared spirit in the melody, were evidences beyond dispute that the traveler through the forests that day was a Mason; for there is a peculiarity, an idiom, in every language not to be disguised by those to whom it is vernacular, nor counterfeited by those who are alien to it. There is this idiom likewise in the Masonic tongue, that although the cowan may even utter the same words of proof as the Craftsman, he can not make them appear as *vernacular.* Lebanon impressed its own image upon its cedars. Thus we say the secrets of Masonry were never exposed; as easily might a rogue exhibit before a public audience *how an honest man acts.*

Does the idea of a Masonic idiom, conveyed in the above sentence, appear to the unenlightened reader incredible? Nay, then, look at a mariner by sea, or, nearer home, at a skillful mechanic planing the wood, driving the nail, hewing the beam, shaping the iron. See him handle his tools. Can you handle them in the same way? Can you teach a third person to handle them mechanic-wise? Then lraw a just comparison, and believe that a Mason may tongue the words sacred to his calling in a style that none who *face the tyler* can possibly imitate.

By such evidences did Brother Otranto justly conceive that the traveler, who was enjoying with such gusto this image of "an old-time Freemason," was himself one who had seen the light and walked therein. So he went briskly up, and with true traveler's cheer hailed him, and proposed that they should journey together. The stranger, a strongly-built man of fifty and upward, dressed from head to foot, from hat to shoes, in home-made garb, as cheerfully assented, in the words, "With pleasure, Brother. I will go with you, on floats, to Joppa, and from thence, by land, to Jerusalem, if you ask it." And the acquaintance was at once formed.

A further examination proved his new friend to be emphatically a homespun native. The bright yellow dye of his garments had been extracted from the abundant sumac (*Rhus glabra*), and fixed by the cheap copperas; the heavy, coarse shoes were fashioned at his own fireside; his hat was the fabric of a neighboring artisan; his shirt spun, woven, sewed by the hands of his daughters, as were all his garments, completed the attire which originally grew from his own soil, and herded and tended by his own care. Many such are yet found in the remote settlements, but their number lessens every day, and the modern theory of division of labor will soon change their habits. The expertness of the widow's son* has few imitations and no equals in this age, and it is deemed a token of talent and skill to be expert in any one of those branches of which Hiram had mastered the whole. Rude as the stranger's covering was, there were marks of wisdom engraven on his face. A knowledge of human nature was not wanting in the comprehensive sweep which his eye took of the form of the new-comer; there was no evidence in him of the boorish simplicity that often accompanies the homespun coat.

In reply to a remark of Mr. Otranto, relative to the pleasure of companionship, he said: "Why, certainly, Brother, there is something to be gained by sociability on such a road as this, where the farms are ten miles apart, and not much to brag of, in the way of farming, at that. They give a man mighty little to see or think of. I reckon, by the way I was bawling out that ballad about Washington, that I was in lack of thought! I am not sure but you were right in that opinion."

"Whatever I thought about it," responded Mr. Otranto, "I was glad to hear a song that set up such a man in the place he deserves, and reminded me so forcibly of my present errand. I am on my way to the seat of government, to attend Grand Lodge."

"And I, sir," replied the stranger, "am journey-

* See 2d Chron. ii: 14: "He was skillful to work in gold and in silver, in brass, in iron, in stone, and in timber, in purple, in blue, and in fine linen, and in crimson; also, to grave any manner of graving, and to find out every device which could be put to him."

ing to the same place, as sheriff of the adjacent county, to render up my annual account, as required by law." "When I caught your words," pursued Brother Otranto, "so forcibly expressing the Masonic virtues of the last generation, I could but wish there were more grafts of the old stock now among us. But, sir, I painfully fear that the days of Masonic heroism are forever passed. The wooden mauls prepared for the builders' purpose seem to have worn out, so that even when we have selected and prepared our blocks they do not fit well in the building!"

"With all deference, sir, to your judgment," was the response, "I must dissent from your views. Within a few years past I have become acquainted with more instances of real heroism, more proofs of honest, unselfish, self-sacrificing devotion to our Institution than is elsewhere on record. In the present excitement against Masonry, you are of course aware of it, sir, the opposition in many quarters has erected a real standard of persecution, so that that which began in friendly persuasion is ending in sharp constraint. Yet there are thousands in the Temple who from its several parts declare they will continue their affiliation, and many who have been prompted by the very crisis, to take a more active participation in Masonic affairs than ever before, even though to do so, demands the sacrifice of houses, and brother and sister, and father and mother, and wife and children, and lands. Sir, this is true patriotism. Fitted with such principles these men are martyrs. While the sun was glowing brightly, it was a small thing to avow membership in our ranks; now it is the work of a hero, in moral exactness, that many do who work in Masonry. I saw such a case recently, you shall hear the particulars of it when we become better acquainted, and to my eye it had more the appearance of an incident like those with which the Book of Martyrs is filled, than an every-day fact. And when this murky cloud, being moved over our heads for divine purposes, shall have passed, and the Craft are called up to receive their wages earned through the burden and heat of the day, their handiwork all approved and their reward ready, you will see that the grafts of the old stock of which I was singing when you overtook me, yet abound among us, and that they have lost nothing of their hereditary worth." All this and more of such from so homespun an individual, led his companion to the conclusion to which the reader doubtless has arrived, that the speaker was familiar not alone with good Masonic work, but with the good Masonic language, in which the acts of the Supreme Architect of the Universe are moralized upon in Masons' lodges.

"But do you actually anticipate with confidence the removal of this cloud?" interrogated the earnest delegate; "and will it flit away in time to save the plants now languishing for the light and warmth of the sun?"

Nothing was ever more prophetic than that reply. "Sir, so sure as there is a God of truth and justice, who presides over the work of human hands, I do anticipate that time, and already I think the day of our redemption is nigh. In my own county, of which as sheriff, I am the executive officer, I see and converse with nearly every one of my fellow-citizens at least once a year, and in that locality I can testify to a happy change. Eighteen months ago there was a dead set made against my re-election because of my acknowledged attachment to Masonry, and my majority was reduced from several hundreds to less than fifty votes. In fact, the subject was so often and so insultingly thrown in my teeth, that I became a jest and by-word even with children. Brats of ten and twelve years of age screamed after me, as I passed,

> Yonder 's swearing Billy Payson,
> Swears whenever he meets a Mason!
> Say, why were you so foolish, Bill,
> To give away your honest will?

and you can hardly imagine how much the doggerel annoyed me. I can laugh now when I think of it, but 'twas neither a laughing nor a little matter then. 'Tis over now; the violence of the assault has ceased. Naked, open attacks have changed to surly, dogged opposition. My friends there, are getting good heart again, and were there an election to come off tomorrow, my late opponent would be grievously worsted. I find from others that this change is already occurring elsewhere, nor need we wonder at it. It is only where politics has been indissolubly wedded with Antimasonry, that Antimasons are active, and it would be contrary to the uniform teachings of history for a party to stand permanently upon such a platform. Sir, I am not clad in the mantle of an Elijah, but should you and I live to see another census taken, not a community can be pointed out in which a respectable majority of the citizens are linked to Antimasonry. I stake the experience of twenty years of active affiliation as a Mason upon this opinion." *

Thus conversing the companions rode onward. Short were the miles, and swift-winged the hours of the journey. A new and more glowing hope had been implanted in the breast of Mr. Otranto. In the place of despair, or at the best, resignation, he had imbibed a determination to assume an aggressive attitude, and lifting up the Masonic banner, now trailing in the dust, to advance against the foe, and even carry the war into their own country.

"For they intended evil against thee," aptly certifies the sweet Singer of Israel, "they intended evil against thee, they imagined a mischievous device which they are not able to perform; therefore shalt thou make them turn their back when thou shalt make ready thine arrows upon thy strings against the face of them."

---

* These were the expressions of one Masonic Brother, conveyed, in 1829, in a letter to another. How well these anticipations were fulfilled, history shows. It was not, however, any proof of prophetic impulse; the science of history has its rules, like those of the mathematics, fixed and reliable. By them, it may be seen, that no combination of evil men is permanent, and that no great political party can be sustained upon a merely negative principle.

CHAPTER II.

In this money-seeking, avaricious and bustling age, something is needed to awaken our *social feelings*, and put them into exercise. The ordinary topics in life fail in this. The excitements of politics and general intelligence, though they may affect our interests, opinions, or prejudices, afford us no sufficient grounds for this purpose; we can not permanently *unite* upon any one of them, and sustain a course of meetings so as to increase our *social* pleasures.

Religion would answer this purpose, were it not for the endless variety of opinions entertained respecting its leading doctrines; a fact which, as it renders it necessary for Christians to form *separate* churches, is fatal to any hope of mankind uniting upon it as a general *social system* or basis.

Under these circumstances, it is an exalted proof of God's goodness that we have a system free from all reasonable objections, perfect in all its parts, and harmonious in all its details; a system exceedingly ancient, exceedingly popular; in a green and flourishing state to-day; a system that has stood fiery trials and survived them; that has endured prosperity, yet retained its original simplicity; that comprehends enough of Christianity to instruct the Christian — enough of the religion of nature to attract the worldling; too costly to be within the profligate's means, yet cheap enough for the industrious; too intricate for the mentally stupid, yet sufficiently plain to the studious; full of ceremony to those who are attracted with rites and forms, yet presenting no ceremony without a direct allusion to solid and important things; mysterious in the extreme to the uninitiated—a system that its votaries call FREEMASONRY. We should bless God every day of our lives that he has permitted us such a treasure as this.

That which was wanting in other topics is found in this. Masonry has proved herself the best of *social* systems, and the mother of them all. However unreasonable it may appear to the cowan, however inexplicable to the initiate, even though the Masonic philosopher himself may not understand the full course of it, yet it is plain that Masonry *does* make its children love and respect one another; and *this* is the foundation of all sociability.

Independently of this native yearning for companionship, which lies deep in the heart of every one except a hermit, there is another inducement for becoming Masons that controls many. We allude to the desire, highly reasonable and proper in itself, to become acquainted with the mysteries that are in Masonry. It is this which attracts to our Fraternity so many lovers of wisdom. All sources of information are undergoing a rigid investigation; their true claims are being exposed; their false ones turned to ridicule.

Whenever we pass through a village, and observe

some upper room with the emblematic square and compass painted on its outer wall, it is easy to conceive a voice issuing thence, and proclaming, "Hither, Oh ye lovers of knowledge! mysteries are here explained to the minds of the wise and good."

The Masonic character of Luther Otranto had not exhibited the principles requisite for this latter branch of Masonry. With all his study and experience, he had not advanced a step beyond the position assigned him the night he was raised to the sublime degree. He had merely memorized the lectures, and acquired the work with mechanical precision. It was fortunate for him (it would be fortunate for thousands like him, it would be the re-modeling of all of us) that he overtook on his long journey such a man as William Payson, who, with all his homespun garb and manners, was the best traveled Mason in the State, and, had he had an education to display it, possessed talents that ranked him with a Marshall, a Livingston, or a Clinton, in a due appreciation of the system.

Every sentence uttered by this deeply-meditative man went to the heart of Mr. Otranto. He began to discover the defects in his own work. The light broke in upon his mind, ray by ray, and he saw, what many a ruler of the lodges might see, that much of the disaster which had befallen the Order at Lowbridge was attributable to his own ignorance. Masonry had not been made to appear the social thing it was. There had been no efforts made to make the lodge-room an interesting spot. There was nothing attracting in its looks; not an engraving on its walls; no library; no carpet upon the floor. It was simply a poorly-warmed, poorly-ventilated apartment in an upper story, with wooden benches, hard as an antimason's heart, naked, cheerless walls, dusty floors, and rude stations. In short, it was the reverse of the great Temple, whose magnificent appearance graced the meeting-place of its warm-hearted builders.

Such being the case, was it wonderful that the young members should prefer the seductive lyceum, or the thronged shelves of the library, or the decorated and social drawing-rooms of Lowbridge, to the cold and barren lodge-room?

But still more painful intelligence broke in upon his mind. He had not imparted that *knowledge* to the neophytes which was promised them before their initiation, and for which they had dispensed such a liberal pecuniary fee. He had practiced a kind of deception upon them. In the publications of Masonry, the manuals, the addresses, the charges, etc., the most glowing promises are made of high mysteries to be opened, useful instruction imparted, enduring affiliation secured. How had these assurances been fulfilled in *his* lodge? With what a scantiness of mysteries, a modicum of wisdom, a slackness of affiliation had his candidates been fed.

But Luther Otranto was a Mason in heart, and to know his error was to cast it off. High resolutions of future usefulness found root in the soil of his mind. He would procure books; he would study to apply the teachings of Masonry; he would commence a course of lectures soon as he returned home, which should lay the links of the Masonic chain together into one grand fetter, from which none of the membership should escape, or desire to escape; he would make the place of meetings a social, cheerful, desirable spot, where the heart might be enlivened and the mind enlightened. Without falling back upon the errors of our Masonic fathers, "of converting the hours of refreshment into hours of intemperance and excess," he would avoid the modern error, almost as injurious, of neglecting physical refreshment altogether, and the moments of recess should be made animated and mirthful with good fare and good music. Those who had cut themselves off from Masonic association through fear of the popular outcry, might go their ways in peace, but the ballot-box should forever bar their return. Those who remained should be encouraged by this new and better plan, to polish their Masonic links, and strengthen the entire chain. This would render the system more alluring to those who were without, and soon another class would be found upon the sacred floor, who should bring among them strength and beauty. Such were the resolves of his mind ere he had been two days in the company of the well-balanced sheriff, master of the work, explorer of the inner lore of Masonry.

Our state of existence is not merely a state of incoming wisdom; there is within it an *opportunity*, constantly recurring, of outgoing practice. The bond which had united the hearts of these two travelers, was soon to have its strength tested in an extraordinary manner.

It has been shown, in the preceding chapter, that Mr. Payson was wending his way to the seat of government, as the executive officer of the county of S——, to render up the annual statement of taxes. In those days it was incumbent for the sheriff to pay over the amount to the State treasurer in specie, and Mr. Payson was now bearing the large amount, principally in gold coin, which constituted the tax money of his county. While preparing to leave home, he had detailed two men to accompany him as guards, for the roads were unsafe, peculiarly so to a traveler freighted as he was. But by some strange accident, fully explained in the sequel, both the men had been taken violently ill the day before the intended departure, and at a time when it was too late to make further arrangements. The stout sheriff being well-armed, and expecting to fall in with Grand Lodge delegates upon the road, started alone, as we have seen.

A party of desperate men had awaited this opportunity to enrich themselves with his golden burden. The illness of the guards was the effect of stupefying medicines administered to them by one of the gang; and no sooner did they find that the sheriff had commenced his journey without company, than they followed him, well-mounted and prepared for the most desperate measures. Coming a few miles behind him, they had made a circuit by means of the country roads, and concealed themselves within a dense thicket in advance.

The circumstances of the attack were these: Mr. Payson had taken from his saddle-bags a copy of a monitor, just then getting into use in the West and South, and was pointing out to his fellow-traveler the distinction between the time-hallowed emblems which have come down to us from the days of Solomon, and even earlier, and those here introduced, with a singular disregard of our Grand Master St. John's injunctions (Revelation xxii: 18), by the author of the book. Like all the older Masons of his day, he was deprecating those exposures of our arcana on things movable, when his horse, whose bridle-rein had fallen loose upon his neck, suddenly started, stopped, snorted, and threw up his head with a violence that knocked the book far out of his master's hand, into the contiguous thicket.

This accident caused him to dismount, while Mr. Otranto rode on some fifty yards in advance. At the instant of his re-mounting, and while yet his body was swayed over the saddle recovering its equilibrium, the highwaymen, whom the horse, with his fine sense of sight and smell, had already discovered, rushed upon him. They were five in number, numerous enough to catch the horse by the head, to ward off the powerful blows of the sheriff, to knock the pistol from his hand ere yet he could level it at either of them, and to strike him by a cruel blow headlong from the saddle.

It was all the work of an instant. A moment

before, and his Mason-brother had seen him erect upon the ground, vigorous, eloquent, cheerful; now, as he turned to learn the cause of the alarm, he beheld the sheriff lying prostrate, a large spout of blood streaming from his head, and coloring the soil to a crimson hue. It was as a dream. Could this broken vessel be the strong and active man from whom he had just parted?

But his meditations were cut short by the movements of the robbers, who leveled their rifles toward him, and demanded an instant surrender, under pain of death. He glanced rapidly around him, and saw that there was indeed no alternative. Before him and on his right arose a steep hill, up which his horse could hardly be urged at a trot. On his left was the almost impassable thicket, terminated, as he could see through the leafless boughs, by a broad stream of water. In his rear the enemy cut off all hopes of retreat, and there lay his mangled Brother, helpless, in their midst. Did not duty demand that he should return to his relief? A bullet that whistled through the top of his hat decided his movement; he rode back, dismounted, and cheerfully gave up his horse to the robbers, asking only for good treatment.

Then there was no further delay on the part of the attacking company; but, as if their plans had been laid to meet every contingency, one rode to the top of the hill in front; another to a considerable distance in the rear, to guard against new-comers; while the rest tied with handkerchiefs the arms of the prisoners, and placed them across their horses' backs.

Within ten minutes from the close of that pleasant conference on Masonry, all was ready to bear the Brothers to captivity or death. Who should say what doom was in reserve for them at the hands of these ferocious men?

How truly it might have been declared of them as of David: "They cried, but there was none to save them, even unto the Lord, but he answered them not." Nevertheless, "the Lord was their helper," though they knew it not; and even now his spirit was operating upon the heart of at least one of these highwaymen, through the influences of Masonry, to save their lives, and restore them to their friends.

The reader will recollect that the halt made by the sheriff, which rendered him so easy a prey, was for the purpose of recovering the monitor, which had been thrown from his hand into the thicket. In drawing his pistol to defend himself, he had again let the book fall, and it had been picked up by the robbers as an object of curiosity. Among the five was one to whom the well-known language of the book spoke in trumpet-tones of warning, of entreaty, of reproach.

While assisting to fasten the limbs of Mr. Otranto, these words, on which his eyes had fallen, came into his mind, "*to your neighbor, in acting upon the square, and doing unto him as you wish he should do unto you.*" In the act of throwing the insensible body of the sheriff upon his horse, this thought, which had been planted in his heart years before, caused him to handle that bleeding head more tenderly, and to dispose of those lithe members more kindly; for though a Mason is never to shut his ear unkindly against the complaints of any of the human race, yet when a Brother is oppressed or suffers, he is in a more peculiar manner called to open his whole soul in love and compassion to him, and to relieve him, without prejudice, according to his capacity. No opportunity of communicating his sympathy was afforded at this time; but a partial determination came over his mind, undefined, yet promising that he would do some kindness to them—he scarcely knew what.

And let it not too much astonish the unenlightened reader that this man, a robber among robbers, engaged in the most desperate act punished by our laws, should have been in possession of Masonic light, or, at the suggestion of a Masonic book, should have brought his mind to such a brotherly determination. Above all things, let no doubt as to the veracity of this tale enter the reader's heart, for we are telling that which we do surely *know* to be true.

That there is many a bad man in the ranks of Masonry, has always been admitted. Why should we be ashamed of it? Is there any association in the world into which hypocrites are not affiliated? Is there any congregation under God's eye where they are not found? Only one, that of the glorified saints in heaven. There *the heart* is read, and no room is left for deceit.

Masons can not read the heart, save through the life. They have but the ordinary rule of humanity, "to judge the tree by its fruits." If the past life has been good, the lodge feels safe in receiving the applicant; for it has a double assurance in reference to the candidate—his own history, and the force of Masonic obligation and instruction. If a man who has been uniformly temperate, brave, prudent, and honest all his life, guided only by the ordinary rules of morality and his early education, can not be enchained to Brotherly Love, Relief and Truth by the powerful fetters of Masonry, there must be something radically defective in his character, which demands more than a mortal's eye to detect. It is no discredit to Masonry that such a man is allowed to affiliate with this Fraternity. It is to the praise of the Order that such material is so generally cast out when the defect becomes evident.

The person of whom we are speaking was known among his companions by the title of Major. What was his real name, the name by which his mother claimed him and the lodge enrolled him, is known only to the Searcher of hearts. In his youth he had been distinguished for his boldness in speaking the truth, coupled with an extraordinary propensity for mischief. This singular contradiction in his character led to these results: that whatever amount of lawlessness he may have perpetrated, he would ingenuously admit the whole on being questioned, and patiently suffer the allotted punishment.

On coming of age, he had applied to the Masonic lodge for initiation, and been promptly blackballed. Waiting a twelvemonth, in accordance with the usual and sound practice of American lodges, he had, nothing daunted, made a second effort, and succeeded in obtaining the first degree; but he was stopped two years on the second, and only obtained the third by a manifest improvement in his life and habits. Although he had become a participant in lodge privileges, yet the uncontrollable spirit manifested in his youth prevented that full confidence which Brethren should repose in one another from being awarded him; and when, in an accidental difficulty that occurred between him and a hired servant, he struck an unintentional blow which resulted in death, scarcely the usual indulgence was allowed him on trial, but he was declared expelled without a dissentient voice. Then he left the country, and became a wanderer. Imbittered against all the world, outlawed for his constitutional irritability, debarred the usual courtesies of one under Masonic charges, he became hardened, lost the fine sense of veracity he formerly possessed, and turned his hand to make a living by unlawful means. Such was the history of Major, as he afterward communicated it to a Masonic ear. In it we see room for two species of application. The Brethren should not have initiated one to whom the use of the *compass* was so difficult; but having raised him, in spite of the weaknesses of his character, to their highest grade, they should have been more lenient to the ebullitions of his spirit, and not pressed his case to such an extremity.*

---

* It is not too much to say that if a lodge receives an applicant who is notoriously faulty, they are bound in common honesty

The reader has seen how Major came to be made a Mason; and now, if he, the reader, is not a Mason, he will wish to learn how this robber, expelled from Masonry, living under an assumed name, at war with society, and cut off from all association with the wise and good, should still feel under the control of Masonic obligations. The answer is ready. Masonic obligations are indissoluble. Expulsion from Masonry, although it casts the member out of the pale of Masonic charity, weakens no tie in him, releases him from no engagement into which he entered toward the Order. This is expressly stipulated at his making. *Once a Mason always a Mason*, is the rule, and no one can escape it. Truth to say, expelled members are not usually anxious to escape it. In the majority of cases that have come under our knowledge, there is more anxiety to pave the way, by kindnesses to Masons and attentions to the proprieties of Masonry, for a return into the Order, than there is to repudiate the solemn pledges made upon their first admission.

Such, likewise, was the case with Major; and the sight of that book, so opportunely presented to his eye, called up vivid memories that were likely to lead to valuable results. And so let us carry on the thread of our incidents.

A short conference among the highwaymen was closed by an order from the leader, a small, active individual, whose strength of arm had been displayed in the cruel blow under which the sheriff still lay

---

to make allowance for the fault, and bear with it in patience. This applies to defects of both mind and body.

insensible. The company closed around the two prisoners, and continuing their sentinels a few hundred yards in advance and in the rear, they rode at a brisk trot for a mile, on the same road the two travelers had just passed over. At a small bridle-path they turned aside from the main track, and then, in single file, pursued their way over that hilly country, until the darkness of night concealed the trace. A halt was then made; the horses were hobbled, and turned out to graze; the captives fastened securely to saplings, but allowed the use of their hands; and the unfortunate sheriff, who had returned to his senses to find himself jolting as a dead pack upon the back of a hard-trotting horse, was allowed the refreshment of cold water to his aching head, dispensed at the hands of Major. A plentiful meal, though rude, was then produced from the wallets of the robbers, and a fair portion bestowed upon the two companions. This being over, a caution was given them to make no attempt at escape, under penalty of instant death; after which the party drew aside a short distance, and entered into a consultation relative to the disposal of the prisoners.

As no negative had been placed upon their conversing with each other, the opportunity was not lost to communicate that mutual sympathy which their situation so much demanded.

How well has the wise man expressed himself: "Iron sharpeneth iron; so a man sharpeneth the face of his friend!" There was no *hope* in the mind of either; for the very necessity into which the robbers had plunged themselves by this desperate act demanded *murder.* Yet the friendly grip of the hand brought warmth to the hearts of both. The glance of the eye, as seen by the log-fire before them, was a gleam of comfort, and the words of the stout-hearted sheriff communicated a glow of resignation to the hearer.

"An end, dear Brother, to all speculation relative to human destiny, will soon be made known to us. The emblems we have studied, the half-glances we have had into the mystery of life and death, the Masonic types relative to something beyond the boundary of time, will soon be cleared up, and *the true light* we have so long sought, and received only in broken rays, will be given us in great abundance. Have patience, Brother, and endure as one whose hope is fixed. What man is he that liveth and shall not see death? If we have been wise, we have long awaited the summons, and if it be now nigh at hand, shall we not be prepared? Our approaching fate can only terrify us according as we have neglected past duties, and missed the great aim of our existence. Wherein we have been faithful, we may rejoice that our reward is so soon to come!"

"What conjectures there will be among our friends! What opinions concerning our fate! What useless search for our remains! Our wives will long refuse to admit their widowhood—our children their orphanage. Our Brethren will be slow to admit our names upon the dead man's roll—long hesitate to give a Masonic funeral service to our memory."

"Were such a fear worthy to find place in the mind of a dying Christian Mason, it would add bitterness to my cup, at this hour, that my disappearance is connected with the loss to the State of so large an amount of money. Such an opportunity of traducing Masonry, through my disappearance, will not be neglected by the enemies of light. But what of that? When our Divine pattern was traduced in all his actions as a knave and an impostor, what matters a word here or a slander there, if only God knows the truth! Such doubts shall not perplex me, dear Brother; such fears shall not terrify me. I see that the conference between yonder ruffians is breaking up. Their conclusions as to our fate may be easily foretold. Brother, this misfortune has befallen you for being in my company; it was not *you* they sought. Forgive me, my friend, for this fate that I have so unwillingly brought upon you."

The hand-grasp that answered this appeal indicated the spirit in which it was received. Then, as the debate, whatever it was, which had been going on among the highwaymen was closing, and one of the party was approaching the place where they sat, bound face to face, the Master of "United Voice Lodge" requested the pious sheriff to offer up a closing prayer. It required but an instant for one who, like Daniel, was accustomed to pray three times every day, to gather up his sacrifice, and offer it there upon the altar of the Lord. It consisted in a heartfelt consecration of body and soul to Him who had given both; it was a sincere humiliation of spirit, in view of sins of omission and commission; it contained a request like that of the dying Stephen, who entreated pardon for his murderers; it concluded with a triumphant claim to heaven's glories, through the merits of Him in whom all may be saved

Oh! there are occasions which justify the assertion of the son of David: "It is better to go to the house of mourning than to go to the house of feasting: the heart of the wise is in the house of mourning." For there are times when from the house of mourning comes out a voice so heaven-toned and heaven-directed, that we are constrained to declare with Jacob, "this is no other but the house of God, and this the gate of heaven!" Such occasions are indulgences to those who have wisdom to use them, and even to the ignorantly vicious; even to such a one as he who had detached himself from the conference, and was leaning upon a tree by their side, while the sheriff prayed; though there was no tone of triumph in such prayer, there was a marked tone of *warning.* It said, *where these and such as these are found, in the spirit-world, you can have no place.*

The prayer ended, the sheriff asked, in a firm voice, "What is your message?" The answer was a significant gesture to the rifle in his hand. "And this man—this man who was only by accident in my company—assuredly he need not die?" A second gesture like the former settled that inquiry, while from the group, who were still at a distance, but within hearing, came the hoarse murmur, which has conveyed the pirate's sentiment in all ages, "Dead men tell no tales!"

Oh, what an error is this! No tales? The dead speechless? The grave without a voice? Of all the mistakes that erring mortals have labored under, this is the most serious, that "dead men tell no tales." Who is it, then, that speak through the murderer's *fear* by day, and his *terror* by night? Who harrows up his conscience, and conjures up the phantoms that pursue him, until he dare not look over his own shoulder, for fear of the shadow that is following? Who is it paints with crimson every green leaf, and fills with a groan or a scream every sweet concord? It is *the dead*, with the dismal tale it is ever telling! There was never a grave dug to receive the mangled remains of the murdered, but what, to the murderer's eye, it was as conspicuous as "a city set upon a hill, that can not be hid." There was never a dead body so concealed by the ruffian's hand, but what some green thing, some *evergreen* thing, would plant itself at the head, and divulge the fatal secret. Ah! the murdered dead rest uneasily. They will not lie alone. They move within their narrow tenements, and extend their sinewy arms, and slumber not in peace until the murderer is cast out of the gate, and put to confession and to death, and laid by their side.

"But," said the hoarse murmur from the ruffianly group, "dead men tell no tales. Kill them both."

Then spoke up the sheriff: "We commend ourselves, Father of Mercies, into thy hands. Cruel men, we submit to our fate, but God grant that, in the day of retribution, this sin likewise may be forgiven you! Our only demand is, that you transmit to our families, by some means or other, a knowledge of our fate. Give us this assurance, and we will die in peace."

CHAPTER III.

It came in our way to mention, in the last chapter, that Mr. Payson, the sheriff, whose pious resignation signalized the termination of that part of the history, had detailed several friends to accompany him, in the capacity of guards, but that a sudden and inscrutable attack of sickness had detained them. This sickness had met them within a few hours of their contemplated departure, too late for the sheriff to secure other help.

It was, perhaps, scarcely prudent in him to commence his journey alone; but human nature is rarely balanced. Those who do to others as they would be done by, look to the world with a touching confidence for reciprocal treatment. Those who have JUSTICE have FORTITUDE, but not always PRUDENCE. The sheriff would not have met the requirements of a Fouché or a Hays in this particular, although by odds the best executive officer his county had ever elected.

Be that as it may, it so happened—*by chance* many a practical atheist would term it—that a couple of friends called at his house, on urgent business, the evening of the day of his departure.

One of them, Mr. Legraph, was the possessor of that one of the cardinal virtues which the sheriff seemed defective in—we mean PRUDENCE; and he had it in such profusion as to leave but little room in his rather diminutive head for the others. He was altogether a man of caution. He spoke mainly in whispers; looked carefully over his shoulder when about to communicate intelligence of the most trivial character; and so fearful was he of divulging the secrets of Masonry, that *he learned as few of them as possible*, for fear that his better-half might somehow worm them out of his slumbers. We need not add that his Brethren made him treasurer of his lodge, or that he looked upon THE KEY in its old symbolic sense—for which see Oliver's Landmarks—and governed himself accordingly.

Brother Legraph was a character, in his way, that, did time permit, should have a larger space. Were it not that human nature has more contradictions than all the metaphysicians, from Brother Dugald Stewart down to Wayland, have developed, we should say that he possessed two characters in one; and that they were timidity in language, and boldness in execution. There was every token of cowardice in his faltering tongue and restless eye, but the very Lion of Numidia was not more earnest in carrying out a plan. For a pabulum to his prudence, he had collected these Scripture passages relative to that "rascally" virtue, as General Lee called it:* "See that ye walk circumspectly. The wise in heart shall be called prudent. The wisdom of the prudent is to understand his way. He that hath knowledge spareth his words. A prudent man concealeth knowledge. The heart of the righteous studieth to answer; but the mouth of the wicked poureth out evil things. The simple believeth every word; but the prudent man looketh well to his going. Keep discretion. Discretion shall preserve thee. The discretion of a man defereth his anger. A fool's wrath is presently known; but a prudent man covereth shame. They afflict the just, they take a bribe, and they turn aside the poor in the gate from their right; therefore the prudent shall keep silence in that time, for it is an evil time. Every prudent man dealeth with knowledge. The heart of the prudent getteth knowledge. The prudent are crowned with knowledge. A prudent man foreseeth the evil, and hideth himself; but the simple pass on, and are punished. Consider your ways. Abstain from all appearance of evil." Armed with such a stock of wisdom as this, it was not strange that when Mr. Legraph called with his friends at the sheriff's house, to forward the annual lodge minutes to the Grand Lodge, that his prudence took the alarm, when he learned that that gentleman

---

* In a paroxysm of rage, General Lee accused General Washington of possessing too large a share of *that rascally virtue, Prudence.*

had already departed with his load of gold coin, and no guard of protection.

This in itself was somewhat alarming. It was more so to hear from the physician that the two cases of sudden illness were cases of victimizing, and that, although the patients might recover, there could be no doubt that real, cold, earnest death had been the intention.

Under these circumstances, what could Mr. Legraph do but call together a dozen of the Masonic Brethren and ask their advice? Having offered his opinion in his own trembling, hesitating manner, that made him look like a slave about to receive thirty-nine stripes for misconduct, what could be more natural than for him to offer to pursue after the sheriff, and kill himself and his horse, if necessary, to overtake him? And what better evidence of his queer consistency could we offer than that, in four hours afterward, he was mounted, with two others, and pursuing the nearest road to the seat of government? The reader will see that help was approaching; but how shall we protract the murder of the two captives until they arrive? Let us see.

The prayer being ended, and the single request being made, which stands at the close of our last chapter, the Brothers prepared for death.

By this time it was well-nigh midnight. There is something about this hour that is frightful to men who have an evil conscience. True, many a murder is committed beneath the vault of night, but it is not from choice that this season is thus made doubly dark. The blow of Cain fell while the sun looked down, and the birds sang over the act. Truth is, the murderer would rather have day and daylight for his trade, though he may heap rubbish over his victim's body, and return at night to bury it.

The group of evil men, who had adopted for their motto "Dead men tell no tales," readily consented to the suggestion, offered by Major, to postpone the deed of death until daylight, and still more willingly allowed him to act as sentinel over them until that time. They withdrew themselves out of sight, built up a large fire, took out the bottles of liquor with which such persons are usually provided, and commenced a carousal, that only ended in a general intoxication.

The sentinel spoke not a word for an hour or two. His resolution to save their lives had been fully formed, but there were many difficulties in the way. The prize for which so much had been hazarded, was now in their grasp; but he did not so much regret the loss of that. Thought was busy in his mind. Through these men, it might be, that he could be restored to society, to *the* society whose fascinations were yet around his memory as a net whose meshes might not be broken by human strength. Possibly the records of the past could be obliterated; he might possibly be restored to the ranks of Brotherhood, among which, spite of the half-averted eye and the partial confidence they had given him, he had had indescribable pleasure. He had repented of his first hasty deed. Oh! readily would he have stricken off that guilty right ear which heard the tantalizing word, and that hand which struck the fatal blow, could such a sacrifice have expiated the offense.

Passing to and fro, in the presence of the two captives, he at length halted, and, catching the sheriff's eye, signaled him with one of those motions which elude the common notice, but can not escape a Mason.

The sheriff acknowledged that he understood it, in the words of the Wise Man: "If thou faint in the day of adversity, thy strength is small; if thou forbear to deliver them that are drawn unto death, and those that are ready to be slain; if thou sayest, Behold, we knew it not, doth not he that pondereth the heart consider it? and he that keepeth thy soul doth he not know it? and shall not he render to every man according to his works?" Such expressive language aroused the mind of his fellow-prisoner, who had been for awhile wrapped in some home-reverie, sweet, but indescribably mournful. He raised his eyes, first to the excited countenance of his brother captive, then following the direction of his to that of the sentinel, who was looking directly upon him. A second signal of the same character as the former met his notice, and was in like manner understood.

And now it was that Mr. Otranto realized a truth that he had often enough advanced in his lodge lectures, as all Lodge Masters must do, but, like thousands of others, had never before truly appreciated. Now it was that he felt a sort of familiarity with this man, as though he had seen him before. There was something in the sign, and in the look accompanying it, which so blended all peculiarities of the man into one, that he saw not the sentinel, the stranger, the rude, rough highwayman, but there stood before him *humanity moralized by Masonry!* In that sign he read a promise (it were treason to our common humanity to doubt its truth) that, come what would, the prisoners should not die without a hand to defend them. He saw not the man, we repeat it, but the character which Masonry had recognized *in* the man, in that hour when she conferred upon him her ancient mysteries. It was as if a member of his own lodge was there; and not more confidently would he have claimed the aid of his own Senior Warden to raise up a fallen Brother, overthrown by violence, than he now demanded: "If so, why are we here in bondage?"

Then the sentinel, carefully assuring himself that the other members of his company were at a safe distance, seated himself before them, and opened all his feelings, and told them his history. He told them of his life; his unfortunate blow; his expulsion from Masonry. He confessed to many an evil deed since his escape from justice, but avowed a desire, not for the first time formed, to withdraw from his present associations, and return to the bosom of society. He swore, by the binding ties of the Order, that the lives of the two captives should be spared, if they would promise to use their influence to have him reinstated into Masonry.

"Withdraw, then, Mr. Major," said the sheriff, "for a little way, and let us two consult together."

The consultation was a long one. The sheriff was doubtful whether a Mason ought to make such a promise. The Master of "United Voice Lodge," thinking probably of his wife, children and liberty, hesitated, but suggested that a probationary period might be proposed to the robber—say two or three years.

The sheriff would not listen to so short a term. Ten years of good conduct, and abundant evidences that Mr. Major had conquered his wild passions, was a moderate probation, considering the responsibility they were incurring.

"But suppose he rejects it?" inquired the Worshipful Master, still musing upon his home.

"Then we are no worse off than we were before. If he has the true Masonic principle, he will see that, in this matter, personal motives can not bias us; and if he has not, then Masonry is freed from an incumbrance. Ten years I will consent to, but would prefer twenty!"

Mr. Major was accordingly called back and informed. It was an interesting sight to witness those two men acting upon a committee of character, as it were, their own lives hanging upon the result of the decision.

The sheriff said: "Sir, we have decided that we can not depart from Masonic propriety, whatever may be the end of it. If you return the fruits of your ill-gotten gains, and take up an honest livelihood, we will befriend you, and our gratitude for the preservation of our lives shall be your security that the law shall not reach you for your past misconduct, if in our power to shield you. You shall have a home in our home, and shall share a child's portion with ours; but to introduce you into the lodge is not for us to promise. There is a way—a narrow one, it must be admitted, and, in your case, a difficult one; but it must be trod by yourself alone. When you first entered Masonry, you had one to conduct you; in your return, should you ever return, you must go alone; we can not help you; but this we will pledge ourselves to do: ten years of honest living, and a victory over that rebellious spirit of yours, shall call to your aid all the influence we possess to further your views; that is all that a Mason can promise, even to save his own life."

The robber resumed his walk, and for a considerable period seemed buried in thought. There is a certain joy in freedom, even in lawless freedom, which it is a sacrifice to give up. The long probation, and the hard struggle which had been laid down as the price of his restoration, staggered him. On the other hand, the very restrictions proposed, and the noble devotion of the two captives, who would rather perish than disgrace their Order, were in themselves high inducements to accept them.* The price of the object

* Why will not the members of lodges see that the very act of rejecting applicants, costly and unpleasant as it may seem, is in reality the very joy and profit of the Order? It is a Masonic guarantee of the highest kind.

made it the more desirable. After long thought, he returned, and cutting the cords which bound the Brothers, declared he had accepted the conditions. He assisted them to rise. It required some efforts to restore the circulation to their limbs, and then, without food or money, the three, thus strangely fraternized, took the course, which the stars indicated, toward tho main road!

Before noon the next day they reached it, foot-sore and exhausted; and it was no small addition to their satisfaction to meet Mr. Legraph and a considerable party, who were searching for them.

It seems that this odd genius had really executed his threat of *killing his horse* while endeavoring to overtake the sheriff. To purchase another was a small thing to one who possessed the *fortiter in re* as largely as Mr. Legraph; and, pending the bargain, he had sent his companion through the adjacent settlements to hire a company of stout fellows, offering them ten dollars each for a week's search.

The spot where the capture was made had been recognized, and a plan of pursuit fairly traced out, when the three tired fugitives came up.

A short delay to procure trusty hounds, and again the sheriff and Mr. Otranto retraced their path, first sending Major away to a safe place, where he would not be detected.

The reader will, of course, understand that the robbers were at no loss to perceive how their victims escaped. Nor was much time lost by those shrewd Ishmaelites in providing for their own safety, so soon as the fact came to light. The large amount of coin, which was the result of their exploit, was divided among the party, and after arranging a convenient rendezvous in another State, they parted in various directions.

The search by the pursuers was long protracted, but all in vain. The place of encampment was found, and, as if to tantalize them, a few pieces of coin, dropped during the hasty division; but the highwaymen, too well accustomed to rapid riding and the deep cave, eluded their grasp.

After several weeks, the sheriff returned home, *a ruined man*. The large rewards offered by the executive, and the intense exertions of himself and other persons interested in the affair, will long be remembered by those conversant with the affairs of that day. It was useless, all.

The sheriff, therefore, sold his farm and possessions, and paying one-half the large debt, begged the lenity of the State for the remainder. He asked for time to pay it—nothing but time. He said nothing of his large family, whose demands for education and support must be met; he said nothing of his gray hairs, and the probability that he would not long be spared; he only petitioned that the legislature would give him ten years' time to liquidate the balance of moneys due the State by the county of S——. After much debate, *it was refused*.

It was refused because Sheriff Payson was a Free mason. The truth afterward came out, that a secret writing had been prepared by the Antimasonic Club at the capital; sent down to the county of S——, to be signed by as many of the opponents of Masonry as could be found unfriendly to the sheriff; and this being circulated privately among the Antimasonic members of the legislature, drew a majority to deny the request. That secret paper was afterward found,* and, as if to prove the assertion of Scripture true, there were upon it the names of one of the sheriff's own brothers, several of his intimate neighbors, and the circuit judge of his district, all pretended friends to the unfortunate man.

So the legislature refused to give the old man a chance to redeem his fallen fortunes. In that refusal, it was plainly said by many, that they did not believe he had been robbed at all. Others declared it was good enough for him to suffer for the carelessness in not taking a sufficient guard for his protection.

Sheriff Payson went to jail as a man who had defrauded the State revenue! In vain Mr. Otranto labored to raise funds sufficient to meet the heavy balance due. His own spare means went no way toward it, and the sheriff would not hear to his selling his property. The people of his county, staggered by the same difficulty—the immensity of his loss—contented themselves with raising a fund to support his family and himself during his impri-

* It is still in possession of the lodge at F——, and preserved as the English preserved the thumb-screws which they took from the Spanish Armada.

sonment. Mr. Legraph took an annual trip to the capital (always making his will and arranging his temporal affairs first) to petition the successive legislatures for the poor man's release.

In the meantime Antimasonry raged high, reached its summit, and when the destructive impulse from *beneath* ceased, it fell as suddenly as a rocket, and as little cared for. Men who had staked their political character on it, looked around one morning and found themselves without a party! The leaders had somehow absented themselves, and when next seen, stood ranged under the banners of one of the others of the regular parties of the nation, with faces as brazen as ever. None could be found who were willing to take it up again, and from that day to this, it has been a carcass loathed or ridiculed, according to the manner in which it is viewed, whose stench pervades the history of ten years of our country.

The death of Antimasonry was the release of the unfortunate sheriff. One of the first acts of "sober, second thought," was a legislative bill to grant him five years' time to settle with the State. The Senate amended the bill by making it twenty-five! Then the House threw the bill away, and originated another, releasing him of the entire balance due. To carry on this handiwork of charity, the Senate *amended that*, and released the whole original claim, which was, in effect, paying back to the sheriff the large amount realized from the sale of his property, and paid by him into the treasury. This was unanimously concurred in, and thus the State honor, though tardily, was fairly cleared up.

The county of S——, which by this time had purged itself of *political* Antimasonry (not *innate* Antimasonry; *that* will abide in the hearts of a certain class of men while sin does), as soon as the jail doors were opened, saw their ingratitude in permitting him to lie there so long, and they elected him, almost unanimously, to his old position. Things smiled henceforward around him. The world, that seemed to think they owed him some sort of redress, paid it in confidence and kind words—sweetest of rewards to a real Mason. Enemies crouched beneath his feet; friends were more friendly, as they found their friendship was likely to serve him. His Masonic Brethren, who had been at the bottom of all the plans that had operated in his release and the support of his family, redoubled their attentions; and Sheriff Payson, with all his presage, and the reaction so evident around him, might have aspired to any popular office with a certainty of election.

He was satisfied, however, with what he had. There was no disposition in his mind to triumph over the fallen party; though it must be admitted that never party fell so far, or presented so abject an appearance, in their day of adversity, as the Antimasonic. With him it was not a triumph of men, but principle; and such a triumph should be heartfelt, but quiet.

One thing had surprised him, and occasioned his kind heart some uneasiness; it was, that since the day of his release from the robbers, he had no intelligence whatever of the repentant Major.

So much confidence had the last act of that singular man inspired in his breast, that he almost regretted he had not held out more flattering hope to him. Ten years had seemed but a little time; but after his weary months in jail, he had learned to set more value upon time, and a shorter probation might have served as good a purpose.

It was painful to think that Major might have despaired, and gone back to sin. Rejoiced as he was to stand under the free heaven, yet the sheriff would have remained another year within those prison walls rather than to have driven him to such an extremity.

There was one circumstance connected with the manner in which he received his means of support, while in the jail, that was odd enough. Twice a year, *on the St. John's days*, while Masons everywhere are assembled to celebrate the birth-days of their patron saints, the loneliness of the sheriff had been cheered by a present of oranges and other tropical fruit, and a purse of gold, both from some mysterious hand. The jailer could give no description of the donor. He came at night, knocked at the jail door, handed his basket to the person who answered, and rode with speed away.

It was very strange; but, although Mr. Payson worked his brains with every imaginable suggestion, he could get no clue to its solution. We suspect the reader has traced it up at a glance.

CHAPTER IV.

It is often asked by those who are galled with our allusions to the political Antimasonry of the last generation, why rake up the buried dead? Even the friends of Masonry ask, why disturb these foul objects, even more hideous in their charnel-house than when they walked the earth to kill and to devour? Our reply shall be to the point.

We rake up the buried to gain a lesson from the dead! Why does the physician, pursuing with a zeal the hidden processes of disease, dissect the body, which, in its very escape from his skill, proves how necessary it is that he should be better armed with wisdom henceforth.

We recall the deeds of Antimasonry: 1. That the children may learn how powerful were the blows that were struck during the days of their fathers. 2. That they may understand how irresistibly powerful in its very inactivity, its inertia, so to speak, was Freemasonry. 3. That we may guard more successfully against *the incomings* of evil, since we have once suffered so severely from them.

Why does the American historian dwell so thrillingly upon British oppression and Colonial fortitude? Is it to excite new animosities between nations long at peace? No; such is not the mission of the teacher. It is rather to warn us to guard well that liberty which cost our fathers so dearly, and to avoid those errors which proved so destructive to others. Even so we apply ourselves to Masonry. We have long ago forgiven our enemies. Even in the war of extermination which they waged against us, we never resisted them. But we intend to remember the afflictions of our fathers, to the end, that we may better guard our sanctuary from fresh assaults. Can the most humane blame us for this?

The remarkable developments of Masonry which led to their escape from death, turned the mind of Mr. Otranto into a new channel. He had been gradually preparing himself for a higher and nobler flight, during the several days that he journied with the sheriff, previous to the attack. But when he saw how the contemplation of death, immediate and horrid in its nature, failed to shake the heart of one, fixed by Masonic as well as Christian principles, and when he came to understand the train of thought which influenced a desperado to resign gold and a lawless life, his admiration swelled into intense wonder. He resolved that, as Masonry had saved his life, Masonry should have all the benefits of that life, so far as they could be given without interfering with his necessary avocations.

His first lesson of improvement related, of course, to himself. He commenced a careful examination of his own defects. He saw that as a Ruler in Israel, he had depended too much upon the *letter* of Masonry. He recollected how rarely he had ever applied the obligations of the system in practical life. He could not remember a single instance in which his lodge had been instructed in the *ethics* of Masonry, although the by-laws demanded a lecture or lectures on some branch of Masonry at every meeting. In trials for breach of discipline, while the printed precepts of Masonry had been brought forward and paraded against the offender, no allusions had ever been made to those unwritten precepts infolded in the symbols, enwrapped in the ceremonies, couched in the allegorical language of the Order. This reduced Masonic trials to the level of an ordinary court of justice, wherein *actions* are only inquired after.* In tracing up the causes for the tremendous evils his Lodge at Lowbridge had suffered in secession, and a general spirit of negligence among its members, he could discover these two as very prominent; taking in material not altogether sound, in the hope to cure its defects, and making Masons of the merely *curious.* Of the twain, the latter injures Masonry the most. Those who become Masons in hopes to improve their morals, though the Order is wronging itself to receive them, do sometimes achieve their desire. But those who enter the sacred courts from motives of curiosity alone, will not only fail in finding that which they seek, but the Order will utterly fail in gaining that reciprocity

---

* It is clear to the author's mind, that in all Lodge trials the question should not be, "What has the party done or said?" so much as "How far has the fraternal spirit of Masonry been violated?" There is every difference in the world between a judicial trial and one of this sort. Will not the Brethren look to it.

of advantage which is always understood in affiliations. So Mr. Otranto discovered, and he now set himself to amendment. He cast out his own *beam* manfully, and with honest grief confessed the error under which he had labored. He sought the *motes* in the eyes of his Brethren with modesty, yet with assiduity and with a determination to cast them out also, not to be shaken.

Opposition from various quarters were not wanting. Such a course of conduct, at first, tends not to peace but a sword. Several applications for demits followed in rapid succession. By strenuous efforts, Mr. Otranto succeeded in the passage of a by-law forbidding demits, save in the event of removals of change of membership.* The uproar that followed reached the ears of the Grand Lodge. That venerable body was agitated for three successive days upon the question, and then, although she did not place it among her edicts for general adoption (would that she had, would that every Grand Lodge would), yet she tacitly admitted the correctness of the principle, by sustaining "United Voice Lodge" in her new by-law. To test the thing still further, two of the members seceded, or rather publicly absolved themselves from all Masonic obligations. Mr. Otranto gained his members over to a vote of expulsion, and himself paid the printer's bill to have the fact announced in several newspapers.

---

*None can doubt the perfect propriety of this as a fundamental measure in the establishment of lodges. But it should not be made to bear an *ex post facto* relation.

This caused a personal attack to be made upon him, in which he suffered considerable injury, but it only animated him the more. He received courage from a regular intercourse with the old sheriff, with his own conscious sense of duty, and from the striking fact that several old Masons long demitted—gentlemen of high character—seeing the battle that was raging between Masonry *pure* and Masonry *mixed*, gave in their petitions for membership and held up his arms.

A new impetus was given to the study of Masonry. Seeing the determination of their Worshipful Master to enforce Masonic duties to their farthest limit, the Brethren began to inquire diligently among themselves as to *what those duties were?* It is a striking fact, that in every instance wherein a contest arose upon the question of stringent application, it came out that the engagements of Masonry are *more binding* and its requirements *more stringent* than Mr. Otranto himself had suggested!

Well has Masonry been styled by a shrewd observer, "A despotism in morals, based on the inherent rule of God." The early use of *the Shoe* on the Tracing Board, ought to convince every enlightened Mason on this head.

Not to weary the reader, the history of "United Voice Lodge," was henceforward written with a flowing pen. One or two attempts were made, it is true, to unseat the skillful rider who was thus alternately curbing and spurring the lodge, apparently at his mere will and pleasure, but neither of them succeeded, and he was at last left in quiet to pursue his plan of reformation.

The influence of all this, soon extended to other lodges. It was evident, first, in changing the slow, dull, inefficient corps of officers, who had slept while the old vessel was dashing to pieces on the breakers, and replacing them with active men of the reforming school.* The early and feeble attempt to disseminate Masonic light in the form of periodical literature began to receive attention. Vices which had been *suffered*, not *encouraged*—excrescences upon the body of the Order, such as profanity and intemperance, (than which no vices can be more injurious to Masonry), began to receive attention, and the physician, where he could not heal, *cut off*. The lodges began to represent themselves more abundantly in the Grand Lodge, and this movement awoke the old mother, who had almost lost herself in lethargy. District officers were appointed to report upon the condition of Masonry, and to record such suggestions as occurred to them in view of the assumed faults of the Brethren. The local influence which had gathered and hardened around the capitol was broken up, and the distant country lodges claimed, and received, their share of Grand Lodge honors.

---

*There are "fogies" in Masonry as in politics. There are men who raise a great outcry when we labor to excite a lodge to action. Men who talk of *innovations*, when, in fact, the worst innovation that Masonry has ever suffered, has been that very sloth and inefficiency to which it was reduced under their administration, so different from the original and fundamental idea of *labor*, *labor*, *labor*.

All this, and more, far more, grew out of the casual meeting of Mr. Otranto with the homespun old sheriff, on his way to the seat of government. Why it should surprise any observer of human events, that "great events from little causes spring," we can not conceive. We have never taken the time and trouble to investigate any important result to its source, without renewed admiration at the minuteness of that source. Thus atoms accumulate and form a world.

A Masonic celebration was announced to take place in S—— county, not far from the residence of Sheriff Payson, and an invitation quite general had been extended to the Brethren. Such things were more in vogue in former days than now. Do those who condemn such meetings on the score of expense, forget that sociability, in its refined sense, is one of the great aims of Masonry? and how are Masons to be sociable if they never meet? and how are we to meet unless the old St. John's days are celebrated? and what do we pay annual dues for, but to purchase sacrifices to keep the fire burning upon our altars?

Among the visitors on the occasion alluded to, was our wide-awake friend, Mr. Otranto, with several of his members, who accompanied him to celebrate the release of the old sheriff from jail. It was a happy occasion, and all the large and general audience enjoyed it, or if there were a few jaundiced faces visible, they belonged to those who saw, in this act, the triumph of the cause whose downfall they had so long predicted.

The speeches being ended, and the bountiful cheer discussed, a meeting was held at the lodgeroom, in which, under the sanctity of closed doors, various matters received attention which do not come under the title of "subjects proper to be committed to writing;" of course we shall pass them over. But there was one topic that it will not be unlawful for us to speak of.

A letter was handed to the Tyler, with a request that the Worshipful Master (Sheriff Payson was at the time in the chair), should read it aloud. It was substantially in these words:

"A Mason expelled for an unpremeditated act of violence, afterward losing his property and risking his life to save two Brother Masons, how many years' probation must he serve before he can be restored?"

"It is my preserver!" shouted the sheriff, as forgetting all the proprieties of time and place, he would have rushed from the lodgeroom, if he had not been restrained, and thus a most unprecedented act happily prevented.

"It is Mr. Major!" echoed Otranto, with the same shameless disregard of propriety. The lodge was immediately called to refreshment, and the visitor invited in.

It was Major, as had been so well suggested. He was dressed in the suit of a sailor, a garb which his sunburnt face and tough hands fully justified; and as he came in, he met the two gentlemen whose lives he had so timely protected, with an overflow of sensibility. Then taking him by the left hand, while the

Worshipful Master of "United Voice Lodge" retained the right, the sheriff, in his own straightforward way, declared how much he was indebted to that man. He gave the history of that dreadful night, when the voice of the two prisoners, condemned to die, went up to heaven's gate. He pointed out the great pecuniary sacrifice that Mr. Major had submitted to, and explained that nothing but a real desire of restoration to Freemasonry and to society, had prompted him in his course. He concluded by asking the lodge to extend their Masonic privileges, as far as they dared to do, and if they could restore him to the Order, to do it without delay. To all this, Mr. Otranto added, Amen.

But the sailor spoke up, and forestalled further action. He gave a sketch of his life since the day he heard that Mr. Payson would go to jail for the loss of the money. Determined that such injustice should not be inflicted, he had gone to the District Attorney, and voluntarily proposed to stand trial for his life, so that the truth might come out. That officer was a Mason, and advised him, instead of pursuing that plan, to go in search of the other four robbers, and endeavor to secure them for justice, in hopes that the spoils might be recovered. He had done so, and followed them at the imminent hazard of his own life, from place to place, until they took passage for the West Indies. In hopes still to accomplish his plan, he had taken service as a common sailor in the West-India vessels. He had risen from post to post, until he now commanded a fine schooner. Twice a year he had returned to S—— county, to inquire how matters were tending relative to the sheriff's affairs, and had always left him a testimonial of his visit at the jail door, but without making himself known. The District Attorney having died shortly after his first visit, he had resigned his intention of standing trial, and in its place conceived the idea of accumulating money enough to pay the sheriff's debt, and thus release him.

He declared before God, that during the years that had passed, in all his vicissitudes and provocations of a sailor's life, he had diligently labored to govern his evil temper, and prepare the way for his restoration to Masonry. He had put a seal upon his lips. He had not been unmindful of his duty to a higher power, but applied himself to the Heavenly Throne for pardon and for grace. He had found peace. For more than a year no storm had disturbed his mind, but amid the wildest turmoil without, all was calmness there.

Nevertheless, he felt a pride now, an honest, *humble* pride, he called it, in sustaining his ten years' trial! He was not willing to reduce the period. He had not come there now to have it reduced, but only to *put in his petition for restoration*, that it might be ready on his return, five, ten, or twenty years hence!

The hearty manner in which all this was said, made a warm impression in his favor, and when he rose to depart, it was with many a tear, many a fraternal wish, many a promise, and, from at least two hearts, many a fond regret.

Time rolls along.

No truth so trite; no fact so evident.

Time rolls along.

The timid Brother Legraph, spite of all his caution, found himself called upon, one afternoon, very unexpectedly to die.

Time rolls along.

The silver-haired sheriff, strong in the hopes that are blazoned forth on the pages of the first great light of Masonry, and symbolized on her trestle-board, was gathered to his fathers in a green old age, and his works do follow him. He died in great peace. The Worshipful Master of "United Voice Lodge," himself coughing out his little remnant in a late stage of consumption, leaned over him, treasured up his last look, reverently closed the curtains of his eyes, and departed homeward, to prepare for his own departure.

Time rolls along.

The consumptive cough soon brought Mr. Otranto to his death-bed, and there was a comfortable sight (comfortable, in view of the grateful affection that prompted it) to be witnessed in that bed-chamber. For, standing around the couch, the outer circle of friendship (the inner being composed of children, and a wife, alas! too soon to be a widow), was a committee of twelve, a committee expressly deputed on behalf of the lodge, *to witness his death*, a committee that had alternated "eight hours for the service of God and a distressed Brother," for more than a week. That committee saw the last movements of his hands toward the children and their mother. They understood it. By a movement of the head they accepted it. They heard the last words upon his trembling lips. They were good words; just such words as the Recording Angel is authorized to write in heaven's books as the expiring words of a Christian Mason. They comforted his mourners. They made the heart of the widow to smile, though her face was sad. They bore his remains to an honored grave, by the side of another grave equally honored, and there the two Brothers, Payson and Otranto, rest side by side, for it was their mutual wish.

Time rolls along.

The remembrance of the robbery, and of the rescue, the imprisonment and the release, had well nigh faded from all hearts. The old jail had been pulled down. New roads to the seat of Government, passing for the most part through dense settlements of people, precluded all danger of robbery, and when the aged spoke of thefts and murders formerly committed on certain parts of the way, it was as though they talked of the old Revolution, or of a certain man, who, on his way to Jericho, fell among thieves.

The lodge at the county-seat of S—— county had built for itself a new and beautiful hall. But three of the members of Sheriff Payson's day remained. Many had died. Many more, in the uneasiness of our Western and Southern habits, had removed to other States. Some, who were formerly the most active, were on the books now as honorary members, physical infirmity preventing them from attending the lodge. Nevertheless, the old charter had been honorably sustained, and the large, well-filled books of the Secretary showed more than one name which had figured conspicuously in the higher ranks of Grand Lodge officials.

At one of the stated meetings, when a full attendance of the lodge was observed, a letter was sent in signed by one F. M. M., to the effect that the undersigned had, many years before that, handed in a petition for restoration to Masonry and membership, in that lodge. That the fee for membership was paid in advance, he had the Secretary's receipt to show, and he referred to the records of a certain date to prove his assertions.

It was Mr. Major, returned after a fifteen years' absence.

The committee appointed to act upon his petition were all dead. But in the archives was found their report, in which they unanimously recommended his restoration to Masonry. The lodge had acted upon that report, as the books showed, and restored him by the same full vote. In connection with the record of the transaction was a copy of the Grand Master's letter, who had been written to upon the subject, in which he unhesitatingly recommended such a step, as both lawful, and, in this case, peculiarly proper.

So the probationer for restoration earned and

received his reward! It was with bent knee and quivering lip that the foreign-looking mariner addressed, in an unknown tongue, that God, whose eye is everywhere over our Order. He had expiated his crimes by all that faith and good works could accomplish. He had wiped out the blot against his name. He stood once more a Mason, Free and *Accepted*, among Masons, and he heard them call him *Brother*, and tell him he was welcome to cast anchor among them for life.

One duty remained, to visit that double grave.

It was a sad disappointment to his generous heart, that neither of those men, who had been instrumental in his reformation, was alive now to give him a welcome back. But he felt that his visit would not be all in vain if he saw their grave. He stood above it, as the sun went down, and lived over again the history of twenty years. Then that man, the wild and lawless youth, the murderer in manhood, the expelled Mason of thirty years' standing, the sailor who was as a rock in the storm, undaunted and foremost in duty, bowed himself upon that broad tablet, and wept as a child. It was a short-lived emotion, for he felt that tears were misplaced over such hopeful dead. So he arose and went his way. There was nothing to detain him there. The dull life of a landsman wearied him. He took a diploma from his Brethren, deposited a large amount of money in the bank, payable to the order of the lodge, and, returning to sea, was never heard of by his admiring friends again.

In recording such incidents as these, the moral lies on the surface. In vain does the opponent of Masonry deny that examples of attachment to Masonry like this exist. They do exist; they are found in every lodge. In vain do some laugh at the spirit of this attachment, and call it frivolous and weak. The same strain of argument would decry all attachments; the love of friendship, of fame, of honor, of woman, of parents. The same spirit of ridicule would weaken every tie that binds society together, and make us all hermits or wolves.

The true explanation of this permanency of Masonic attachment, found in every enlightened Mason, is, that Masonry is so wonderfully (we do not say inexplicably), adapted to our mental constitution. This was admitted by one of the virulent writers of the last generation; but he endeavored to blunt the point of the admission, by adapting it to our *corrupt* nature. We deny that. The incidents of the sketch deny it. The circumstances of every Masonic sketch deny it. There can not be a case mentioned in which Masonic light pointed to a deed of lawlessness or wrong. As well say that Christianity instituted the Inquisition as to assert it. As well attribute every result of persecution or hypocrisy to the practice of religion as to assert it.

Freemasonry is a circle, with the Holy Writings in the center. Every action committed by a Mason, contrary to the letter and spirit of Scripture, is un-Masonic. With this in view, if the reader fails to gather our moral, as he reads, we despair of making it clear to him.

We lay down the pen, warm with the recollection that many a lodge in the United States has an *Otranto* for its Worshipful Master, and that the number is rapidly increasing, as the light of the press becomes blended with the light of Masonry.

We lay it down, animated with the thought that many a grave over which we tread has a *Payson*, whose company we shall share when this division, soon to attempt the passage of the flood, shall join that one which is safely over.

We look onward, with our back to the west and south on the right; we look upward, with the heavenly east in view, and reflecting how many are there, seated in the Grand Lodge, whom we have loved and mourned for, we say prayerfully and humbly, "Even so, Lord Jesus! Come quickly!"

The Broken Column Unbroken.

A TALE OF MASONIC RESISTANCE.

Inscribed to R. W. Bro. John Warren Hunt,
OF MADISON, WISCONSIN.

THE "Morgan Affair," as it was popularly termed, or rather the Antimasonic *boil*, which came to a head — a bad sore it was for all parties—between 1826 and 1836, was the *experimentum crucis* of Freemasonry in America. It was "the time that tried men's (Masons') souls." The Institution of Freemasonry had previously stood all manner of persecutions from *the ruling powers*, political and religious, and stood them well; but now it was doomed to encounter persecution from *the people*. It had met *argument* and defeated it; now it must meet *ridicule*. It had buffeted opposition in countries where the light of the press has never been diffused, and in countries where the press is muzzled; now it must buffet it in a land of free press, and its old, but not decayed, hulk must èndure the full broadsides of missiles, large and small, from pellets to forty-two pounders, poured upon it in the full blaze of an organized, *scientific* war. It was the *experimentum crucis*, we repeat, of the system. It answered the queries often enough propounded: Has Masonry a mission in this free country? Can it withstand the indignant opposition of an outraged people?

And it is because this Antimasonic warfare of 1826 to 1836 *was* the *experimentum crucis* of the system, that we write so much concerning it. When by the approbation of the ancient fraternity we were first encouraged to turn our pen to Freemasonry, and seek from its inexhaustible fields subjects for Essay and Sketch, we discovered how available was this department of the great subject to our purpose. We saw that as the Revolution of 1776 was to the United States, as the Exodus to the Israelites, as the Hegira to the Moslem, so was this era to Freemasonry—a date from which future historians will reckon, and a treasury from which will be drawn proofs of its adamantine powers of resistance, the invincibility of its inertia, the undying nature of its principles, the genial character of its attachment in the soul of its votaries, and its perfect adaptedness as well to the citizens of a free country, in an enlightened age, as to the subjects of despots in the days of darkness.

Among the incidents of this gloomy yet triumphant period, we transcribe from our memorandum book the following, furnished us by one of the actors, who yet lives to tell it with an enjoyment that age seems never to lessen.

In Eastern Ohio there are places where, to this day (1854), a man can not be popular if he is a Freemason. The circuit-rider, sent by his bishop to his twelve months' work in that "neck of woods," must say nothing of his Masonry, if peradventure, like the rest of his enterprising company, he is a Brother among us.* Two to one, the petition will go up to "Annual Conference" for a preacher "who is not connected with any of the secret societies;" and unless they get him, they grumble.

Lest our readers may think we exaggerate, read what "the Committee on Secret Societies" reported, June 13, 1854 (not 1654, as a person would suppose, from the bigoted, behind-the-age tone of the recommendation), to the "Joint Evangelical Lutheran Synod of Ohio and adjacent States," which met in Thompson's township, Seneca county, Ohio. The committee reported as follows: "The Synod regards as unchurchly all societies out of the church, and particularly secret societies, whenever they aim to accomplish those objects which the Christian Church, according to the Word of God, has and ever must have in view; because they are not only rendered unnecessary by the establishment of the church, but because they are calculated to produce indifference toward the kingdom of Christ, and, in many cases, entire estrangement from Christianity, and even gross infidelity. In future, we will admit no one into our connection who belongs to said societies." This report was adopted, only two members, to their honor

---

* We have some curious statistics on this subject, furnished us by a bishop of the Methodist Episcopal Church. In certain conferences, the non-masonic preachers compare in numbers with the Masonic as the "number of them that lapped" (Judg. vii: 6) did to the bulk of Gideon's army.

be it recorded, the Revs. Henkel and H. Heincke, entering a protest, particularly against the last clause. We should think the citizens of Seneca county, Ohio, would think twice before they would invite "The Joint Evangelical" to sit among them a second time.

But to the story. In one of the villages of Eastern Ohio, there was a peculiarly malignant spirit of Antimasonry manifested, and about the year 1830 it gained its hight. It amounted to as much as its votaries dared to do. To deface the outside of the lodge-hall with obscene emblems (the symbology of Antimasonry—foul as Baal-peor's, and very much the same figures, too); to blacken the character of Masons; to buy up Giddings' Almanacs by the cart-load, and give them away to all who would read them; to vote against all "who had the mark of the beast in their foreheads" (as the Rev. Mr. Slidel elegantly expressed it, in his memorable sermon from Rev. xix: 20); to separate father and son, pastor and people, husband and wife, partner senior and partner junior, the upper and lower millstone, the antagonistic blades of scissors, and all other separable things, upon this important question; these and similar acts were the fitting works of the crew that ruled, and the sheep that *were* ruled, in ——— county, Eastern Ohio, about the year of grace 1830.

A few years before that period, about the time that Lafayette visited the United States, and the Masonic Fraternity generally were roused up to extraordinary feeling by his sentiments of approval and attachment to Masonry, one of the most zealous and enlightened members of *the Institution* (there was but one secret society in the United States at that time, so that the adjective Masonic was seldom used and never necessary) died suddenly, and under circumstances that awakened the profoundest sensations of the Brethren, his co-members. They built a costly monument to his memory, and selected the highest knoll in the burial-ground as its site. It was the broken column upon a platform of three steps; in fact, the same figure that is given in the Monitor in the third degree.

There the beautiful monument stood, undisturbed, for several years, and glittered in the sunlight, or glowed under moonbeams, to the eye of every traveler, early or late, who journeyed from the southwest toward the county-seat of ——— county. It became the center of various other Masonic graves. Death is ever at work; and as his work thinned out the ranks of the lodge to which the deceased had belonged, processions were seen to wind slowly thitherward with melancholy loads, and around "the weeping Virgin" stout-hearted men were seen to weep, and by the side of the broken column they laid other columns, broken in like manner, until a group, silent but suggestive, was formed of the Fraternal dead.

This elegant monument became the scene of the incident we are describing. During the crisis of the fever so often referred to, it was a standing eyesore, a stench in the pure nostrils of Antimasonry. To tower so high, to glare so brightly, to cry out its lessons so loudly, that every beholder was in a manner *compelled* to hear them, and all this, too, in a time when their honest, disinterested efforts had almost rendered Freemasonry *a broken column*—the thought was insupportable. An order of court was petitioned for to remove it, but the presiding judicial was too conscientious to grant that, though he had been elected as an Antimason. Then the parties consulted a lawyer, to know the damage of openly tearing it down; but that proving several figures too high for their pecuniary ability, they decided at last upon convening under the shadow of night for the purpose. The plot came to the ears of a Brother Mason through the instrumentality of an old lady, who, though she had been in the chimney corner too deaf for twenty years to hear much, had her auditory nerves wonderfully keen when anything was stirring in regard to a society to which all three of her deceased husbands had belonged. The Brother Mason, of course, communicated it to the rest, and a counter-plot was devised, as ingenious as anything in the strategy of Brother N. Bonaparte, of Corsica.

The malignant Antimasons met, to the number of three, one wet, dark, cold night, and, with Masons' tools, went together to the graveyard. The very nature of their errand demanded silence, and a silent party in a dark night is necessarily a superstitious one. By the time they got half-way from the graveyard gate to the doomed monument, every grave had its ghost perched upon it, and every puff of wind emitted its sigh. If the reader will try the plan of entering a well-peopled graveyard, after midnight, upon an unholy errand, he will exactly realize the pleasant feelings of these three ruffians. They soon found themselves walking so close together as actually to impede one another's steps, whereupon one of them fell headlong, and screamed as his hand came in contact with something cold as a dead man's forehead. It was no fancy, as the result proved, that made the other two hear a subdued chuckle, in response, from behind a gallows-looking oak hard by.

The party had barely arrived at the broken monument, and settled their hats upon their heads, which had been pushed off by their electrified hair, when blankets were thrown over them; and, in spite of their agonizing attempts to scream, they were silenced, thrown down, gagged, and bound, in a space of time quite miraculous in its brevity.

Who committed the act was not known for ten years afterward; but those three night-walkers were found by their anxious friends, next morning, in the court-house, with corncobs arranged horizontally in their open jaws; their hands and feet tied with their own suspenders; and their bodies completely tattooed with all the emblems of seven degrees of Masonry, done in monochromatic—that is, in lunar caustic. The color came out by a few weeks' vigorous rubbing, but no second attempt was ever made upon the integrity of the monument, and the Broken Column stands Unbroken yet.

The Five Orders of Architecture in Brentford Lodge.

A TALE OF SPECULATIVE ARCHITECTURE.

Inscribed to R. W. Bro. William D. Ferris,
OF DOVER, MISSISSIPPI.

ORDER FIRST.

BROTHER LEMUEL FAIRFAX OF THE TUSCAN ORDER.

IN those handy little compends of Masonic doctrine, styled Masonic Manuals, Monitors, Charts, Trestleboards, etc., there is an admirable spirit of *stevedoring** displayed, by means of which a great mass of themes is compressed within the smallest possible amount of space. The use of such books is invaluable if applied in the way of *suggestion.* There are *texts* in them for a thousand Masonic lectures. Every paragraph, indeed, is a text from which an intelligent Master may draw to feed and enlighten a willing membership. The only use of them that we feel called upon to deprecate, in this connection, is *as lectures.* The Manuals, be it recollected, do not and were not designed to

* The business of a *stevedore* is to pack the various articles that make up a ship's cargo into the confined space of the hold—*multum in parvo.*—*Vide* WEBSTER'S DICTIONARY.

supply lectures, but to *suggest* them. If used in the former sense, they are the laziest and least useful works in the world, and will as certainly bring about a low state of Masonic intelligence in the lodge, as would the mere occasional reading of a few proof texts in the pulpit, without commentary or preaching, lead to a speedy dullness of spiritual matters in the church.

Among the subjects so briefly but comprehensively conveyed in the Manuals, is that of "Orders in Architecture." This theme is expounded to Fellow-craft Masons on their way to the Middle Chamber of King Solomon's Temple; and, when properly worked up by the Senior Deacon, forms an elegant lecture, and one well calculated to impress the hearer with a sense of the scientific character of the Masonic Institution. To assist Senior Deacons, and afford to the general reader some idea of what this subject is capable, we present a series of tales, to include respectively the Five Orders in Architecture, the Tuscan, Doric, Ionic, Corinthian, and Composite. And our first shall be "Brother Lemuel Fairfax of the Tuscan Order."

But, to start fairly with our subject, let us inquire, What do the Manuals *suggest* upon this head? From Webb's Freemasons' Monitor, the original of them all, we quote: "By Order in Architecture is meant a system of all the members, proportions, and ornaments of columns and pilasters; or it is a regular arrangement of the projecting parts of a building, which, united with those of a column, form a beautiful, perfect, and complete whole." This is very well given, and proves its author, Preston, to have been as elegant in diction as he was clear in conveyance. One other quotation seems necessary here, something to justify our application of architectural terms to the qualities of men. It is the paragraph which describes "the moral advantages of geometry;" and, should we find space, we shall introduce it in some other number of this series; if not, we refer the reader to his own Monitor at home, where he can readily find it.

"The TUSCAN is the most simple and solid of the Five Orders," says our standard. "It was invented in Tuscany, whence it derives its name. Its column is seven diameters high, and its capital, base, and entablature have but few moldings. The simplicity of the construction of this column renders it eligible where ornament would be superfluous." This is a monitorial sketch of the Tuscan Order in Architecture; but if he had had Brother Lemuel Fairfax, the Junior Deacon of Brentford Lodge, in his mind when he wrote it, and if he had seen him as often sitting in the south-west of his lodge as we have done, and if he had been his guest week-days and Sundays as frequently as we have been, he could not better have described that estimable man and Mason, than this. It will be our agreeable duty to make the proper application of his words.

"The simplicity of the construction of this column [Brother Lemuel Fairfax, of course] renders it [him] eligible where ornament would be superfluous." That's a fact, as everybody will admit who knows him. There is an admirable simplicity in the getting up of the man, as well as in the way he dresses, acts, and speaks. His nose, for instance, is as nearly flat as "the projecting part" of a man's face may lawfully be. His eyes and ears are small and unobtrusive, and the whole contour of his body is suggestive of a man who does not wish to impose himself unduly upon anybody. The same idea is conveyed in his dress, which is a kind of medium style between the first habiliments worn by Father Adam in the garden and the last worn by Brother Lorenzo Dow in his ministry. To complete the picture, Brother Fairfax delights in the *yea, yea, nay, nay* fashion of conversation, and believes that whatsoever is more than these cometh of evil.

Such is the Tuscan column in Brentford Lodge. Wherever it was invented, it is clearly one of the oldest of the Five Orders, and contains the elements of them all, just as every good block of stone has the elements of the most elegant statue in it.

That Brother Fairfax is the most "*solid* of the Five Orders of Architecture" in Brentford Lodge, we can readily demonstrate. He is *all* Mason; he belongs to no "secret society" save the Masonic. Nay, though the Linkumfoodles, when they organized their lodge at Brentford, in 1849, offered him inducements—remission of fees, full benefits, speedy promotion, a sure card—he declined their allurements (allurements which, for a time, *de*luded one or two of Brentford's columns, as we shall see further on), and declared himself "solid," and a Mason "clear through." His Masonry keeps him single. Though of a domestic turn—did you ever see a real good Mason that wasn't? no!—he has never married, never offered to marry. Not that his homeliness prevents. There is a score of ladies around Brentford, so rumor says, not one of whom would consider his face for a moment if the Tuscan column would but propound to her the four-word query, styled "popping the question." But Brother Fairfax is too "solid" a Mason to marry, though our Sister, the Queen of Sheba herself, were to make his acquaintance. He finds, so he says, in the workings of Masonry, a safe medium for diffusing those wages which a due adherence to the principles of Masonry secures for him. Being a tanner by trade, as you would naturally suppose by looking at his shocking bad boots, and a most successful one, as such an honest, conscientious mechanic is certain to be, let him live anywhere between Dan and Beersheba, he coins money, and lays it up; but he lays it up "where neither moth nor rust can corrupt, and where thieves do not break through nor steal." In his treasury, this "solid" Mason has safely hoarded the wages of twenty-six years. Happy man, whose wealth secures him the largest interest the (divine) law allows, while yet it gives him no trouble, from year to year, either in collecting the interest or protecting the principal!

At Brother Thirteen's academy, at Brentford, are five orphan children, whose board, clothing and tuition are paid in advance. Look at Brother Thirteen's ledger, page 68, and under the letter F you will find the name of the individual who does it. When the Tuscan column falls, there will be none but God to act the father to those sweet little boys and girls.

At the Widow Leach's there is a pile of wood that will outlast the winter, late and pinching though it may be, as it has been early and pinching. Yet Sister Leach did not pay for it, nor pay for hauling it, nor pay for cutting it. The wagon that bore it, the ax that cut it, were marked with the initials "L. F.;" and the man who did the labor gets fifteen dollars a month for his services, from the party whose "column is seven diameters high, and whose capital, base and entablature have but few moldings." Precious few moldings has Brother Lemuel Fairfax; but if you had seen him, as we did, when the widow thanked him for the wood, you would have thought, as we did, that he had the face of an angel, flat as his nose may be.

It is a singular fact that the Tuscan column never has been able to learn the lectures. Why it is so we can not divine. He knows the Ten Commandments—or at least we presume he does—for he keeps them well; and he knows the Lord's Prayer, for we have heard him say it while — but that 's telling. But the ritual of the lectures, he says, he can't memorize. He wedged in a few of them while he was taking the degrees, just enough, of course, to get off the checkered pavement into the middle chamber, and so on; and he *has* managed, after a labor which, he says, is greater than taking the hair off of three dozen flint-hides, to learn by heart the responses of the Junior Deacon; but, verbally speaking, his education is incomplete. The jewel and the rod of the Junior Deacon are all he will ever be entitled to; to carry messages, and to exercise due vigilance, the highest employments that can be committed to his trust.

But, as we observed before, "the simplicity of the construction of this column renders it eligible where ornament would be superfluous." Who wants the Junior Deacon to be a Solomon, or the son of a Solomon? Brother Fairfax fills every station which the wisdom of the Master assigns him with perfect accuracy. Is it a place on a committee of inquiry, never were such examinations known as *he* institutes; and if there 's a hole in the applicant's moral garments as large as a hen would peck, he finds it, and proclaims it. Is he on a committee of discipline, he pursues the offender, according to the Constitution of his Grand Lodge, with impartial and unrelenting severity. It is not until called upon with the rest *to pronounce sentence*, that he knows such a word as *mercy* in his Masonic vocabulary. Is it a committee of charity to which he is called, luckily for the lodge he is not its *Treasurer* instead of Junior Deacon, for he would never wait "the order of the Worshipful Master with the consent of the Brethren;" but, impelled by the movements of his own noble heart, would pour out its funds as liberally as he yields his sympathies. Distress can not pass him unrelieved. If anything will call him out of his coffin when we encircle him there, prior to casting the evergreen and clod upon him, it will be our tears, our sorrowful words, our swelling hearts. If not too far away for return, his spirit can hardly bear the scene, and he will come back.

Ah, thou faithful man! as thus I sit and write of thee, the broad waters of the Mississippi swelling around me, the rush of steam from the escape-pipes awakening the echoes of the hills; as thus I sit alone this midnight hour, in the cabin to which, for a week's journey, I am consigned, my fellow-passengers all retired to their slumbers, I hug to myself the pleasing recollection that thou and I are one in Masonry. Thou in the south-west, at the widow's cot, in the home of sickness, leading the orphan, strengthening the feeble; thou, in the field of life, fast-ripening for the harvest of the Lord, secure in the reception of the long-promised wages; I, in my long, weary, ah! weary journeyings, anticipating what may never be fulfilled, and hoping for what may never come to pass—thou and I, upon this great platform of Freemasonry, are one. One in purpose, one in labor, shall we not be one in the reward?

Yes, faithful frere, they who worked together in the quarries of Zarthan went up together to the Holy City, to assist in dedicating the Temple of the Lord; they who pined together at Babylon, and "by the rivers of Babylon there sat down and wept when they remembered Zion," went up together, though over a rough and rugged way to the Golden Hill; they who walked and wearied with their Lord, rejoined him after his resurrection; and so shall we. We who have wrought in quarry, hill, and temple together, who have floated together to Joppa, and thence conveyed our burdens, in sweet companionship, to Jerusalem, will not be separated when the day of disbursing wages shall have arrived. Together, singing, we shall go, and from our unerring Master together shall receive "according to that which we have done, whether it be good, or whether it be evil!"

ORDER SECOND.

BROTHER FRANK ASHDOD OF THE DORIC ORDER.

By Speculative Masonry, it is said, we learn to subdue the passions, to act upon the square, keep a tongue of good report, maintain secrecy, and practice charity. It is so far interwoven with religion, as to lay us under obligations to pay that rational homage to the Deity which at once constitutes our duty and our happiness. It leads the contemplative to view with reverence and admiration the glorious works of creation, and inspires him with the most exalted ideas of the perfection of his Divine Creator. . . . This is admirably well said; it affords a fair compend of that whole moral and religious system so long preserved, cherished and applied under the name of *Craft Masonry*.

Among the leading members, the *pillars* as they are fairly named, of Brentford Lodge, may be mentioned Brother Frank Ashdod. He is appropriately styled its *Doric* column, and as such we shall describe him. His name, it must be admitted, smacks a little of the philistine, and, so far as a name can go, is calculated to prejudice one somewhat against the man; but when we consider that one's name, like his hair, is inherited, and that it is a burden he bears without being responsible for it, we shall pay no regard to that; for, laying the name aside, there is no Mason in Brentford so worthy to be styled a "Doric" as Brother Ashdod, the Junior Warden. Let us examine the text-book for a definition of the *Doric* Order:

"The *Doric*, which is plain and natural, is the most ancient, and was invented by the Greeks. Its column is eight diameters high, and has seldom any ornaments, on base or capital, except moldings; though the frieze is distinguished by triglyphs and metopes, and triglyphs compose the ornament of the frieze. The solid composition of this Order gives it a preference in structures where strength and a noble simplicity are chiefly required. The Doric is the best proportioned of all the Orders. The several parts of which it is composed are founded on the natural position of solid bodies. In its first invention it was more simple than in its present state. In after times, when it began to be adorned, it gained the name of *Doric;* for when it was constructed in its primitive and solid form, the name of *Tuscan* was conferred on it. Hence, the Tuscan precedes the Doric in rank on account of its resemblance to that pillar in its original state."

It is said that the Doric Order was formed after the model of a strong, robust man. This statement is correct, as you may see by visiting Brentford Lodge with us at its next stated meeting (third Monday in each month). Brother Ashdod being in the South, where he has been ever since 1850, and will be until he dies, you will see one of the finest specimens of humanity you ever looked at. Whether it is the contrast presented between him and that ridiculous-looking Brother Fairfax, the Junior Deacon, on his left, who is as homely as he is sound, or whether it is the contrast presented between him and that magnificent wooden pillar of the Corinthian Order on his right, we can not say, but the fact is indisputable that Brother Ashdod is the most stalwart Mason in Brentford. And this may be further illustrated by making the acquaintance of his wife, who is the smallest fairy of a creature that ever stole the heart of a giant. How singular that our great, gross Brethren always stumble over these little female specimens of humanity! But so it is; and we are able by this unerring law exactly to compute the weight and size of Sister Delilah, to whom Brother Samson lost his heart, his hair, and finally his eyesight; but that 's immaterial.

It is somewhat fortunate, or at least it *was* fortunate a few years ago, at the revival of Brentford Lodge, after the Antimasonic excitement had subsided, that Brother Ashdod is a man of so much physical ability; and for this reason—when the old lodge went down, in 1829, the members nearly all took to drink. What is the reason of this remarkable fact in Masonic history, we are unable to say; but the truth is indisputable, that the old boys, the most of them, about 1820 to 1826, loved liquor much too well either for their good or that of Freemasonry; and when the "Morgan Itch" spread over the land, many of those who did not secede took to the bottle. Missing the old restraints of Masonic discipline, or philosophically attempting to drown their mortification in wine, or perhaps because they naturally loved it, they gave a marked impetus to the liquor trade, which it has maintained to the present day. Now, when the lodges began to revive again, these Brethren, whose noses had become as red as pokeberries, and their livers badly inflamed, were presented at once as subjects for Masonic discipline. This was the case particularly in Brentford. Six old Brethren, two of whom had been initiated by Thomas Smith Webb before we were born, and a third who had been called "Brother E—d—r" by Brother George Washington himself, in 1796, had become perfect sots, as discreditable to their families as they were dishonorable to the Masonic Order, of which they daily boasted themselves to be members. Something had to be done with them, for no person, however much he might respect Masonry, would petition the lodge for Masonic light, and run the risk of being styled *Brother* by these filthy old boys. At every meeting their misconduct was reported, and a conference was held as to the course the lodge should take with them. Their long and formerly faithful services, their noble liberality, their love for Masonry, for which they were willing to die (or do anything else save *live*), and their repeated pledges of amendment, embarrassed the case more than the superficial reader can imagine.

Has the reader ever reflected that King Solomon, the great founder of our Institution, left no rule on record whereby a block may be *taken from* the wall? Directions in abundance there are for selecting the blocks, preparing the blocks, conveying the blocks, elevating the blocks, cementing the blocks in the wall, but none for taking them out again. After the cement hardens; after other blocks have been built around and over them; in short, after they become, to all intents and purposes, a part of the wall, then if we are called upon to take them away, and throw them away, *hoc opus, hic labor!* we have no rules to work by. Then, if we discover flaws and defects, the whole enterprise must stop, until, at a great destruction to the wall, and at the risk of throwing down the whole structure, we can draw out that which should have never been placed there, and hurl from the sanctuary that which it was almost blasphemy to have borne there.

Well, this was the difficulty in Brentford Lodge. These old men failing to improve themselves, and contriving to disgrace the Institution at whose portals they stood, like Gog and Magog, hideous and disgusting, it was absolutely necessary that they should be pulled out of the wall, and hove over among the rubbish. And here we see the advantage of having a strong and determined man, like Brother Ashdod, for Junior Warden of Brentford Lodge; for it was his duty to present the offenders to the notice of the lodge, and prosecute them for their offenses. It was his duty—and he did it, despite their clamors, and the clamors of their large and respectable connection; despite the threats of their sons to use personal violence upon the Masons if their fathers were expelled—to have the honor and purity of Masonry vindicated at every hazard, and he did it. Through all the regular grades of punishment—reprimands, suspensions, brief and protracted, and finally expulsions from the Order—he pursued them. Being joined with Brother Lemuel Fairfax, that lion-hearted Mason, whose praises we sung in our last, he pursued them unrelentingly; and finally, by their own obstinacy, contumacy, and wickedness, they were, one by one, dragged out of the Temple, and thrown over the battlements into the valley of Jehosophat, where they still remain. Well for them, in view of that alarming passage in Scripture concerning drunkards, they do not find their next remove into the neighboring valley of Gehenna, which is Hell.

More than once in this disagreeable, this disgusting part of his duty, Brother Ashdod found the advantage of his great bodily strength. When attacked by the two sons of Brother E—d—r, and threatened with "the d—dest flogging he ever got in his life," he was enabled to place one of the assailants under his feet, the other over the fence, in a moist place called a ditch, and there to restrain them by bodily force until they promised to cease the quarrel. This was fortunate for the young men, as well as for Ashdod, for the rebuff they met with operated so powerfully upon their minds, as to excite an ardent respect for the Institution thus bravely defended, and before three years expired each of them became a Mason! Didn't Judah E—d—r himself tell us the circumstance? and haven't we met him in a Masters' Lodge?

Again: old Brother C—p—d, the day after he was expelled—he is dead now, and there is no harm in telling it—got extraordinarily drunk—so drunk as to forget an important point, and every point save the point of his sword-cane, and attacked Brother Frank Ashdod, the Junior Warden, with intent to take his life. He pursued Brother Ashdod, who would, of course, rather run than to fight an infuriated old man, Mason as he had been for forty years, he pursued him, we say, from one room to another in the hotel, until he cornered him, and then placing the point of that diabolical implement to his left breast, proceeded deliberately to run him through. Fortunately for both of them, Brother Ashdod was strong enough to turn aside the point, to take away the weapon, to throw it out of the window, and then, leading the would-be-murderer home, to dismiss him uninjured at his own doorway, as his brave, good heart prompted him.

With all his manly perfections, Brother Ashdod is "plain and natural," as the definition of the Doric column requires. He has "seldom any ornaments on base or capital, except moldings, though the frieze is distinguished by triglyphs and metopes, and triglyphs compose the ornaments of the frieze;" (not that we pretend to know what *triglyphs* and *metopes* are—and we never saw any one who did—but they are certainly applicable to Brother Ashdod!) and we can conscientiously affirm, from our own personal observation, that his "solid composition gives him a preference in structures where strength and a noble simplicity are chiefly required." We confess that we *have* seen him once or twice wearing a Masonic pin—it was in the shape of a column, a neat little thing made of eighteen carat gold—but in general he is satisfied to exhibit the graces of his own person without any meretricious ornaments. There is nothing finer than his appearance, as we remarked it one day when we presided over Brentford Lodge at the burial of a Brother; his portly bearing, with the Junior Warden's pillar reaching outward on his left arm, the Hiram grasped in his right hand, the plumb suspended upon his broad chest, everybody remarked it as we walked in procession to the grave. We could not help recalling a part of the definition of the Doric Order just then, and saying to ourselves, "the several parts of which this man is composed are founded on the natural position of bodies;" for so they were. And when arrived at the grave, and taking a handful of the loose mold, we divided it with the Wardens, as is our wont, and beckoned to the Junior Warden to do his part, with what simplicity and fervor he dropped the clay upon the coffin, quite concealed as it was by the pile of sprigs a hundred hands had tossed upon it, and pronounced his appropriate part, "dust to dust!"

It is scarcely necessary to add, that the charges delivered, and the duties enjoined upon him at his installation, form a part of his very religion. He feels that the PLUMB admonishes Masons to walk uprightly in their several stations; to hold the scale of justice in equal poise; to observe the just medium between intemperance and pleasure, and to make their passions and prejudices coincide with the line of their duty. He realizes that to him is committed the superintendence of the Craft during the hours of refreshment, and it is, therefore, indispensably necessary that *he* should not only be temperate and discreet in the indulgence of his own inclinations, but carefully observe that none of the Craft be suffered to convert the purposes of refreshment into intemperance and excess. He is too well acquainted with the principles of Masonry to warrant any distrust that he will be found wanting in the discharge of his duties. What he has seen praiseworthy in others he carefully imitates; and what in them has appeared defective he does in himself amend. He is an example of good order and regularity, feeling that it is only by a due regard to the laws in his own conduct that he can expect obedience to them from others. He assiduously assists the Master in the discharge of his trust, and diffuses light and imparts knowledge to all who are placed under his care. In the absence of the two officers above him he succeeds to higher duties, his acquirements being such as that the Craft never suffers for want of proper instruction.

ORDER THIRD.

BROTHER JOSEPH CONCORAN OF THE IONIC ORDER.

OUR subject, like all others within the compass of Masonic inquiry, partakes of the raciness and ripeness of age. From the first formation of society, says an orthodox guide, order in architecture may be traced. When the rigor of seasons obliged men to contrive shelter from the inclemency of the weather, we learn that they first planted trees on end, and then laid others across to support a covering. The bands which connected those trees from top to bottom are said to have given rise to the idea of the base and capital of pillars; and from this simple hint, originally, proceeded the more improved art of architecture.

But has the reader ever considered that all this attention to "Order," in Masonry, this precision in proportions, this scrupulous exactitude of admeasurements, was directed to *the eye*, and had reference to the "chief support" of BEAUTY, so well enforced in the Entered Apprentice's Lecture? yet it was even so. The stern old artisan of Tyre, who thought it not hard to die for the honor of his Craft, was the type, not of Wisdom or of Strength, but of *Beauty*, and his name and works, not less than his glorious end, are remembered, and will be remembered, even above the others.

The Ionic Order, in Brentford Lodge, is aptly represented by Brother Joseph Concoran, the Senior Warden, as all who know him will admit on perusal of the following definition of that Order: "The IONIC bears a kind of mean proportion between the more solid and delicate Orders. Its column is nine diameters high; its capital is adorned with volutes, and its cornice has dentils. There is both delicacy and ingenuity displayed in this pillar, the invention of which is attributed to the Ionians, as the famous temple of Diana at Ephesus was of this Order. It is said to have been formed after the model of an agreeable young woman, of an elegant shape, dressed in her hair; as a contrast to the Doric Order, which was formed after that of a strong, robust man."

Brother Concoran is a man who has little or none of John the Baptist about him. Dress him in camel's hair and he would be a ridiculous spectacle. Place him in the deserts beyond Jordan, and he would infallibly get lost. Attempt to feed him on locusts and wild honey, and he would starve to death. In point of fact, he was never made for things of that sort, as you will see by observing him in his seat in the West. How thin his figure!—it is nine diameters high—how pale, though beautiful, his face! It is as pale as a woman's, and almost as fair. But give him a fair showing with John the Evangelist, and you will soon discover his merits. The key to his character is *love, Brotherly love;* this is his pabulum, his stimulus.

Looking over his family Bible, one day, we were struck with the dilapidated condition of the *latter* portion of it. Such texts as these were nearly rubbed out by frequent use, as we have seen at a country hotel, a State map greasy and worn nearly through at the spot representing the locality: "The wisdom that is from above is first pure, then peaceable, gentle, and easy to be entreated, full of mercy and good fruits, without partiality and without hypocrisy." "Pure religion and undefiled before God and the Father, is this: To visit the fatherless and widows in their affliction, and keep himself unspotted from the world." But while these portions of his copy of the New Testament were almost illegible from frequent use, those terrible laws thundering wrath upon people who deserved all that they got and more, those passages, we mean, which occupy so much of the older Scriptures, seem to have had no attractions for him; for we found a one dollar bill alongside the eighteenth chapter of Genesis that looked as if it had been there ever since Brother Lafayette's visit, in 1825. If a man's daily reading is any index to his character, this will give us an insight into his. He is modeled upon that second of the "Lines Parallel," who died at Jerusalem, and his motto is: "By the exercise of Brotherly Love we are taught to regard the whole human species as one family; the high, the low, the rich, the poor; who, as created by one Almighty Parent, and inhabitants of the same planet, are to aid, support, and protect each other. On this principle Masonry unites men of every country, sect, and opinion, and conciliates true friendship among those who might otherwise have remained at a perpetual distance." Good words.

With all this loving soul, and the tenderness of nature that is its proof and crown, it is not strange that there is a tinge of melancholy in the manner of Brother Concoran, induced, perhaps, by much ill-health and various trials into which the vicissitudes of life have plunged him. It is with an appropriateness then, somewhat unusual, that he wears *the Level*, which is his Jewel and badge of office, and contemplates its lessons: "That we are descended from the same stock, partake of the same nature, and share the same hope; and though distinctions among men are necessary to preserve subordination, yet no eminence of station should make us forget that we are Brethren. He who is placed on the lowest spoke of fortune's wheel may be entitled to our regard; because a time will come, and the wisest knows not how soon, when all distinctions but that of goodness will cease, and death, the grand leveler of human greatness, reduce us to the same state." These melancholy, yet healthful thoughts, are often expressed by him before the lodge, at such times as, just prior to its close, the Master calls aloud to him to pay the Craft their wages, if any be due them, and see that none go away dissatisfied. At such times, we say, he calls upon the Brethren to consider the uncertainty of human life, the immutable certainty of death, and the variety of all human pursuits. He directs them to fix their eyes on the last sad scene, and view life stripped of its ornaments and exposed in its natural meanness, that they may be persuaded of the utter emptiness of these delusions. In the grave, he asserts, all fallacies are detected, all ranks are leveled, all distinctions are done away. But when saddened by such words, the Brethren turn toward the door as if about to wend their way in silence homeward, he calls them back, reminds them affectionately that after labor comes refreshment, and at the table raises a friendly and brotherly sound above them all. Doubtless that is the way John the Baptist did before him. After preaching his fraternal sentiments in language that can never die, we are perfectly convinced that that loving Evangelist gave at the symposium, which followed the best toast, and most likely, the best song of the occasion. Disprove it who can!

"There is both delicacy and ingenuity displayed in this pillar." Brother Concoran, in other words, has cultivated a taste for the more graceful in science and literature. The adornments of the lodge are all of his devising. That group of laborers at work in the quarries; those lofty cedars; the heavy raft, nigh shipwrecked off the coast of Joppa; the tasteful imagery in which are so ingeniously blended the implements of Operative, with the charges of Speculative Masonry—all these are his. The Scriptural mottoes upon the wall, selected not at random, but with a thoughtful sense of their application to Masonry, are his. The furniture was modeled, piece by piece, under his eye. The five pillars illustrating the five Orders of Architecture, the only set we ever saw whose proportions are accurate, are of his own estimate. You can not look at any part of the hall without seeing something of that delicacy and ingenuity which belong to him as the type of the Ionic Order.

Again, you see traces of this mental elegance in the records, the by-laws, and the reports made the Grand Lodge by Brentford Lodge. The by-laws, particularly, are clothed in the loveliest sentiments that even Masonry affords, and the typographical adornments in which they are presented are worthy of them. The annual returns are prepared by Brother Concoran's own hand—Brother Scribendi not being a neat pensman, though an accurate one—and are models of elegance. This runs again into the patterns of the aprons and collars, the rods and gavels, the jewels and carpets, and in whatever else, neatness, grace, and beauty may be made adjuncts to utility. All this goes to illustrate that his capital is adorned with volutes and his cornice with dentils.

King David had such men as Brother Concoran in view, when he said: "Behold, how good and how pleasant it is *for brethren to dwell together in unity.* It is like the precious ointment upon the head, that ran down upon the beard, even Aaron's beard, that went down to the skirts of his garment: as the dew of Hermon, and as the dew that descended upon the mountains of Zion; for there the Lord commanded the blessing, even life forevermore"—and it is such pictures of fraternal happiness that every visitor to Brentford Lodge will witness. On the occasion of our first call there, we were an admiring witness of the following incident, which we give in token thereof. A feud, savage as a Corsican's and durable as a Scotchman's, was in fervid action between the families of the Ravels, at Brentford, and the Comyns, at Belfast, some ten miles away; and Brother Concoran had set himself, in the spirit of love, to heal it. It was a large, a bad, an offensive sore. Cousins and brothers-in-law, and chattering old maids, and obstinate men and women generally, had become jumbled up in the turmoil, until the skein was so snarled that you couldn't find the end of the thread. The good Senior Warden made several passes at the case without success. As no two of the parties in dispute looked at the subject in the same light, there was, of course, no common ground upon which they could meet to settle it. The attempt, therefore, appeared as futile as to settle a general plug-muss in a snake-den at the approach of spring.

It was accomplished, however, by means of Masonry, and in this way. Old Hugh Comyn, of Belfast, was an original member of Belfast Lodge, and would do anything that he thought Masonry required of him, yea, even if the sacrifice had been as great as Brother Jephthah's was. Being an ardent bob-a-sheely of Brother Concoran's, he accepted an invitation to come over and see a "raising" at Brentford. Now the party to be raised was no other than Tom Ravel, who, of all the Ravels, was the one most offensive to Old Hugh; but the latter, being short-sighted to an extreme, didn't recognize him till the work was done, and not until, in accordance with a blessed usage in that Lodge, he went up with the rest of them to shake hands with him. Imagine the scene as we saw it! Tom, seeing the old gentleman walking smilingly up, with his fin extended horizontally before him, supposed him desirous of healing the feud, and though much surprised at the suddenness of the thing, being an impulsive, generous fellow, he sprang forward, clasped his hand nervously, and burst into tears! Old Hugh, electrified at the tears, astonished at the discovery of who the party was, and troubled at soul at a few words Concoran slipped into his ear just at the instant, ("Beloved, if God so loved us, we ought also to love one another,") threw his left arm round Tom's neck and cried aloud! There never was such a scene before or since; the general excitement was so great that the Tyler was compelled to open the windows, by which means the thing got out, and before daylight it was all over town that the Comyns and Ravels had made it up by the means of Masonry! They did so, and are now good friends, thanks to the guile with which the loving Brother deluded them to their lasting good.

One thing is pretty certain, and we must not forbear to tell it—the health of this good Brother, the type of the Ionic Order, is such that he is plainly but a little while for this world. There will be a scene of no common interest when Brother Concoran dies and is buried. It will be good, we think, to be there. His last view will be from a Pisgah as high as Nebo, and the sky will be cloudless, as he surveys the Promised Land, to tell the solemnized group around, the good sights of the vision. Should we outlive him—ah! the tremendous query, *shall we?*—should our flickering wick burn a little longer than his, it will be a sacred duty to go and join the hundreds who love, respect, and admire him as we do, in the last rites of Masonry. This much we have promised him and ourselves.

ORDER FOURTH.

BROTHER HENRY EVANS OF THE CORINTHIAN ORDER.

It is for this, the richest of the Five Orders, that masterpiece of art, represented in Brentford Lodge by that polished shaft of Masonry, Brother Henry Evans, the Worshipful Master and Past Grand Master—it is for this we have reserved our quotations from Brother Webb's Monitor, relative to the moral advantages of geometry in a Masonic sense. The reader must not pass them over, even though they may appear a little tedious; for there is nothing that Webb, or rather Preston before him, ever wrote more worthy a Mason's notice. "Geometry, the first and noblest of sciences, is the basis on which the superstructure of Freemasonry is erected. By geometry we may curiously trace nature, through her various windings, to her most concealed recesses. By it we discover the power, wisdom, and goodness of the Grand Artificer of the Universe, and view with delight the proportions which connect this vast machine. By it we discover how the planets move in their respective orbits, and demonstrate their various revolutions. By it we account for the return of the seasons, and the variety of scenes which each season displays to the discerning eye. Numberless worlds are around us, all framed by the same Divine Artist, which roll through the vast expanse, and are all conducted by the same unerring law of nature.

"A survey of nature, and the observation of her beautiful proportions, first determined man to imitate the Divine plan, and study symmetry and order. This gave rise to societies, and birth to every useful art. The architect began to design; and the plans which he laid down, being improved by time and experience, have produced works which are the admiration of every eye.

"The lapse of time, the ruthless hand of ignorance, and the devastations of war, have laid waste and destroyed many valuable monuments of antiquity, on which the utmost exertions of human genius have been employed. Even the Temple of Solomon, so spacious and magnificent, and constructed by so many celebrated artists, escaped not the unsparing ravages of barbarous force. Freemasonry, notwithstanding, has still survived. The attentive ear receives the sound from the instructive tongue, and the mysteries of Masonry are safely lodged in the repository of faithful breasts. Tools and implements of architecture, and symbolic emblems most expressive, are selected by the Fraternity to imprint on the mind wise and serious truths; and thus, through a succession of ages, are transmitted unimpaired the most excellent tenets of our profession."

Thus forcible and eloquent are the vital lessons presented to us through the medium of Masonry.

To show the application of all this to our type of the Corinthian Order, Brother Henry Evans, it is only necessary to give the definition:

"The Corinthian, the richest of the Five Orders, is deemed a masterpiece of art. Its column is ten diameters high, and its capital is adorned with two rows of leaves and eight volutes, which sustain the abacus. The frieze is ornamented with curious devices; the cornice with dentils and modillions. This Order is used in stately and superb structures.

"It was invented in Corinth, by Callimachus, who is said to have taken the hint of the capital of this pillar from the following remarkable circumstance: Accidentally passing by the tomb of a young lady, he perceived a basket of toys, covered with a tile, placed over an acanthus root, having been left there by her nurse. As the branches grew up, they encompassed the basket, until arriving at the tile, they met with an obstruction and bent downward. Callimachus, struck with the object, set about imitating the figure. The vase of the capital he made to represent the basket; the abacus the tile; and the volutes the bending leaves."

Among the curious topics which, of late years, have elicited debate among Masonic writers is this, whether great talents and enlarged fame give a man any peculiar merit in the sight of Masonry? Some have argued, from the radical theory promulgated in our lectures, that all men are absolutely equal in the sight of God, and therefore entitled to equal regard as Masons. This argument is not borne out by facts. So far as the Divine love and attention are concerned, we are not called upon to decide; yet, from the diverse circumstances under which we find humanity placed, it would not be illogical to say that the Heavenly Father shows his own preferences in many things that conduce to the happiness of men. But, so far as Masonry is concerned, it is clear to our mind that very decided distinctions are and ought to be made in relation to applicants — distinctions based upon their moral, social, and religious eminence in the world. For instance, after the revival of Masonry about Brentford, and the proposition to re-organize the old lodge there, Brother Henry Evans made known his desire to become attached to the Order. He was a man who had held the highest distinctions in his native State, having been a judge, governor of the State, and president of a college. His great wealth, universal popularity, and uncommon learning were so many means of usefulness and honor as he employed them. Now, when he announced his wish to attain to Masonic honors, no second thought was required. What was the use of the farce of a committee of inquiry? He had been tried in the furnace of public opinion for twenty years, and found true and sincere. Therefore the Brethren unanimously signed a petition to the Grand Master, who came down in person and initiated, passed, and raised him by dispensation. The Brethren of Brentford Lodge took up the case where the Grand Master left it—elected him a Warden at the first election, and Worshipful Master at the second. Then he fell into the hands of the Grand Lodge, which, at the first bound, indorsed public opinion by making Judge Evans Grand Master. There being nothing higher than that, at least on this side of Jordan, the Honorable Brother fell back upon Brentford Lodge, which repeated its evidences of confidence and attachment by re-electing him Master, nominally for a year, but actually, so it is privately understood by the members, *ad vitam*, for life.

This little sketch of the accomplished Master of Brentford Lodge will explain somewhat of the uncommon respect we evince when we speak of him. Brother Evans is a great man. It is good to sit in the lodge when he presides. "Blessed art thou, O Lodge!" thought we, the last time we paid a visit there, while contemplating the man and his ways, "when thy king is the son of nobles, and thy princes eat in due season for strength and not for drunkenness!" As the lily among thorns, as the apple-tree among the trees of the wood, as the Corinthian among the Orders of Architecture, so towers this wise and good man among his Brethren—"beautiful as Tirseh, comely as Jerusalem, terrible as an army with banners." Such language, fulsome and extravagant as it may sound, does but feebly represent the veneration inspired in the heart of all his Brethren by this distinguished officer.

The Grand Lodge having, in the regular order of succession, committed to his care the superintendence and government of his Brethren who compose Brentford Lodge, he is thoroughly sensible of the obligations that devolve upon him as their head, and of his responsibility for the faithful discharge of the important duties annexed to the office. The honor, reputation, and usefulness of the lodge, he feels, materially depend upon the skill and assiduity with which he manages its concerns, while the happiness of its members is promoted in proportion to the zeal and ability with which he propagates the general principles of the Institution.

For a pattern of imitation, he takes the luminary of nature, which, rising in the east, regularly diffuses light and luster to all within the circle. In like manner, it is his province to spread and communicate light and instruction to the Brethren of his lodge, and this is his unremitted care. Forcibly he impresses upon them the dignity and high importance of Masonry, and often and seriously admonishes them never to disgrace it. Out of the lodge, he charges them to practice those duties which they are taught in it; and requires them, by amiable, discreet, and virtuous conduct, to convince mankind of the goodness of the Institution. It is his theory, that, by this course of conduct, Masonry may be so elevated, that when a person is said to be a member of it, the world may know that he is one to whom the burdened heart may pour out its sorrows; to whom distress may prefer its suit; whose hand is guided by justice, and his heart expanded by benevolence. These injunctions to others, being accurately drawn out from his own life, enables him to acquit himself with honor and reputation, and inspire a hope that he shall lay up a crown of rejoicing, to continue when time shall be no more.

This Corinthian column, the pride and glory of Brentford Lodge, attracts the admiration of every wayfarer; and it is a small and natural change from admiring *him* to admiring the *Institution* he represents. Thus it happens that, according to the Grand Lecturer's report, "no lodge in all that Masonic district is enjoying such outward and material prosperity as this." The increase of membership, though the door of admission is jealously narrowed and guarded, and the rejections are numerous, is very great, from year to year, and composed of the best material in and about Brentford. What wonder! Are not those who enjoy the daily friendship of Brother Evans *out of* the lodge, the individuals most likely to desire to pursue his friendship *within it?* Go to. If you would have the better class of men among the applicants at your doors, place in the ranks of leaders those of your members who correspond with that class, prudently recollecting that "like begets like," and that the Institution is mainly judged through those who are its heads. It is a small matter for you at least to put your best foot foremost.

It were quite superfluous to say that this accomplished leader in Israel spares none of the appliances of the Masonic trade in qualifying himself and his lodge for the best work, while the subject of adornments, and the graces and beauties of Masonry, are safely left with the Senior Warden, as we detailed in our last sketch; and while the topics of discipline and government in general are confided trustingly to the Junior Warden, as also we have said before, Brother Evans takes it upon himself to see that the tools of speculative Masonry are abundantly furnished to the membership, kept bright and sharp in use, and their use from time to time explained. We mean, of course, that all the advantages of Masonic literature, and of that oral instruction which has its immovable basis in Masonic literature, are abundantly furnished to the Masons of Brentford Lodge. Its library is the best in the State. Its collection of the current literature of the Craft, the journals, the proceedings of the greater and lesser bodies, the addresses upon all Masonic occasions, etc., is respectable, and is daily increasing. The Orator of the lodge gives a half-hour oration at every meeting. Each degree conferred is the theme of lengthy and most interesting discourses from the Master, whose proxy the Orator is. The festivals are always made occasions of Masonic profit, by intelligent addresses delivered either in or out of the lodge; and, most sensible of all, each advancing Brother is advised and expected to acquire a respectable amount of Masonic information from these various publications as a qualification for higher degrees.

Our theme is an endless one, but its moral may be condensed into this word of exhortation: "Put your Corinthian column in the East!" There are many lodges that linger, fail, and die from a disregard of this plain law of common sense; many lodges, possessing more than one Corinthian column of the kind alluded to in the definition, "the richest of the Orders, masterpieces of art," that, by a strange blindness, elevate columns of the inferior orders, or of no orders at all save bastard orders, and discover their error only in their dying hours. We would be found warning our Brethren against so fatal a mistake. Though every lodge may not have its Evans, yet every lodge has some Brother in its membership of the class of which Evans is but a type; or, failing in this, that lodge ought to die, and must die. The doctrine that all Masons are equal, and equally qualified to rule and govern their Brethren, is as false as that all men are equally wise, equally strong, and equally beautiful. Those who have acted upon such a theory, have discovered the error sooner or later. We would that those who honor our poor efforts with a perusal, may be spared the sacrifices which experience upon this head demands, and be advised by those who, having suffered, are qualified to teach.

ORDER FIFTH.

BROTHER BOWLING FANT, OF THE COMPOSITE ORDER.

HAVING come to the last number in our series of Orders, it may be as well to observe, lest an undue prominence be given to this modern and factitious Order, termed the Composite, that the ancient and original Orders of architecture revered by Masons, are no more than three, the *Doric*, *Ionic*, and *Corinthian*, which were invented by the Greeks. To these the Romans have added two, the *Tuscan*, which they made plainer than the Doric, and the *Composite*, which was more ornamental, if not more beautiful than the Corinthian. The first three Orders alone, however, show invention and particular character, and essentially differ from each other; the two others have nothing but what is borrowed, and differ only accidentally; the Tuscan is the Doric in its earliest state; and the Composite is the Corinthian enriched with the Ionic. To the Greeks, therefore, and not to the Romans, we are indebted for what is great, judicious, and distinct in architecture.

These remarks, furnished us from Webb's Monitorial Lectures, lead us naturally to the definition of the Composite Order, and show us its application in Brentford Lodge to Brother Bowling Fant, the Senior Deacon: "The Composite is compounded of the other Orders, and was contrived by the Romans. Its capital has the two rows of leaves of the Corinthian and the volutes of the Ionic. Its column has quarter-rounds, as the Tuscan and Doric Orders; is ten diameters high, and its cornices has dentils or simple modillions. This pillar is generally found in buildings where strength, elegance, and beauty are displayed."

In reply to this last remark, we are not prepared to deny that there is a sort of specious beauty, an outside elegance, about the Composite Order, when seen with an untrained eye, or that its strength may be as great as anything which is ten diameters high could be expected to be,—but we do say that no one, who loves purity in Masonry, can esteem it in comparison with the other Orders. It is a bastard, nay worse, a hybrid in architecture. It is not merely an unauthorized alteration from an acknowledged scientific type, but the hybrid progeny of two Orders, which, by the unvarying laws of architectural physiology might never be conjoined. It is as though a Brother had wedded his sister, and they begat it.

This, we are sorry to be compelled to say, is exactly the case with Brother Bowling Fant, the Senior Deacon of Brentford Lodge, whose Masonic character comes last upon the tapis. He is a bastard, if not a hybrid Mason. He was first of all an Orangeman in Ireland; from that he slid naturally, but not gracefully, into Odd-Fellowship. When the rage for drinking cold water on the square came about, he joined in chronological order: 1. The Washingtonians; 2. The Sons of Temperance; 3. The Rechabites; 4. The Templars of Temperance. Having run through the Temperance gamut, he was next a Red Man, and as the Druids met in Red Man's Hall, he became a Druid. Of course he was one of the earliest of the Know-nothings, and as he was fortunately able to talk a modicum of Dutch, he went over from that on the other side of the ridge and became a Sag Nicht. *Last of all he tried Masonry!*

One advantage, to be sure, the costly experience gives him,—an advantage that the Worshipful Master, Brother Evans, was not slow to detect,—he makes a good Senior Deacon! To give him his due, this Hybrid of a Mason makes one of the most graceful, fluent, and impressive Senior Deacons we have ever seen; and Brentford Lodge is justly proud of him in that capacity. Having a happy facility of memorizing, he can give all the monitorial lectures of the three degrees without glancing at the book. Having seen such an immense variety of applications of the Masonic emblems and lectures in the various imitative societies to which he has belonged, he is able to season his part well with such variations as add grace and novelty thereto. And this makes him popular with those with whom he has to do in an official capacity.

But it is the peculiarity of the Composite Order, which was compounded of the other Orders, and contrived by the Romans, that it will not bear minute inspection. This putting the two rows of leaves of the Corinthian with the volutes of the Ionic, and adding the quarter-rounds of the Tuscan and Doric Orders, is only calculated to attract the eye, but can not please the mind. It is like those hideous drawings on Chinese boards, in which the several parts may be sufficiently graceful and pleasing, but *the whole* is execrable. In studying the character of Brother Fant, the thought irresistibly intrudes: How long before he will try some other society? There can be no confidence put in a man who only tabernacles in a place for a few months or years, and then pulls up stakes and is off to fresh fields and pastures new. Compare the case of Brother Lemuel Fairfax, that thorough Mason described in the first paper of this series, with the one before us. The former is *all Mason*. He knows nothing higher, broader, deeper; he looks to a Masonic lip to give him a remembrance among men after he is dead. Like a faithful husband, who, the longer he lives with the bride of his youth, the more firmly he becomes attached to her, and who only hopes that, of the twain, she may not be the first called away; so Brother Fairfax, having early given his heart to Masonry, looks to it to be the attachment of his declining years. But the latter embraces Masonry only as one of a harem of concubines. He has toyed with the meretricious charms of the others until they have palled upon his appetite, and his fervor in Masonry, his last conquest, is likely to be as short-lived as it is excessive. View, we say, the contrast, and act the judge between them.

The practical weakness of Brother Fant, in a Masonic point of view, may be shown by a few examples. He can not be restrained from arguing the wondrous merits of Masonry in every company, disregarding that caution in the Ancient Charges which forbids it; and great evils have grown out of it. He was so accustomed to do this in the Temperance societies that it is bred in his bone. He has introduced much confusion in the Temple, and more than once brought himself under the Junior Warden's notice by proselyting for applicants, contrary to the express injunctions of the Order. The discovery was made by the honest refusal of one or two to declare, in the anteroom, that, "Unbiased by friends, and uninfluenced by mercenary motives, they freely and voluntarily offered themselves candidates for the mysteries of Masonry." He was so accustomed to proselyting among the Odd-Fellows—where he was acknowledged to be the greatest drummer out of Philadelphia—that he can not, he will not relinquish the practice. Its pursuit will some day pass him ignominiously out of the South gate.

He is excessively incautious in his use of pen and ink in relation to the private matters of the Institution. Having come from societies using written Rituals, the invincible repugnance of Symbolic Masons to anything of that sort has no counterpart in his breast. When he dies, the parties who open his private cabinet will find some queer manuscripts, which, though they can work no actual injury to the Masonic Order, will leave serious imputations upon his memory. What would you think of a man who would deliberately record and recklessly preserve the minutiæ of his nuptial night?

His tongue is unmasonically glib in relation to the particular business of the Lodge. He not only usurps the business of the Secretary, who, of right, should give certain notifications to proper parties, but he makes those notifications to parties who are not entitled to have them, and others that should be made to no one out of the Lodge. It was the habit in some of the societies to which he belonged, to do this thing. They boasted that their only secret was a simple means of recognition, and challenged the whole world to examine and approve all their proceedings. Is it strange that the introduction of such a heresy into his Lodge has created an uproar? Yet the habit is so deeply rooted in the man that it is apparently incurable.

Finally, this unmasonic jumbling up of orders and systems in the Composite, is seen in the looseness of the tie that binds Brother Fant to the Masonic Institution. The spirit with which he entered it was of the same uncemented character. "He was going to join the Masons," he said. "He had been thinking for some time that he would join the Masons." "He would try them awhile, any-how;" and his opinion of the tie is, evidently, that it may be dissolved at pleasure. He calls a diploma a "withdrawal card," and views it as one. Whenever he gets tired of the Institution, which he can hardly fail to do in time, he will "take out a withdrawal card," and consider his connection with the Institution virtually at an end. Thus *the shoe*, in his mind, has no force; the *cable-tow* no meaning; *the trowel* no utility. What of wisdom, strength, or beauty, can be expected of such a Mason? Suppose a Lodge, officered by three such men, one in the East, one in the West, one in the South—could there be any doubt as to its fate? In all the strength of our great Institution, as it is developed in the United States, we have found nothing added by the class represented here under the appropriate type of the Composite Order.

We close our series by an earnest recommendation to every Brother to pursue these topics on a scale more nearly commensurate with their merits than is usually done. There is not a paragraph in the lectures, exoteric or esoteric, but what contains the germ of a valuable essay, and will reward the student for his labors. Some of us like them in the form of tale and pleasing sketch; it is for that class, mainly, that this series is written. The intelligent mind will readily penetrate the flimsy gauze we have thrown over important truths, and receive them in their purity. Others best appreciate Masonic knowledge in other forms—the recent awakening of mind among our Fraternity promises a thorough exploration of every vein, and the presentation of truth in every form. As an illustration of the highly symbolic language of our lectures, take the following: "By Operative Masonry we allude to a proper application of the useful rules of architecture, whence a structure will derive figure, strength, and beauty, and whence will result a due proportion and a just correspondence in all its parts. It furnishes us with dwellings and convenient shelters from the vicissitudes and inclemencies of seasons; and while it displays the effects of human wisdom, as well in the choice as in the arrangement of sundry materials of which an edifice is composed, it demonstrates that a fund of science and industry is implanted in man for the best, most salutary, and beneficent purposes." In this paragraph is the key to the series of sketches we are just concluding, and in it is material for an unlimited number of exhibitions in every form of the amenities of our beloved Institution.

Brother: Your zeal for our Institution, the progress you have made in our mysteries, and your steady conformity to our useful regulations, have pointed you out as a proper object for this peculiar mark of our favor.

Duty and honor, now alike, bind you to be faithful to every trust; to support the dignity of your character on all occasions; and strenuously to enforce, by precept and example, a steady obedience to the tenets of Freemasonry. Exemplary conduct on your part will convince the world that merit is the just title to our privileges, and that on you our favors have not been undeservedly bestowed.

In this respectable character you are authorized

to correct the irregularities of your misinformed Brethren; to fortify their minds with resolution against the snares of the insidious; and to guard them against every allurement to vicious practices. To preserve unsullied the reputation of the Fraternity ought to be your care; and, therefore, it becomes your province to caution the inexperienced against a breach of fidelity. To your inferiors in rank or office you are to recommend obedience and submission; to your equals, courtesy and affability; to your superiors, kindness and condescension. Universal benevolence you are zealously to inculcate; and, by the regularity of your own conduct, endeavor to remove every aspersion against the venerable Institution. Our ancient landmarks you are carefully to preserve, and not suffer them on any pretence to be infringed, or countenance a deviation from our established customs.

Your honor and reputation are concerned in supporting with dignity the respectable character you now bear. Let no motive, therefore, make you swerve from your duty, violate your vows, or betray your trust; but be true and faithful, and imitate the example of that celebrated Artist whom you have this evening represented. Thus you will render yourself deserving of the honor which we have conferred, and worthy of the confidence we have reposed in you.

Bob White and his Lectures.

A TALE OF THE PURSUIT OF KNOWLEDGE UNDER DIFFICULTIES.

Inscribed to Brother John Ransom,
OF ST. JOHNS, MICHIGAN.

BROTHER BOB WHITE, or as we call him in the lodge, *Robert Ebenezer Flake White*, had got his first degree and liked it, as himself declared, "*right smart.*" In fact, to pursue his own phraseology. "*It rather took his persimmon*"—or, to vary the figure with another of his happy hyperboles, "*It wed his injun patch clean out.*" By all which expressions we understand his approval of Freemasonry in general, and that portion of it learned on the ground-floor of King Solomon's Temple in particular.

It *is* whispered, however, that Bob had stretched his verity a little when he declared in his petition "that he had long entertained a favorable opinion of Freemasonry." Certain it is, he had read Bernard, Morgan, and Crafts, as found in the library of Rev. Zerubbabel Cash, the hard-shelled pastor of Corcoe Church; and 'tis very unlikely that the man who peruses that trio with the hard-shell faith (Bob had been himself a hard-shell of the stoniest sort), 'tis very unlikely, we say, that his opinion of Masonry could be anything but hostile. Be that as it may, however, Bob petitioned, was elected, forked over, and was initiated, as we remarked in the very first paragraph of this sketch.

His initiation (or as Bob, who is not a classical scholar, pronounced the word, *inishooashun*), being complete, Bob became free to acknowledge that the thing wasn't what he had expected. It was better, *a heap*—more solemn, more impressive—in its moral bearings, more like Bible teachings, which, to Bob's credit, be it observed, he especially delighted in. What he could gather from once hearing the lectures, pleased him so well that he determined to get the sensation duplicated soon as possible; and the very next day after his *inishooashun* aforesaid, he started out for that purpose. His adventures in the quest will form a solid foundation for this veritable article.

Bob's appearance as a traveler was not impressive. Brought up under the severest requisitions of *home manufactures*, he thought no pantaloons so comfortable, no coat and vest so elegant, as those made of wool clipped from sheep raised on his own land—said wool being spun and woven by his own wife's hands—said garment cut and sewed by the same. Following this line of political faith, Bob's hat was necessarily of the manufacture of Tom Looby, of Loobyville, close by, who (not to be guilty of slandering a Brother Mason) knows nothing of Genin or Oakford—his boots acknowledged the workmanship of Coney, Mrs. Smith's nigger, and the rest of his wardrobe corresponded. However a man's politics or his purse may be strengthened by it, his appearance is not improved by this style of dress, especially where, as in Bob's case, the craftsmen, to wit: Mrs. White, Tom Looby, and the nigger Coney, are but dabsters at their respective arts.

Bob rode a mule. Glorying in a stomach that knew nothing of neuralgia, and a temper placid as a Quaker's, he could bear with the animal's infirmities without a token of impatience. Thus mounted, thus dressed, see him, then, on his way to get lectured.

First to Past Master Sloane's. Not at home. Nobody is ever at home in the country. Either they are in the field at work, or in the woods hunting, or out borrowing something of their neighbors. The Past Master was engaged in the latter vocation, and Bob followed him to Parvin's, whither he had gone to borrow a file. Arrived there, he took Sloane down into the spring-house, three hundred yards from anywhere, looked cautiously around on all sides, and told him his business. Past Master Sloane colored up to the eyes, hesitated, blundered, prevaricated, and, finally, came out with the humiliating confession that *he was too rusty*. Hadn't conferred a degree in five years. Couldn't attend lodge regularly. Go to Brother Hamburg's.

Bob was dampened. What! a Past Master not able to give the lectures! Why, they told him the night before, that the Master of a lodge was the representative of King Solomon, and had *all* the light! and here was Brother Sloane, the very man who organized the lodge only six years before, and after whom the lodge had been named, without *any* light! Discouraging. Bob asked him, suppose he was going to travel, how would he pass himself? To which the rusty Brother pettishly replied, he didn't expect to travel any more! Whereat Bob sawed him off with the inquiry, how would he examine a visiting Brother who should call on him for that purpose? And the Past Master was prudent enough to make no reply.

Astride his mule again, Bob took a bee-line for Brother Hamburg's. This Brother had once been a pillar in his lodge. First at the hall, at every meeting, he was known to be efficient for any post in which he was placed; the last to leave the hall, he was the enlightened center of a circle that remained for instruction's sake for hours after the lodge was closed. But Brother Hamburg had become a changed man. In a journey to another State, he had fallen in with a green sprout from the Masonic tree, whose fruitage was not of the old graft. How it ever came to pass that the sound branch was thus ingrafted, we have in other places and often tried to tell. So it is, the enlightened eye can detect these *foreign sprouts* amid the foliage. But Brother Hamburg was deluded, ate of the clandestine fruit, was gratified with its, to us, insipid flower, and from that moment his Masonic usefulness was gone. He came home professing, like Eve, "that his eyes were opened, knowing good from evil."—(Genesis iii: 5.) He approached his Brethren as an innovator. He declared that Masonry was naked and needed covering; and, to set the example, he had sewed for himself fig leaves and tied them around him. To drop the allegory, he preached "improvement in the Masonic system—improvement in the lectures—improvement in the work—improvement in the grammar—improvement even in the means of Masonic recognition!" He became troublesome to his Brethren in consequence, and a clique-leader. Imagine Bob's astonishment, then, when on approaching Brother Hamburg to get the standard lectures, he received, instead, a tirade against the work, as the lodge was practicing it, and a recommendation to Bob "to pay no attention to it, but acquire it on the improved plan!" The staggered neophyte yet shrewdly inquired, how will Masons in other States know us then, if we adopt a new way? To which it was responded, "Our way is so much better than theirs, they will soon acquire it." But in the meantime? "In the meantime we shall be engaged in a good work, that of perfecting the glorious system of Masonry, conforming it to the improved age in which we live, bringing it up to the standard of other affiliated societies, supplying the vacant links in it, and furnishing to the world something that is the acme of all that is glorious, fraternal, and pure!" Has the Grand Lodge adopted this work? "No; but they will." Are you not afraid the old Masons will oppose it? "Let them do it. In a few years they will be out of the way!"

Bob rode off to Brother Haszard, the Junior Warden. It was six miles distant and the day was cold, but Bob felt not the air, nor thought a moment of the miles. He was brooding over the words of Brother Hamburg. There is something so tempting in the thought of becoming *a reformer*, that the young Mason is easily carried away with it. More than once, Brother Bob stopped his mule and almost turned back, but better thoughts prevailed, and he reached the gate of the Junior Warden, determined to make another effort.

Brother Haszard was called a bright Mason, and was glad to see Bob, and glad to lecture him; more by token. He was lying up with rheumatism and couldn't get out. So, after talking about everything else he could think of, and trading mules with him, in which latter operation he got to windward, he sent his wife to a neighbor's and his children to the nigger-quarters, and commenced the lecture.

* * * * * * *

But, expostulated Bob, I was told there is *a rational explanation* to all this! "Well, didn't I give you a rational explanation? Don't I tell you what these emblems mean?" Why, no—yes—you told me what the emblems meant, but you didn't say why they meant it. You explain the emblems, but you don't say what the emblems explain. Isn't there something more? "Nothing more in your degree. You must go higher?" But—but—how does this system improve a man's morality? What have I learned yet that has anything to do with morality? "Go higher, Bob, go higher, and you will get the idea."

Poor Bob started home. The Junior Warden, as you and I can see, excellent reader, was a mere stick-in-the-mud of a Mason. He knew no more of Masonry, than a man can know of the comforts of a domestic fireside by examining a brick that came out of the chimney thereof. *He*, lecture on Masonry! as well a lad lecture on Rhetoric who has just learned his alphabet by rote.

Poor Bob started home sad and disappointed. His mule partook of his depression, and became soured in temper and vicious. Consequently, just as the Entered Apprentice was going by the house of Mrs. Harrison—old Brother Harrison's widow—you knew Brother Harrison—the brute took advantage of a fit of musing into which its rider had fallen, and threw him off, kicked him as he was falling, and jumped on his carcass after he was down.

Bob was carried into the widow's house and laid upon the widow's bed, from which he never rose until Spring. The long nights spent in pain from his fractured ribs, taught him patience, resignation, and fortitude; the visits of the Brethren who stood sentinel by him for two months, instructed him in Brotherly Love and Relief; other and still more precious truths were inculcated through his blessed fall, and *thus Bob White got lectured.*

The Junior Warden, discovering Bob's disappointment at *his* system of lecturing, took the hint and looked *behind* the looking-glass—to wit, the emblems. What he saw there, ask us not; but it changed the Masonic character of the whole man.

The Past Master took shame to himself for his rust, and, applying the mental file, got bright, and, before Bob's fifth rib knitted to his sternum, could lecture like a Solomon. He always declared that to Bob's sick-bed he was indebted for the suggestion and the opportunity of improving his Masonic character.

But Brother Hamburg was past improving. He had tasted the forbidden fruit, and to the paths of innocence and unsophisticated truth there was no return for him. He became conspicuous elsewhere, and Freemasonry lost him. Expelled for contumacy, his appeal to the Grand Lodge was a bitter accusation against Masons and Masonry in general, and a particular commentary upon the dangers of innovation.

So soon as his fifth rib knitted, Bob was taken in triumph to the lodge and passed into the Middle Chamber like a shot. It was a joyful scene. Everybody was glad. Even old Aleck Gooseberry, the Tyler, who, having prophesied that Bob would die, didn't like to have his prediction fail—even old Aleck smiled when Bob "tuck him by the paw-paw and shuck it till it hurt." Widow Harrison, who had lost thirty-one pounds weight nursing Bob these two months, made a new Bible-cushion for the occasion to *swar* him on! "Masons swar, don't they?" yelpt old Mother Harrison, and echo answered *swar*. And so, as we said before, Bob White got lectured.

The Leak in the Lodge.

A TALE OF MASONIC CAUTION.

Inscribed to Bro. the Hon. J. L. Smedley,
OF HARRODSBURG, KENTUCKY.

THERE is a leak in Mirror Lodge, beyond all doubt or controversy. Bats do not communicate Masonic intelligence; mice and night-flying insects are powerless to divulge its secrets; the days of ghosts and fairies are long past. Yet they only, with three-and-twenty Masons, heard the fact communicated that "Brother Bendle was about to be tried for slandering Brother Shaw's wife;" and, for all that, the fact has become as well-known throughout the village of Scorpio, and has excited as much speculation, as the fact that Fillmore and Buchanan were opposing candidates for the Presidency. The only explanation to this that we can give is, *there is a leak.*

Nor is this the first instance upon record of a leak in a Masonic lodge. Far from it. We wish it was; but our memorandum-book too truthfully reveals a number of them, more or less *unpluggable.* There is one, for instance, in Cotchecon Lodge, through which has oozed the unpleasant fact, "that Barney Lenter was blackballed, in May last, by *seven* votes."

There is one in Doleg Lodge, at this very time, whose dimensions are frightfully large, and out of which has lately trickled the intelligence, "that Mrs. Soaper's claim for charity was refused because her husband was only a Fellow-craft when he died." There is one also in Rusoy Lodge, at this minute, through which regularly leaks everything curious and interesting that happens there, and a great deal still more curious and more interesting that *never* happens there. These leaks, though unpluggable, are not then altogether undiscoverable. The one in Cotchecon Lodge, for instance, is owing to ——; but we are not justified in telling all we know; and we spare Brother —— the humiliation of a public exposure. (Only we will say this, if our wife were to ask us as many foolish questions, when we come home from the lodge late at night, as Mrs. ——, our Brother's wife, asks him, we would use our privileges as a husband, and *command* her tongue. That 's poz.)

But the Leak in Mirror Lodge; it is as much worse than these so lightly touched upon above, as the consequences that have grown out of it are more grievous. The fact "that the lodge is about to try Brother Bendle for slandering Brother Shaw's wife," is, in reality, no fact at all. The true state of the case is, that *somebody* had been handling that estimable lady's character very shamefully, and as public opinion had fixed the charge upon Brother Bendle (for the very conclusive reason that there is no other Mason in the neighborhood upon whom to fix it), the said Brother *requested the lodge* to investigate the matter, with a view to bear favorably upon public sentiment, so that his innocence may be made manifest; and this, too, against the wishes, against the better judgment of the Junior Warden, who has to bring the charges, and of every member of the lodge, who is as confident of his innocence as of their own.

Yet the consequences of the Leak are, that Brother Bendle's church looks askant at him, because he is under Masonic discipline; Brother Bendle's partner, who is *not* a Mason, and, for physical reasons, never can be, is talking of dissolving their mercantile connection on account of the scandal; the Scipio "Investigator" (weekly, two dollars per annum, in advance) teems with insinuations against Brother Bendle, as a "calumniator of female innocence;" and, worst of all, Mrs. Bendle, that estimable woman, the daughter of old Father Cornish, can not be persuaded but that her faithless lord has committed one of the seven mortal sins, "else why should the Masons be trying him?"

You see now, sharp-eyed reader, what evil things have run out of this Leak, and what the importance of its being properly and expeditiously plugged.

"To search for a leak on ship-board, you must stop the trip, keel the ship over to larboard or starboard till her bottom is exposed, and then examine her with all your might for the place where the calking is defective." So, when Brother Gunther, Worshipful Master of Mirror Lodge, wrote to us, with a statement of the facts of the case, and craved our advice, we responded. Not understanding our allegorical but sublime way of dispensing light, however, Brother Gunther wrote again, reminding us that his "was a Masonic, not a commercial question," and wanting to know what he should do. Descending, with as good a grace as we could command, to the level of his comprehension, we explained: "Stop all work of the lodge; question the Brethren individually; spot the suspected Brother;" and this was so plain that even Brother Gunther understood it.

The attentive Master immediately acted upon our advice. He locked the charter up in his bureau at home; refused to open the lodge for three months; called upon each member individually, and put him to the torture; examined witnesses, particularly Mrs. Assyd, wife of Brother Assyd, the Tyler (suspected of having a *pivot* tongue, *id est*, one hung in the middle, and movable, as a jewel, at either end); Miss Moggoly, daughter of Brother Obed Moggoly (known to have Allyn's Ritual in her possession, and believed to put her religious trust therein); and old Mother Thoroughblood. These three were particularly selected as being most likely to point out the Leak, or the *Leaker*, if such a one there was. But Gunther might as well have asked the right-hand pillar at the entrance of King Solomon's Temple as to have questioned these females. Nay, in fact, he had better; for the aforesaid pillar might symbolically have told him a great deal more than he knows, or, it is likely, ever will know. But Mrs. Assyd simply told him that *her* husband staid out too late at the lodge for *her* good, and if he didn't come home earlier hereafter, the lodge might find him in lodgings, for all *she* cared; Miss Moggoly, instead of enlightening him in relation to the Leak, put the leak *into* him, as Sam Slick would call it, by inquiring whether the ceremony on page 79 of Allyn's Ritual is *exactly* the way Past Masters are made; and Mother Thoroughblood told him to get out of the house, and not be asking her any of his *consulting* questions! And that's all that Gunther gained from those three witnesses.

It has been our hap to investigate a great many hard questions, and if we have been able to settle a few of them, by dint of time, patience, and perseverance, no wonder, seeing we have failed in so many. But when, by vote of Mirror Lodge (we are an honorary member of that lodge, you know), "the intelligent," etc., etc., "was requested, in the abundance of his," etc., etc., "to advise his loving," etc., etc., "members of Mirror Lodge, how to conduct themselves in this emergency," etc., etc., we acknowledged we were *almost* cornered. The Master had tried every nook and corner to get testimony that would convict somebody of unmasonically publishing the proceedings of the lodge; and the nearest he had come to it, was to prove that Brother Sore, the carpenter, had inadvertently observed one day, in public, that the one step to the Junior Warden's station was an inch and a half higher than Brother —— had advised. And what could be made out of that? After sternly rebuking Brother Sore, however, in open lodge, so as to get our hand in, we set to work.

Was there any place overhead where a cowan or eavesdropper could conceal himself? To answer this, Brother Sore broke open one of the planks in the weather-boarding, and let out such a drift of bats into the lodge-room as convinced us that no man could hide himself in that loft.

Was there any means of reaching a window by ladder during the meetings of the lodge? This was satisfactorily answered in the negative. What then? Nobody could answer; and we all went to bed, intending to pursue the investigation next day.

That night we were put in the same room with Franklin Harper, that gross man in the flesh, whose weight is said to be unknown. Brother Harper eats as though he had the dyspepsia, and digests it afterward as though he hadn't. Being good company, we entertained him, after retiring to bed, with several chaste and agreeable anecdotes — so agreeable, in point of fact, that the Brother slightly shook the building, which was of brick, laughing at them. Our stock being exhausted, we let the obese Brother go to sleep, which he did instantaneously, and immediately afterward opened all his nasal batteries with the most fearful snores.

As we can not endure snoring, we lay awake, and, for a cheerful entertainment, ran over in our mind the demonstration to the Forty-seventh Problem of Euclid, which we had been trying to elucidate to the lodge that night, in connection with the Eureka

Hiatus. But we had hardly got to the fourth step in the demonstration, when, to our surprise, Brother Harper stopped snoring, and began to *talk in his sleep!* At first he spoke of the girls, as every fellow does who somnambulizes; but then, to our admiration, he took up Masonry. He talked of the case that had so bothered us; explained its difficulties as, as, as—well, as we ourselves could have done it; and insinuated, in a maudlin sort of way, that there *was* an explanation, "if Brother —— only could get at it." Then he spoke of more private matters still; and only that Brother Franklin Harper knows little or nothing of Masonry—and probably never will, he being so obese—the very mischief might have been played by the sleep-talker.

Here was the Leak in Mirror Lodge with a vengeance! We hurried down to the lower story, called up all the Masons in the house, and gratified them with the evidence which so well accounted for their difficulties.

It is unnecessary to detail all that followed; but, at the next Grand Lodge, Brother Gunther informed us, with great glee, that Brother Harper had been put upon a cracker-and-milk diet, and had married Miss Moggoly—the latter event allowing little or no sleep to talk *in*, and the former giving him little or nothing to talk *about*.

So the Leak in Mirror Lodge is plugged, after all.

Three Episodes in the Masonic History of Loring Hahded.

A TALE OF IMPERFECT MATERIALS.

Inscribed to Bro. J. Adams Allen,
OF KALAMAZOO, MICH., GRAND MASTER.

EPISODE FIRST.

LORING "JOINS THE MASONS."

WHY did Loring Hahded "jyne the Masons?" is an inquiry that has been often made, but never answered. His wife, with true Caudleian perseverance and tact, propounded it; his neighbors propounded it; the members of the Fraternity who visited Tillibellover Lodge propounded it; we propounded it; and when *we* ask anything, the answer is bound to come. So we take pride in saying that *we have the truth of the matter.*

But we are greatly tempted not to tell it. Why shouldn't we keep some things to ourself? Other folks do. Our readers who are in possession of golden facts like this, withhold them from us and from the world. Old Masons, who are getting older every day, and are reminded of their graves by every *arbor vitæ* bush they see, permit the reminiscences of their Masonic youth to perish in them, and won't communicate. Why, we cry again, should not *we* be allowed the privilege of knowing something that nobody else knows?

But the temptation vanishes, and a more liberal spirit possesses our heart, when we reflect upon the pleasure we shall impart to our patronizing thousands by communicating to them what no other Masonic writer has—what no Grand Master ever alluded to in an opening address—what no Com. For. Cor. ever argued, or settled, or declared, or doubted, or done anything else to—why, in short, Loring Hahded became a member of the A. and H. F. of F. and A. M.'s. We cry with Solomon, when the old builder was introduced to him, h-u-r-a-m-e-n, we have found it!

Loring Hahded had an observing disposition. He had ridden the mail, in his youth, from Tillibellover P. O. to Hog Haslet and back, and this had enabled him to see the world. He had seen a steamboat; had swapped horses eight times in one month (commencing with a four-year-old and twelve dollars, and terminating with a twelve-year-old and four dollars); had heard a member *for* Congress make a speech; and was a subscriber to two (lottery) newspapers. All these rare advantages Loring possessed over the ordinary mortals, his neighbors.

This observant disposition it was that first turned Loring's attention to Masonry. When Tillibellover Lodge was first organized, Loring had been one of those who opposed it. He had aided in spreading the scandalous rumor that it was for purposes of gambling and intemperance that the Brothers met.

His hands had handled the brush, that spread the paint, that painted the vulgarity, that insulted the house that the Masons built. Two or three lies, that nobody but an old mail-rider who had seen the world would have thought of telling, had been traced up to Loring Hahded—lies in which the honor of Masons and the chastity of their wives and daughters were involved. This seems like a queer introduction to our story, but it is in reality *the preparation.* We will presently take you in.

This observant disposition, to which we have so admiringly alluded, had led Loring to mark various instances in which Masonry benefited its votaries. He had particularly stored away in his mind the five following, to wit:

Case First.—A man with a family had driven up one day to the Tillibellover tavern (over the blacksmith-shop—sign of the gingercake and bottle), and called out the landlord by some very singular words. The landlord was known to be a Mason of one degree at least, if not more; and the way he pranced around and waited on that family, after the utterance of those cabalistic words, convinced all the by-standers, among whom happened to be Loring Hahded, that there was *Masonry* in it. Thinks Loring to himself, wouldn't it be nice to belong to a society like this, so that I could get waited upon in that way?

Case Second.—Parson Lightfoot, well-known to be a Mason (didn't he deliver the address last June, which was three years ago published in the ——, where all the Masonic addresses are published?) only preached once in a while at Tillibellover church, while the Rev. Mr. Scrump, who was *anything but* a Mason, did it weekly; yet when Lightfoot held forth, everybody, the Masons in particular, attended, while Scrump commanded less than a score of hearers. Loring had observed this, and his native shrewdness led him to the conclusion, wouldn't it be nice to belong to a society that backs up a preacher that way?

CASE THIRD.—Mrs. Pelletreau, widow of the deceased Brother Simon Bolivar Pelletreau, who was killed at the raising of Brother Finn's barn, was very poor. In plain truth, Brother Pelletreau had left her nothing in creation to go upon but a gang of little children and a mule. Yet the widow never lacked for anything; her crib always had corn in it; her smoke-house, meat; her children went cleanly to school; her shawl was a Bay State article, that cost ten-fifty at Blaster's. Of course, all this was the result of her relationship to Masonry. True, she divided her time, Mason-like, into three parts, giving one to sewing for people who would pay her for it; one to sewing for herself and children; and the third to light work, such as cooking, washing, etc.; yet general rumor, an infallible guide about Tillibellover, declared that Masonry supported her, and we don't dispute it. Loring Hahded had observed the pleasant way this Mason's widow got along, and he had often thought, wouldn't it be nice to belong to a society that takes such good care of the wimming?

CASE FOURTH.—The lodge at Tillibellover meets

Saturday night, on or after the full moon. It is a tradition of great age around Tillibellover, that whisky is far the pleasantest in flavor in the full of the moon. Coupling this and that together, Loring and his class early concluded that one prime object of Masonic meetings was imbibition, and that whisky, a fluid that Loring keenly favored, was the tap. True, they had never been able to prove exactly that any whisky or other oxygenized fluid was carried in the lodge; but, if not, why lock the door? Neither was it satisfactorily demonstrated that the Brothers were ever any the worse for their carouses. But what of that? Hasn't Masonry its secrets? and one of them may be how to disguise the breath!—who knows? With these observations, Loring had decided, wouldn't it be nice to belong to a society that shows you how to drink like a gentleman, and nobody ever know it but themselves?

Case Fifth.—Loring had observed, as everybody else does, that Masons go not to law with each other (Loring was, commercially speaking, in embarrassed circumstances); are not known to quarrel and fight (Loring often indulged in gymnastics of an illegal character); are rarely heard to make slanderous charges against each other (Loring's character was ragged, and the truth made it worse); gave each other good counsel gratis when demanded (Loring paid five dollars a clip for what he got); always have a spare quarter to loan a Brother Mason (Loring rarely had that amount of metal in his possession); and these facts brewing in his head, brought him logically to the conclusion, wouldn't it be nice now to belong to a society that does so much for its members?

The secret, then, of Loring Hahded's Masonic fraternization is, that *he coveted its personal advantages.* He joined it—the phrase, though one that in general we strongly disapprove, is appropriate here—he *joined it* as the mistletoe joins the oak; as the ivy joins the elm; as the leech joins the leg; as the tick joins the passer-by. He reached up to it and clomb in, but in so doing *he pulled it down part of the way to him.* Philosophers, who know all about such things, say, if you tie a rope to one of the moon's horns, and draw yourself up to it, you tip Luna a little over. Just so with Loring Hahded; he flung his cable-tow up to Tillibellover Lodge; the Brethren were weak enough to seize it, instead of letting it fall back; they tied it to a ring in the wall, and Loring shinned up, bending the lodge over, racking it, and cracking the roof in the act, so that it leaked ever afterward.

But, asks Sister Maria, and Sister Charlotte, and Sister Henrietta, and four hundred other Sisters who read this tale, why *did* the lodge take such a Hahded in? Ah, good ladies, answer it yourselves. Why did you, Sister Maria, take for your first husband that dirty dog of a Flegan? and you, Sister Charlotte, how came you to marry the cowan who got drunk tri-weekly? Ah, ha! now we have you. You, whose happiness is involved in making marital selections, you marry such flawy blocks as they are, and then ask us sarcastically why we took Hahded in!

But to gratify the inquiry, which we knew you would make, we wrote to Brother Axeltry, Master of Tillibellover Lodge, "Why did you accept Loring Hahded?" He replied: "For eleven distinct reasons, which, as there were only eleven of us present that night, was a reason apiece. The first was—we were a pack of d—— (*drastic* was the word he used, being a physician) fools. The other ten I will give you some other time." That 's it. Tillibellover Lodge was made up of d—— (drastic) fools, who didn't know when they were well off. They had nineteen excellent fellows in their membership, and they thought they could manage one j—k—s; hence Hahded!

But we didn't set out, understand us, to excuse the lodge. We commenced this episode to show why Loring Hahded became a Mason; and you will admit that, as far as he was concerned in the transaction, it showed as much good sense as ever an ex-mail-rider exhibited. To this day we can but conclude, as we did the night we visited Tillibellover Lodge, and saw him sitting there eating pecans while the work of the third degree was going on, that it proved there was one sensible mind entered that drastic membership when Loring Hahded became a Mason.

EPISODE SECOND.

LORING DEMITS.

Tillibellover Lodge lost Loring from its membership before the moon had fulled and waned thirteen times. And why did Loring Hahded demit? Having set ourselves up as a target for all manner of interrogative arrows, we find ourselves assailed on all sides by the inquiry, *Why did Loring Hahded demit?* We have taken the pen to answer it. We turn first to our Index Rerum—that treasure-house of ten thousand times ten thousand thoughts that have flickered in this brain in all the years gone by—that coffin-full of buried hopes, which, to read, makes us sigh and weep that we were ever young, or that we have ever got old—we open our *Index Rerum*, and under the three heads: I. *Inexplicable blunders.* P. *Parsimony of the wind-shaken cedars.* E. *Who should be Excluded?* we see the answers. Isn't it handy, this Index Rerum? Why, when Brother Heugague wrote us last year, to know what preparations he should make for his trial, (he being under charges for striking a Master Mason,) we found a reply put to his query under these two heads: R. *Repentance.* A. *Make Acknowledgements*, and he did it like a good fellow, as he is!

Loring Hahded was not overly pleased with the ceremonies, etc., of his initiation. He had rather anticipated something diabolical; indeed, had prepared himself therefor, by spiritous applications inwardly, of which his breath smelled outwardly, as averred the Senior Deacon when it was all over, and failing in his expectations, had expressed his disappointment by refusing to listen to the Master's lectures explanatory to the work, thus pleasantly biting off his own nose to spite his face. The second degree pleased him still less, he being of the opinion, prevalent among the *hard heads* generally, that something "quick and d-v-l-sh," is the very jig of human existence. The corn, wine, and oil of the Fellow Craft, failed to impart to his mind either nourishment, refreshment, or joy. With the Master's degree, however, he was considerably better gratified; and, it must be acknowledged, to the credit of that traditionary grade, had the other two but been as spicy and juicy, Loring had never grumbled at Freemasonry. But, upon the whole, he was not favorably impressed with the secrets of Ancient York Masonry, and not having the funds (or the character), to go higher, Masonry, incontinently lost him from her membership.

But there were various other reasons, which, as an honest historian, we are bound to specify, for his withdrawal from the lodge. The reader will remark, that, although we chronicle the fact of Loring's disappointment at the non-impressiveness of the ceremonies of Masonry, we have not said he was disappointed in its availability to every-day life, or its practicalness as a social system between man and man. We dared not say that; for, in good truth,

Loring Hahded found Masonry even more practical, pecuniarily and socially, than he had anticipated. For instance, Brother Josh. Cohoes, to whom he had long been indebted in a small bill of horse-shoeing, promptly offered him a year's extension, without solicitation, and that, too, the very day after he touched the checkered pavement. Brother Bill Sloogan lent him five dollars to pay his doctor's bill, the week he passed into the middle chamber; and before the lodge closed which raised him to the Sublime Degree, a subscription was made up, which resulted in fifteen dollars, principally in cash, to give him a start at his trade. Therefore, he had no reason, nor did he ever pretend to have a reason in the conduct of his co-members, for demitting so soon as he did from the ranks. His real motives we are about to narrate:

First, Loring attended the Masonic burial of Brother Ahishar Peters. It was an occasion of unusual interest. More than fourscore Brothers were in attendance. The Deputy Grand Master, the Right Warden, Brother Lincumdoddie, came fifty miles on purpose to officiate. The Rev. Levi Lawbstice made the oration, and a pathetic one it was. After the return to the lodge, a series of obituary resolutions, commendatory and regretful, were unanimously adopted, in which all the virtues of the human character were made to adorn the manes of the deceased Brother Peters, and money was appropriated to erect a suitable testimonial over his remains. Now, Loring knew that Peters had been a *demitted Mason* for well-nigh seven years;—had paid no lodge dues, done no lodge duties, honored no Masonic principles; but on the contrary, done all that his example could do to break down the very organization through which Masonry has its stability. And Loring thought to himself—for he was an observant man, as we had occasion to observe in our opening chapter—"If a man can get all these honors and attentions after neglecting Masonry for seven years, why not I, too? I will save my two dollars a year and demit." And so he did. Why shouldn't he, sure enough? When a lodge offers such rich premiums to its members to demit, what fool of us wouldn't jump at the bait, and withdraw as soon as possible? We take shame to ourselves for our stupidity in not following Hahded's example long ago.

Second, Loring Hahded found the duty of attending lodge at its regular meetings too onerous. The idea of giving up one evening a month to Masonic duties was hard enough of itself, but when the fact of the regular meetings of the lodge occuring on the same days with the monthly races at Tailup, is taken into consideration, the real severity of the case is seen. Loring experienced it in its utmost rigor. At three successive meetings he absented himself from Tailup, though he was one of the standing judges of the races; his son, Solomon, bet off half his possessions, and, of course, lost it in consequence of his father's absence, and so plainly was ruin staring him in the face, through this untoward neglect of business, that Loring was compelled, by due respect to the interests of himself and family, to discontinue his attendance on the lodge. And if not an attendant on the lodge, why retain his membership? Why should *he* pay for candles or fuel, and the Tyler's fee, and the Secretary's fee, and this, and that, and the other, if he couldn't be there to get the benefit of it? And worst of all, when the lodge got to making a monthly appropriation of twenty-five cents, for refreshments, in pursuance of sound advice, and Loring *never* got "nerry a cracker," as he pathetically declared, how could it be expected that *his* funds should go toward feasting and rioting for other people's stomachs? Therefore, Loring demitted.

Third, There was a man in Tillibellover Lodge that Loring didn't like. He was a good man enough in himself, but his candidate for constable wasn't *Loring's* candidate, his religious sentiments were opposed to Loring's, and his advice had prevented Tom Spirty from marrying Loring's half-sister. These facts, and others of a kindred character, had naturally imbittered Loring against him; and he hadn't been a Master Mason a week, before he had told every one of his twenty co-members how much he disliked old Phil Gorer. So when the other two sound and wise reasons we have specified, had brought his mind almost to the demitting point, this grudge of his against Gorer turned the scale, and determined him to withdraw. He reasoned in this way: "Oughtn't Masons to be all of one mind? Can they be expected to keep their obligations to one another, if they are not? Hadn't we better separate, when we can't *gee* together better than I and Gorer kin?" On stating his objections to the Worshipful Master, that worthy rather fortified his previous resolution to demit, by the remark that he (Hahded) was not looking at this thing in a Masonic light—whereat Hahded declared that it was evident the Master was a Gorer man, and the sooner he (Hahded) got his demit the better for all parties.

By the way, how curious it is, that when an argument occurs between a Hahded and his Brethren, they always take sides against him. This illustrates the general injustice with which the Masonic Craft treat their weaker Brethren.

Fourth, A motive for demitting, of prime importance to Hahded, lay in the two dollars per annum dues, which the by-laws of the lodge enjoined. This, metaphorically speaking, stuck in his crop. It was a large sum to be expended in this way. Why, the annual fee of membership to the Tailup Jockey Club was only *five* dollars, and that gave you all the privileges of the ground, a seat in the judges' stand for your wife, and other advantages too numerous to mention. Two dollars a year! "Thunder!" as Mrs. Hahded emphatically observed, "'t would buy a new dress pattern of calliker!" Not that Loring would have considered two dollars a year much to *receive*, but it was an awful sum to *pay out*, especially when demitted Masons drew more deeply and frequently from the treasury of Tillibellover Lodge than the members thereof. Loring really felt, when he paid his first half-yearly installment, that he was taking the bread out of the mouths of his little ones, and he said so. But when the Secretary called on him for a second dollar at the close of the year, the cup of his complaint overflowed. He paid it, but with an inward malediction. He took a receipt, with a determination it should be the last. And before the lodge closed that night, he was recorded on the books, "as having applied for a demit, and all dues being paid, and no charges against him, he, the said Loring Hahded, shall have his demit," etc.

EPISODE THIRD.

LORING SECEDES.

THERE is a certain book, old and but little valued by many, yet full of life and light, of which one of the sentiments is, "Men do not gather grapes of *thorns*, or figs of *thistles*." We recommend the perusal of this sentiment, together with a few hundred other sentiments from the same source, to the attention of the members of Tillibellover Lodge, which no longer numbers among its members or its subjects the distinguished Loring Hahded. For should they take. our advice, and be influenced by such old-fashioned axioms as the one cited, they would spare themselves, and us, and all other good Masons, the mortification of episodes like these we are writing. The thorns and thistles in our Masonic field—how came they there? Who introduced them? who planted them? who watered them? and who, oh foolish ones! looked for grapes and figs to grow upon their branches?

Why, you, Worshipful Master of Tillibellover Lodge, you helped in this nice piece of business; and you, Brothers A B and C D, who recommended Hahded's petition, you brought the briar-roots and the thistle-seed into the lodge; and you, all the others who were present on the night of the ballot, you helped to plant and set them out; and, when the second ballot was taken, you watered them; and so you kept on until they got a hold in the earth, and then, oh you silly nineteen constituent members of Tillibellover Lodge! you all set your empty noodles expecting to find figs and grapes! Didn't you find them—in a horn! Didn't Hahded yield rich clusters of grapes, like the grapes of Eschol, and drums of figs, like the figs of Smyrna, in reward for your agricultural feats in his behalf? Oh! yes, to be sure he did—enough of them to set up a fruit-shop with—in a horn!

And Loring Hahded seceded. Foolish fellow, did you say? Nay, verily, Brother Dismukes, he was the most sensible man among you. He was a sensible man for trying to get *into* the Order—more sensible for *demitting*—most sensible for *seceding;* and the only symptoms of weakness visible in the affair were those exhibited by yourself and your co-members.

Why look at this thing a moment! Do you remember, Brother Dismukes, how, in episode first, we specified the five reasons which induced Loring to become a Mason, and each one of them sound as a nut? There is no proof of the fellow's weakness in them; and in our luminous exhibit of the motives that prompted his demitting, is there a flaw in them? No. The whole sum and substance of the matter is, that Loring saw he could make something, first by joining the Masons, and then by demitting from their membership; and his love of mammon led him on the scent, true as a greyhound's nose. We admire and respect such a character as Loring for pursuing, in his little sphere, his self-interest, and making no mistake, from alpha to omega, in the whole matter.

Our admiration of his character increases still more when we contemplate the motive of his secession. After he demitted from Tillibellover Lodge, he joined the church; and when we say the church, we mean *the* church. Churches there are many—enough, indeed, to suit every taste, from the man who thinks fathering a child one of the mortal sins, to the man who feels unwilling to die before he has begotten two-score—but it is *the church* which was favored in the calling Loring Hahded *brother.*

Shall we describe *the* church? We must, for all the Hahded connection as naturally tend to its membership as the Junior Warden tends to the South. It is *the* Christian family that unchristianizes all the other Christian families; *the* ecclesiastical body that talks most about making the Bible the infallible guide, and studies it the least; the—the—in short, *the Hardshells!*

Imagine Loring a Hardshell! Imagine the day he joined the church! Imagine the rejoicings over him, from the Rev. Brother who claimed the merit of converting him, down to the meekest member of his flock! Imagine Loring giving in his experience, and telling how deluded he had been in joining the Masons, and how "unchurchly" he had found them, and what little *real enjoyment* he had experienced in their membership!

Don't laugh, Brother Thoughtless, but imagine yourself there, listening and looking on, while this farce was enacting, and say wouldn't you feel belittled at the very thought of Masonry, when such vagabonds as Loring Hahded could *get into* our Order, and be allowed to *demit* in good standing, and then, worst of all, be permitted to *secede* because "he hadn't had any spiritual enjoyment in it?" Faugh! our very nostrils are outraged, and we almost want to secede ourselves.

Oh! Worshipful Master, Wardens and Brethren of Tillibellover Lodge, what a wound you have inflicted on the whole body of Masonry! Not merely upon your own miserable lodge—would it had died, like an untimely birth, before it ever saw the light—not only upon that insignificant corner of the Temple in which *you* are at work, but upon *the whole enterprise*, the whole body of builders, and the whole amplitude of the building. Repent in sackcloth and ashes, and promise never to repeat the grievous error. 'Tis the only restitution now. The aforesaid Hahded, the filthy, low-minded Loring, has got your secrets, and he tells them, so far as he can understand them—fortunately, that is not far enough to enlighten others—whenever he thinks he can injure you by it; but the worst harm he can do to you, is to make it known to the world that such a man can be a Mason. Oh! Master, Wardens and Brethren, be warned in future, and keep such men out.

How many there were who were Masons in September, 1826, and who, in September, 1827, were, like Hahded, seceders from the ranks! And why? Because as they became Masons for lucre, for self-interest, through hypocrisy, and by the crimimal negligence of the Brotherhood, so they went out from us whenever their self-interest predominated to turn the index outward. What mystery is there in all that sad, sad lesson of the Antimasonic warfare? None at all. 'Tis plain as light. And that lesson will be acted over again, before this generation passes away, unless we are spared the just punishment which Providence inflicted upon our fathers. *We* deserve all that *they* received; and if we have not received it, it is because we have been more favored.

We close as we began, with the divine axiom, "Men do not gather grapes of thorns, or figs of thistles." No man of judgment ever looks for them on such stocks. If our lodges would have the grapes of harmony and the figs of joy, they must plant vines and trees of the right species, nourish them tenderly, water them kindly, prune them seasonably, and, in due time, rich and abundant will be the fruitage. So mote it be.

The Peace-Maker.

A TALE OF MASONIC CONCILIATION.

Inscribed to R. W. Bro. Hiram Bassett,
OF MAYSVILLE, KENTUCKY.

"Blessed are THE PEACE-MAKERS, for they shall be called the children of God."

THE county of Barrett, State of ——, had long been the scene of bickering and strife. Viewing its lovely plains and fertile valleys, the admiring traveler would little have imagined that the residents of those peaceful cottages and more aspiring halls were the subjects of feuds, scarcely less bitter than those which brought ravage and death to the other continent in days of old. Yet so it was, and we will rehearse the cause.

A few years before our story opens, there had been a presidential contest. The numbers in the opposing ranks were nearly equal, and the contest was sustained with a virulence remarkable even in this quadrennially agitated, though always prosperous, republic. Though the fever of the strife was broken, evil results remained. Like other fevers, it had left the system in a state of chronic derangement, that

threatened every hour a new and fatal outbreak. To change the figure, the parties whose votes and voices had been employed in the effort to build up or pull down, had become known as acknowledged enemies to each other, even to the bitter end. It is rarely the case in our political history that a presidential election leads to such lasting consequences.

The secret of this state of affairs may be found in that peculiarly anti-republican and demoralizing vice, which has sprung up within a half-score years past, known as *betting upon the election*. Colonel Hoganny, for instance, had laid a wager of his finest horse, the roan that had borne him in safety so long, that M—— would be elected, while Squire Seaver put in his, the large black mare, pride of his soul, against it. Stimulated by this desperate issue on the part of the two most prominent men in the county, the followers and imitators of both backed up their judgment until many a horse, which its owner ill could spare, and many another piece of property, was staked upon a question to be decided by millions of votes over half a continent. Settlement day came, and while one party was elated to ridiculous pride, which offended the losing party, and extravagance, which soon wasted the ill-gotten gains, the other was depressed foolishly low by the loss, and ready, morosely, to quarrel upon the slightest provocation with the winners. Quarrels led to fights, which had cost one valuable life already, and threatened more.

A year had rolled around, and the election of sheriff reäwakened the evil spirit which could hardly be said to have slumbered, so easily was it aroused by the slightest cause. An extraordinary amount of electioneering, and a corresponding looseness of morality, had been practiced, and now that the day of voting was only a week distant, it was a matter of nice discrimination which of the two contending candidates would command the largest suffrage. Betting had been practiced here also, and thousands of property was involved in the question. One man had bought a cow of his neighbor, to be paid for at a double price if Ayres should win in the race for the sheriffalty, but at no price at all if defeated; another, an enterprising storekeeper, had sold out a handsome assortment of moth-eaten hats upon the same noble principle. Schoolmasters had bet the amount of their school bills; blacksmiths their shop accounts; nay, Colin Schlump, the fisherman who seined Lake Lively three times a week, and peddled the spoils, was peddling his spoils at fifty cents a fish *if* Zaney got the biggest vote, and nothing if he didn't. This was the state of affairs in the good county of Barrett a week before the election. Bad enough it was.

Nor must the reader suppose there were none who labored to change this aspect of things for the better. There were many good men, Christians, Christian ministers, men of note, and philanthropy, and eloquence, who spared no pains to show up the inevitable consequences of these foolish feuds, and to point out the sin before God the parties were committing in pursuing their fatal quarrels. It amounted, however, to but little. If convinced, the parties only yielded sufficiently to promise in a surly and hopeless manner. "If the other party would make acknowledgments, and own up," they would do so and so; but as they very well knew the other party would do no such thing, the pledge counted for nothing, and was so understood.

Now, there had moved into Barrett county, the present year, an old man, who was originally styled Charles Barlough, but for euphony, or, as the westerners call it, *for short*, he had received from his friends the agreeable appellation of *Charley Barley*, by which name, not to be out of the fashion, we will call him likewise. Charley Barley had been a land-surveyor all his life, and fortunately for the little Barleys, of which he had a glorious crop, had early invested a large portion of his surveying fees in lands, which, when he quit the "stick-stuck" business, and began to look after them a little, he found to be valuable beyond his wildest expectations. In fact, Charley Barley was rich geologically—that is, "by the rise of the soil"—and he had moved his family, as aforesaid, to take care of his lands.

Charley was a Freemason. Of course he was that, or we never should have selected him for our hero. But he was a genuine Freemason, such as the Callises, the Geislers, the Bertisors, the Welds, the Scribes, and others, of whom we love to write. Charley Barley being a Freemason, was likewise a peace-maker. Whether he thought he had a mission that way, we do not know nor care, but if he had, and if he knew that he had, he couldn't have performed the duties of the missionary office more faithfully, unremittingly and unselfishly than he did. Just ask about him in Madison county, where he moved from, will you? and count if you can, the number of reference cases and compromises in which he was concerned there for twenty years. Ask Blacklock, the leading lawyer at the county seat, and he will curse when he speaks of the promising cases that Charley's propensities nipped in the bud. Having said this much of Charley Barley, we need not add that he was a Christian. A man reared up in this Christian land, who was educated from the Bible, and loved it, and prayed over it, and practiced upon it, as Charley Barley did, was *bound* to be a Christian, and so he was. He may not have been very deep in his theory, but he was very broad in his practice, so 'twas well balanced at last.

Charley Barley had suffered many a heartache in witnessing the miserable state of things, politically speaking, in Barrett county. He saw that Church influence was a nullity; that old friendships were severed like tow, and the moral and social interests of the county were all going to the dogs under this foolish political excitement. He saw and he grieved. How was it to be remedied?

He had been to both parties, the Hogannys and the Seavers, and plead with them for peace' sake, and for virtue's sake, and for God's sake, to stop the thing where it was. Seaver only said, "he'd quit if Hoganny would," while Hoganny merely intimated, "he'd blow off when Seaver had done blowed off"—and so it went.

The week preceding the election day was actually spent by Charley Barley perambulating the county on his holy errand, but Wednesday, Thursday, Friday came, and for the life of him he could not perceive that he had made a single step toward effecting his purpose. A happy accident at last gave him a clue, which, like a faithful fellow as he was, he followed out to complete success.

Squire Seaver was by birth an Irishman, by education an Irish gentleman, and no fool of a scholar at that. In his native country, up to the year of his majority and for ten years afterward, he had mingled in such society as ample wealth, a high talent, and a respectable lineage insure a man in old Ireland. As a matter of course he was a Mason, as all that class in the Emerald Isle are, and as a Mason, had held such official stations as had made him conversant with the obligations of the Order. By a train of disasters he had lost his possessions, consequently emigrated to America, as all distressed Irishmen do, and to the West as all distressed Irishmen ought to, to commence life anew. Here, immersed in business, he had let the mystic tie hang loosely about him, and made no profession at all of his brotherhood. This fact explains why Charley Barley, who was picking up all the items floating about that would enable him to accomplish his great purpose of *peace-making*, had never learned of his being a Freemason. Judge of his surprise then, in looking over an old Album on Squire Seaver's table on Friday, as he made his last visit of reconciliation, to see the following document regularly worded and engrossed upon parchment:

"GRAND LODGE OF IRELAND:

"We, the Chiefs of the Enlightened men of the Most Ancient and Right Worshipful Lodge of St. Johns, do hereby certify, that Brother Carrick Seaver, of Lodge 75, has been initiated in all the degrees of our mysteries, and has performed all his works among us to the entire satisfaction of all the Brethren. Therefore, we desire all the Right Worshipful Lodges of the universe, and all true Accepted Masons, to recognize, and admit him as such. In testimony, whereof, we have delivered him this present certificate, sealed by our Secretary with the seal of our lodge, and that it may not be of any use to any one else, but unto the said Brother Seaver, he has signed his name in the margin. Given in the Grand Lodge at Dublin," etc.

After perusing this, the mind of Brother Charley became animated. His week's disappointment counted for nothing, as he conceived a project for making the discovery available. A few questions in a quiet way induced Seaver to admit that he *had been a* Freemason in Ireland, but so long out, etc.—rusty, etc.—forgot everything, etc.—just as all careless Masons say in similar circumstances.

Charley Barley posted off to Colonel Hoganny's fast as his mule could pace, and spent the night with him. Colonel Hoganny was a suspended Mason of long standing, and we are ashamed to say suspended in this old Virginia Lodge, for non-payment of dues. In fact, he had been suspended so long as to have lost all (Masonic) vitality, and he might safely have been cut down as dead, and his body given over to the (Masonic) surgeons. Charley Barley knew of the circumstances, and to leak the secret out, had been corresponding with the old Virginia Lodge to get him reinstated. But of this the Colonel as yet knew nothing at all. To tell the truth, when the old Virginia Lodge finally sent the certificate of reinstatement in acknowledgement of Charley's pressing request, and inclosure of nine dollars and twenty-five cents, and presented it to Hoganny, he was as much astonished as he ever was in his life. But not to anticipate.

Charley Barley staid Friday night at the Colonel's and Saturday till noon, and talked Masonry with him. Now you never saw an old Mason, suspended or not, but what likes to *talk* Masonry—no, and you never will. Grandma can remember the days when she went sleighriding with her beaux, yes, and she loves to chatter on the subject, though she has forgot everything that has happened since George Washington's time. Hoganny has seen many evil years since the last night his heart swelled with Masonic emotion, but when Charley Barley in his pleasant way began to call over some of the pleasures of the lodge, etc., it touched him to the core.

Charley was trying, he said, to get up a lodge at the county seat of Barrett, and asked Colonel Hoganny if he would go into it? He never let on that he knew the Colonel was a suspended Mason, but took care in conversing with him not to touch upon the arcana. Though for the matter of that, Hoganny had been so long out of the profession, that Charley Barley might have talked any gibberish to him, and he wouldn't have known the difference. He asked Colonel Hoganny if he wouldn't join in and help start a lodge, and Colonel Hoganny said he would. It was agreed, then, that as Monday was election day, when everybody would be at the county seat, they would have a sort of convention in the Grand Jury rooms before the polls opened, and make the necessary arrangements to get the thing started.

Saturday and Sunday, Charley Barley rode through the county at tip-top speed—it was a holy errand—and Monday morning by daylight he was at the county seat with his plans all matured.

Seaver came with his party to the polls ready for all sorts of a fight—Hoganny with ditto ready for ditto. At nine o'clock, Charley Barley had them both in the Grand Jury room, together with six others, of whom, singularly enough, three were Hoganny's, and three were Seaver's men, and all hands were at work preparing to organize the new lodge. Colonel Hoganny didn't know before, that Squire Seaver was a Mason, and Squire Seaver had been equally as ignorant concerning Colonel Hoganny. Billy Floogan had no idea that Dempsey Hoister was one—Saul Austin whispered to Felix Poopy, that he would never have shot his (Poopy's) dog had he known *he* was a Mason, and Poopy, who had intended to lick Austin that very hour, good-naturedly whispered back that 'twas of no consequence, though, to tell the truth, he would rather have lost his old woman than his dog. Hoganny found himself on a committee of two with Seaver, both sitting on the same bench thick as thieves, and counting up the ways and means.

The result was, there was no fighting that day—all bets were withdrawn, feuds were compromised, a Masonic lodge was started, and you will find it on the catalogue of the Grand Lodge of ———, as "Peacemaker's Lodge." Look and see.

Brother Bauer from Berlin.

A TALE OF THE MEANS OF MASONIC RECOGNITION.

Inscribed to Bro. Henry George Warren,
OF LONDON, ENGLAND, PUBLISHER OF THE FREEMASONS' MAGAZINE.

BENEVOLENCE LODGE, at Papyrus, has a difficult question before it to-night. A great deal of seriousness is manifested among the thirty odd members present, and it is seriousness, too, that is queerly intermixed with a *puzzlement*, which proves that a new question has been sprung upon them. Brother Brownlow, the Master, who has the run of common subjects so well that he is said to be able to—and sometimes does—decide them in his sleep, while sitting stiffly under the letter G, sits now as uneasily in his chair as Job might be supposed to have done on his potsherds when his boils were in their worst condition. He (Brownlow) divides his time by looking over old Nos. of the ———, which lie about, whispering over his right shoulder to the man of the keys, and over his left to the man of the pens, but, sooth to say, he gets but little light from either.

Around the stove, which, of course, is in the Northwest—around the stove, we say, stand Brothers Juris and Prudence, those two promising young lawyers lately turned into Masons with the shell of their profession still sticking to their backs. These young brethren, as everybody knows, are as full of Masonic law as Hiram Abiff's trestleboard was full of designs, and in spite of the well-known modesty of their vocation, they are not backward to communicate it. It is said of Brother Juris, that while yet in darkness he argued a law point with the Senior Deacon; and it is said of Brother Prudence that he *never* got the lecture on the Third Degree in full, because he contradicted Brother Brownlow so much while giving it. Around the stove stand these promising young brethren, engaged most earnestly in violating the rule (*Ancient Charges, Chapter VI*) which declares, "You are not to hold private committees, or separate conversation, without leave from the Master," and seeking with all their might for a fitting thought that should throw light on this dark question. Oh, that they might be the first to elucidate it!—then would they triumph over that slow coach Brownlow, over that *death-on-innovations* Brother Cocke, yes, over the renowned ——— itself. *Then* would Juris be elected W. M., and Prudence S. W., and Benevolence Lodge would be fitly officered for once in its life, and—and—the famous problem, relating to the cocoa-nut, be solved forever.

Old *death-on-innovations* Cocke, as he loves to be styled, is in a brown study. His eyes show it—his mouth—eke his hands. His very apron has slipped from its orthodoxy, and hangs cross-wise over his abdomen, as though one side of him had suffered a paralytic shock, and shrunk. You may be sure it is no common difficulty that affects Cocke. A faithful service in Freemasonry, ever since 1817, has enabled him to gather up rare treasures of Masonic light, applicable to the ninety-nine cases that usually come up before Masonic lodges. But this is the hundredth.

The other thirty Brethren, present to-night, sit in various stages of distress. Some exhibit a sort of skepticism upon their faces, as though in doubt of the ability of their W. M. to adjudicate this question. One is making a pencil memorandum of the affairs to send to Brother ———; one mentally determines that he will pump ——— on the theme; a third resolves "to bring it up before the Grand Lodge next G. A. C.,"—but no device nor work is found among the thirty which goes to unravel this skein so knotty.

The question is this: The landlord of the Ollock's House, Brother Braham Willis, a good fellow and a true, has reported that there is stopping with him a Dutch gentleman—all foreigners with him are *Dutch*, but not all *gentlemen;* no, "not by a long chalk"—a Dutch gentleman who called there a few days back to spend the Sabbath, was taken sick during Sabbath hours, while at church, and "now lies flat with the typhoid fever. No one knows him; his baggage only contains some clothing and a few Dutch manuscripts, which nobody in Papyrus can read; and, worst of all, he has n't a picayune about him." (This latter expression denotes, if our memory serves us right, that the poor gentleman is entirely divested of all metallic substances; a horrid condition, as we are personally aware, to be in!) The landlord, therefore, reports the case to the lodge, and asks some help to pay his board bills, together with a pretty salty account of nurses, a saltier one of doctors, with the probable saltiest one of undertakers. Brother Braham Willis is a poor man himself, and while he does all he can to relieve human distress, he acknowledges to-night that he is not able to do much.

But we are mistaken; this is not the perplexity of the case. It is a small matter to move "that the Committee of Charity"—composed, of course, of the Master and Wardens—"have plenary power in the case to appropriate the lodge funds."

Seconded—adopted unanimously.

It is a small thing for Benevolence Lodge to agree to give even as much as fifty dollars at a time, when necessary to serve God in that way. The real difficulty is this.

It is this: Among the manuscripts of the unfortunate foreigner, already alluded to, is one engrossed upon parchment, which, to a man up in the third degree, looks amazingly like a Masonic diploma. It is sealed heavily, the wax bearing no faint impression of Masonic symbols. It is signed by three and four, in the usual manner of such documents, and countersigned in the margin. The collocation of words, though the words themselves are in an unknown tongue, accords with the plan universal among American Masons;—and, best of all, around the margin of the document may be seen, elegantly drawn by the pen, the following standard symbols of the Masonic Craft: The Lamb; the Twenty-four inch Gauge; Gavel; Clouded Canopy; Ladder; Bible; Square; Compass; Mosaic Pavement; Indented Tessel; Blazing Star; two Ashlars; Trestle-board; Point in circle; Plumb; Level; Globes; Pillars of Five Orders of Architecture; Trowel; Pot of Incense; Bee Hive; Book of Constitution and Sword; Sword and Heart; All-Seeing Eye; Anchor and Ark; Euclid's Problem; Hour Glass; Scythe; Three Steps; these, and various other emblems, more frequently seen in the symbology of the European Craft than the American.

In addition to this reputed diploma, there is found in the trunk of the sick gentleman an apron, apparently Masonic, cut square, bound with blue, of the material most fitting of all for a Masonic apron; and on the back of this apron is written, in queer chirography, the words, "Louis Bauer,—Berlin," as though they were designed to convey the owner's name.

And the question is, ought the lodge, upon these ambiguous evidences, to consider Mr. Louis Bauer a Mason, and to treat him as such?

Looking at the matter in a Blackstone point of view, as Brothers J. and P. do, the query stands, can we test a man a Brother without the aid of his tongue and hand?

'T is an interesting theme. It embraces the queries: Can a widow lady prove her claim to Masonic attentions by an exhibition of her deceased husband's

Masonic possessions? Can the family of a Brother Mason prove their Masonic claims in his absence? and others of the same class.

* * * * *

The subject is opened in due time for debate, and for three mortal hours the debate is continued. The W. M., putting Brother Cocke in the chair, brings forward all that he has ever seen in the ——— on this topic, but acknowledges he finds nothing conclusive there.

Brother Cocke, giving up the gavel again to Brother Brownlow, admits himself stumped, as having never, since 1817, met with exactly such a case. He remembered when Brother Lafayette came over from France;—but then Lafayette could speak our language, so the illustration is not apposite. He recalls the fact of Captain James Riley, relieved by Brother Sidi Hamet;—but then Riley was wide awake and able to communicate with Hamet by hand and voice, while Mr. Louis Bauer can do neither. He refers to Brother Lorrison, shipwrecked on the coast of France, and unable to *parler* a single word of *Français*;—but then the French Brethren refused to have anything to do with him because he had lost his diploma in the salt water, so the cases are not parallel. He concludes, as before remarked, by acknowledging himself stumped, and so sits down.

Brother Juris then rises and makes a declamatory effort of the first water. He almost outdoes himself and quite outdoes his audience. He is eloquent,—sublime. He gives statistical details of distressed

Masons, their widows and orphans, within this Grand Lodge jurisdiction; enumerates feelingly the various sorts of woes to which all Masons are subject; enters into a precise calculation how far the funds then in the lodge treasury, and those that may safely be anticipated, will fall short of relieving so much distress, and concludes with earnestly deprecating any expense in relation to a man who can not even prove himself to be a Mason.

Brother Prudence follows in nearly the same track. He inquires vociferously, how can the lodge justify itself before the Grand Lodge for recognizing a man under the circumstances in which Mr. Bauer is placed? How can the lodge justify itself before the community for taking up a foreigner who may be a thief, murderer, or anything else that is bad, and adopting his case as its own? How can any Brother justify to his own conscience the etc., etc., etc.? Finally, he advises, and it is the only piece of advice the lodge has yet received upon the subject, that they wait till the sick man becomes able to communicate with them, and then decide whether they will recognize him or not.

So the question is put and carried, two voting in the affirmative, nine in the negative. The ordinary business of the lodge being then hastily transacted, the fraters parted, but with looks that plainly expressed a chronic state of puzzlement, aggravated by the feeling that somehow or other, the sick man had not received Masonic treatment in the conclusions to which the lodge had arrived. It is an ill feeling to feel, as every one will admit, that we have done wrong, and still worse to feel that we can not give the wrong a name. Such was the feeling of Benevolence Lodge.

Brother Brownlow hurried home to examine the earlier files of the ——; Brother Cocke to look over Preston, the only book in *his* collection; Brothers Juris and Prudence to play out the rubber of chess, and chuckle over the facility with which old *death-on-innovations* Cocke had been dumb-founded in the debate.

The Committee on Charity—to wit: the Worshipful Master, Senior Warden, and Junior Warden, who, in all well-regulated lodges, fill, as everybody knows, that benevolent bill—hurried early next morning upon their errand of love. No dusty cobwebs of law choked *their* charitable throats as they inquired of the sleepy landlord, "How is Brother Bauer of Berlin this morning?" For though Brownlow, the Master, has vainly searched the files of the —— since May, 1853, for an elucidation of the problem before them; and though neither of the Wardens has an idea upon the subject as big as a beech-nut; and though Cocke has pierced Preston through and through to find law that will win in this conjuncture; yet the demands of a sick, enfeebled stranger are acknowledged without a question, and the Committee on Charity will take care of "Brother Bauer of Berlin," whether he is a Freemason, or whether his diploma and lambskin are tokens of membership in the "Feegle-cloob," the "Climer-housyn," or any other form of Dutch Odd-Fellowship known to that ingenious nation. They will take care of him, and see that he has all things needful, and bury him decently if he dies, and take pains to apprise his foreign friends of his death, and all that, just as any set of kind-hearted fellows will do, whether "Feegles," "Housyns," or only Freemasons. As to the matter of that, if "Brother Bauer of Berlin" had fallen under the observation of John C. Spencer, Billy Seward, and Pliny Merrick, at the hottest point of their Mason-hunting, and being sick and distressed, a stranger in a strange land, had appealed to them for aid, he would have got it, blistered Antimasons as they were; for humanity has its Freemasonry, and poverty and sickness are its indisputable signs and tokens.

To the query, "How is Brother Bauer of Berlin this morning?" the sleepy landlord, who has been up all night, shakes his head doubtfully. A great deal of force in head-shaking! No wonder the deaf and dumb man succeeds so well in the world, considering that he has fingers, eyes, and a movable head. There is more than one man we know, who, for all ordinary purposes, would be really better off, in point of the graces, were his means of communication confined to a loose noddle and flexible fingers. Talk of Masonry as an artificial thing! Why, the universal language of eyes, fingers, and nodding heads forms a Masonry more ancient than Jubal and Jabal, and one that will last after faith is lost in sight, and hope ends in fruition.

Brother Braham Willis, by his head, indicates "worse; he can't live long," which brings a paleness over the committee's cheeks, and adds swiftness to their feet, as they hurry up the stairs to the poor invalid's room. No mockery of knocking is necessary there. Retirement, solitude, decency, modesty—all these are the demands of reason; but the reason which of wont had tenanted the frame of Brother Bauer has now fled, and his room may be entered by any one at pleasure.

Some *have* entered it already. Brother Juris is already there, so is Brother Prudence. It was a point of boasting for them to get there before the committee, and they gained it. They have already looked at the poor semi-corpse on the pallet; have already heard the two or three syllables he whispers occasionally, which sound to them like "lieber" and "Mädchen," but which might as well sound like anything else in the German dictionary, for all that Juris and Prudence can make out of them; have already decided in their own minds, and noisily affirmed it, too, to the two or three other Brethren present, that "'t will never do to *recognize* this fellow as a Mason without something more definite than they have had yet;" have already fixed up a polemic on the subject to throw at the head of Brother Brownlow just as soon as he will listen to it. And somebody else has entered the room—no less a body than an enormous dog, a black spaniel—who, with a tender look at his sick master, and anon a sour look at Juris, who is making more noise in his argument than he (the spaniel) thinks proper to a sick-chamber, has taken possession of the foot of the bed, as if by prescriptive right, which no doubt he has. Brother Bauer of Berlin, once opening his eyes, and staring straight forward, sees the tender look of the dog, and acknowledges, by an answering glance, that it does him good, which no doubt it does.

Enter with us, benevolent reader, into the spirit of this scene. The poor and dying man; the group around; the faithful dog, who (we use the pronoun with intention) looks upon his master, according to the idea of Brother Robert Burns, as *his god;* the friendly landlord, willing but unable; the sorrowful wife of the landlord, Sister Willis, mighty in Dorcas societies, and in the work of good-will, and in kitchen and parlor, who has come in also, to smooth the bed-clothes and fix the pillow, as none but God's favorite children, the women, can do it. Gaze upon all this, and as you give passage to the obtrusive tear and swelling sigh, acknowledge that there is a Masonry in sickness and in death which makes all men brothers.

But the difficulty, sprung in our last chapter, is not solved. Standing there by his bedside, not one of those Masons can say in his conscience, "This is *my Brother* in the mystic art; living, I will love him—dying, I will respect him." On the contrary, the more plainly death becomes visible in his eye or on his face, the more puzzling is the doubt. The only means of recognition afforded the committee thus far is the apron and diploma, and this, at the best, whatever our foreign Brethren may think, are no more than so many letters of introduction and recommendation to the traveling Brother.

16

An hour passes, and then the doctor, a stern old man, who has the merit of always telling the most unpalatable truths in the most unpalatable way, declares "the Dutchman is dying;" and, according to his invariable custom in such cases, dashes off home to let him die without hinderance. The shock—a natural shock, one can no more fail to be impressed by such intelligence than he can fail to be affected by a charge of electricity—is felt by all the group. An increased tenderness is visible in the countenance of each; voices drop to whispers; movements are made on tip-toe; Brother Juris, observing a disposition in Brother Prudence to raise his objections to the last argument too loudly, catches the prevailing tone, and cautions him to silence. The group gather closer around to see him die—the Brothers, the weeping landlady, and the faithful dog.

It is a kind Providence that gives to many a person a moment of reason, and a little strength in the dying hour, to communicate his last wishes to surviving friends. Without it, we all are so prone to postpone needful matters, we should leave undone the things which ought to be done even more than we do; without such a Providence as this, Brother Bauer could never have been recognized by the Masons of Benevolence Lodge as a genuine Brother, and this true sketch had never been written.

In the little interval between the stupor of disease and the stupor of death, the eyes of the sick man were fairly opened. They fell first, as before, upon the dog, but there was an expression of anxiety in those eyes not removed by the sight of that wistful, loving, honest face. It was not removed by the low, earnest whine with which the animal acknowledged his master's gaze. It was not removed by the womanly face and hand of Sister Willis, who strove, by many a womanly art, to express her sympathy for his condition, and her desire to alleviate it. It was not to be removed by any class of friends whose types were of such.

Brother Brownlow bethought him then of the Masonic apron, which still lay upon the table after its exposure last night. It was no great display of intellect to be sure, yet to no other person in the room had the idea occurred that these things, the apron and the diploma, might be made a medium of communication between the living and the dying, and effect, partially at least, the very object all the group were desiring to attain—*the recognition of the man as a Mason.*

He held the apron up in view of those anxious eyes, and lo! a glance of meaning shot from them. The attentive sister marked it, and with a well-instructed prudence, and a meaning smile to the Brothers, retired from the room. The smile implied, "it is not dog or woman he wants—it is Freemasons." And so it was. * * * * * * *

Not a sign is known to ancient Masonry which he did not give, as he perceived the closing group, intelligent and responsive. The tongue obeyed, for the instant, his command, and gave, in low but distinct utterance, the mystic sounds. The hand, feeble to all other uses, was yet nervous enough for that pressure which demands and implies so much. And when, after all this, the exhausted man fell backward into the skeleton arms open to receive him, and the weeping group closed his eyes and straightened his limbs for a long repose, it was remarked by each, as a pleasant thing to contemplate, that no anxiety was mingled now with that placid look which death had lent him; but all things, in eye, mouth, and lineaments, told of the gratifying sensation—oh! how gratifying, what tongue can tell?—experienced by the stranger who has found friends and brothers in this his hour of utmost need.

Benevolence Lodge at Papyrus, is quite as perplexed as before. It is rarely the case that death lessens human complications; he rather increases them as an enemy, and makes the confusion worse confounded. Few such men there are as the Past Master of Alexandria Lodge, Virginia—he whom men have entered in history as the apprentice, the craft, and the master, *George Washington*—who, from early habits, left all his business matters regularly entered, balanced, and posted *up to the previous Saturday.* Rather, the most of those who have joined themselves to the "Silent Lodge," whence there is none that come away, have left their accounts unbalanced, and their business awry.

It was so with Brother Bauer, of Berlin. Is it not so, kind reader, with you? Had he lived, he would have recovered; had he recovered from the present crisis, he would have proved his right to Masonic burial, while, at the same time, no Masonic burial would have been required of the lodge. But he was gone, and darkness was upon the face of the history—a vail thicker than the neat linen which Sister Willis, with holy care, had spread over his poor face; a darkness as palpable as that which filled the atmosphere, through which the poor dog looked and whined, wondering as a reasoning creature might have done, and distressed at his master's silence. Who was he? was he a Mason in reality? Had the lodge a *right* to bury him? was it their *duty*?

Viewing the matter merely as an illustration of human consistency, it was pleasant to hear these questions answered emphatically in the negative by Brother Juris, and even more emphatically by Brother Prudence, those saints in Masonic precept. They had, in fact, lashed themselves up to a virtuous skepticism profitable to contemplate. Listen to Brother John Juris's arguments, as the Brethren, in lodge assembled, listened to them the next morning:

"Taking this editor's own explications of Masonic law"—he was alluding, dear reader, to a certain writer on Masonic law, not unbeknown to you, whose hopes are all at *Jerusalem*, ancient and sound, and what not!—"taking it as law as quoted, it requires three classes of proofs to establish the fact of a man's Masonry. The first link in the chain, is, *a solemn declaration*, and this link is wanting. This, the very first proof, the most important, because the first—the most important, because in many cases it is necessarily the *only* proof; this link, which would give an examining committee, or you, Brother Junior Warden, who, according to the old monitor, are officially the examining committee, a basis on which to ground an examination, and an apology for a poor examination, if need be; this link, I say, and in duty bound, am compelled again and again to reiterate, is wanting. Now, we have no more right to believe, and I no more *do* believe that this man Brawler was a Mason, than I believe his dog is." All this, with great gesticulation, one-half his words in small caps, the other half in italics, and peppered with the exclamation points that come from both cases.

To which Brother Prudence—"Worshipful Sir"—he was altogether too independent a Brother Prudence, mind you, to say "Master"—"Worshipful Sir, I would like to ask, and if you or the Brethren here will permit me to do it, I *will* ask, at the risk, doubtless, of exciting a sneer on the faces of *some*"—here a sardonic contortion that looked like contempt for all sneers and sneerers, especially the latter—"at the risk, I say, of being sneered at for my ignorance; for I am free to admit, here and elsewhere, that I do not draw my inspiration from Masonic newspapers or editors, do not profess to learn Masonry from printer's ink"—sardonic expression again, which, if the poor editor alluded to had witnessed, he had never raised his head again—"I will ask of you, my Brethren, here present"——"Address yourself to the chair, Brother Prudence," promptly said Worshipful Brother Brownlow, successfully attempting to subdue his tendency to yarn—"To you, then, Sir, I address this query, and I beg it may be recorded on the minutes of this meeting, can you reconcile it to yourselves as a lodge, and can you justify yourselves as a lodge, before the Grand Lodge, in giving this man Masonic burial? If you can, I am free to say, *I* can not. I am free to say, you may take any pauper, yes, Sir, a pauper from the County Poor House, and, because he has somehow learned, probably in a clandestine way, your grips and signs, and because he has somehow got a Masonic apron and diploma, you may give him Masonic burial with just as much right as this man Border. Where is Masonry tending, Sir? to what end is it hastening, when such irregularities as this are allowed? In my little experience"—it was, indeed, a little one, and daily growing no larger—"in my limited experience I have been instructed to demand due trial, etc. Now, have we had it? I ask you, Sir, *have* we had it? I ask you, Brethren" ——"Address yourself to the chair, Brother Prudence," again enjoined the attentive Master, evincing no passions, save ennui and regret. "I ask, have we had it? And suppose we go out before the world to bury this man Borer. Suppose we improve this occasion, and perform the funeral rites over him. Suppose, afterward, it turns out that he never was lawfully in receipt of our secrets, or that he had been expelled from the Masonic body. How should we look then? how would you, Sir, look then? and what sort of a face could we present at the Grand

Lodge, when the report of this stupendous irregularity came up? I hope, Sir, this lodge will not desecrate itself and this glorious Institution, by assuming, for 'tis all mere assumption, that the man was a Mason, and burying him as such. For myself, I tell you freely, I will not turn out in the procession, and, if I am subjected to the discipline of Masonry for it, then I will appeal to the Grand Master."

Now, if the reader presumes that all this sketch, or any other Masonic sketch that we give him, is imaginary, let him cast the notion at once from his mind. The thing actually happened as it is recorded. These speeches, silly or not, as you choose to call them, were made—nobody is hurt now at the telling, for Brothers Juris and Prudence have given up Masonry, and are now members of another Secret Society, where they are burning and shining lights—and great was the perplexity caused thereby. Masons, good Masons, are a cautious and discreet people; a true Mason, indeed, is a child of Prudence, but not unfrequently those qualities are in excess.

Brother Cocke arose. Cocke is a *real* orator. Not in the way of words—I am bound to admit Juris could talk the horns off of him, Prudence could talk him into an untimely grave—but, in the way of stevedoring a great many thoughts into the narrow hold of a few sentences. I have no account of his address on this occasion; but he said, that while he admitted the so-called defect in the chain of evidence alluded to, yet he believed Brother Bauer *was* a

Mason—and sternly did he rebuke the liberties with the name which the two Brethren had taken—and, as such, he was in favor of burying him. He gave it as his opinion, based upon nearly forty years' experience, that no dying man could *act* the accepted Mason as *that* dead man had, unless he *were* one, lawfully begotten, lawfully reared by and among Brothers and fellows. He brought tears, when he declared, in his figurative way, that, seeing the dog had already been sarcastically alluded to, he would as soon believe that poor animal a hypocrite, in pretending to love the deceased foreigner, as that a deception had been practiced upon them by the deceased. For his part, he should insist that the Worshipful Master summon the lodge, for what was all they could now do for the Brother, *the funeral service.*

Old Father Hymnic followed. He is a man—or rather *was*, for he has since followed Brother Bauer, of Berlin, to another sphere—he was a man who rarely spoke, partly because he said he could learn more by listening, but this is somewhat doubtful, and partly because he stammered. Now, however, in his slow and laborious way—it is a way that makes you listen, despite yourself—he plead for the dead man's privilege of Masonic rites. He said that he, Father Hymnic, had himself become a Mason in his old age, to gain loving and respectful burial. For none, he affirmed, know the true use of a dead man, save Masons. *They* lay them away, he said, embalmed in balsam, incorruptible against the day they shall be wanted. *They* lay them with faces looking upward and eastward—how eloquently he rendered himself here!—because, from the elevated Orient the Master will appear to hail his sleeping Craftsmen, and call them to their new and better work. So he plead, that the Masons of Benevolence Lodge should take that sleeping Mason yonder, and embalm him with the mystical ceremonies older than Egypt's. That they should bear him, in fitting procession, to a resting-place, opened in the Masonic portion of the cemetery. That they should place him there, in proper position, to receive more light in Masonry, when the Supreme Grand Master should think proper to communicate it. It is my obligation, said he; and he uttered much more. And such talk as this, good reader, though it was borrowed, unwittingly, perhaps, from writers before him, and, though there was nothing, perhaps nothing at all original in it, so far as the venerable Hymnic was concerned, told with powerful effect upon the lodge. What! would they cheerfully vote their money to bury him, because they believed him a Mason, and would they refuse to lay him, Craftsmen-like, before the Master of men, by the side of those who had gone this way before him!

The upshot of it was, that, the next morning at ten o'clock, the village of Papyrus closed its doors for a few hours, while the Masons—a most popular and influential set among the Papyrians—bore their dead slowly down the street to the cemetery. How shall I say it of Brothers Juris and Prudence? their law office alone was seen to be open, and a gossiping old woman said afterward, that those two pillars of society were engaged at a game of chess as the dead went by. But the dead was not rendered unhappy by their indifference. The poor dog, who walked sadly under the bier, never raised his head to observe it. Gossips soon forgot it. Do you forgive it, and forget it, too.

They laid him right, poor Brother Bauer, of Berlin, as they had been often taught to lay dead Brothers right. He will rise properly when the signal is given. Side by side with six others, who are lying right by his side, he will rise, and the rank will stand steady before the Master, all silent and inert though now they be. He lies right. Grovel, and bore, and gnaw as you may, foul earth-worms; bear him piece to piece to your holes, yet know that you can not affect his resurrection. He lies right; he will rise right.

And though the mystery was never solved, who, or what, or whence this stranger, who came to Papyrus only to enter one of its graves—and though Benevolence Lodge will probably never have an assurance upon the subject, who can say they committed an error in laying that dead man right, against the resurrection day?

Yourself, intelligent reader, being the judge, for I deem you to be a Mason, were they right or wrong?

By the craving for decent interment which all men evince; by hopes having reference to a future state, which inspiration has implanted within human breasts; by the dead who have been raised by divine power, as witnesses to the truth of the doctrine of the resurrection; by symbolic illustrations often repeated in our lodges; by tried and trusty blocks in our foundation walls; by answers to prayer never denied by a prayer-hearing, and prayer-loving, and prayer-answering Deity, the great I AM, willing, as he declares, to be daily importuned by mortals; let the Masonic dead have Masonic burial! Give no ear to those teachers who denounce this tried doctrine of Masonic philosophy! They who leave the tenement of flesh trusting in the power of God to reunite soul and body, shall know their former homes again!

The Badgered Witness.

A TALE OF TESTIMONY.

Inscribed to Bro. George W. Bartlett,
OF SALEM, INDIANA.

THE question how far a witness is compelled to answer inquiries put to him at the bar remains unsettled. To judge by John Q. Adams's theory (as expounded in his "Letters on Masonry"), one would suppose there was no reservation on this head. Yet it is well-known there is: the confidence of the confessional, state secrets generally, the communications of criminals to their attorneys, and all testimony which would criminate the witness, are exceptions, so acknowledged in all courts, and by none better understood than Adams himself.

'T is true, a person is obliged *to tell the whole truth* before he knows how much of the truth he will be required or permitted to tell; but it is well understood, in judicial cases, that the party who summoned the witness only desires that portion of his testimony which favors *his own cause*, while the opposite party watches, with hawk's eyes, for an opportunity to seal his lips, so that the whole truth may *not* appear. Between the two, did ever a witness tell the whole truth? Is there not, more or less, *mental reservation* in all witnesses as to certain parts of the testimony? The following is in illustration:

In a trial that occurred somewhere in New York, during the Antimasonic warfare of 1826–36, a witness had been subpenaed, who was expected to give highly important testimony for *the defendant*, in proving title to a large tract of land which was in dispute. The plaintiff's counsel were, of course, anxious to stop the mouth of evidence that could injure their case so much; and when they learned that the witness, as well as the defendant, was a Royal Arch Mason, they seized upon the fact as a snub at the outset.

No sooner was Mr. Perry summoned to the witness-box, than one of the circuit bullies accosted him in his harshest manner, and the following conversation took place:

"What's your name, sir?"

"Perry."

"What else beside Perry?"

"Barnabas W. Perry."

"Well, Mr. Barnabas W. Perry, are you the same Barnabas W. Perry whose name is recorded here?"—pointing to a catalogue of the members of a neighboring chapter—"the same Perry, did you say?"

"I did n't say anything on that subject."

"Well, then, say something now. Are you the same Barnabas W. Perry? Come, out with it!"

"My name is Barnabas W. Perry, as I told you; that's as much as serves to identify me, I suppose.

I appeal to the court for protection against this man's insolence."

Here the judge, who had been slightly dozing, woke up suddenly, and asked what was the matter?

"Here is a witness, sir, who refuses to testify as to his name, please your honor," said Bully.

"Is that so?" inquired the judge, with surprise.

"I told him that my name was Barnabas W. Perry, judge, and then I appealed to the court to protect me from his rude and insulting questions."

Here a gray-haired attorney rose to clear the puzzled mind of the court by an explanation.

"Mr. Perry was inquired of as to whether he was the same person whose name appears there in a certain printed catalogue, please the court."

"And did you decline to reply?" asked his honor.

"I did decline, judge, both on account of the insulting tone the counsel adopted, and because the question is not at all relevant to anything which I have to relate concerning this suit."

"Remember your oath, sir," interposed Bully, fiercely. "I demand, on your oath, are you the same Barnabas W. Perry?"

"My oath, sir, has reference to my subpena, and says nothing about any Royal Arch catalogue," responded the badgered witness; "therefore I shall not reply."

"You must answer the counsel's questions," observed the judge, mildly; for Mr. Perry was an intimate friend, and a man of weight. "Witnesses are not allowed to be judges of relevancy. Give your evidence, and if irrelevant to the case, the court will order it to be ruled out. Unless you declare on oath that you can not answer this question without criminating yourself, the court must insist upon your replying."

After a moment's pause, during which bully looked with an air of triumph toward the jury, Mr. Perry further expostulated:

"No, judge, I am not in the least afraid of criminating myself; but I have frequently been summoned as a juror before you, and I have always observed that when witnesses were insulted by insnaring and improper questions, the bench interposed. Now, the question asked me is one that, in its connection, is plainly designed to convey a reproach. I was summoned here to testify concerning a land title. The first question asked me is, am I a Royal Arch Mason? I claim your protection, judge, and decline to answer."

And not another word would the badgered individual say, though the bully foamed and the court threatened. In the upshot, he was imprisoned for contempt of court.

Being a gentleman of considerable distinction, he was visited by members of the bar, who labored with all their might to change his mind, and the judge himself condescended to apply to him through the jail-door. All in vain.

At last, as the suit could not progress without him, counsel consented to waive the question, and Mr. Perry was released to answer *relevant* questions.

The Duel.

A TALE OF MASONIC INTERPOSITION.

Inscribed to M. W. Harvey T. Wilson,
OF SHERBURN, KY., GRAND MASTER.

"When thou givest him not warning, nor speakest to warn the wicked from his wicked way, to save his life, his blood will I require at thine hands."

DURING the campaign in Northern Mexico, which resulted in the capture of Monterey, there were various outbreaks among the American soldiers, in which they avenged themselves upon the inhabitants, by acts of cruelty and injustice, for the annoyances they experienced from the guerrilla bands.

It is not to be doubted that the guerrilla warfare is one well calculated in itself to stimulate revenge, even to ferocity. To be waylaid at every step; to be shot down like wild beasts, even in sight of camp; to sleep in hourly expectation of the fatal dagger; to drink water and eat bread at the imminent risk of poison from the desperadoes that infested the country—these were provocations to a furious retaliation, especially from an unscrupulous soldiery. But vengeance is blind. It sates itself without discrimination when its unholy fires are once lighted, and the nearest unfortunate is too often made the victim upon its unhallowed altars. Well does the genius of Masonry deprecate the whole business of war. In the campaign above referred to, the blood of innocent persons often flowed; the humble roof of many a harmless family blazed over the cruel torch.

Among other recorded acts of atrocity, a case had occurred in which a whole Mexican family was butchered by a lawless party from the American camp.

By what individuals this dreadful guilt was perpetrated, or from what precise motive, was never ascertained; but suspicions pointed out certain members of Captain Y——'s company of ——— State volunteers, and such, to this day, is the general sentiment.

Some members of that company having, a short time afterward, met the members of Captain A——'s company, from the same State, insulting charges were made, connected with this affair. Hot recriminations followed, and in a few minutes a general fight was in progress among scores of men. Fortunately, none had deadly weapons in their hands, or much blood would have flowed.

Ah! it was wise in the great King to forbid ax, hammer, and all metal tools in the building of the sacred fane. Our statute that prohibits wearing concealed weapons, is founded broadly in WISDOM.

No lives, then, were lost, but several of the party were cruelly beaten, and the tumult was at its hight, when a couple of officers, summoned by the din, came simultaneously upon the ground, and ordered the men to their quarters. They were both lieutenants, and, as it happened, one from each of the companies in dispute. Unfortunately, these gentlemen had not been on friendly terms for several weeks, and some words hastily dropped by R—— were caught up by B——, as personally insulting. When we are at outs with a person, we readily distort everything he says. A hot retort followed; replication of an offensive nature flew back and forth, and the result was a challenge; a duel to the death with pistols, at sunset, a gunshot from the camp!

Seconds were selected; testamentary papers signed; letters of farewell to friends beloved.

As the sun went glowingly down beyond the Cordilleras, the opponents—both in the prime of days and hopes—met in the little glade that had been designated for the scene of blood. God had never created it for such a sanguinary purpose. It was an opening in the musquit and prickly pear, of about an acre in extent. The thick wire-grass of the country made a mat below, while above them was the blue vault of the rainless sky of that clime.

Was that blue arch to behold that verdant mat dyed scarlet? The ground was speedily marked out; the parties were placed in positions; not a tremor visible; no paleness; no desire to spare or be spared. Ah, no! hatred had done her worst work, and usurped the spirit's throne.

The weapons were skillfully loaded and pointed, and now only *the word* was wanting for Satan's triumph. "Let there be death, and there was death," might well be inscribed on every duelist's tomb.

Although the fact of the challenge had been carefully concealed, yet a report of such things will struggle out despite of all precaution, and, to the great annoyance of the parties, a considerable crowd of spectators had collected, and were lining the edge of the little opening, and waiting with breathless expectation for the result. It was still more perplexing that others were continually arriving from the camp, for the probability was imminent that notice of the intended duel would reach the commanding officer, in which event the whole affair would be summarily stopped.

Among others who came running into the opening, just as the parties were placed, was Captain F——, lately in command of a company in the regiment to which the lieutenants belonged, but badly wounded at the battle of Resaca de la Palma, and consequently absent for several months on leave. Captain F—— was a mutual friend of the contending parties, and, of course, shocked to hear, upon his arrival in camp, that a deadly duel was in progress between them. As he bore letters and kind messages to each from absent friends, he engaged a soldier to show him the way, and hurried, as we have seen, to the spot. He was barely in time.

"Now, my dear young friend R——," he began, "my excellent friend B——, let me say a word before you shoot. Here's a letter for you, R——, from your mother. You certainly won't refuse to read it. B——, I've a message for your particular ear. Come, come, boys, I'm just from home!"

Home! what a word is home! It is the symbol for a host of lovers. The extended pistol-hands were dropped; the places in which their seconds had stationed them were vacated; and, forgetful of the rules of the duello, the two who were thus lawlessly pursuing each other's life, hurried up to their mutual friend, and each had claimed the first news.

"Nay, nay," good-humoredly responded that gentleman, "I left the letters in camp; and as for news, I do n't feel easy to tell news under these circumstances. Stay, there's a late paper from home; read it, friend B——, while I deliver a very particular message here aside to R——." And, to the surprise of the spectators and disgust of the seconds, who had never heard of such a thing before, his request was acceded to—one of the lieutenants sitting down to read the newspaper, while the other, with colored cheeks, heard a kind word, warm from the heart of his betrothed. Then Captain F—— called up B—— to the conference, and a long conversation ensued between the three, but what was said by the humane mediator, what arguments he answered, or what acknowledgments passed between the parties, can not here be spoken of.

The two seconds, foaming and fretting, and almost ready to fight each other in their disappointment, were now called up, and the debate became exciting. What had before passed in earnest whispers, was now heard by the nearest spectators to take such a form as this: "I offer that"—"I accept that"—"that's true"—"I did n't mean"—"I only intended." Then, as a winding up to the whole, all parties turned into a furious shaking of hands. Then went up a general shout from the little area, for the soldiers were as much rejoiced at the reconciliation as the good captain himself; and then the blue heavens looked down again upon the vacant spot.

A splendid supper was given the next night, and the best toast drank, the one that excited the loudest cheers and drained the deepest goblets, was offered by the colonel of the regiment: "Gentlemen, drink with me the health of *the healer* and *the reconciler*, whose fraternal thought spared the flow of brothers' blood!"

By this we presume all parties to this singular affair must have been Masons.

Staying the Hands.

A TALE OF PIRACY.

Inscribed to R. W. Harman G. Reynolds,

OF SPRINGFIELD, ILLINOIS.

IN relating a circumstance wherein Freemasonry is exhibited in the hands of pirates, we are called upon to explain by way of prelude—for a moral community will demand it—how it happens that such an abandoned class are authorized to enter our holy precincts? The wonder does not lie in the fact that pirates acknowledge a Masonic appeal when it is made, but in the circumstance of their understanding such appeals at all. Romancers like Marryatt—in his "Peter Simple," for instance, where he has made one of the most abandoned jail-birds in all England the *Master of his lodge*—are not expected to know anything more of this matter than they can work up into their "thrilling tales" or "interesting sketches." Others, whose knowledge of Freemasonry is embraced in the terms "clap-trap" (see "Mysteries of London"), or "tomfoolery" (see a late Philadelphia weekly), may deride what they can not understand, and the reading world will set them down for what they are really worth. But he who undertakes to dilate on Masonry in its practical application to society, must expect to be catechised on this head, and prepare himself accordingly.

That many pirates and freebooters, especially among the Spaniards and Moors, were and are Masons, is incontrovertible. That they are, in general, quick to answer the appeals of suffering humanity, when offered through the medium of a Mason, is acknowledged by every one who has had occasion to try the experiment. That in the matter of relief to Brother Masons they are even more than ordinarily benevolent, may reasonably be admitted. It remains to explain how they become Masons at all.

Freemasonry, though universal and unchangeable in its forms and ceremonies, is susceptible of various applications, as it is worked up by various hands. Thus, in some European countries, it was made, for a time at least, a conservator of the aristocracy; in England, a bulwark of royalty; in Mexico, a shield of patriotism. It has served as a friend of sociability and a teacher of temperance; as a relief association; as a stern dispenser of justice; as a trial of fortitude and a test of prudence. This multiform character it has sustained, in general, by means of *mutilation*. Divested of its equalizing, democratic character—and Masonry, in truth, is a perfect model of democracy—it becomes a convenient tool to despotism, as in Prussia; divested of its grand religious principles, it will subserve the purposes of deism, as with Voltaire and the French clique of the last century; worked up with modern elegances and modern philosophy, it becomes a gewgaw to catch the multitude, as in many of the French forms; divested of its morality, it may be applied even to the convenience of a pirate, as in the case we are about to relate.

It is asked, if Masonry possesses this protean character, who will guarantee its integrity and stability, and that it will not do more evil than good? The answer is ready. No principle is to be judged of by its abuse, but by its use. Nothing has been more abused than religion, the grandest principle of all; yet none but a skeptic, and an ignorant one at that, will attribute the evils of bigotry and misdirected enthusiasm to religion. Masonry has been, is, and doubtless will be, misdirected and abused in divers ways; but it will be, as with religion, by mutilating its members; it will be by divesting it of its grandest principles, and leaving only the relief, the social feature, and its universality.

How shall the evil be cured? Answer, by teaching, through lecture and through print, what Masonry *is*. By dispelling the thick cloud of ignorance that enshrouds not only the enemies, but the friends of Masonry; not only the cowan, but the affiliated; not only the camp of the foe, but the tabernacle of the priest. By proving that Masonry dismembered is not Masonry, any more than a dismembered individual can be made a Mason; but that Masonry is a whole, and must be so taught and practiced.

Pirates can not be Masons in a high and complete sense. They may learn some of our signs, and may recognize them, and recognize their duty in obeying and answering them; they may be able to speak some of our language, and be the better for what they have learned; but a real Mason is *free;* prepared first in heart; restrained in all his passions; taking unlawfully from no man; laboring in an honest vocation; and ever sustaining the word of God between the palms of his hands. Such men are never pirates.

But how do pirates gain admission into Masonic lodges? Into chartered lodges they never do enter. No person made clandestinely—that is, out of the fold of a just and *legally* constituted lodge—can be admitted even as a visitor. No person whose character, age, calling, etc., are not avouched by persons known to the lodge, can legally be made a Mason. But in various parts of the world, especially in the loosely organized society of Northern Africa and the Spanish West Indies, and in countries generally where the Papal Church has secular power, and all secret associations are interdicted, there are many extraordinary, and, in a sense, illegal lodges, in which men are made Masons for restricted purposes, and without that thorough inquiry into their character and qualifications which the true system of Masonry presupposes. Among these, the freebooter and the highwayman may sometimes even have entrance. Nay, such a man may be the principal agent in organizing this clandestine body, as best knowing how advantageous the relief principle may be to him and his in times of difficulty.

This is a fair explanation of the subject, and one to which the most rabid opponent of Masonry ought not to object. As well blame chaste, wedded love for the evils of licentiousness; as well accuse honest commerce and economy for the sins of theft; as well attribute to legal self-preservation the horrors of murder, as to accuse honest, lawful Masonry of these sins of abuse. The better the subject, the worse its abuse.

It was about the year 1820, that the schooner Brilliant sailed from a West Indian port to the coast of South America, having on board such a cargo as the tropics yield, for the use of less favored climes. The various inlets of the islands were at that time infested by bands of pirates, who took every opportunity to attack the unarmed traders. Their common method was to lie on the sand-beaches, and watch the passing vessels until a calm; then to dash out in their armed boats, capture the defenseless craft, murder the crew, hurry the most valuable parts of the cargo ashore, and finish the work of hell by burning the unfortunate vessel; or else they would mark the position of a coaster as night came on, and while the crew was sleeping off the fatigues of the day, guarded by a single sentinel only, they would approach with muffled oars, surround the doomed object on every side, and, at a given signal, rush in, and carry all before them by boarding, ere half the crew could tumble up to the defense. In every case, the piratical dogma, "Dead men tell no tales," was made absolute. Nothing but joining the buccaneers unreservedly could save the prisoner's life, nor were the officers permitted even this privilege. The females were reserved for a fate worse—how much worse!—than death. So general, indeed, was the dread of this, that numerous instances are on record where fathers stabbed their daughters, husbands their wives, and brothers their sisters, rather than suffer them to pass the horrid ordeal of banded lust.

The Brilliant spread her canvas to the breeze, and short and profitable was her trip to the destined port. Loaded for the return voyage, her prow was turned northward, and the hearts of officers and men were already bounding with the hope of a speedy and safe conclusion to the trip. There is something in the idea of a well-built, well-rigged, well-conditioned craft, that excites the admiration of a seaman. He sees such a uniformity of design and of plan in the whole affair, from the laying down of the keel to the tying of the last fastening in the running-gear, that he feels no surprise at the intense affection for his ship, which is the characteristic of a mariner. He experiences the same emotion at the consideration of speculative architecture (even as our brethren felt amid the details of their practical architecture), and he recognizes the fraternity of sympathy. This explains to the mind, although purblind historians can not explain, because they can not feel it, how it happens that the Phœnicians, first of sailors, should also have been first of builders, and renowned for the strength of their fraternal links, the basis of the Solomonic Masonry. On this principle, the principle of *handicraft*, there is a confraternity of *labor* everywhere.

But the schooner Brilliant was destined to illustrate something more than handicraft or operative Masonry ere she reached her port; and although there was great peril in her way, there was also a great triumph to be realized, as the reader shall see.

Among the officers was a gentleman whose name shall be narrowed down to the initial B——, who was on board as acting supercargo. This young man, afterward a Jewish Rabbi and a Masonic Brother, was at that time passing through his season of experience, the results of which, in a talented mind, are not only to implant useful thoughts, but to eradicate educational errors. *His* errors of education, however, related principally to Masonry, concerning which he had imbibed a strong distrust. The few instances in which he had remarked Masonic application had not been fortunate ones; and Mr. B——, at that time, might have been described as a somewhat marked Antimason, not offensively so, but so to the serious detriment of the Order wherever his influence extended.

Captain V——, who had charge of the schooner, was a plain Englishman, whose highest talent consisted in his seamanship; between whom and his supercargo as little intercourse existed as an entire diversity of habit, taste, and experience could well afford.

Toward the close of a certain day, the wind being fair for port, the crew were strolling about the deck in that listless, unoccupied manner, usual in such cases. Our Mr. B—— was sitting in the little cabin, with a Hebrew volume before him, in which he was mayhap considering the past glories or the promised triumph of his now far-scattered nation; or he was haply attuning his voice to one of those wild and pathetic chants which form the synagogue worship, as they once formed the temple and the tabernacle worship, of his people, in ancient days.

In the midst of this, his attention was claimed by the captain, who called down the gangway, "A suspicious sail to windward, Mr. B——. Looks most remarkably like a freebooter!" This startling announcement cut short his musings, and caused him to hurry on deck. There was the stranger vessel, but a few miles to windward, with all her wings spread, and steering, straight as an eagle to his prey, toward the little Brilliant. Such a course left few doubts as to some evil intentions; and the doubts, if any, soon became certainties; for the report of a gun, and the sight of a cannon-ball skipping but a few cables' length ahead, was too clear for dispute. The Brilliant hove to just as the stranger was aiming another messenger to speak her purpose nearer home. Suddenly the naked gaff was furnished with a large flag, which, unrolling, displayed the awful *skull and cross-bones*, emblems of the pirate's trade. A general paleness was instantly diffused over every countenance in the schooner. The boldest hearts sank. A thought of home and friends was choked up by the consideration of the horrors before them. The old captain, with an impatient stamp and a muttered curse, turned to his crew, and advised them—"No resistance, my lads, no concealment; give the ruffians all they ask for, and possibly they may let us off the easier." But it was evident he lacked the comfort of his own words, and expected no mercy. The supercargo went below to arrange his papers, and returned, bringing up the manifest of the schooner's cargo, just as the pirate captain and a score of his crew came up the sides. A murderous band, in good sooth, they were. Of all nations, the selected devils; of all tongues, the foulest of speech; their malicious eyes and ferocious words spoke of nothing but death, the horrid symbol of their flag-staff. A heavy cutlass flashed in every hand; a row of pistols gleamed from every belt; the handle of a poinard protruded from every breast; while the scars visible on many exposed portions of their bodies and limbs, spoke of murderous combats with lead and steel, where the weakest go to the wall.

The first orders of the pirate chief, spoken in Spanish, were a sufficient indication of his intentions. While one of his subordinates went to the helm, and a part broke open the hatchways, and commenced to hoist out the cargo upon deck, the remainder seized the crew of the Brilliant, bound them hand and foot, and tied ropes round their necks, preparatory to swinging them aloft at a given signal from the chief.

The time occupied in this manner, although short in reality, seemed to those doomed men long as it was painful. Standing upon tip-toe, well-nigh strangled with the ropes, intentionally jostled, from time to time, by their tormentors, as they passed to and fro in their employment, and expecting every moment to be their last, it was the very agony of death. The display of the manifest in the supercargo's hand had not saved him from the general fate. Indeed, the pirate captain had but glanced scornfully at the document, unable to read English, as it appeared, and cast it upon the deck.

Among the other boxes brought out of the hold and cabin to be opened, was a large chest. The lid being wrenched off, there were displayed, on the top of the clothing and other matters, a Mason's painted apron, a diploma, and other paraphernalia of the Order. These met the eye of the chief, who instantly inquired, in a voice of thunder (still in Spanish), "Whose chest is this?" No one of the crew save Mr. B—— could speak that tongue. He replied, as well as his strangled condition would permit, that the chest referred to was the captain's. A signal from the chief caused the release of that officer and Mr. B——, both of whom were ordered down below, where the pirate immediately joined them. The ferocious eye gleamed with an unusual fire.

He threw himself into a position strange to the young supercargo, who could only observe in the twilight that his officer answered it in a similar way. Then the chief, with a yell that more resembled the howl of a beast than the voice of a human being, threw his arms around Captain V——'s neck, embraced and kissed him. After a pause, he suddenly disengaged himself, stepped a pace or two back, and turning to Mr. B——, commanded him, "Ask him why he did n't let me know?" This being interpreted to Captain V——, he answered, with a stammering tongue and mortified manner, "that he forgot all about it!" The pirate, with his eyes flashing fire, and his mouth churning foam and fury, stepped furiously up to him, and with a blow on the side of his head felled him to the floor. Then raising him up, he again kissed him. After this, he ordered Mr. B——, with the most furious curses, in Spanish—a language prolific in words of blasphemy and foul epithets—"Tell the rascal that he well-nigh caused me to break my obligations; and never, no, never, so long as he lives, never again lead a Brother Mason so near into danger as that;" and the fondest words and embraces were lavished, by turns mingled with such awful imprecations and fierce threats as well-nigh caused the hearer to lose his own senses with terror.

All this time the poor captives were standing half-choked around the sides of the vessel; but now the pirate went on deck and ordered them all cast loose, and further pillage to cease. Not only that, but the boats alongside, which had been loaded with the specie and the choicest portions of the freight, were hastily unloaded, and one of them which had left the schooner's side, was recalled for the same purpose. The men were summoned from below, and the hatches replaced; chests and boxes were covered, and everything reinstated as nearly as could be done consistently with the great speed at which the pirates labored.

And now the Mason chief approached Captain

V——, and taking his hand kindly, directed Mr. B—— to assure him "that he loved him like a brother; that it was his own fault (Captain V.'s) that the mischief had gone so far; for, had he known his relationship, he (the chief) would have forfeited his own life before he would have harmed him; that now he could go without another word, only his crew were greatly in want of provisions, and if he would spare him a few barrels of meat and some vegetables, he would give him an order upon a house in Havana for payment; if not, let him say so, and there was an end of it." It is needless to say that the locker was freely opened, and the ship-stores divided with his fraternal captor; likewise, that any thought of payment was indignantly spurned. A parting glass was drank together in the cabin, and with one more embrace, and many a brotherly word, the ferocious visitor departed with his men.

But even then, so anxious was the pirate for their welfare, that, after reaching his own cabin, he hailed the Brilliant, and ordered her to delay her course, while he went below and wrote her a protection. This document being sent back by the jolly-boat, the vessels parted with mutual cheers. The protection was long preserved by Mr. B——. It expressed, in brief terms, the fact that the schooner Brilliant, Captain V——, had been visited in such a latitude and longitude, at such a date, by himself, and overhauled, and that she was exempt from further inquiry by the Free Rovers, on the score of certain emblematical marks inserted in the margin.

The signature was embellished with a full display of the ornaments of which Spanish writers are so diffuse.

No further accident, however, delayed the voyage, nor was the pirate's protection put to that test which it would doubtless have passed through triumphantly.

Sitting together in the cabin, at their evening meal, the supercargo, whose curiosity had as yet received no stay, impatiently demanded of Captain V—— what it all meant, and what circumstance had thus turned the tiger into the lamb?

"It was Freemasonry, and nothing else," answered the captain. "The pirate chief was a Brother Mason, that 's all; and he felt that he dared not harm me, or take my property."

Observing a look of distrust in the countenance of Mr. B——, he went on to show him, by the paraphernalia in the chest, and the emblems marked in the margin of the written protection, that his statement was true, and that the preservation of the Brilliant and her crew was attributable to this circumstance, and to this alone.

We need not add that this one practical fact removed a thousand absurd prejudices, however acquired, from the young man's mind; nor will the reader be surprised to learn that, ere the moon had twice more waxed and waned, he had commenced his mystic journey toward the sanctum of the temple. That journey was prosecuted with diligence and discretion. Each step was carefully weighed and considered; each degree was made thorough and secure ere the next was attempted; and thus, in due time, being permitted the survey of the inner mysteries, his prepared and enlarged mind could comprehend what his delighted ears received.

No further intelligence was ever received concerning the pirate chief; but in his ferocious and demoniacal career, unmasonic and inhuman as it was, there nevertheless existed one green spot, which must, in his gloomy pauses, have yielded him a ray of comfort—the preservation of the schooner Brilliant and her crew on account of his attachment to Freemasonry!

The Tongue too Silent.

A TALE OF MASONIC ADOPTION.

Inscribed to R. W. Bro. S. Blanchard,
OF TECUMSEH, MICHIGAN.

WE are about to relate another scene from our personal experience. The man who will open his eyes and ears as he journeys with the great caravan of humanity, needs nor book nor mouth to tell him how exceedingly wondrous is truth. We see far less of it in the more serious, than in the more romantic works of the shelf, for they who deal in it in pureness must needs write with a ghostly pen. What authors give us such flights of fancy as the scriptural ones? Yet scriptural truths are pure. Who so far from the cut-and-dried logic of the schools as the writers of divine laws?—yet they write for the mass and for all time. We will continue to deal in truths as they enter our knowledge,—in as nearly the same garb, that is to say, as they reach us, and the finical may turn away with scholastic horror if he choose, and ask for statuary clothed in more fashionable array.

Come with me, to-day, to the river bank, kind reader, and let us gather some plain truths as they occur before our eyes. It is a chilly morning, forsooth, and in spite of our winter coats and wind-proof gloves, the blood stagnates and the muscles stiffen in the January blast—hardens the water wherever it may chance to fall—reverberates the frozen clod under our heel as we walk. In frosty clouds the vapor gathers from our breath and settles around us, too heavy to mount upward. It is the coldest morning of the peculiarly inclement month of December, 1851, and we are in a spot at which the blasts from the great prairies gather and accomplish their boreal work.

Before us is a busy scene. A great steamer is landing a portion of her enormous load at the wharf-boat, her steam bellowing loudly through her escape-pipes the while, as if impatient at the necessary delay. Rapidly the debarkation of passengers and the transfer of packages is accomplished, for time is precious and it waits for no man.

Soon the signal is made for departure—another—a third; and with a parting groan from the pipes and a graceful bend with the current, the monarch passes from the shore and down the river, and is lost to view.

There is little time for greeting among these people thus cast so hastily ashore. Those who have become partially acquainted through an intercourse of three or four days, close their acquaintance with a parting nod, or, rarely, a shake of the hand and a kind word, and part never more to meet. Some are cheered at landing by a friend, whose waving hand was visible to their eager eye even before they reached the wharf. Such are seen to hasten, arm linked in arm, to a place where, doubtless, the fire is burning cheerfully for them and kind welcomes await them, of which, even now, with bended head and absorbed attention, they gather a foretaste. But the most pass off the wharf-boat and up the bank without any external show of joy or sorrrow at the change from the river life of half a week to this in the growing town of ——, with which they seem well familiar.

All this has transpired in less than the half hour we have been writing it. Interested as we were with a scene which, though familiar, can never lose its interest to an observing mind, we scarcely note the increasing pain beneath our gloves and boots until our companion, with an ejaculation of distress, more common by half than proper, calls our attention to his own sufferings, and, by a natural transition, to our own. We prefer the glowing stove of the wharf-boat, nigh at hand, to the more distant, though more tasty fire-place of our hotel.

The usual group around such a center of heat presents but little to attract our eye. Certainly, in the language of a wharf-boat there is nothing to attract the ear of a Freemason who reveres God's name, for it is made up of such a skeleton of profanity that were *that* removed it could not stand alone. One object, however, *does* attract the eye, and as we gaze with wonder upon it, there does presently reach our ear a sentence that is interesting to us.

For there, upon a trunk, marked *Matilda Dewey*, sits a young woman, already a mother, and, as the most stupid of this wharf-boat crowd has already noticed with sneers, soon to become a mother yet again. As we entered, two of us, she looked anxiously to each in turn, as if to find in our faces some lineament with which she was familiar; but, with an expression of disappointment, turned her face away. Presently, remarking that we were watching her, and possibly reading our interest in our looks—for we were thinking as we gazed upon her, how hard is woman's lot in an hour of misfortune, yet how uncomplaining she can endure—she asked us in words so low that we were obliged to move closer and request her to repeat them, "Did I know Henry Dewey in this place?"

Unable to satisfy her inquiries, we inquired privately of the clerk concerning her. His reply was so far from being satisfactory that—we blush even now when we recall the circumstance—we turned disappointed away and with our companion left the boat.

A week passed and we were again in the town of ———, when, in a cabin, a mere shanty, such as foreigners only can build around our better domiciles, we saw, as we rode to a distant part of the town, a face that we remembered, no other than the face of the young woman whom we had first seen on the wharf-boat. She recognized us as promptly, and, as we involuntarily drew in our reins with surprise, she repeated the question asked before, "Did I know Henry Dewey in this place? or would I aid a poor woman to seek for her brother there?" It is among the acts long since repented of, that, influenced by the slanderous insinuations whispered in our ear by the clerk a week before, we replied coldly and in the negative, and rode on. Heaven forgive us—we thought her a base woman, though every feature in her countenance spoke of suffering virtue and modest worth. So easily are we biased by a slanderous tongue.

It was in the heat of summer and the dust thereof, that we again saw Matilda Dewey. She had wandered some fifty miles into the interior, in search, as it afterward came out, of her brother, and there her money and her strength both becoming exhausted, she had found refuge in a hospitable family and given birth to her child. We were lecturing in the lodge in the vicinity, and as Major F. was a member of it, as the heads of all hospitable families in that region are, our visit to him brought us once more in contact with Matilda. She was greatly changed for the worse. Her little one was dead and she was fast following it to the grave. She had failed to discover her brother, and had given up the search, having business of more importance now upon her hands.

An hour's conversation with her revealed that, which, if we had known it, we had rather lost an eye than to have overlooked or slighted her so at first. Her husband, as she could readily prove, was a Mason. She had all his Masonic evidences, costumes, etc., even to the By-laws of his lodge—in which his name appeared as an officer—his Masonic engraved medal and diploma; and, withal, she had the ordinary evidences of Adoptive Masonry. There could be no manner of doubt that she was a *Mason's widow*, and whoever conversed with her an hour without convincing himself that she was *a worthy one*, must have been a brute.

We do not propose to give the details of her history, for they are not necessary to our story. She has gone before a tribunal now that will judge her lightly, and to a home where she will be a welcome guest. Our only purpose in culling these facts from the pages of our diary is to deduce some practical thoughts for ourself and our readers for future benefit.

Had that woman been instructed in her obvious, indisputable privileges as a Mason's widow—made herself known as such—had she exhibited any little token of a Masonic character that would barely have caught the eye without shocking the mind with a brazen effrontery—had she allowed herself any sign, any movement known only to Masons and their female relatives—the mischief had not been done. Our ears would not have been poisoned with a scandalous imputation, and our readiness to relieve the distressed, which, in spite of this suspicious exception, is a fixed principle within us, would have been exercised in behalf of that unfortunate widow. And O, what grief, what anguish had been spared to a virtuous woman!

Suppose when Boaz looked inquiringly toward the form of Ruth in the barley-field, near Bethlehem, and asked his overseer concerning her, that the latter had replied with such an imputation! How would the generous purpose of the wealthy husbandman have been stayed, and he turned away with pain, peradventure with scorn! Such was the case with ourself in the incident cited.

Those who possess the peculiar tender and inalienable privileges of a Mason's widow, do an injustice to the fraternity whose hearts are ever opened to their wants, not to avail themselves of the offered kindness. For it is a service of no light order to afford the Brethren the opportunity to do these acts. One such is of more avail in teaching the younger members of the Order its real spirit, in awakening dormant sympathies throughout the whole circle, and in opening the ways of charity, than a score of the more common incidents in the history of a lodge. Let us instruct our wives and daughters, then, in these privileges of theirs. Let us familiarize their minds in the practical details of Masonic benevolence; and when the misfortune comes—as it came to poor Matilda Dewey—as it may come, dear reader, to *your* wife or *ours*—they will know that it is no disgrace to claim that which only awaits their call, and so enable the ancient Brotherhood to realize that it is more blessed to give than to receive.

The Great Dedication Day of King Solomon's Temple.

Inscribed to R. W. Bro. H. L. Hosmer,
OF TOLEDO, OHIO.

CHAPTER I.

THE HALL OF RECEPTION.

"EXCEPT the Lord build the house, they labor in vain that build it." "For my brethren and companions' sakes, I will now say, Peace be within thee." "For in the time of trouble he shall hide me in his pavilion; in the secret of his tabernacle shall he hide me; he shall set me up upon a rock."

We live again in the mighty past when we invoke such a subject as this. We honor our own uncorrupted tastes when we reject the impure fountains so freely opened to us; the romance, the wild unnatural novel, the licentious sketch, that pander to and increase the vicious habit of modern reading; when we reject all such as these, and address ourselves to one pure and undefiled, offered to us in the Scripture; to one that directs us to the fountain of life, for sustenance and enjoyment; to one rich enough to comprehend Revelation, Tradition, Reference, Type, Anti-Type, Prophecy, and Fulfillment; to one that challenges us to consider a TEMPLE, the most costly, the most beautiful, the most perfect, the most sacred, the most venerable, ever contemplated, executed, or beautified by man.

To one whose *shadow* filled the earth, whose *purpose* was no less than that of fixing Jehovah, the light and life of heaven, in a tenement of earth; whose *site* so wisely chosen, refreshes our memory with the faith of a Patriarch, the repentance of a King, the sacrifice of a Redeemer; whose *preparation* exhausted the treasures of the wealthiest and the zeal of the mightiest; whose *pattern*, conceived in the Divine mind, was traced by the finger and communicated in writing by the Spirit of God, that Spirit which can not err; whose *builders*, divinely selected, divinely inspired, were divinely strengthened and sustained; whose *completion* left nothing wanting, introduced nothing superfluous; whose *dedication* called down from heaven the fire of approval and the cloud of acceptance; whose *memory* is both the pride and sting of the Hebrew as he walks his homeless, aimless way upon the earth.

It is good for the young, laying up a store of useful knowledge, to be taught concerning Messiah's temple and Jehovah's altar.

It is good for the Christian, searching out the ways of God with man; for the worldling, seeking the sublime and the beautiful; for the philosopher, craving all knowledge that is high and ennobling, to be informed upon a topic like this.

And how much does it recommend itself to the descendants of that noble band of Gibbeonites whose hands erected the wall, adorned the edifice, and laid the cap-stone high in its place, amid shouting and joy. Brother Masons! join us in contemplating the Temple of King Solomon!

Bright rose the sun of Palestine on the eventful day of dedication. Gloriously his beams flew back from the mountain-tops, and from the clear current of Jordan, and from the marble sides and golden roof of the stately fane, this day to be consecrated to Jehovah, the living God.

Millions who thronged the streets and dwellings of Jerusalem, or encamped "upon the hills round about her," or grouped around Gihon's sweet fountain, or crowded themselves beneath the dense foliage of the Mount of Olives, or pitched their tents upon the banks of the waters of Siloah "flowing softly," offered an ejaculatory prayer, as their heads left the verdant sod or the harder material which had formed their rude couch and pillow, and that prayer was for a blessing upon this Dedication Day.

In the camp of the stone-squarers, there were congratulations and gleams of gratified pride, and swelling hearts, the re-action of long years of anxiety and toil.

The Hebrew monarch gathered up his self-possession (never did he need it more than now) from the soul-wrapt prayers, the cheering visions, the profound meditations, and the half-trembling anticipations of a sleepless night, and came forth from his most retired apartment in the palace of David, on Zion, to meet his officers and distribute his orders for the day.

Those officers, like himself, had kept unbroken vigil the livelong night. Like himself, too, they exhibited in their solemn speech and fervid eye, tokens of profound anxiety as to the day's great work.

A goodly band they were; their names are recorded by an inspired pen; their characters are forever engraved upon the tablets of our hearts.

Foremost among them stood Zabuel, the son of Nathan, principal officer, first among his equals, honored by that appellation employed but once in the history of Jewish royalty, "The king's friend."* His part it was, by day and night, to draw nighest the pious king, to share most largely in his heaven-directed wisdom, to pitch his cot at the door of his sleeping apartment, and to communicate his matured thoughts to his fellow-officers.

In *his* light, things without figure became figured. His fervency and zeal were known of all.

Upon the fringed borders of his garments was seen the ribbon of blue, constant remembrance of God's commandments, a visible warning against forbidden indulgences. Other symbolic representations were upon his clothing and suspended to his neck, that spoke of mysteries into which he had been

---

* 1 Kings iv: 5.

inducted, rewards for his devotion to his royal and select master, the king.

And there stood Adoniram, the son of Abda, chief of the thirty thousand; * whose arduous and thankless task of reconciling the Jews to their unprecedented labor was happily ended. † He rejoiced that morning that the din of axes should no longer echo from Lebanon's side, 'mid the rebellious murmurings of his men. Upon his rugged face flitted no shadow of the fearful fate that awaited him long afterward, under the foolish King Rehoboam. ‡

Once more he took his honored station with those who waited in the presence of their Lord, and forgot the snowy peaks, the forest gloom, and the painful anxieties of the hard service past.

Side by side with his distinguished brother Zabud, was Azariah, principal officer, medium of communication with the large and well-born company of officials that filled the courts of the palace. As thus they waited, hand in hand, to greet the monarch at his approach, none nobler than these two sons of Nathan were in that king's realm.

And there was the eldest-born of Zadock, the priest, the second Azariah, between whom and his compeers no envy or jealousy was ever found, though

---

* 1 Kings xiii and xiv.

† Oliver's Landmarks, Vol. 1, Lect. 15, quotes Michælis's "Laws of Moses, 1203," as follows: "Solomon attempted an innovation which might have been very obnoxious to the Israelites in putting them to this kind of work in which foreigners only had been heretofore employed."

‡ 1 Kings xii and xviii.

rivals in the favor and affection of the king. Each felt rewarded by the approval of him to whom all looked for instruction and reward.

Dressed in the simple robes of their profession—yet more honored than their brethren, the Levites—with the sacred rolls of the Laws reverently extended in their hands, stood the two sons of Shisba, Elihoreph and Ahiah, the Scribes. Their charge it was to copy from the ancient manuscripts, choice passages to be worn in the phylacteries of the Hebrews, and to preserve the most accurate enumeration of the sentences, words, and even letters of the law. Very safe in the hands of these trusty sons of Shisba, was the heavenly trestle-board that revealed the designs of God. Attached to their persons were the implements of their profession, the erasing stone, sponge, ink-horn, and knife.

The recorder, Jehoshaphat, son of Ahilud, occupied a conspicuous place in the apartment, surrounded by a band of subordinate officers, who bore the ponderous tomes that contained the records of the building craft. These records, now closed, had occupied his undivided attention for more than seven years. His hair had grown gray and his eyesight dim, as he pored night and day over those pages, anxiously correcting the slightest error, or tracing out every possible excess or deficiency in the payments.

But his eyes would now find relief, and the short remnant of his days be spent quietly beneath the protecting shadow of him for whom he had toiled so faithfully.

Girded with the sword of might, his stern eye gleaming meteor-like, his lofty form towering over his comrades, was the brave son of Jehoida, Benaiah, Captain of the Host. What was there within the limit of mortal strength that this strong and resolute chieftain would not accomplish for one, before whose royal face his haughty eye, that quailed not before Philistine or Egyptian, fell gently as the mother's upon her cradled babe!

All these had left their stations at daylight under charge of their respective lieutenants, and hastened to pay early homage to their master, and to receive his last directions for the duties of the day.

In the rear were the twelve officers whom Solomon had placed over all Israel, to provide victuals for the royal household.* This task, in itself immensely arduous,† had been vastly increased by the necessity for making preparation for the dedication and the subsequent festival. The storehouses in Jerusalem had been filled to overflowing.‡ The fertility of Mount Ephraim, between the plain of Esdraelon and the city of the great king, had been well-nigh exhausted for the immense supply. The grapes of Eschcol, the fat herds of Bashan, the desert dates, the pomegranates, apricots, and peaches of Maan, the corn, wine, and oil of every plain and hillside from the river to the sea, had been gathered, spreading joy through the immense population of the city, yet leaving no lack behind. Two of these officers

---

*1 Kings iv and vii. †Ib. iv: 22, etc. ‡Ib. viii: 63, etc.

were even now anticipating the royal reward that awaited their faithful purveyorship.*

Centrally, the cynosure of other illustrious groups, objects of general admiration and respect, were Nathan the prophet (honored in receiving the first communication of the royal David's intention to erect this temple, now so happily completed by his son), and Zadock, High Priest, since the deserved degradation of Abiathar, and the death of his ferocious advocate, Joab.

The former stood wrapt in one of the brightest visions of his seership. The glance of the temple-glories through the centuries to come, was well-nigh too brilliant for his mind. He stood and trembled, yet blessed God.

Upon the other glittered the costly and magnificent robes of the Jewish High Priesthood. His robe of expiation, a plain linen garment, girded about with a belt, was now concealed by the Ephod, or "Garment of gold," which announced the great day of the nation. This was curiously wrought, with golden wire, and with threads of blue, purple, and scarlet, brought from the regions beyond Persia. An onyx stone gleamed from each shoulder, and bore the names of six tribes.

Suspended in front, by a wrought chain of gold, was the mysterious breastplate, adorned with twelve precious stones, and immovably fixed by its upper corners to the Ephod.

---

* 1 Kings iv, xi, and xv.

Therein were seen the emerald, jasper, amethyst, beryl, onyx, chrysolite, ligure, carbuncle, topaz, sardonyx, sapphire, and agate, and thence sparkled out the spirit when rightly addressed by the ministers of religion. On his lofty miter were those words, suggestive of so much that was important for man to remember: HOLINESS TO THE LORD. Around him waited an attendant train of priests, each worthy of respect and obedience, but lost in the superior blaze of their chief.

Standing by the wall, as if alien to the spirit of this scene, was a Phœnician mariner, one deeply in the confidence of Hiram, King of Tyre. His garments, so unlike those around him, and the lineaments of his countenance, would have bespoken him a foreigner, even though the singular notes of his voice, replying to a kind remark from Zabud, had not denoted his nationality.

Such, then, was the audience that awaited the monarch of Israel as he entered the hall of reception on the morning of Dedication. Such the groups, that with downcast eye and words subdued to softness and respect, made him welcome to that proudest day of his life.

There was no Babel among those faithful men, no confusion of tongues, no clashing of ambitious interests. The wisdom of their superior and the holy work in which they had so long been employed, had hallowed all their desires, until they had attained to the same tongue—the tongue of peace, love, and unity.

King Solomon came forth! Well was that man worthy of his servants' deference and loyal respect. In every trait of character, in every phase presented us by history or tradition, in every attribute, mental, moral, or physical, this young and ardent monarch was a paragon of excellence. God's promise to David, soothing his wounded heart, and compensating him for his own rejection as a temple-builder, pointed out the man of Peace,* Solomon, his son, as the person whose hands should lay the corner-stone—whose eyes should behold the cap-stone of the great Temple.

Solomon was a man of consummate wisdom, most wonderful for the age in which he lived, but unmatched in any age. How acquired, the tongue of history speaketh not, but its scope was broad enough to embrace all that man had known.

"Solomon's wisdom," says Holy Writ, "excelled the wisdom of all the children of the east country and all the wisdom of Egypt. For he was wiser than all men; than Ethan, the Exhahite, and Heman, and Chalcol, and Darda, the sons of Mahal. He spoke three thousand proverbs, and his songs were a thousand and five, and he spoke of trees, from the cedar-tree that is in Lebanon, even unto the hyssop that springeth out of the wall; he spoke also of beasts, and of fowls, and of creeping things, and of fishes."† Nor were these requirements as so much

---

* The word Solomon signifies peace or peaceful.

† 1 Kings iv: 30, etc.

selfish wealth, hoarded up and concealed. None were so profuse in intellectual beneficence as he. "There came of all people to hear the wisdom of Solomon, from all kings of the earth which had heard of his wisdom;"* and none went away dissatisfied. There was that in the composition of this philosopher's mind, not often met with in the wisest, *an aptness to teach*, as precise as the knowledge itself was general, and this gave him peculiar merit in an age when knowledge was conveyed in ambiguous style, and rarely to any save the select few.

The wealth of Israel's young monarch was not more remarkable than his piety. At the age which we are describing, he was verily the servant of God; he lived but for Jehovah; he studied, wrote, toiled only for his honor.

His knowledge of men, not a common trait in the character of kings, was like that of the divinity. His heart, closed and locked to all other eyes but that of God, was revealed in the conscious look, as the man stood under the searching gaze of Solomon. Plots, conspiracies, disloyalties, what were they to him? as the chaff before the gale, or the fog before the piercing sun! Whether it was two mothers contending for the living babe; or a band of conspirators weeping out a late confession; or a tyrannical governor giving account of his official acts; or a steward rendering up his stewardship; the stammering tongue confessed, even against the culprit's will, unable to endure the fire of the royal eye.

---

* 1 Kings iv: 34.

Ah, would that the man of Peace had died at the close of that Dedication Day!. Then had we been spared the evil of his latter days. Then had our hearts never been pained with the sad story of mental ubiquity, mental degradation, and physical debasement!

Then had this day of triumph been his last day, and though his sun had set at noon, yet the memory of it had glowed forever!

King Solomon came forth! What marvel that the admiring, almost adoring Jews, who saw in him the nation honored and fast rising to the pinnacle of human greatness, should have adopted Solomon as their model of all that is wise, magnificent, and great! What marvel that *the fraternal bands* whose operative skill he had so wonderfully vitalized into a moral system, making of "dead works" a living faith, and giving them to see in THAT which they ignorantly worshiped, a shadow of Jehovah, should have substituted for their idol the source of wisdom as it was humanized in Solomon.

King Solomon came forth. His morning devotions had been worthy of the man and the occasion. He had found God very nigh to his soul in the retirement of that chamber, and though he was pale with the very intensity of his thoughts, yet there was a consciousness of power in his eye, that well became the man.

Upon his tablets were freshly inscribed some of those golden aphorisms that have gilded the aphorisms of every subsequent age, and do make up the pure gold of every system of ethics that is acknowledged by the wise and good. Such phrases as these were there: "The light of the righteous rejoiceth."* "When it goeth well with the righteous the city rejoiceth."† "The desire of the righteous is only good."‡ "Righteousness exalteth a nation."§ "Whoso walketh upright shall be saved."|| "The wicked flee when no man pursueth, but the righteous are bold as a lion;"¶ and many more that inspired men have seized upon and the Spirit of God has indorsed.

He approached the foremost group with encouraging words and looks of cheer. Bowing respectfully before the High Priest, he addressed to him at low breath his first salutations, then dismissed him with every mark of attention. He took the wrinkled hand of the aged prophet, and laying them reverently upon his own head, asked a blessing for the day.

He received it, a blessing for things temporal and things spiritual. He inquired of his health, then gave him into the tender charge of his confidant, Zabud, that he might receive all needed assistance at the approaching ceremonies.

To the other officers, the warriors, scribes, purveyors, and supervisors, he spoke in a clear, self-possessed tone, and gave explicit orders relative to their duties and stations; then sent them away.

To the noble representatives of his ally and brother, Hiram, King of Tyre, he presented a sealed missive,

---

* Proverbs xiii: 9. † Ib. xi: 10. ‡ Ib. xi: 23.
§ Ib. xiv: 34. || Ib. xxviii: 19. ¶ Ib. xxviii: 1.

that told kind remembrances and morning cheer to his royal friend.

This duty was ended. The reception hall was cleared, save of the servants, and the king returned to his apartment to gird himself for the day.

CHAPTER II.

THE PROCESSION.

"LORD, I have loved the habitation of thy house. But will God indeed dwell upon the earth? Lo, the heavens and the heaven of heavens can not contain thee!" "We have heard with our ears, O, God. Our fathers have told us what work thou didst in their day, in the times of old."

AT ten o'clock on the fortunate day of the month Ethanim, which is the seventh month of the year, corresponding with our 4004 A. L., 1004 B. C., the procession to dedicate Jehovah's fane was formed. The Grand Marshal was that indomitable son of Jehoida, Benaiah, Captain of the Host. Assisted by an immense corps of aids, who had been carefully tutored for weeks past as to their respective charges, he arranged the head of the column so that it could file out of the palace of David, on Mount Zion, at precisely two hours before high twelve. Such an array of the living was never seen. The innumerable dead who will journey together toward the Throne will only equal its numbers. Our thoughts, habituated to the consideration of lesser quantities of tens, and hundreds, and thousands, can not easily admit the idea of millions, yet within that long drawn procession which wound, as an immense river, through the streets of Jerusalem, there were not less than five millions of human beings, besides a countless company of animals for the national sacrifice.

For the king had summoned the elders of Israel and all the tribes, the chief of the fathers of the children of Israel, unto Jerusalem, to bring up the Ark of the Covenant of the Lord out of the city of David, which is Zion.* He had also invited his subjects from every tribe, on either side of Jordan, and from the distant lands into which they had journeyed from motives of interest or curiosity, to leave their dwellings and their pleasures, and join him in consecrating the sacred edifice. "To the end," he said, "that our children and our children's children may have it as their inheritance that their fathers stood on Mount Moriah and witnessed the first sacrifice upon the brazen altar of its sanctuary."

An invitation had, in like manner, been forwarded to every king, prince, and potentate, upon the earth; requesting them, either in person or by deputy, to join the princes of Israel in honoring the universal Lord.†

The obedience to the summons and the acceptance

---

* 2 Chronicles v: 1.

† This fact, overlooked by many historians, assists us to account for the very general traditions relative to Solomon and his Temple.

of the right royal invitation, were alike cheerful and general.

Accompanied as the generous call had been, with the assurance that all visitors, whether Jews or Gentiles, should be entertained at the king's cost while at Jerusalem, there was nothing to hinder the poorest Jew from making the journey and tarrying at the capital. The fame of tho youthful monarch, which had already attracted the wise and the skillful to his feet; the rumors relative to his unequaled Temple, which had gone abroad; and the inward sense of worship due to Him who had cleft sea and river, that his people might advance to fulfill their glorious destiny, conspired to attract a delegation from every court.

Then came up men, women and children, from all the parts of Judea, until the land was totally depopulated. The angel of health had flown over their homes until there was not one sick, not one dying. The young placed their hands in the palms of their parents, and with elastic steps undertook the journey. The aged braced themselves steadfastly upon their staff, and leaned hopefully forward, and they commenced the march. Israel's Helper was with them, and though every road and by-way was thronged with travelers Zionward advancing, no accident met even the weakest.

There came up grave judges, dignified rulers, gray-haired teachers, all grades and classes of men leveled into one, at the command of religious duty.

There came up kings with long trains of attendants; embassadors and delegates; the potentates of mighty nations; men who ruled in despotism, and men who ruled at the choice of the governed; the occupants of the throne of luxury robed in purple, and they who presided over the rude congress of semi-barbarians.

And as these strangers caused the hilly roads of Palestine to glitter with the unaccustomed pageantry, they listened eagerly to many a tale concerning the chosen people, they had never heard before. They listened concerning David, whose heart was after the heart of God, raised from being a shepherd of sheep to lead the armies of Israel, and to go in and out before them as their king. And they wondered at his dying charge: "Thou, Solomon, my son, know thou the God of thy father, and serve him with a perfect heart and with a willing mind: for the Lord searcheth all hearts, and understandeth all the imaginations of the thoughts: if thou seek him, he will be found of thee; but if thou forsake him, he will cast thee off forever." *

They heard of Saul, slain by the hateful Philistines for his hardness of heart and obstinacy; and of Jepthah, friendless and childless, though honored of the nation for his valiant services; and of Joshua, captain of the millions who had come to repossess the land of their fathers, after centuries of absence and bondage; and of Moses, the meek and faithful one, who governed those millions for forty years, and

* 1 Chronicles xxviii: 9.

received at the Divine hand that code of laws which forms the basis of all subsequent legislation; and of his conference with God on Sinai's burning top.

With gleaming eyes, the Jews recounted these traditions of their fathers to the illustrious strangers, and when the catalogue was done, it was with an honest pride that they affirmed that all the piety of David, the courage of Jepthah, the meekness of Moses, and a wisdom far above the sons of men, were concentrated in the person of the present king, Solomon, whose stupendous temple walls would soon peer above the hills, and mark the termination of their journey.

Thus animated and thus enlightened, the millions of Jews and strangers had assembled at Jerusalem, and awaited the marshaling of the grand procession, to occupy their respective stations.

The order of the day was the offspring of Solomon's own mind.* A reference was made to it by a still wiser, one thousand years afterward, in the words: "The last shall be first and the first last."

First came an array of Janitors and Purveyors, the former with naked blades—indicative of power—men of vigilance and discretion. The latter consisted of Baana, Abinadab, Ahimaaz, Baanah, Jehoshaphat, Shimei, Geber, and the sons of Hur, of Dekar, of Hesed, of Abinadab, and of Geber, in all twelve, with their subordinates, who had been set

* All Masonic processions, which are or ought to be modeled upon a common plan, are essentially but copies of the one now to be described.

over all Israel to provide victuals for the king and his household: "each man his month in a year made provision;" with these marched the multitudes of animals provided for the sacrifices, consisting in part of "two and twenty thousand oxen, and a hundred and twenty thousand sheep," * for a peace-offering to the God of Israel, as commanded through his servant Moses.

Flanking the advance guards came the trumpeters, several thousand in number,† who, at stated intervals, blew loud blasts, according to the signals given them. And so, through the gates of David's palace of cedar, marched the head of the procession.

Following them came Huramen, the Grand Architect, a man of great age, venerable for his years and skill, selected to complete the work which one wiser than he had brought nigh to its consummation.

Hand in hand, following him, marched by twos the various subordinates of the Grand Architect, who bore the well-known Trestle-Board and the various architectural implements, especially the plumb, square, and level of the mason's trade. Each one of those was a man destined to write his name deeply in some vast project ere he died; some palace, temple, or pyramid, that should prove him to have marked well the lessons of his unequaled master. Foreigners they were, men of Phœnicia, whose dress, visage,

---

* 1 Kings viii: 63.

† There were two hundred thousand trumpets made to be used in the Temple service, and forty thousand other musical instruments.

and speech, pointed them out as a part of those to whom the promises relative to the Gentiles were applicable.

The Grand Architect and his deputies were followed closely by the Grand Secretary, Jehoshaphat, son of Ahibud, of whom we have spoken in a former chapter, and the Grand Treasurer, both supported by the numerous officials attached to their respective offices. The symbols of pen and key betokened then, as now, the high trust reposed in these distinguished men.

All eyes among the spectators were turned upon the group immediately following these.

In their hands they bore what had the semblance of columns upon a miniature scale, but there were striking differences in the proportions and adornments of these objects. For while some were plain and even rude, though strong, others were elaborately carved, and their shafts gracefully slender, even unto weakness. They were models of the various orders of architecture used in constructing the Temple.

A burning taper that appeared dim beneath the bright sun of Palestine, was borne next in the mighty procession.

Following this was a band led by the chief Scribes, Elihoraph and Ahiah, who bore between them a copy of the Holy Writings. The eyes of all this detachment were cast reverentially down, and their whole demeanor gave evidence that they esteemed this as the best gift of God to man.

Upon the golden cushion on which the sacred roll

was borne, lay emblems of speculative architecture, strikingly appropriate in connection with the day, and the purpose which had called out the assembly.

As the casket for this richest of treasures, *the Holy Ark of the Covenant* came next, borne by its staves in the hands of four reverend ministers of God, what a thrill passed through the mind of every one who looked upon that sacred chest! What a history, rich with the incidents of four hundred and eighty years, was connected with it. Its construction by the heaven-guided Aholiah and Bezaleel: the source from which its precious material had been acquired; its emblematic form, size, and adornments; the inexplicable cherubim hovering above its mercy-seat; its contents; the remembrance of the cloudy and fiery pillar which had so long guarded it; its memorable halt in the bed of Jordan; its sevenfold circuit around the doomed walls of Jericho; its capture by the Philistines, and its remarkable restoration to the true worshipers. The thoughts of each well-instructed beholder ran from topic to topic through this long chain of events, as the awe-inspiring box was borne along, and the eager eye was rendered all the more eager, as it was understood that this was the last time the ark would ever be borne in a public procession.* The sensation resembled that of a surviving friend taking his last look of a beloved object.

* Various legends exist as to the final disposition of the Ark. That it was taken from the Temple at its destruction by Nebuchadnezzar, and carefully concealed in a cave in Mount Pisgah, was

More burning tapers followed after the ark. It was well that the first great light of life should be accompanied with emblems of physical illumination. The importance of this kind of practical teaching was never overlooked by King Solomon.

A large vacancy was allowed here, and then came the head of the Tyrian division, which preceded in honor all the representatives of foreign powers.

The pompous court of Hiram, the merchant king, led the way. There was no end to the display of precious gems and metals that glittered from the vestments of this splendid company. All that a navy which visited every accessible coast in the world, could collect of rarities, was brought out on this occasion. Two hundred and forty years had the strong walls of Tyre defied every invader; during the prosperous reigns of ten monarchs, the treasury of the kingdom had been waxing exceeding rich. The brotherly covenant that had existed for forty years between Hiram and David, had been fraternally tendered to Solomon, and as freely accepted.

A generous loan of money had been made to the latter, to strengthen his hands for the great work he was then commencing.* One hundred and fifty-three thousand six hundred of the most skillful artisans in all Phœnicia, were, in the same noble

---

believed by many. Others assert that it was drawn up miraculously into heaven. Some of the Hebrews believe it may still be discovered.

*1 Kings x: 14.

spirit, tendered him to perform the work.* And most acceptable of all, the aged and experienced Hiram, chief of builders, wisest of designers, the pride of the nation, was sent up to Jerusalem to crown a long life of honor by placing his name upon the walls of Jehovah's Temple.

Now he came, that powerful and wealthy monarch, with all his retinue, men of severe countenances, who had steered the prows of his vessels westward to the unnamed islands, northward to the land of tin,† southward to the stormy cape, eastward to the mysterious Ophir; men of might, who had led his armies in many a battle along his extended coast; men of architectural rank, whose names lie in cartouch and symbol in the north-east corner of many a grand edifice so beautiful, that time looking upon those works erected for eternity, hesitates to place one finger of his destructive hands upon their walls; and last of his train the eighty thousand artificers in marble, and metal, and wood, with their seventy thousand assistants, all ranked in orderly manner under the overseers. Each of these latter bore the implements of his degree. Each wore his masonic badge in a manner to designate at a glance to the instructed, the state of his masonic advancement. But whatever the implement or however the badge, there was a gleam of triumph in the eye of each, that spoke of a long-expected, now realized

---

*2 Chronicles ii: 17. †Cornwall in England.

object, toward which the hopes of years had all gravitated, upon which the honors and rewards of the future would all be founded.

These having passed, a place was formed for the attendants of the great king.

And now, every eye that had shrunk from barbaric splendor, or been dazzled by divine emblems, that had admired the gratified builders, or trembled before the majesty of kings, settled with a look of intense curiosity upon the person of King Solomon.

In the prime of youth, at that boundary line between hopeful youth and thoughtful manhood, but full of the unexampled honors of his name, walked the pious son of David. The fire of his eye was quenched in deep devotion. As he walked he prayed, wrapping his face in his royal mantle, and with his head drooping like a rose leaf in a heavy dew.

On his right royal head rested the golden crown worn erewhile by his father David. The thoughtful king well understood that upon this proudest day of his life, his subjects would be gratified to see this token of him, who, for nearly half a century, had governed them in God's fear.

And as he passed, his feet so reluctantly moving that the eye could scarcely note his advance, the mothers of Israel, who were grouped upon every threshold, who crowded every casement, who swarmed like bees upon every housetop, raised the hands of their little ones and pointed them to his person. Every head was uncovered before him. Every knee of aged or young bowed in reverential regard. A muttered prayer for the Wise King arose from millions; a spontaneous offering of affection more precious than the richest gift of kings.

In his right hand was one of those simple emblems whose explanation is in every man's mouth. It was the miniature representative of that architectural implement, the earliest used in the quarries, the latest used in the finished wall; the only implement whose sound was permitted (and that only upon a systematic plan and for peaceful purposes) to break that awful silence amid which one hundred and fifty thousand men labored for thirty-six months.* All who saw this little implement of ivory in the royal hand, comprehended its meaning; it was the will and pleasure of him who wielded it to be considered as a builder most eminent in the ranks of speculative architecture.

Thus the king passed magnificently over the same pavement which had felt the tread of the repentant king of the last reign, as he fled in anguish before his evil-hearted son, Absalom.† The same pathway had been trodden eight hundred years before by the feet of a father—the father of the faithful and recipient of the promise—bound to the hill-top to sacrifice his beloved child in accordance with the Divine command.‡ Nor was either of these events absent from the mind of those thoughtful scribes whose part it was to record and to instruct.

So the king passed on, and as those who remained

*1 Kings vi: 7. †2 Samuel xv: 23. ‡Genesis xxii: 9.

at the palace on Zion stationed themselves upon the turrets of the building, and looked eastwardly and northwardly, they saw that the almost interminable procession, which three hours before had begun to file out of the palace gate, had seven times encircled the whole hill Moriah, as a glittering serpent, and now stood still, the van-guard and rear-guard having come together at the grand entrance on the south of the Temple.

Then, from every part of the assembly burst forth in one grand chorus, the strains of Israel. Then the ten score thousand trumpets sounded a blast whose welcome reached the heavens to which they were directed, and divine embassadors charged with a grand commission, that day looked down to see if it were not the proper time. Then the songs of the son of Jesse, attuned to glorious melody by his own sweet harp, and made household words to millions, were pealed forth as never before or since were heard. Then sackbut and cymbal, timbrel and flute, and every form of wind or string instrument known to the age, shook with the enkindled zeal of the performers.

Again all was hushed. At a given signal every voice and instrument ceased to sound, and then it was known that the king was about to enter the gate of the Temple.

Of all the labors of human wealth and power devoted to worship, the Temple on Mount Moriah was the most mighty. Compared with this the most famous shrines of the great kingdoms of idolatry—

the fane of the Ephesian Diana, the master-piece of Ionian splendor; the Temples of Hercules, that exhausted the skill and the wealth of Phœnicia; the edifices of Delphi; of Minerva of the Acropolis; of the Capitoline Jove; of Sancta Sophia in the Rome of Constantine; of the still more splendid structure in which the third Rome worships—compared with this they were but dreams and shadows; they were but insignificant before the grandeur, the dazzling beauty, the almost unearthly glory of that Temple, that once crowned the Mount of Vision of the City of the Lord.

The court of the Gentiles circled the whole. There was a fortress of the whitest marble, with its wall rising six hundred feet from the valley, its kingly entrance worthy the fame even of Solomon; the innumerable and stately dwellings for the priests and officers of the Temple, and above them, glittering like a succession of diadems, those alabaster porticoes and colonnades in which the chiefs and sages of the Jews were to sit, instructing the people, or to walk to breathe the pure air, and gaze on the grandeur of a landscape which swept the whole amphitheatre of the mountains. Rising above this stupendous boundary was the court of the Jewish women, separated by its porphyry pillars and richly-sculptured wall; above this the separated court of the men; still higher the court of the priests; and highest, the crowning splendor of all, the central TEMPLE, the place of the Sanctuary and of the Holy of Holies, covered with plates of gold, its roof planted with lofty spear-heads of gold, the most precious marbles and metals everywhere flashing back the day, till Mount Moriah stood forth to the eye of the stranger approaching Jerusalem, as often described in subsequent ages, "a mountain of snow studded with jewels!"*

The south gate, through which the King now passed (the rear of the procession in which the monarch had thus far been stationed, was becoming the head), although not so costly as that upon the east, was more majestic. It opened into a portico having three aisles, the lateral ones being each forty-five feet in height, the central passage ninety feet.

First within this lofty aisle entered the king, followed by his friendly ally of Tyre and the band of builders. These latter spread themselves out to the right and left, occupying with the royal visitors and representatives of princes, the more eligible positions of that first or outer court; for the time had come when even those whose hands erected the Temple of Jehovah, might not enter it any more.

Passing through, the King of Israel entered the second court, the place of the Jewish women, and the third, the court of the Jews. Both of these were speedily filled to overflowing by the various tribes, according to a preconcerted arrangement, although the main courts were made to contain more than three hundred thousand people.

---

* This vivid description of the Temple we have transferred, with some alterations, from "Salathiel."

Rising as he approached the central Temple, resuming his equanimity as he drew nearer to the great task allotted to him, the monarch advanced around the third court, until he stood in the large area fronting the mystic pillar, Jachin and Boaz, which guarded the eastern entrance. Here he halted, and again the bursts of music rent the skies. Again the melodies of the warrior-king mingled and swelled from the hearts of millions, and then all was still again.

Solomon was about to tread the checkered pavement and to enter the sanctuary.

The re-arrangement of the procession had brought the High Priest, the Ark of the Covenant, and the ministers whose turn it was in course to minister before the Lord, immediately in the rear of the king. The Levites, with the sacrificial knives raised over the heads of the victims, awaited the command from their spiritual chief to strike the fatal blow. Incense smoked upon the golden altar, and sent its delicious and penetrating fragrance into every part of the Temple courts. The clear sun streamed its crimson rays along the walls and the roof. Every voice was hushed, every heart was still, for it was the moment, the expected point of time, in which the Lord should acknowledge this great enterprise by some visible mark of his favor.

CHAPTER III.

THE CLOUD AND THE DEDICATION PRAYER.

"WITHOUT faith it is impossible to please God: for he that cometh to God, must believe that he is, and that he is a rewarder of them that diligently seek him." "Behold, how good and how pleasant it is for brethren to dwell together in unity." "I know that the Lord is great, and that our Lord is above all gods."

Two score lusty hands were grasping each gate of that eastern entrance. Those massive doors, of olive wood overlaid with gold, which the strength of a Sampson could hardly have moved on their hinges, stood between the monarch and the sanctuary. The gate-keepers awaited his signal to roll them back. But the motion was delayed. The stillness that had gone over the multitude as deep as midnight, was protracted. King Solomon was lost in silent prayer. The High Priest, who stood nearest to him, saw his form quivering beneath his royal robes. He saw the crown of David sink until it had well-nigh fallen to the pavement. He heard the muttered words which conveyed to the Divine ear all that the swellings of that pious heart contained. Moved by a spirit of sympathetic piety he bowed his own head, and prayed for grace for Israel's king.

Grace and strength were given him at last. The crown was upraised again; the quivering ceased; and with firmness he made the signal for throwing back the mighty portals. The stout forms of the keepers were instantly applied to the task, and, as a mountain that slowly and reluctantly yields before the irresistible power of an earthquake, so did these mighty masses of wood and metal yield before their strength.

The entrance to the sanctuary was now clear, and King Solomon advanced.

Passing between the golden altar, the table of the shew-bread, and the ten candlesticks of gold,* he approached the curtain which separated the Holy Place from the Holy of Holies. It was looped up, and that apartment, with all its contents, was clearly exposed to view. It was a room only twenty cubits square, and twenty cubits in height. The walls and ceiling, covered with plates of beaten gold, were engraved with figures of palm-trees, open flowers, and cherubim,† skillfully executed. Jewels of the largest size and purest water were arranged in astonishing profusion on the walls. They were set in symbolic groups upon the ceiling; they sparkled in mysterious forms upon the sides of the room; they gleamed brilliantly from every corner; and wherever a ray of light infringed upon any object, it was sent back dispersed in prismatic colors by those well-cut gems.

In the center of the apartment was the altar, made to be the honored recipient of the Ark of the Covenant. Over that altar stood the two Cherubim, of image work. The wings of these were twenty cubits

---

*2 Chronicles iv: 7. †1 Kings vi: 29.

long, each wing being five cubits; they extended from wall to wall. They stood on their feet, and their faces were inward.

Nothing in the whole Temple was calculated to excite sentiments of awe, so much as these strange images. Their position in the very center of the *Sanctum Sanctorum*, as if they were its guardians; their heads fashioned after those of human beings, which were bent reverently inward and downward, as though they loved to behold the mercy-seat which they shielded; their eagle wings extended as for flight; their strong limbs of a lion; and their feet shaped like those of oxen—all these, gleaming with the color of pure gold, and fixed in solemn silence, as for a vigil of a thousand years, never failed to impress a holy fear upon the beholder.

Into this apartment, passing under the folds of the looped-up veil of blue, and purple, and crimson, and fine linen, and wrought cherubim thereon,* which was soon to be lowered as a shield against all prying eyes, the king advanced to the front of the altar; then led a circuit, the priests and the ark-bearers following, until he had compassed the room seven times, with the altar on his right hand.

Then the ark was placed upon the altar; the staves by which it had been borne from the foot of Sinai, through the desert, through Jordan, through all the battle-fields of Canaan, were drawn out never to be replaced. The ark was safely seated beneath the

---

*2 Chronicles iii: 14.

wings of the cherubim, and the staves laid aside as useless things. So shall our limbs, which have borne our weary bodies through all the pilgrimage of life, be consigned to a perpetual rest, when we, as vessels consecrated to God, shall be deposited in the divine *sanctum* above.

The Holiest Place was then vacated. Beginning with the least, the apartment was soon left alone, save for the presence of the High Priest and King. The former casting a glance around to see that all things were properly disposed, then passed out, treading backward, and lowered the curtain as he went.

Solomon, alone and for the last time, knelt before that altar and looked upon that ark. Henceforth, none but the High Priest (and he but once a year) could raise that consecrated veil to enter that awful place. Many a fraternal meeting with the living and the dead had he enjoyed in that apartment, but those convocations were now ended. Many a season of spiritual refreshment had he enjoyed in that retired place, but those seasons would return no more. It was a solemn reflection that to him; all the glory and beauty of the *Sanctum Sanctorum*, in which had been displayed his highest skill, his most profuse bounty, were henceforth to be as things of the past.

One more prayer, one more glance, at altar, ark, cherubim, golden walls, palm-trees, open flowers and jewels, and the king resigned himself to depart. He passed beneath the curtain, and saw these things nevermore.

By this time the priests and the ark-bearers stood in groups near the outer gates of the Holy Place.

Through the open portals could be seen, standing at the east end of the altar, the vast company of the Levites which were the singers, all of them of Asaph, of Heman, of Jeduthun, with their sons and brethren, being arrayed in white linen, having cymbals, and psalteries, and harps; and in a band drawn to one side, was a chosen party of one hundred and twenty priests, holding golden trumpets, ready to sound.* The moment had come when, by unanimous consent, all waited for some Divine token of acceptance. A solemn look of expectation was on every face. The appearance of the king as he came among them, increased this intensity of feeling, until it became even painful.

And then there began to gather around them the wings of some awful, inexplicable darkness! A gloom as of midnight, a darkness as of Egypt, which first occupying the now closed *Sanctum*, began to roll from beneath the curtain as a cloud of dense smoke, moved toward them. The person of Solomon was first hidden from view; then the splendid garments of the High Priest, who stood by the table of the shew-bread, was lost to their sight.

The outer folds of this strange gloom went past them to the gates, floated out at all the windows, crept up the marble walls outside, and shut in the

---

*2 Chronicles v: 14.

whole building, until it met and settled upon the golden roof above.

The signal was Divine! The millions who waited without accepted it with one accord. The one hundred and twenty golden trumpets on the south-east corner of the grand sacrificial altar were the first to sound. The singers of Heman, Asaph, and Jeduthun, took up their song of praise. Then, tribe by tribe, thundered forth all Israel, from all the courts of the Temple, from all the streets of Jerusalem, from the slopes of the surrounding hills, until, "the great stones, costly stones, and hewed stones which were laid in the foundation of the house"* moved beneath the mighty accord.

"It came even to pass," says the Word that can not lie, "as the trumpeters and singers were as one to make one sound to be heard in praising and thanking the LORD; and when they lifted up their voice with the trumpets, and cymbals, and instruments of music, and praised the LORD, saying, FOR HE IS GOOD; FOR HIS MERCY ENDURETH FOREVER: that then the house was filled with a cloud, even the house of the LORD; so that the priests could not stand to minister by reason of the cloud; for the glory of the LORD had filled the house of God."†

With fearful haste fled the janitors, the ark-bearers, and the priests, and passing between the mystic pillars, Jachin and Boaz, they joined the groups

---

* 1 Kings v: 17. † 2 Chronicles v: 13, 14.

around the sacrificial altar. More slowly, but with faces pale with emotion, came out the High Priest and King Solomon, and placing themselves beside a brazen scaffold five cubits long, and five cubits broad, and three cubits high, which the king had caused to be erected there,* they joined their own voices, as drops to the mighty ocean of sound that was heaving around them.

The view from that spot and at that moment was sublime. The banners of the Twelve Tribes, antique, respected as memorials of four hundred years, flags under which they had conquered at Jericho, at Ascalon, at Jabesh-Giled, at Aroer, were tossing to and fro as trees in a mighty gale. Kings in foreign garb stood bare-headed, their crowns laid reverently in the dust before this indisputable manifestation of Jehovah; their banners covered with every emblem that mythology could claim, every animal, every memorial connected with their history and soldiership, gilded serpents, lions, women, gods, genii, stars, diadems, and imperial busts, bowed down as unworthy to stand erect in the Divine presence; their subjects crouched in terror at this unheard-of event. Sages from every land were conferring together in voices lost in the general uproar, and storing their memories with every particular of this event, that could enrich the traditions of future ages.

Women were holding their children aloft that they might see the cloud, that by this time entirely con-

* 2 Chronicles vi: 13.

cealed the Temple. The chiefs of the tribes extended their almond-rods above their heads to encourage their respective followers to a still louder strain, and the sun of Palestine shone smilingly down over all.

King Solomon ascended the scaffold and stood in the view of all Israel. He spoke: "The Lord hath said that he would dwell in the thick darkness, but I have built an house of habitation for Thee, and a place for Thy dwelling forever." This was said with his face toward the cloud-enveloped sanctuary, of which only the typical pillars were now visible. Then he turned his face southward, and northward, and eastward, and raising up his hands—at which signal the immense volume of sound suddenly ceased, and Israel became silent as the grave—he solemnly blessed his assembled people, in the name of the most high God. "The eternal God be thy refuge," he said, "and underneath thee be the everlasting arms." He pronounced upon them there, the canonized blessings of the city; of the field; of the fruit of the body and the fruit of the ground; the fruit of the cattle; the increase of kine and the flocks of sheep; of the basket and of the store; coming in and going out. He declared that the enemy approaching one way should flee seven ways before them. That a good-will from heaven should settle upon their storehouses and upon all that they attempted. That the Lord should make them plenteous in all things; should open unto them his good treasure and the heavens to give them rain. That they should lend to many nations, and borrow from none. That they should be head of all and above all, living in settled peace and dying in glorious hope.*

The words, in that clear air, went plainly to the ears and hearts of millions.

And he furthermore addressed them in these words: "Blessed be the LORD God of Israel, who hath with his hands fulfilled that which he spake with his mouth to my father David, saying: Since the day that I brought forth my people out of the land of Egypt, I chose no city among all the tribes of Israel to build an house in, that my name might be there; neither chose I any man to be a ruler over my people Israel; but I have chosen Jerusalem that my name might be there; and have chosen David to be over my people Israel. Now, it was in the heart of David my father, to build an house for the name of the LORD God of Israel. But the Lord said to David my father, forasmuch as it was in thine heart to build an house for my name, thou didst well in that it was in thine heart; notwithstanding, thou shalt not build the house; but thy son which shall come forth out of thy loins, he shall build the house for my name. The LORD, therefore, hath performed the word that he hath spoken; for I am risen up in the room of David my father, and am set on the throne of Israel as the Lord promised, and have built the house for the name of the LORD God of Israel; and in it I have put the ark, wherein is the covenant of the Lord that he made with the people of Israel."

* Deuteronomy xxviii.

To this honest acknowledgment that all bounties and grace come from God, a sentiment of accordance went through the people; for it was good to confess this thing before the kings and philosophers of the heathen; it was well that tradition, which was to preserve the day's wonders, should add this act of worship to the rest.

And now came the Dedication Prayer.

It was to this that the thoughts of many a sleepless night had been sanctified. For this, the written history of God's dealings with his nation, with all the nations of the earth, had been examined, and the experience of his own life rendered subservient. All that man, under the dispensation of the day, could ask of God, was to be comprehended in it; while the purposes for which the Temple was erected and the importance of its long preservation by the chosen people, must not be omitted.

Therefore, kneeling down on his knees before all the congregation of Israel, and spreading forth his hands toward heaven, he said: "O Lord God of Israel, there is no God like thee, in the heavens nor in the earth; which keepest covenant and showest mercy unto thy servants that walk before thee with all their hearts; thou which hast kept with thy servant David, my father, that which thou promised him, saying: There shall not fail thee a man in my sight to sit upon the throne of Israel; yet so that thy children take heed to their way to walk in my law, as thou hast walked before me. Now then, O LORD

God of Israel, let thy word be verified which thou hast spoken unto thy servant David."

Magnificent caption to the sublime prayer that followed.

How must the hearts of that fraternal band have echoed the words: "*There is no God like Thee!*" of that fraternal band, who, for more than seven years had forsaken home and kindred to labor on this work! By day they had been scorched with summer heat or chilled by winter cold; by night their softest pillow had been the ground; no relaxation of labor had they known;* no cheerful visits to friends; early to labor, late to rest; their grand stimulus of exertion, the hope that their eyes should not be closed in death until they had beheld this auspicious dedication; well might they echo their Grand Master's words: "*There is no God like Thee, in the heavens nor in the earth!*"

But here a doubt intruded into the heart of the royal worshiper. A question of locality arose and raised up a skeptical thought, despite his remarkable faith. His tongue uttered the thought, "But will God in very deed dwell with men on the earth?" The righteousness of Jehovah; the utter worthlessness of mankind; the vastness of *His* habitation; the insignificance of *ours*—was it remarkable that

---

* The fact recorded by Josephus, that during the building of the Temple there was no rain fell in the daytime to interrupt the labor, gives additional testimony to the severity of the toil, since no rest days were known save the Sabbaths.

even Solomon's mind staggered for an instant under the thought: "Behold, heaven and the heaven of heavens can not contain thee; how much less this house that I have built!"*

It was but a moment, however, a little moment of unbelief. The remembrance of the promise that the LORD would assuredly put his name there, gave new force to his words, and he advanced further in the Prayer of Dedication.

"Have respect, therefore, to the prayer of thy servant, and to his supplication, O Lord my God, to hearken unto the cry and the prayer which thy servant prayeth before thee: that thine eyes may be open upon this house day and night, upon the place whereof thou hast said that *thou wouldst put thy name there;* to hearken unto the prayer which thy servant prayeth toward this place. Hearken, therefore, unto the supplications of thy servant, and of thy people Israel, which they shall make toward this place; hear them from thy dwelling-place, even from heaven; and when thou hearest, forgive!"

The various petitions which the inspired king here offered up, are seven in number. The fifth is expressly applicable to the stranger, the dweller in a foreign land. Five parts refer to misfortunes liable to befall the people of God, and to the remedy for those ills. The remaining portion relates to the punishment for perjury, the most daring of offenses against God.

---

* 2 Chronicles vi: 18.

Relieved now of all mental embarrassments and doubts, and warmed up with his high mission as the mouth-piece of that immense multitude, the king proceeded:

"If a man sin against his neighbor, and an oath be laid upon him to make him swear, and the oath come before thine altar in this house, then hear thou from heaven, and do and judge thy servants by requiting the wicked, by recompensing his way upon his own head; and by justifying the righteous, by giving him according to his righteousness."

Thus was the Temple made a testing-place of truth, in which no liar could stand, before whose altar all deceit should be revealed.

"And if thy people Israel be put to the worse before the enemy, because they have sinned against thee, and shall return and confess thy name, and pray and make supplication before thee in this house; then hear them from the heavens, and forgive the sin of thy people Israel, and bring them again unto the land which thou gavest to them and to their fathers."

The national experience of four hundred and eighty years had taught the king that no expectation of Divine help need be entertained, save by those whose sins are covered through repentance and faith.

"When the heaven is shut up and there is no rain because they have sinned against thee; yet if they pray toward this place and confess thy name, and turn from their sin when thou dost afflict them; then hear them from heaven and forgive the sin of thy servants and of thy people Israel, when thou hast taught them the good way wherein they should walk; and send rain upon thy land which thou hast given unto thy people for an inheritance."

"If there be dearth in the land, if there be pestilence, if there be blasting or mildew; locusts or caterpillars; if their enemies besiege them in the cities of their land; whatsoever sore or whatsoever sickness there be; then what prayer or what supplication soever shall be made of any man, or of all thy people Israel; when every one shall know his own sore and his own grief, and shall spread forth his hands in this house, then hear them from heaven, thy dwelling-place, and forgive; and render unto every man according unto all his ways, whose heart thou knowest (for thou only knowest the hearts of the children of men); that they may fear thee, to walk in thy ways, so long as they live in the land which thou gavest unto our fathers."

Thus far the king had made petition only for his own people. Was there not a place in that great soul for the whole of mankind? There was:

"Moreover, *concerning the stranger which is not of the people of Israel*, but is come from a far country for thy great name's sake, and thy mighty hand, and thy stretched-out arm; if they come and pray in this house, then hear them from the heavens, even thy dwelling-place, and do according to all that the stranger calleth to thee for; that all people of the earth may know thy name and fear thee, as doth thy people Israel, and may know that this house which I have built is called by thy name."

"If thy people go out to war against their enemies by the way that thou shalt send them, and they pray unto thee toward this city which thou hast chosen, and the house which I have built for thy name; then hear thou from the heavens their prayer and their supplication, and maintain their cause."

"If they sin against thee (for there is no man which sinneth not), and thou be angry with them and deliver them over before their enemies, and they carry them away captives unto a land far off or near; yet, if they bethink themselves in the land whither they are carried away captive, and turn and pray unto thee in the land of their captivity, saying: We have sinned, we have done amiss, and have dealt wickedly; if they return to thee with all their heart, and with all their soul, in the land of their captivity, whither they have carried them away captives, and pray toward their land, which thou gavest unto their fathers, and toward the city which thou hast chosen, and toward the house which I have built for thy name; then hear thou from the heavens, even from thy dwelling-place, their prayer and their supplications, and maintain their cause, and forgive thy people which have sinned against thee."

Such were the petitions registered in heaven that day, from the heart of assembled Israel. For, at the close of each, the voice of the multitude went up as the mingled roar of many waters in the grand AMEN! AMEN!! AMEN!!!

Then, in a still louder key, his face flushed with excitement, his hands quivering as he held them upward toward Heaven's throne, the impassioned speaker concluded:

"Now, my God, let, I beseech thee, thine eyes be open and let thine ears be attent unto the prayer that is made in this place. Now, therefore, arise, O LORD God, into thy resting-place, thou and the ark of thy strength: let thy priests, O LORD God, be clothed with salvation, and let thy saints rejoice in goodness. O LORD God, turn not away the face of thine anointed: remember the mercies of David thy servant."

And the Dedication Prayer was done.

CHAPTER IV.

THE FIRE AND THE DEPARTURE.

"THY right hand hath holden me up." "Surely goodness and mercy shall follow me all the days of my life: and I will dwell in the house of the Lord forever." "Praise ye the LORD. Praise, O ye servants of the LORD, praise the name of the LORD."

THE last mighty AMEN, AMEN, AMEN, reverberated through the defiles of Judah's hills, and Solomon arose from his praying. Every sentiment of adoration had been exhausted; every petition had been comprehended. The sublimest form of devotion that the Spirit of God had ever kindled up in a human heart, had been uttered. It was recorded in the presence of angels, by an angel's pen, that they might know of what human piety is capable. It was recorded by the Scribes, who were the historians of Israel, to the end that it might be laid up in the archives of the nation. It was recorded by many "a stranger who had come out of a far-distant country" (sages upon whose lips hung the wisdom of a nation), to the end that a memorial of this day's transactions should have a place in every record-chamber on earth; and in the fragments of lore that have come down to this latter generation, may be traced the pious sentiments which they bore away in their copies of that prayer.

It was recorded by the secretaries of those fraternal companies, whose system, skill, and handiworkmanship had raised the edifice, which, through this prayer, they had beheld consecrated. This explains how that every lodge of speculative Freemasons in the wide world possesses the religious sentiments embraced in that unparalleled form of devotion, and thus they complete the harmony in their *dedication* which runs through every other portion of their moral structure.

Thus, then, the first part of the ceremony, that of placing the Ark of the Covenant within the Holiest Place, had been accomplished, and the descent of *the cloud* betokened the Divine approval.

The prayer had been uttered, whose acceptance at the heavenly throne was proven by the religious glow upon the countenance of every Jew present.

There was yet remaining the offering up of sacrifices upon the great altar, "twenty cubits being the length thereof, and twenty cubits the breadth thereof, and ten cubits the hight thereof." * This, the last great care of that illustrious day, was now to be undertaken.

In the vast molten sea, which held six thousand gallons, the priests who waited in course this day, had purified themselves for the work of national sacrifices. This great font was "ten cubits from brim to brim, round in compass, and five cubits the hight thereof; and a line of thirty cubits did compass it round about. And under it was the similitude of oxen which did compass it round about, ten in a cubit, compassing the sea round about. Two rows of oxen were cast when it was cast. It stood upon twelve oxen, three looking toward the north, and three looking toward the west, and three looking toward the south, and three looking toward the east; and the sea was set above upon them, and all their hinder parts were inward. And the thickness of it was an handbreadth, and the brim of it like the work of the brim of a cup, with flowers of lilies; and it received and held three thousand baths." †

King Solomon descended from the scaffold and approached the altar. Around it was now congregated the multitude of offerings which had been brought up by all the people to be sacrificed.

A liberality almost unbounded, had been exercised by all for the occasion. From the king himself (whose princely gift consisted of two and twenty

---

* 2 Chronicles iv: 1. † 2 Chronicles iv: 2.

thousand oxen and one hundred and twenty thousand sheep), to the desolate widow, whose poverty yielded nothing but the turtle-doves, all had come up to Jerusalem provided with some objects for sacrifice and offering.

Beautifully select they were; beautiful in colors and proportions; precious in value; the best of the best; there was no blemish or evil-favoredness found at all in them.*

All had had respect to the commandment connected with the prophecy this day fulfilled, delivered through Moses so long before: "Unto the place which the Lord your God shall choose out of all your tribes to put his name there, even unto his habitation, shall ye seek, and thither thou shalt come, and thither ye shall bring your burnt-offerings, and your sacrifices, and your tithes, and heave-offerings of your hand, and your vows, and your freewill-offerings, and the firstlings of your herds and of your flocks." †

The ceremony of sacrifice was symbolic in all its parts. It pertained alone to the sacerdotal order, and during its accomplishment, the king, like the lowliest of his subjects, stood apart.

The High Priest, the spokesman of the nation, laid off the golden garments, and appeared in the linen vesture, which were the holy garments.‡ He took a young bullock for a sin-offering, and a ram for a burnt-offering; these were out of the portion presented to the sons of Levi.

---

* Deuteronomy xvii: 1. † Ib. xii: 5, etc. ‡ Ib. xvi: 4.

From the general stock he then selected two kids of the goats for a sin-offering, and one ram for the burnt-offering. For an atonement for himself and his house he first offered a bullock. The two goats being presented before the Lord were then made subjects for lots, one lot being cast for the Lord, the other lot for the scape-goat; the former was brought forward and offered, the other sent into the wilderness (first having the hands of the High Priest laid upon his head, and confession made of the national iniquities), to bear away those iniquities into a land not inhabited.

The High Priest then took a censor full of burning coals from off the altar, and his hands full of sweet incense beaten small, and entered that lonely place within the veil, still dark with the overshadowing of that awful cloud. He put the incense upon the fire before the Lord; and of the blood of the bullock he sprinkled with his finger seven times upon the mercy-seat eastward. In like manner did he with the goat upon which the death lot had fallen, offering up, bearing its blood within the veil, and sprinkling it therewith seven times.

Returning to the great altar, he cleansed it and hallowed it from the uncleanness of the children of Israel, by the same sevenfold sprinkling.

These preliminary exercises being performed, it only remained for the Levites to complete the great sacrifice. Then bled the veins of thousands of cattle, and tens of thousands of feathered things. Then flowed the blood, type of a blood yet to flow for the sons of men, so precious, that one drop would outweigh the value of a world. Then cried aloud in their last agonies, the brute multitude doomed in their innocence to die for the guilt of others, even as One, the Divine model of Innocence, should yet cry aloud in his last anguish, and protest against the hard-heartedness of men.

The number of officiating priests being very great, the sacrifice, vast indeed, and costly as became such a nation, was soon accomplished.

The piles were heaped upon the altar until it could contain no more. Then great heaps were made around it, and the work being done, the ministers washed themselves free from the blood and pollution, and awaited further commands. The twelve brazen oxen which bore the immense sea upon their backs, and looked with stolid eyes to the north and the west, and the south and the east, were not more silent at their stations now than the band of ministers who bore upon their inquiring faces the words: "What will God work?"

By this time the Temple was partially freed from its murky investiture. The golden roof gleamed brilliantly under the rays, now turned eastwardly in their direction. The mystic pillars displayed their tall forms with distinctness, and proclaimed aloud the lessons with which they were fraught to the initiated. "These were each eighteen cubits high, and a line of twelve cubits did compass either of them about. Two chapiters of molten brass were set upon the tops of the pillars, each five cubits in height; and nets of checker-work and wreaths of chain-work for the chapiters, seven for each. There were two rows round about the net-work of each, to cover the chapiters upon the top with pomegranates. And the chapiters were of lily-work, in the porch four cubits. And the chapiters had pomegranates also above, over against the belly which was by the net-work; and the pomegranates were two hundred, in rows round about upon the other chapiters. These pillars were set up in the porch of the Temple; and the right pillar was called Jachin, and the left Boaz, and upon the top of the pillars was lily-work."*

Fresh from their molds, "in the clay ground, in the plain of Jordan, between Succoth and Zarthan,"† these wonderful columns glowed and smiled in the bright sunbeams, as though no adverse fate, no destructive hammers, no foeman's profane hand, should ever come nigh them.‡

The ancient olives, that even then gave their name to the hill on the other side of the brook Kedron, sent a green, cheerful hue, to match the bright golden of the Temple. But not a breath of air stirred their leaves or made music among their boughs.

Far in the south-east, lay sullen and voiceless, that Dead Sea whose face bore upon it a history of eight hundred years. Its silent dwellers, the phantoms, fiends, and images of horror, who possessed no tongue to tell the awful doom of Sodom and Gomorrah, in whose streets lay their submerged dwellings,

* 1 Kings vii: 15 to 21. † 1 Kings vii: 46. ‡ Jeremiah lii: 17.

were not more silent this moment than the millions who filled Jerusalem.

The silence began to be painful. The king had again ascended the brazen scaffold, but his subjects and his visitors looked to him in vain for a signal that should dispel it. He cast his look above. At this thoughtful gesture, those who were set apart with trumpets, and with harps, with psalteries, and with cymbals, raised their instruments nervously, as if prepared to sound.

"Now THE FIRE came down from heaven, and consumed the burnt-offerings and the sacrifices." "And when all the children of Israel saw how the fire came down, and the glory of the Lord upon the house, they bowed themselves with their faces to the ground upon the pavement, and worshiped and praised the Lord, saying: FOR HE IS GOOD; FOR HIS MERCY ENDURETH FOREVER!" *

So the king and all the people dedicated the house of God.

Once more the voice of the nation swelled upward, in one unanimous outpouring of praise.

Once more the clang of metal, and the blast of air, and the dulcet notes of strings, were made accordant in glorifying God.

Once more the grand structure built for a thousand ages, built for a God whose measure is in eternity, shook from foundation-stone to apex with the earthquake of human adoration.

---

* 2 Chronicles vii: 1.

Once more banners tossed, and kingly crowns were laid humbly before the feet of the wearers, and heathen standards were bowed low, and philosophers conferred together of him, the first, the last, the God of gods!

O! on that triumphant day, when the people at last arrived to a full consciousness of their importance as the chosen seed, what full measure of gratitude did Israel offer? Why was there ever a weaker song, a less concordant strain, upraised from that holy hill?

What evil spirit, in unlucky hour, dropped the seeds of human pride into that young, noble heart, that swelled with such piety that hour before Jehovah?

The work was done.

The vast pile of sacrifices, which, a moment before concealed all the great altar from every eye, was now but a residuum of ashes, to be scattered at the hands of the priests to the four winds of heaven.

The work was done.

The trumpets of the guards sounded the signal of recall. The Captain of the Host took his position as before, and the long procession, which had folded itself as a glittering serpent, seven times round the Temple, began slowly to unwind.

The same order was preserved as at the approach, until the king reached the gates of his own palace; then, as a mighty enchantment, the great assembly was dispersed.

A feast was commenced which lasted seven days.

All the abundance of that land of milk and honey was dispensed at the king's cost, and none were allowed to go empty away.

Twice a day public audience was held in the king's palace, where the visiting princes, and the delegates of national governments, together with all the wise and the learned who sought to see Solomon, and to hear of his wisdom, were freely admitted.

Seated upon a magnificent throne, and surrounded by the chivalry that had honored the court of his father David, he welcomed all comers, speaking fluently to each in his own tongue, and inviting those who would, to ask him questions.

Many a profound difficulty, weighty, inexplicable to all others, yielded before the eye of his mind. Many a problem pregnant with a thousand issues, was solved by him so readily that the proposers shamed themselves that they had occupied his attention with topics so light.

Many a question of jurisprudence was brought forward, and his answers, each one a golden maxim, are found to this day incorporated in the laws which have governed nations for thousands of years.

With each of his royal visitors he entered into intimate relations, whose counterparts exist in all nations, symbolized in figures; developed in ceremonies; working glory to God in the highest; on earth peace, good-will toward men; and embracing within themselves the elements of perpetuity while there is a moral edifice to be erected, or a vice to be stricken off the souls of men.

From sunrise to high twelve; from the hour of resuming labor to the going down of the sun in the west, the fraternal bands of builders, whose hands were now at rest, labored mystically to reward the good and true for labor done. The mystic gavels resounded; the emblematic jewels gleamed; the watchful Tyler exercised his vigilance, and now was perfected that GRAND MORAL SYSTEM OF FREEMASONRY which, from the days of Adam, mankind had been incessantly building up.

Its materials, the virtuous and the laborious; *its master builders*, the Enochs, the Noahs, the Abrahams, the Moseses, the Joshuas; SOLOMON, KING OF ISRAEL, set up the cap-stone in the last arch, and under God, accepted the dedication thereof.

There was not a *signal* connected with it which did not point either to man's extremity, or to God's opportunity.

There was not a *grip* which did not speak of human relations that demand human sympathies.

There was not a *word* that did not tell of power, permanency, or wisdom, as the result of active, thorough devotion.

There was not a *ceremony* which was not full of instruction upon the great divisions of human knowledge; its grand aims were for the first time clearly conveyed in the speaking terms, *fraternity*, *devotion*, *information*.

And day after day the blood of victims smoked around the great altar, and the fire, preserved from that divinely communicated on the Dedication

Day, was kindled to consume the offerings piously made.

"A certain rate was offered every day, offering according to the commandment of Moses," and from this time the sacrifices began, "on the Sabbaths, and on the new moons, and on the solemn feasts, three times in the year, even in the feast of unleavened bread, and in the feast of weeks, and in the feast of tabernacles."

So the work and the dedication were alike completed. The very great congregation "from the entering in of Hamath unto the river of Egypt," was entertained in his own royal manner, for seven days, and in the eighth day they made a solemn assembly, "for they kept the dedication of the altar seven days, and the feast seven days. And on the three-and-twentieth day of the seventh month, he sent the people away into their tents, glad and merry in heart for the goodness that the Lord had showed unto David, and to Solomon, and to Israel his people." *

The assembly at the parting hour, was truly a solemn scene, and full of that pathos which is in the whole thought of *farewell forever.*

There were kind words from the king, messages of princely respect, tokens of remembrance and love.

There were tears of affection from his subjects, prayers for his welfare, offers of devotion to his service.

---

*2 Chronicles vii: 9, etc.

Again the roads of Palestine were crowded with pedestrians, but all with their backs turned upon the golden city. Each traveler as he arrived at some point which was to shut out from his view the whole scene, paused, turned, drank in a last draught of its matchless glories, and so departed.

Last of all came the breaking up of the system of Builders, cemented by ties of ninety months' entwining, which had carried through this great work so successfully. What was said in that tyled assembly, that model and origin of all Grand Lodges; what was promised for the future; what tokens of love, broken tesseras, exchanges of pledges passed from hand to hand, from lip to lip, from heart to heart, can not be recorded in any vernacular; yet it is indelibly impressed upon many a loving heart.

They parted. The ships at Joppa were loaded with their freightage. Carmel witnessed their orderly bands winding around his base, and pursuing their way, along the sea-shore, northward. Lebanon saw them in groups, encamping night after night, each camp still nigher home. Then a city came forth to meet them, and to hail the return of their king; then a nation extended its arms to welcome them back, and so they reached their homes.

Years passed away. They were scattered everywhere, but everywhere at work; everywhere transforming shapeless material into forms of exquisite art; everywhere extending the knowledge they had earned by so long and arduous an apprenticeship; everywhere conjoining the knowledge of *moral* with that of *operative* Masonry; everywhere distinguished to the eye by the badge of their profession, and known to the world by the honorary appellation of *Solomon's Builders.* Your hand, Brother! The builder is still at work!

A Night in the Lodge-Room.

A TALE OF MASONIC HUMORS.

Lovingly Inscribed to Bro. Benj. N. Webster,
OF RICHMOND, KY.

HAVE we ever related our incident of *the night at Aluminum Lodge?* · Probably not. Rather than look over our files to see, we will jot down the whole circumstances just as they occurred; and here they are.

We had met the trusty Brethren of Aluminum by previous appointment, that night. O, how long ago that night seems to us, when we look back upon it now! Not a gray hair sparkled on our head, not a wrinkle marked our face then. Nearly every man who faced us that stormy night at Aluminum, has since that night faced his coffin-lid, his God, and his final doom.

We had lectured them—we repeat, that very night. We had expatiated on *the landmarks*, and very patiently did those plain, honest brothers and fellows listen to us on the landmarks. Who couldn't lecture to men who listen as well as they did? We had glanced over *the covenants*—ah, what freedom of speech we used to have in those days on the covenants! Who of our old pupils but that remembers our explication of S.H.O.C.S; and the tenth point; and the Texas "emergency;" and the Louisiana Teuton, with his feeble appreciation of a Divine trust; and all those things with which we beguiled the passing hours, and impressed mnemonically the various points of our subject upon the minds of our hearers.

We had told a few score chaste and delicate anecdotes, such as charmed the knights at Chicago one evening, about the turning of the sun, not many years since—and not until low XII. was announced on our watch, which lay open before us, did we close up our discourse, and prepare to retire.

After eating the half dozen cold hens, ponderous in their fatness, that had been provided for the occasion, garnished, we must not neglect to say, with biscuit admirable in toughness, and coffee mighty in strength, we opened the door at the head of those steep and narrow stairs outside the building, to depart, when behold an impediment, an impossibility! Some ungodly youth—*they* will never arrive to the years of discretion—had pulled down those clattering old steps (it must have been while we were telling that "do-you-feel-anything?" yarn of ours, or some of us would have heard the fall), and the twenty-eight of us Freemasons were prisoners in the third story of an isolated brick house! Worse than that, it had been raining cats and dogs for the last twelve hours, and the whole country—the lodge-hall stood on low ground, where lodge-halls never *ought* to stand—hill and dale, was under water! Here was a pretty state of things! The look of consternation that passed around the twenty-eight of us, was pitiable to behold. Old Jimmy Davids, who had an appointment to preach and immerse some people the next morning, used a scriptural phrase far out of its scriptural connection. Jack Evans (they all called him *Ivins*, we remember), murmured something about his wife, which we thought we understood, having one ourself. Langley Feex groaned bitterly in relation to some business of his, which he solemnly vowed would go to "wrack and ruin," if he was n't at home by chicken-crowing to attend to it. While Obed Brown, the schoolmaster, was worst of all in his objurgations, though otherwise a moral man; for the next day was examination with him, and he had twenty-five miles to ride.

We spoke:—Brethren of Aluminum Lodge, listen to me. (We had knocked every one of them down before we commenced.) I, too, sorrow for this disappointment, and were those impious juveniles who have cast our Jacob's ladder so rudely to the earth, but so much nearer heaven than they ever *will* get, *my hand* would pummel and *my foot* impress itself upon the fleshier portions of their persons, and I should feel justified in these exhibitions of my wrath. But what matters grieving? We are all—all here. We can't go home till morning, till daylight doth appear. Why not make a night of it? There is yet coffee in the pot (it was a six-gallon vessel full, so strong that Brother Shaggs' tuning-fork, which he accidentally dropped into it, floated), and vast wrecks of the cold hens and seven baskets full of the fragments of biscuit. There is an inexhaustible fund of Masonic anecdote too in this repertorium of mine (alluding to our finely-organized cranium). You are not half full of Masonic food yet. Let us make a night of it?

"Agreed!" "That's right!" "Go it!" "Amen!" "Yes, yes!" "So mote it be!" Such, and others, were the friendly interjections that in a torrent of enthusiasm followed our speech. A rush was incontinently made to the hens, whose mighty skeletons were presently heard cracking within the dental apparatus of twenty-eight pair of jaws, until there was n't a pope's nose left of the half dozen. Coffee, whose specific gravity far exceeded the scale of Liebig, was swallowed in such inconsiderate quantities, that none of us slept quietly for a week afterward; and then, grouping around the stove, with vests, suspenders, and boots loosened, the twenty-seven good fellows of Aluminum took a deadly stare at us as a hint to begin. We were in for it now, beyond all question. Seven hours of amusement and instruction we stood pledged to afford them. So opening our jackknife, mounting those *large* goggles we used to wear (Bro. M. Webb, *you* remember them?) elevating our pedal extremities on a chair, so that the blood might easily flow back to the heart when necessary, we gracefully waved our jackknife at the awaiting group as if to intimate the profoundest silence, and began a "Night in the Lodge-room."

Brethren:—Albeit not myself addicted to the use of narcotics, yet I like the smell of tobacco, par-

ticularly from a corn-cob pipe. Our celebrated Brother, Andrew Jackson, of whom you have all heard—("Hurrah for Jackson!" shouted thirteen of the twenty-seven, without reflecting upon the enormity of the crime; and "Hip, hip, hurrah, for Jackson!" yelled the other fourteen before we could bring them to order. We frowned slightly, but with a pleasant look shook our jackknife at the whole of them, as a token of warning not to do it again, and recommenced.)

All political allusions, in the lodge, my Brethren, are expressly prohibited in our regulations. For what sayeth the Ancient Law under this head? Brother Coldstreet, *you* can quote it from memory; pray do so? Upon this, Brother Alonzo Coldstreet arose and recited the regulation, thus: "We are of all nations, tongues, kindreds, and languages, and are resolved against *all politics*, as what never yet conduced to the welfare of the lodge, nor ever will." (Well he might quote this from memory, for he had made it a point ever since his initiation the preceding year, to repeat the whole of the Ancient Charges over his box of tin—he is a tinner by trade—twice a day, and ever will.)

You observe, my Brethren, we resumed, what the law is, and you will now see how improper such exclamations as those you just now uttered—for they could only have proceeded from the most ardent political feelings. As was once remarked by our distinguished and veteran Brother, Henry Clay. ("Hurrah for Clay!" shouted twenty-one of the twenty-seven, and "Huzza for Harry of the West!" splittingly screamed the other six; whereat the whole crowd jumped up in a high state of excitement, upsetting the stove, and ran and shook our hands till they hurt. We frowned again, but, if possible, more pleasantly than before, assisted in righting up the stove, and, after some difficulty, found our jackknife, caused silence to return, and resumed.)

I was about to say, my Brethren, that I admire the smell of burning tobacco, particularly from *cob-pipes*, and if any of you would wish to smoke while I am entertaining you, pray consider yourselves entirely at liberty to do so. It is likely, however, that only a few of you will wish to do so.

Only a few of them did; that is, only twenty-four; the other three having already commenced. (By the way, that little *finesse* of ours about *cob-pipes*, we take it, was rather neatly managed, for we knew very well by the bulge in their coat pockets, that every Mason among them had brought a cob or two from home for pipe purposes.) Very soon the twenty-seven were peacefully at work at their calumets, and from that moment we saw no more of them till daylight. Indeed, we have sometimes had our doubts, reflecting upon the intensity of that fog, whether Aluminum Lodge-room has ever been cleared of smoke since. We recollect how, in a Tennessee lodge one night, we were *raising* a candidate and *lost him* in the tobacco smoke; nor have we ever been able to affirm positively to this day, that we ever did finish off the right man that night! But we must take care not to digress in our story.

And now, my Brethren, that you are comfortable, I will relate to you

Our First Story,

OF THE TIMELY WARNING.

It is an incident in which a plug of tobacco enabled me once to give a Brother Mason a useful Masonic warning. ("Lord bless me!" we heard old Jimmy Davids say in the fog. "Who ever hearn tell of such a mejum as that before?" We knocked David down, and proceeded.) It was about a year since; I was traveling on a stern-wheeler from Cairo to Memphis, and a slow and painful conveyance it proved to me. The bill of fare was frightfully scanty, the bedding bug-haunted, the company profligate. Gambling was going on from sunrise to midnight, and every hour or two, a fight settled the game. After which, a new "deck of keerds," as the gamblers uncouthly styled them, was "fotch on," and another round began, to terminate as before.

Among the passengers, I had observed a young man of that gentle, amiable cast of countenance which young men even at this day sometimes wear, who have been raised in pious families, under the hands of loving mothers and praying fathers. How such a man got to the gambling-table, I have never ascertained, but rising one night awhile before twelve, after vainly attempting to snatch sleep among the roaches and more offensive vermin, I discovered him there excited with liquor, furiously excited with the gamblers' madness—worse than delirium tremens itself—and in a rapid process of being plucked by the experienced scoundrels around him. The sight shocked me. I was quite unprepared for it. Through my conversation with him the previous day, I was confident he knew little or nothing of cards, a thing easily enough seen by the way, in his awkward style of handling them, and that he would not rise from that dangerous place while he had a dime left in his pocket. After standing by for a considerable time, during which, dollar after dollar disappeared from his pile to enlarge that of his opponent's, I took a chair close by him, and leaned my elbows upon the table in real distress. A square piece of tobacco lay there, a "plug," I think, such things are called (" A hand," murmured somebody from the fog), with a knife by it. Mechanically I took them up, and began thoughtlessly to chip the edges of the tobacco. While doing so, the young man reached his hands in my direction for the pack of cards, it being his deal, and exposed his wristbands to my view. By the flash of the candles, I observed that they were fastened with gold studs, having Masonic emblems—the square and compass—on them, a sign I never fail to see, when within my purview.

A thought occurred to me. *This is a Mason. I will warn him of his danger!* So with the knife I cut deeply in the tobacco the same emblems, the square and compass, and laying it down with the knife before him, as if I supposed they were his property, I arose and left the table. I could see that his eye caught the emblem instantly, and that he understood me.

It was a curious thing to observe him then. He went on dealing the cards, but so listlessly and carelessly as to forfeit the deal. He laid his forehead in his hands thoughtfully, and his hands upon the table. Once or twice he counted his little pile of money, now reduced to a very trifle. He got up for a drink of water, and walked in an uncertain manner to and fro, sat down again, played his game out, and by the evident co-operation of his adversaries, won it. Got up again, drank, and took a longer walk. Played again, and won. And then, as with a power given him at that instant from on high, he threw down his cards with startling vehemence, fell on his knees, raised his hands aloft to heaven, and with a mighty voice repeated an oath that he would "*never*, NEVER, NEVER gamble again, so help me God!"

I sat by his side all that night bathing his head with cold water, and that saved him, I think, from a terrible attack of brain-fever; saved him for a lovely girl to whom he was even then betrothed; saved him to be the father of as charming a child as ever sprung like an olive-shoot by human feet; saved him to become one of the best officers in one of the best Grand Lodges in the land; saved him to become one of my best correspondents and truest friends—a Mason, with whom I hope at the resurrection-day to rise.

Nor is this the whole of the story—(we hastened to say this, because there were evident signs of excitement among the twenty-seven men in the fog, and they were only waiting a pause in me to break forth)—for one of the gamblers, to whom the knife and tobacco really belonged, seeing the square and compass cut on his plug ("hand," corrected somebody in the fog), sat with me all that night at my brotherly work; avowed himself too a Mason; declared, in language more ardent than was necessary (for, under other circumstances, I should have called it blasphemy), that "had he known the young gentleman was a Mason, he was essentially d — d, if he would have played a game with him," and the next morning, learning the exact amount that had been won, collected it up from the others, and restored it to him. That gambler took a step in the right direction, consequent upon the rebukes, compliments, and counsels, which, combined in equal doses, I administered to him, and quit the river forever, opened a drinking-saloon, opened a book-store, became a grain dealer, a dry-goods merchant, and made money at all these things, was elected sheriff of the county, and still holds that position; and, to conclude the story, I still have the plug ("hand," from the fog) in my possession, with the original *square* and *compass* cut upon it!

Great and noisy were the plaudits from the fog, drowning the thunder of the rain upon the roof.

Everybody talked at once, and Alonzo Coldstreet was heard indistinctly to be quoting from Webb's Monitor, a work he was just then commencing to memorize: "By secret and inviolable signs, carefully preserved among the fraternity throughout the world, Masonry becomes a universal language. Hence, many advantages are gained; the distant Chinese, the wild Arab, and the American savage will embrace a brother Briton, Frank, or German; and will know that beside the common ties of humanity there is still a stronger tie of obligation to induce him to kind and friendly offices. The spirit of the fulminating priest will be tamed; and a moral brother, though of a different persuasion, engage his esteem. Thus, through the influence of Masonry which is reconcilable to the best policy, all those disputes which embitter life and sour the tempers of men are avoided; while the common good, the general design of the craft, is zealously pursued."

Our Second Story,

OF THE THREE BROTHERS.

SCARCELY did the company wait the end of Brother Coldstreet's quotations, however, ere a shout of—"Another story! give us some more of it!" arose. The twenty-seven pipes which had gone out, amid the obliviousness of the moment, were refilled and relighted, and the smokers leaned back on their benches, amid fearful clouds, for another set-to. Putting our well-developed cranium for a moment out of the window, professedly to see how the weather was doing, but in point of fact to get a breath of fresh air; we stuck the point of our jack-knife into the table, as if to indicate our point of departure, and loosened the reins of our memory in the following style:

It was early after my own initiation, only two years or thereabout, and I was longing, as all young Masons are, to comprehend that most difficult and most beautiful of Masonic subjects, *the philosophy of the third degree.* I had failed thus far to get a competent instructor. One professional lecturer whom I employed at considerable expense to elucidate the theme for my private benefit, knew no more about it than— Well, I won't say how little he *did* know; but the most circular form of the Arabic numerals exactly expresses the amount of his Masonic attainments, as well in the third as in the three degrees of Masonry. Others, old and young, to whom I applied to untie the various knots that had confused my mind, could only *cut* them, Alexander-fashion, by denying that there was any mystery at all in them! So I went on my perplexed way, getting a ray or two here and there (and more from Dr. Oliver's writings than any other source), until I had the good fortune to fall in with a master mind, no less a person than Brother Charles Scott, just then issuing his first work, "The Analogy of Ancient Craft Masonry to Natural and Revealed Religion;" and whose singular abilities in this direction had so excited the attention of his Mississippi brethren as to cause his early elevation to the Grand Mastership of that State. It was at Jackson, and in his own lodge, that I first witnessed his manner of governing the craft and heard his master-piece of Masonic philosophy, *the symbolism of the third degree.* I can never forget the impression made that hour upon my mind. What a direction was that hour given to my Masonic career, past and future, can only be known in the mind of Omnipotence.

Brother Scott began by recapitulating the ceremonial itself. Interlinking its various parts with much ingenuity, he drew the image of a great tragedy worthy the mind and attention of a Shakspeare, in which the incidents all led to the same proper conclusion, and of which the whole made up a drama of great naturalness, pathos, and life. I have often taken this view of the third degree in my subsequent course as a professional lecturer, and always find while passing through it, that I am indebted for my best passages to my recollections of Brother Scott's lecture that night. I have read the best tragedies of Shakspeare and other dramatists, but have not found a subject so well adapted to be the masterpiece of human passion already intensified for the histrionic art, as the legend of the third degree.

Following upon this, Brother Scott spiritualized the whole. Incident after incident so naturally following each other in the action of the drama, was shown up in equal naturalness in relation to the moral and spirit life as a Mason. We were taught—but why recapitulate the truths unfolded in that splendid effort of a giant mind. You have heard me to-night pursuing the same theme; and my model was shaped upon his. Few, I apprehend, ever heard him upon that subject, without acquiring a lasting respect equally for the philosopher and his theme.

But I have a story to tell in this connection. A year or two afterward, sojourning in another State, I chanced upon a lodge in which were three brothers, all of one birth, physically as well as Masonically. They were pointed out to me by the Brethren present not only as remarkable for the fact that they were born the same hour and initiated at the same ceremony, but because there was a curious incident connected with their Masonic beginning. It seems that they were formerly members of the same denomination, a denomination whose principal enemies (the world, the flesh, and the devil) are symbolized to their heated minds under the name of "Masonry." Though meek and mild in a general way, yet the three brothers were wrathful and bitter in the extreme in relation to all matters connected with the subject of Masonry. Neither Masonry nor Masons had any favor in their sight. In their monthly meetings, when called upon for "remarks" and "suggestions," their burden was "this outrageous Order, and the way it was spreading and deluding the young men of their flock."

In fact it *was* playing havoc among their young men. Every meeting or two some degenerate son of a hardshell sire came home late, looking thoughtful, intellectual, and happy, and acknowledged in reply to the pressing questions as to his recent whereabouts, that "he had been to the Masons' lodge!" Report said that the eldest born of one of the three brothers was contemplating the same rash, daring, and blasphemous step.

To counteract the effect that these accessions to Masonry were having upon the church, a special meeting was called, preachers were invited from a distance, and the word went out that a general demolishment of Freemasonry might be anticipated.

To prepare for the occasion various works were ordered at the expense of the ecclesiastical treasury, and Morgan's "Illustrations," Bernard's "Light," and Craft's "Key" were the profitable results. These were carefully studied, their little discrepancies harmonized as well as possible, and the proper passages, mostly from the foot-notes, penciled for use. But now occurred the curious incident which I promised you, in which Brother Scott had a part. Some brother Mason in the neighborhood, not having the fear of the Church before his eyes, took a copy of Scott's Analogy that belonged to himself, tore out the lectures upon the third degree, and sewing them up, mailed them to the clerk of the church as a veritable antimasonic document. He having hastily perused it, laid it with the others, and so the matter rested until the day of debate arrived.

A great audience assembled, which the large church room scarcely held. The preachers were numerous, and it was difficult to say who were the most interested—the Masons or the members of the church.

Passage after passage from Morgan was read and commented upon by the moderator, who, warming with his theme, next took up the *Analogy*, supposing it to be Bernard's work, and declared that he should now show up "the ungodly doctrines, the diabolical tendencies, and the unchurchly practices" of the Freemasons in their true colors. He then read a few pages aloud. Being a man of some intellect, and charmed with the language and sentiment, forgetting the occasion, he continued to read aloud until he actually finished the whole—winding up with that magnificent peroration worthy of Cicero himself. The congregation was electrified. The profoundest silence had been maintained during the whole hour, and when the moderator ceased and looked blankly around, as if recalled to himself, a general murmur of admiration went round the church; but when a gentleman arose, who was known to all present as the Master of the neighboring lodge, and stated that "he could not consent for the foes of Masonry to claim *this work* as their own, because it was the production of Mr. Scott, one of the most learned men and jurists in the country, and a devoted and high Mason," terrible was the uproar. The moderator was interrupted, hustled, and insulted. Several verbal combats, that nearly ended in muscular exhibitions, occurred, and the meeting broke up in a row.

Our three gentlemen went home in deep thought. They were men of true principle, and already saw that some great error had been committed. "Let us not fight against the truth," they said to one another, "lest peradventure we be consumed." They procured the entire volume, of which the fragment had accomplished so much, and read it carefully—prayerfully. It worked a total change of sentiment. It set them upon further reading and further reflection. They sought the Master of the neighboring lodge for information, and what he told them they accepted as the truth. Finally, they united with the Fraternity cheerfully, suffering the expulsion from the Church which promptly and naturally followed; and so it was that I saw them sitting together in my visit to that lodge. The incident was so remarkable as to work a great reformation in that community, softening down the tone of prejudice formerly so hard and obstinate, and inducing more than one of the church members to follow the example that had been set them.

The reception of this incident was equally enthusiastic with the other, and one of the twenty-seven in the fog, recalling an anecdote he had heard us relate some months before, asked it for the benefit of the others. We acceded and commenced

Our Third Story,

OF THE CONQUEST OF A LADY.

It is the manner in which Abner Lowenthal became a Mason that I am about to explain to you. Brother Lowenthal was a man of considerable distinction in the county of ———. For many years he had held the office of County Judge, was the Commissioner of Public Schools, and occupied other posts of distinction among his fellow-countrymen. At almost every session of the Legislature he was elected to either the upper or lower House (as our British friends term it; though, for the matter of that, it is *low* enough to belong to either of them nowadays); and, had he been mean enough, he could readily have secured the office of Congressman. Happily, however, he was not sufficiently reduced for that. (Murmurs of dissatisfaction from the fog. One of the twenty-seven had run for Congress once and was elected. Another had a father badly beaten at the last election. We hurried on with the story.) In all respects he was the model of a gentleman, and when Preamble Lodge, F. A. M., was established U. D. in his county, it was naturally hoped by the zealous eight, whose names were in the petition, that Esquire Lowenthal would be found among the applicants for Masonic light.

And so he was, but his application was long protracted on account of his wife. Mrs. L. (formerly Miss Sharp, of Lockport, N. Y., a schoolmistress) had been raised up according to the strictest principles of antimasonry. At Lockport, whence poor Bruce was torn for that sad incarceration (twenty-eight months in the Canandaigua jail), the public feeling was for a while intensely positive against the Craft. At every fireside hung a devilish little engine of an explosive character labeled "Giddins' Antimasonic Almanac." The newspaper reading of the place was a pleasant compound of bitter partisanism, more bitter sectarianism, and most bitter antimasonry. The young lady had been so long fed upon this pleasant pabulum, that it is no wonder she was decided in her antimasonic opinions. It is only wonderful that ever a boy or girl raised in Western New York, between 1826 and 1836, became a Mason or a Mason's wife at all.

Mr. Lowenthal was an outspoken man in all his ways, and freely acknowledged his desire to unite himself with the Fraternity just then making an establishment in his county. The announcement was met with an opposition upon his wife's part that astonished him. She did not go into hysterics (that is reserved for the heroines of novels), but she loosened her tongue, as female tongues are sometimes loosened, and ran over all the elements of feminine logic, making miraculous combinations of its rules and principles, and ended every breath with a declaration that if "he (her husband) joined them (the Masons), she (Mrs. L.) would crave a divorce, leave the country, and die." So decided was the little lady as to stagger her husband, and cause many a serious thought as he sat in his judicial post at the county seat, or in his place at the country church.

I was written to upon the subject to suggest a plan by which the lady could be reconciled to his initiation. My counsel was that "he should go on and take his three degrees quietly and trust to his wife's 'sober, second thought,' and affection for her husband to receive him again into favor." This plan was agreed to, and I put myself to some trouble to be present and officiate. It was a cold wintery night, the room exceedingly uncomfortable, and the attendance sparse. I have rarely ever suffered so much in person as during the three hours I passed with those zealous brethren of Preamble U. D; but when Mr. Lowenthal was introduced, and the ceremonies of his initiation begun, I at once forgot all the disagreeabilities of my position. There was that in his face which spoke the man of dignity, authority, and thoughtful decision. He seemed born to command, and I selected him at once as one who would, in due season, if Masonry met his rational favor, become a *Master in Israel*, and even sit upon the Grand Lodge daïs, the governor of the entire Craft. His intelligent eye spoke volumes. In the lengthy and elaborate lectures with which, according to my invariable occasion, I closed the subject, he followed me with a perfect understanding, and often seemed to anticipate my words, and mentally to enlarge upon my meaning. We parted, and I met him but once more, *when he lay in his coffin.*

His wife was not informed of the step he had taken until he became a Master Mason. The news was then broken to her, by my suggestion, in the following manner: A party of gentlemen and ladies met at her house, in which, as if by accident, every man was a Mason, and every lady a Mason's wife. After refreshments had been served, one of the gentlemen, a preacher venerable for age and piety, proposed to give them a little lecture on Masonry. This was readily responded to, and by none more greedily than Mrs. L., who had all the curiosity of her sex. The reverend brother opened with some happy remarks upon "the advantages of Freemasonry to its votaries," showing how it inclined men to be temperate, brave, prudent, and just, and inculcated the most moral and religious sentiments at every step. He then ingeniously, and without exciting suspicion as to his intentions, turned his subject so as to show that the female sex are if possible more practically interested in the Masonic institution than the male, and that ladies ought to be the warmest friends that Masonry possesses. This, you know, my Brethren, is not hard to do. Ladies are helpless, dependent, and needy, and require the strong arm, the wise counsel, and the business tact of men. He showed them that the worthy wives and daughters of Master Masons, traveling among strangers, had an acknowledged claim upon the sympathy, counsel, and pecuniary aid of every Master Mason with whom they came in contact, and related some most touching incidents in which their application, under such circumstances, had led to the happiest results.

The only difficulty in this case, the old man remarked, is the want of the means of making themselves known to the Fraternity. So many impostors of both sexes are afloat upon the great wave of modern travel, that the mere word of the strange lady, however honest she may appear to be, and however distressed, can not, with propriety, be taken. The lady needs some secret token, some sign or password, *something known only to herself and the Freemasons*, by which she may be easily and certainly recognized, and, when recognized, relieved. It was easy to see that the ladies present comprehended the difficulty, for they looked quite downcast, and none more so than Mrs. Lowenthal, that such great advantages as Masonry offered to the female sex should be forfeited for the want of those means of mutual recognition of which he had spoken.

But now a light came over their countenances, and sweet smiles wreathed their dear lips, as the reverend Brother informed them that there *was* a method, practical, easy, general in its application, and to which every Mason's wife, widow, sister, and daughter is entitled, which, under any circumstances of distress, may be made available; that there was a degree entitled *The Eastern Star*, pure, graceful, and religious, which has its signs, passes, and means of recognition, which have been tried in a thousand instances, and proved to be exactly what a lady needs in the cases mentioned; and that if any of the ladies present were entitled to this beautiful and important instruction, he was ready and willing to impart it.

An inquiry was forthwith made, and the surprising truth came out that Mrs. Lowenthal was the only woman in the company whose husband was not a Mason! This was truly unfortunate. She evidently wanted the degree, and all present were disposed to gratify her. A private conversation with her husband was held, and a second with the old preacher, whereat she was heard to declare that "if he (her husband) actually wanted to join them (the Masons), she (Mrs. L.) would no longer object." It was, of course, an easy matter to grant her the privilege of receiving the degree with the rest, and when it was ended she was the loudest to aver that "it (the Eastern Star Degree) was, beyond all question, the prettiest thing that she (Mrs. L.) had ever heard." There was no delay now in imparting the news to her that she *was* a Mason's wife, for her good man had been *raised* five months before, and, greatly to the joy and relief of all present, she declared her entire approbation of his course.

But I said I never saw Brother Lowenthal but once after his initiation, and then *he was in his coffin.* I received the intelligence of his death while lecturing at no great distance, and hastened to pay the last sad tribute. I arrived barely in time. I headed the mystic procession, journeying three times round his grave, leaving it on the right. I directed the public grand honors, and it was like a beautiful piece of mechanism, the movements of that funeral group, as they joined me by three times three. I dropped the first handful of mold upon the lid that covered that noble face and shut in those intelligent eyes. I supported that now fainting widow to her coach, accompanied her to her dwelling, whispered the first words of sympathy and encouragement in her ear. And afterward, as my mind recurred to the entire scene, painful yet hopeful and even triumphant, I noted down upon my solitary road these lines, commemorative of the fact that *I had seen him but twice;*

I saw him *first* one snowy winter night—
But summer's fire glowed in his honest breast—
An humble seeker for Masonic light,
A pilgrim yearning for Masonic rest:
From the bright Orient southward to the West,
Darkly he journeyed, while our eyes inquired
If form, and heart, and garb, *fulfilled the test?*
From the ordeal he came as one inspired,
And glad among us stood, enlightened and inspired.

Once more I saw him—but his eyes were hid,
Hoodwinked by death; as with an iron hand
His limbs were fettered; 'neath the coffin-lid
The strong man lay extended, and his hand
Whose grip had thrilled me, ah! how dead it spanned
His pulseless breast; yet round our Brother's head
Thrice we encircled, but with grief unmanned;
And with respectful tenderness we spread
Upon his breast *green twigs*, fit presents for the dead.

For he had *journeyed further*, learned a lore
Profounder, drank in purer light than we—
And of desired treasure gathered more
Than dwells in all the mines of Masonry.
What unto us is vailed in mystery,
Was *real* to him, and by his Master's side,
"Knowing as he was known," *the dead was free!*
Therefore, we paid our homage to the dead,
And "we shall meet again, our Brother dear!" we said.

And we *shall* meet again; not as in quest
Of light Masonic, nor as in that time
When last I saw him pallid in his rest;
But in a lodge transcendently sublime!
Where death shall ring no funeral chime,
Nor weeping band shall compass round its dead,
But light and life inspire an endless hymn.
Ah! happy we, whose very graves do shed
Effulgent hope and joy as by their brinks we tread!

It was here, too, that I was first induced to contrast the curious fact that in all cases where music and processions are employed in the burial of the Masonic dead, there is a marked contrast, based upon sound traditional reasons, between the manner and measure of *approach to, and departure from* the grave. This thought I conceive I have worked rather neatly into these lines:

How *sad to the grave* are our feet slowly tending,
  The cold form of one whom we loved, on the bier!
What sighs swell our hearts while above him we're bending,
  And shudder to think we must part with him here!
Ah, gloomy is life when our friend has departed!
  Ah, weary the pathway to travel alone!
There's little remaineth to cheer the lone hearted,
  Oppressed with the burden, "the loved one is gone!"

But *glad from the grave* are our feet homeward tending,
  Though death's cold embraces our Brother restrain!
Hope springs from the hillock above which we're bending,
  And whispers "Rejoice! you shall meet him again!
Death's midnight is sad, but there cometh the morning;
  The pathway is cold, but its ending is nigh."
Then patient we wait till the glorious dawning,
  That's told in our emblems of life in the sky!

The sounds in the fog at this stage of proceeding were those of sympathy and concern. We could distinguish the blowing of various noses on Adam's handkerchief, and thought we detected a note or two of blubbering. Knowing that this would never do, for the night was not half out yet, and the rain had taken new heart, we conceived the idea of a story of a strictly comical nature, for which we confess we drew more upon fancy than recollection. It was highly successful. The stove was again upset, this time by Brother Whitehouse, the ex-Congressman, a great fat man, heavier than the Duke of Sussex, who (Brother W.) always found a difficulty when he had a laugh in him of more than ordinary dimensions, of getting it out without pain. In such cases it was his habit to clutch hold right and left of whatever was at hand, and by this effort of the muscles to brace himself up for the explosion. His pillars of Ashdod in the present case were Brothers Rays and Fyve, who, being themselves in a high state of cachinnation, were in a relaxed condition of muscle, and could n't support a falling Brother. So over they went, the stove at the bottom, Rays next, with his nose in the opening where the stove-pipe properly belonged, Fyve on him with one bootless foot in the glowing embers, and the ex-Congressman pleasantly acting what he called, in parliamentary language, a "ryder" upon the whole. It being very foggy around them, several minutes elapsed before they were sorted out, during which Fyve's foot and Rays' nose became intensely charged with caloric.

It is not our purpose to relate this anecdote. To tell the honest truth, we don't remember it well enough; but the reader may do as we did, invent one of his own and imagine the catastrophe which followed it. The room being quiet again and a new set of cob-pipes dug out, the old ones being quite burned through, the whole twenty-eight, at our suggestion, united in singing the following ode, which, if the author ever gets his due, will—we won't say what amount of fame and glory he *will* get:

Ask, and ye shall receive:
Seek, ye shall surely find:
Knock, ye shall no resistance meet,
If come with ready mind.
For all that ask, and ask aright,
Are welcome to our lodge to-night.

Lay down the bow and spear:
Resign the sword and shield:
Forget the arts of warfare here,
The arms of peace to wield.
For all that seek, and seek aright,
Are welcome to our lodge to-night.

Bring hither thoughts of peace:
Bring hither words of love:
Diffuse the pure and holy joy
That cometh from above.
For all that knock, and knock aright,
Are welcome to our lodge to-night.

Ask help of Him that's high:
Seek grace of Him that's true:
Knock patiently, the hand is nigh,
Will open unto you.
For all that ask, seek, knock, aright,
Are welcome to our lodge to-night.

This warmed us all up, and naturally led to "Burns' Farewell," which was delivered to *Bonny Doon* with such a gusto that the fire-bells rung in the village as we shouted (encoring it *four times*):

One last request permit me here,
When yearly ye assemble a',
One round—

(Good gracious, did ever poet feel as keenly or express his feelings as naturally as Brother Robert Burns!)

One round—I ask it with a tear—
To him, the bard, that's far awa'!

The fire-bells having ceased, we were constrained to exercise our power of enforcing silence, and having knocked the entire twenty-seven down, again we blessed them with—

Our Fourth Story,

OF CHARITY NO HUMBUG.

A GOOD, but juvenile and extremely verdant little lodge, in the State of G——, had suffered frightfully since its birth, from the depredations of itinerant men and women. How this people manage it, I don't know, but there is some sort of secret communication among traveling impostors, the world over, and where they find good cultivable soil, they flock in numbers to the farming of it. They had discovered by means of their U. G. Telegraph Line, that Impartation Lodge, the one in question, was young, verdant, feeble, and generous; and they contrived to be represented, somehow, at every meeting thereof. At one time it was in the shape of a Brother "whose clerk had choused him out of his money and run away." He was in pursuit of the rascal, and only needed twenty dollars, which he would promptly return. He got the twenty dollars, and returned it in a horn. The next month a man came along, a Past Grand Something, who had been lying at the point of death, he said (but anybody not greener than May clover would have said, "at the orifice of a whisky-jug"), in a neighboring town, and expended his funds, which, however, was a small matter, for as soon as he got home, which he could easily do upon twenty-three dollars and a half, exact calculation, "he would draw it from the Grand Treasurer, add six dollars and fifty cents to the amount, as a donation to the charity-fund of Impartation Lodge, and remit the whole by the earliest mail." Of course, he got the twenty-three fifty, and remitted it by a mail so early that it never reached its place of destination at all.

The third case, as one of the brethren feelingly observed to us, was "railly too bad." Of course, it was a woman, of course a widow, of course with six children (widows applying for Masonic charity are limited to six), and, of course, she was trying to "get back to them." Her husband had been a *high Mason* (it was afterward ascertained that he was hung at Vicksburg); had given millions to the cause of Masonry, and, she intimated her opinion (though she would not insist upon it, as it was merely a woman's notion), had impoverished his family by his generosity in that direction. "How much would do her?" Well, here was a little memorandum. Here was the landlord's bill, and she needed some shoes, and the stage-fare, etc., etc. Upon the whole she thought probably thirty dollars would take her to her children, the youngest of whom, she said it with a tear, was not a healthy child, and she sometimes doubted whether it would live to grow up. But the other five would live, and she would teach them to pray nightly for her benefactors, the dear Masons of Impartation Lodge.

The dear Masons of Impartation Lodge of course raised the thirty dollars, borrowing it on the strength of a joint-note, bought the shoes (sevens), paid the hotel-keeper and the stage-fare, etc., and saw her safely off to her little flock, whom she doubtless some day or other reached; though they heard of her visiting seventy odd lodges right straight along, and this must have occupied several months of her journey. Of course they made no calculation of getting *that* money back, but it was delightful to discover, as they did, that her whole story was a lie, and she a humbug, her husband a gambler, hung by a mob, and her children yet unborn.

Other cases similar to these occurred, until the dear Brothers of Impartation Lodge began to doubt one another's integrity, to look upon every traveling Mason as an impostor, and to suspect that the Masonic institution itself was but a nest of unclean birds. Attempting to stand upon the perpendicular of caution, they, in fact, began to lean *backward.* It was at this time that a stranger, from Georgia, knocked at the door of the lodge, as a visitor. He stood a fine examination and was admitted. Asking permission, at a proper moment, he declared that he was on his way, on horseback, from Iowa to

Georgia, when at the last village, a few miles back, his horse had lain down and died, leaving him on foot with but little money to pursue his way; that learning of the vicinity of a Masonic lodge open that night, he had hurried hither on foot, to ask a temporary loan to purchase another horse, promising to refund the amount so soon as he arrived home.

It is needless to say he did n't get it; but one of the members who had accidentally read the Ancient Charges upon this subject, averred that it was the duty of the Lodge to give him *work*, or tell him where he could get it. Brother Coldstreet, please to quote the passage in question.

"*Behavior toward a strange Brother.*

"You are cautiously to examine him in such a method as prudence shall teach you, that you may not be imposed upon by an ignorant, false pretender, whom you are to reject with contempt and derision, and beware of giving him any hints of knowledge.

"But if you discover him to be a true and genuine Brother, you are to respect him accordingly; and if he is in want you must relieve him if you can, or else direct him how he may be relieved. You must employ him some days, or else recommend him to be employed. But you are not charged to do beyond your ability; only to prefer a poor Brother that is a good man and true, before any other poor people in the same circumstances."

Exactly so; and that was the passage, or a part of which, one of the members, having accidentally read, so opportunely quoted on that occasion. Learning that the visitor was a blacksmith, and having just then several companies of cavalry horses to be shod for the Mexican campaign, he offered, in the generosity of his heart, to give one of them to the Georgia Brother as a job, and to pay him at the rate of three dollars per day for executing it. Some of the Brethren, a little pricked in conscience, thought, may be—perhaps—it might be better, etc., etc.; but the result was, that he was sent for to the anteroom, whither he had retired, and the proposition made him in a semi-sheepish manner by the Master.

To the astonishment of every one present, he accepted it, and gladly. It *was* remarkable, for I hardly knew a case like it. It is so much easier to beg than work! However, I am stating facts as they occurred. He *did* take the job, and went to work, like another Tubal Cain, that very night, on the nails, of which, before morning, he had a peck or two done. He hammered away at the rate of two divisions on his guage, every twenty-four hours. He did his work well. This his employer was bound to acknowledge, having got three severe kicks while too critically inspecting it. He scarcely took time to eat or sleep. Withal, he continued at it so uncomplaining, and looked so cheerful, and even happy, that the Brethren of the lodge, neglecting their own business, got into the way of coming to the shop to stare at him, as though the sight of an honest Mason in distress was a phenomenon not to be too lightly esteemed. Drinks, and chaws, and pleasant chats, were offered him every hour, but all most courteously declined "for want of time to enjoy them."

The thing couldn't last. The feelings of the Brethren got every day warmer and higher in his favor, and their stings of conscience more and more acute, as they watched him. Whenever his mild blue eye fell upon one of their faces for an instant, the party hid himself, ashamed. The Master was compelled to call a meeting of the lodge.

At that meeting all concurred, save one, in opinion, that a horse should be bought for the strange Brother, and he sent home to Georgia at once. The one exception was from the Brother who had loaned the thirty dollars to the Mason's widow a few months before, and who was in a condition to fight any man who alluded to it. He suggested, rather morosely, that the fellow was probably a bigger rascal than the rest, only more cunning and hypocritical. For this remark, he was ordered out of the lodge, and would have been promptly expelled without trial, Grand Lodge or no Grand Lodge, but for his humble submission, confession, and apology. One hundred dollars was raised by subscription and deposited on the altar, within ten minutes afterward, the morose Brother cheerfully contributing twenty-five dollars for his share, and a committee was sent down to the shop to bring the Georgia Brother up. This they accomplished after a struggle, for he was anxious to finish another horse that afternoon, and he was introduced with his grimy, honest, blacksmith's leathern apron on, his face dingy with soot and dank with sweat, his hands hard and black as the very iron he had been shaping. The action of the lodge was then explained to him, and he was induced, but with some difficulty, to take the money and throw up his cavalry job. He started home bright and early the next morning, and, I need not add, sent back to Impartation Lodge a glorious letter of thanks and kind wishes, with a small parallelogram of paper in it, which, upon one end, displayed the Roman letter C.

This story was well received. The fog gave forth sounds expressive of the warmest approbation, and the ex-Congressmen was heard to say, as if addressing old Jimmy Davids close by, that "there is an *anthem* of fraternal feeling, whose grand and heavenly notes have been pealing since the day the matchless Solomon arranged the deathless harmony. Myriads who are making their solemn march toward the boundary of time, *understand the music*, and join their voices to the accord. They seize the echo as it rolls back to them from the myriads who have gone beyond their straining sight into the shadows of the unknown world; they teach the key-note and the pitch to those who *are* to follow after them, and thus Friendship's music is never silent, its secret is never lost. The air will never cease to vibrate with it until time shall be no more." But it sounded very much, to us, like a part of some speech he had previously delivered, and we have no doubt it was. At any rate, the effect of the story was much of that sort; for, upon the suggestion of Brother Gabriel, the Secretary, the case was incidentally mentioned of the widow Libby, whose cabin had been burned a few nights before, and it being well known that *she* was a Mason's widow, for Brother Libby had died in worthy and full membership, it was suggested to us then and there to lift a collection in her favor. This was done, and we took our own hat around, thrusting it here and there into the fog as we could see a spark of fire indicating a pipe, and withdrawing it whenever we heard anything drop. It is none of the reader's business how much the Widow Libby made out of us that night, but there was a yellow piece, evidently the gift of the ex-Congressman, and a smaller one, whose donor shall be nameless, and enough more to buy two hundredweight of meal at the highest retail price. So much for the story of Impartation Lodge. We had often enough seen the effect of a good anecdote upon the pocket before, but this was a case worth noting. In one instance, we heard the Master of a lodge tell a most moving thing (we shall always believe he manufactured it out of whole cloth) about some object of distress he had once witnessed, and when he got our eyeballs generally to glistening, he suggested the case of a widow close by, who was sick, poor, and heartbroken. The old man proposed himself to make a small contribution in her favor, but warned the lodge that no one must give *over five cents*, and, to secure that amount, ordered the ballot-box around, beginning with himself. When his five cents fell in, a singular phenomenon was remarked by all of us, viz.: that that diminutive coin rattled as if accompanied by several others, and fell to the bottom with a weight rarely known to such little pieces. This, of course, however, was all in our imagination. We followed his example literally, each depositing *exactly five cents*, and then the box was brought back again to the east. Before opening it, however, the Master directed another old Brother present, who tried to preach sometimes, to open the Scriptures, then displayed at Ecclesiastes xii, at 1 Kings xvii, commencing at the tenth verse. He did so, and our wondering ears heard the word of God, as follows:

"Elijah arose and went to Zarephath. And when he came to the gate of the city, behold, the widow woman was there gathering of sticks, and he called to her, and said, Fetch me, I pray thee, a little water in a vessel, that I may drink.

"And as she was going to fetch it, he called to her, and said, Bring me, I pray thee, a morsel of bread in thine hand.

"And she said, As the Lord thy God liveth, I have not a cake, but an handful of meal in a barrel, and a little oil in a cruse; and behold, I am gathering two sticks, that I may go in and dress it for me and my son, that we may eat it, and die.

"And Elijah said unto her, Fear not; go and do as thou hast said: but make me thereof a little cake first, and bring it unto me, and after make for thee and for thy son.

"For thus saith the Lord God of Israel, The barrel of meal shall not waste, neither shall the cruse of oil fail, until the day that the Lord sendeth rain upon the earth.

"And she went and did according to the saying of Elijah: and she, and he, and her house, did eat many days.

"And the barrel of meal wasted not, neither did the cruse of oil fail, according to the word of the Lord, which he spake by Elijah."

A dead silence followed this reading, which was broken with startling effect by the voice of the old Brother who sometimes tried to preach, who, at a wink from the Master, commenced a prayer which would scarcely have passed muster in Her Majesty's

Chapel, but moved all present to tears. So far as we can recall it now, it reviewed the case of the poor widow, her barrel and cruse, and her miraculous supply, and besought of God, in terms calculated to move the Divine heart, that "a blessing, similar in kind, if not in degree," might be vouchsafed to each one "then in Divine presence," who had "stood in the place of God" toward the "widow and the fatherless" that night. The ballot-box was then opened, and although there were but thirty-eight of us present, all told, and at five cents each there should have been only one dollar and ninety cents in the box, yet, by some inexplicable circumstance, never explained, the collection was more than twelve times that amount!

We told this anecdote, following on our Impartation story, and the thing tickled the twenty-seven mightily. Of course, in that number, there was at least one shallow-pated fellow, and he (it was Isham Borneo, a man of feeble intellect) was silly enough to suggest, talking to Billy Davids, that "he knowed better than all that five-cent story come to — *he* knowed they must have drapt more 'n half a *dollar* a a-piece. You could n't fool him," etc., etc.; but he was stopped by the ex-Congressman, who exhorted him "not to make a natural Billy of himself," and we took the floor again.

The ex-Congressman remarked that he had understood we were in the habit of making memoranda from our reading, and the conversation of men as we meet them, and from our own reflections from hour to hour; and asked, if it was so, would we be so urbane as to read to the lodge from the last page of our memorandum-book? Readily assenting, we gathered the representatives of the three lesser lights on the table before us, opened our well-thumbed book, and read as follows:

"That Masons are bound to spread the mantle of charity over the failings of their Brethren, remembering that the wisest have erred, and that each is liable to fall, does not conflict with the maxim that discipline must be dealt to the refractory. It is those who, being often counseled, obstinately persist in error, who are the proper subjects of discipline in the lodge; and the lodge that neglects to reprimand, suspend, or expel (the only grades of punishment known to the institution), inflicts a fatal wound upon itself.

"Steadiness of purpose overcomes difficulties; gives the strength of a happy conscience; imparts dignity and honor to the character, and insures success. Many a Master, profoundly discouraged at the outset with the weight of ignorance and obstinacy opposing him, has found in steadiness of purpose, a victory as glorious to himself as profitable to those upon whose minds he is at work.....The goodness of God consists in his justice, wisdom, truth, and mercy. How proper, then, that whenever his adorable name is uttered in the performance of our mystic rites, we should all—from the youngest Entered Apprentice to the Worshipful Master—with reverence most humbly bow?....It was an ancient practice among Masons, while working the lectures, to close every section with a toast. This is still continued among many foreign Masons.

"More than one episode occurred on the fearful battle-field of Buena Vista, in which Masonry bore its wonted part. An American officer borne down in the fatal ravine by the press of foes, made the mystic sign. It was recognized by a Mexican officer, who rushed obediently forward to the rescue, but in vain. Before he could interpose his hand, the bayonet had done its work..... The Masonic apron belonging to Washington, is now the property of the Grand Lodge of Pennsylvania; a lock of his hair is in the possession, carefully inclosed in a golden casket, of the Grand Lodge of Massachusetts. Much of his Masonic regalia may be seen in the hall of the old lodge at Alexandria, Va

The ex-Congressman thanked us, and requested us to go on with,

Our Fifth Story,

OF THE HAUNTED LODGE.

THE hour of *three past Low xii*, is a good time, my Brethren, for tales of *diablerie*, witchcraft, and terror. At this very moment every ghost that is ever permitted to circumambulate his own grave, is engaged in that interesting work. Satan, if allowed to walk the earth, is walking it now, at a 2.40 pace. Murdered men, outraged and murdered women, strangled and murdered infants, if ever permitted to fly about the country and shriek, and scare travelers, are doing those very things at this moment. ("O Lord"—from Jimmy Davids in the fog—"don't talk that way!") Frightful shapes, if ever allowed to hide behind stumps, and gibber at belated Masons, are hiding and gibbering at them now. Dying wretches waiting for death to come and lay his bony hands upon their throats, won't wait long at this hour. For down by the sea-coast, were you there, you would see 't is about the turn of the tide, and the skeleton monster is passing swiftly over the earth, from bed to bed, relaxing jaws, stopping hearts' flow, glazing eyes, silencing tongues, doing his work heartlessly, cruelly, murderously; and the cries, and tears, and curses of bereft mortals, follow on his track. ("Then, my Brethren, let us imitate the good man in his virtuous conduct, his unfeigned piety to his God, and his inflexible fidelity to his trust, that, like him, we may welcome the grim tyrant Death, and receive him as a kind messenger sent by our Supreme Grand Master, to translate us from this imperfect, to that all-perfect, glorious, and celestial lodge above," etc., etc. Thus, and more, exhorted Brother Coldstreet from the fog, animated thereto by the horrid reflections our remarks had awakened within his breast. A dead silence from the other twenty-six, and a general cessation of smoking.)

At this solemn moment then, my Brethren, how appropriate that I should tell you a regular *ghost story.* It shall be no claptrap. I won't humbug you with the story of the lodge that broke up one night without ceremony, on account of a mysterious noise that muttered "*Death!* DEATH!! DEATH!!!" from the roof; nor the procession which on its way to the grave was dispersed suddenly by a fearful shriek from the coffin; nor will I move your manly hearts by the mysterious taps that used to be heard on the walls of Fagin Lodge on the third Saturday night of each month, and so annoyed the members that they changed their meetings to the second Saturday, when the tapper ceased. Likewise I will spare you the recital of that fearful incident of the *Shapeless Horror* that broke up Caracturus Lodge by its regular appearance at their communications, and the

Shrieking Voice which followed the Master of Oriental Lodge wherever he went, and finally caused his resignation, and the *Devilish Din* that I heard myself when Carbon Chapter held its first meeting; and the *Shifting Skull* that moved across the table one night in the sight of all of us, and terrified me in particular most horribly. These things are not all substantiated as they should be, and I prefer to leave them out. ("Gracious goodness, Brother Morris, do stop that sort of talk!" from old Billy again. "I shan't dare to go out of nights for a month!" Sounds of scornful laughter from young Doctor Griggson in the fog, who, it is said, sleeps on skeletons, and keeps his medicines in a coffin as a fancy cupboard. "Hold your tongue, and let him go on," from the ex-Congressman.)

Sparing you anything of that sort, then, as unworthy such an intellectual group, I will describe an incident, every item of which I can substantiate from my personal knowledge.

There is in a neighboring State a village which I will call for form's sake, *Chestnutville.* It is peculiar in its locality and historical surroundings. On three sides of it flows Floyd Creek, in size almost a river. The peninsula thus formed was the graveyard of the aborigines for countless ages, and its very earth is the ashes of departed mortals. In the bricks burned from its clay, you may see human teeth, and the marks of the fragments of human skulls. ("Bless my heart; isn't that too much?" from the fog again.) Upon the smooth face of its beech-trees are drawn all manner of horrible imaginings, tortured captives, merciless torturers, devilish contrivances for exaggerating human pain. The bed of the creek abounds in human skeletons. The muscles attach themselves to bony structures; the catfish poke out their counterfeit angle-worms from the eye-cavities of skulls ("Mighty horrors!"—old Billy, once more); the little boys fishing, fish up infants' frames, and old men's single pieces. It is emphatically a locality of horrors.

The literature of *Chestnutville* partakes of a ghastly tone. During the Sabbath I spent there I found *The Pirates' Own Book* read in Sunday-school, while the Rev. Obadiah Sturn preached from the text of the *Witch of Endor*, and sang a paraphrase of Satan's appearing among the sons of the Lord to ask permission to tempt Job. The prayer-meeting that night was the most fearful exhibition of suggested horrors possible to conceive of. Children generally were born at Chestnutville with *marked* countenances, the prevailing superstition somehow affecting the health of their mothers and depreciating from their personal appearance.

It was my lot to give a course of lectures at *Chestnutville*, and a fearful job I had of it. I think an extra tinge of melancholy was added by that three days' work to my bile. I have shirked grave-yards ever since, and a skull and cross-bones give me a tremor formerly unknown to me. The first night of my lectures I took a scare from observing that the brethren, when they left the lodge, all went in a body down the same road, though they lived in different directions, and kept shoulder-to-shoulder order as compactly as a flock of blackbirds. On our way to the village I observed a dilapidated skeleton of a building off to the right, in an old field, and was surprised to see that none of the Brethren would look in that direction. I asked them what building it was, and the Master in reply hoarsely whispered, "For the land's sake, hush, till we get by it!" This was sufficiently startling, but when the company had all passed this place, they separated with an understanding that I was not to be told what it meant till I got to bed.

The story was that the old building had once been the lodge-room, and that it was haunted. That every Tuesday night the raps of the gavel were distinctly heard in it from about seven until midnight. That an old decrepit negro, whose cabin was in a corner of the field, said he could sometimes hear "drefful sounds," such as, "Why in the west, Brother?" and such as that; and that, when the raps ceased about midnight, there followed bursts of laughter and reveling as if a company of jolly ghosts were having a regular time of it. All this was whispered in my ear after I went to bed, and the result in my own mind was, that I covered up my head under the blanket, left my candle burning till it burned out, and then gave myself up to a fit of the horrors that lasted till daylight.

The next morning I took an early walk in the direction of the haunted lodge, calling first on the old negro to gather, if possible, something clearer on the subject, before pursuing my investigation into the building itself. The African was a grizzly-headed old fellow, cunning as a fox, and had, doubtless, stolen more chickens than any hundred of that class of canines. At first he was shy of me, but, upon the presentation of a quarter and a plug of tobacco, which I had brought along for the purpose, he became more communicative. He declared the story was all true; that every Tuesday night "dreffal sounds" were heard there, and that when the wind blew in his direction he could recognize much of what passed. Upon my closer interrogatories, he repeated many expressions, which, though none of them appertained to the secrets of Masonry, were such as are peculiar to a Mason's lodge, and convinced me that he was thus far telling the truth. Yet the old darkey evidently did n't tell the whole story; and though he solemnly avowed his belief that it was "all fants that made dem orful noises," there was a cunning twinkle in his eye that denied his words. Not wishing, however, to excite his suspicions that I disbelieved him, I bid him good-morning, and went toward the old building, closely watched, as I could see, by the old negro. It was a cheerful-looking edifice. In every corner of it, shells, formerly plowed up from the old field, had been piled. Some of them had been stuck in the angles of "the walls," some were garnishing stakes set up around the building, and all of them grinned at me in the early sun as if to convey a friendly good-morning. Huge thigh bones, dry and pallid as pokestalks, lay here in confusion, and the whole scene recalled to mind the vision of the Valley of Dry Bones introduced into one of our Manuals.

The stairs which mounted to the second story, in which was the old lodge-room, were very much decayed and dangerous to use. Yet, by clinging carefully to the wall, I lifted myself over them, and stood in the once consecrated room, where a generation now moldering with the dead, had once worked the delightful work of Masonry. Here was the scene of many a circumambulation. Here many a gratified Brother had been led between the brazen pillars, and up the mystic stairway, and into the middle chamber. Here many a proof of fidelity unto death had been exemplified. Here had hung the Divine Symbol. Here had stood many a young Brother to receive those first instructions on which to build his future moral and Masonic edifice.

I examined carefully for signs of recent visitations, not by ghosts, but by men. The stairway was evidently too feeble for man's step, and there was a deep mold of fungi upon it, proving that mine was the first foot that had trodden it for many a day. But a hole in the floor, at the south-east corner of the room, presented suspicious indications of having been used as a place of entrance, the wall below it being smoothed as if by the knees and elbows of the climber, and the marks of hands visible on the edge of the rotten planks that constituted the floor. A rag of broadcloth, too, which had been torn from some man's coat was even then sticking upon the edge of a nail.

The three stations were still standing as they had been left years before, and a cheap square box in the center, which had once done service as an altar. Upon turning this over, I found, to my surprise, a large Bible, fresh and clean, and the square and compass of heavy silver lying in it. Looking a little closer, I discovered, hanging upon a nail inside of the box, a *charter* for a lodge, regularly signed, filled out, and sealed, which bore date many years previous. Upon the three stations were new and heavy gavels, and the indentations upon the soft plank proved that they had been used by no fleshless hand. Noting these things carefully, I swung myself down the aperture, and went quietly to breakfast.

The day was spent in lecturing, during which I marked nothing peculiar in the manner of the Brethren, except their taste for the funeral service over any other portions of my instruction. If my memory serves me, I went over that ceremony eight times while with them. No allusion was made by any one to the Haunted Lodge, and I abstained from any remarks or questioning on the subject; but I selected, in my mind's eye, two of the Brothers, the Junior Deacon and Tyler, and resolved that that very night, it being Tuesday, we would settle the question of *the haunted lodge* together.

To get the time, I worked all day, at double tides, at my lectures, and having set nearly all of them to sleep by nine at night, was readily excused for the rest of the evening. I had hinted to my two selected friends that I wanted to see them at my room privately that night after the lectures were over, and when we arrived there I locked the door and laid open my business. I told them there was some stupendous humbug or other existing about that old building, described what I had seen, impressed upon their minds the disgrace of leaving such a curious affair unexplained, and asked them to accompany me that very hour to the place. ("Father of grace!" groaned old Billy Davids. "Did you go?")

It was funny to mark their evident unwillingness, struggling with the shame of being deemed cowards, and an ardent curiosity to solve the riddle. With much inward reservation they professed a willingness to accompany me, provided they were led into no danger. Calling for some strong coffee, which we drank freely, and borrowing each a pair of pistols, but without informing the landlord of our purpose, we slipped quietly out of the hotel and went to that corner of the deserted field. The raps from the *haunted house* were sounding loud and long! ("Merciful protector!" "Don't interrupt the house," responded the ex-Congressman.)

As I had anticipated, the old negro was absent from the cabin, but a good fire was burning there; a broadcloth overcoat hung on a chair before it, as if to dry, and a pair of boots lay on the floor, too small by half for the negro's feet. These things I pointed out to my now trembling companions, as important links in the chain of development soon to be made, and encouraged them in the belief that the only ghosts we should find in the *haunted lodge*, were such as had worn those garments. Taking a rapid circuit to come in from the further side of the field, toward which the wind was blowing briskly, we swiftly approached the old building. The Masonic expressions which had been repeated to me that morning by tho negro, could now be plainly heard, and the gavels rang merrily between them. The foot of some heavy person passed rapidly to and fro over the floor of the old lodge-room, and shook it until at times it seemed about to give way under the weight. There was no light in any part of the building, nor after going round it two or three times, could we find any persons outside.

The old negro, however, was asleep on the earth-floor within. We sprung upon him, overpowered him, tied his hands together, and gagged his mouth, but not until in his struggles he had given warning to the person above, who instantly ceased the work in which he had been so mysteriously engaged. Having dragged the old negro out of the building, we hastened to place ourselves, with cocked pistols, one at the opening in the floor, one at the foot of the decayed stairway, and the third as a general sentinel to circumambulate the building. Having thus cut off all means of escape, I called out to the person overhead, whoever he was, to come down, assuring him that no harm was intended him; but that if he did not, we would summon the people of the village and have him brought down by force. The threat was effectual. A clear manly voice was heard in the loft accepting the terms of surrender, and asking me if I was a Freemason? Upon my reply in the affirmative, and giving my name, he said "he had long expected me, and was only keeping the lodge alive till I should come." He then handed me down the Bible, gavels, and charter, and quietly descended, took my hand, and walked arm-in-arm with me to the cabin, followed by the old negro, whom we had by this time released. Arrived there within the influence of the fire-light, I found him a man of about sixty years of age, physically in good health and strength, but mentally quite off the balance. His thoughts ran connectedly upon no subject but Masonry; upon all others he was in the most idiotic manner flighty and obscure. He readily answered my interrogatories when he was made, what lodges he had visited, and why he pursued the mystic work in such an out-of-the-way place, time, and manner; and having surrendered up his charter to me, admitting my right to demand it, and avowing "that he had only been working under it until I should come and take charge of it," he pledged himself to do so no more.

Having got the poor maniac to sleep, we then demanded of the old negro, in a threatening manner, why he had allowed the neighbors to be so long humbugged by this affair when he could have set them right at a word. Upon which the black gave us the whole story as follows: The deranged person, whose name we may as well call Carroll, was his former master.

Mr. Carroll had been a government officer in another State some years before, in which capacity he had committed a great defalcation and then absconded. His negroes and other property had been sold for the benefit of his securities, and the one in question, being very decrepit and useless, had been bought by some humane person, who had removed with him to Chestnutville, given him his freedom and a small annuity, and settled him there for life. Some ten years afterward, his former master had suddenly appeared to him, from what quarter he never knew, and asked his protection and support. This the faithful black cheerfully gave, and he had shared with him his little means of sustenance ever since. The negro had soon discovered that Mr. Carroll was deranged, and it was not long until he found him strolling off at nights to the deserted lodge-room, where he would practice ceremonies of which the old black knew nothing more than that they scared the neighbors around, and gave a bad reputation to the house.

I will not dwell upon all the little circumstances of this case, nor explain how Mr. Carroll secured the old charter, etc. The lodge was privately informed of the facts so far as we could gather them from the negro, and means were taken to aid him in his honest and benevolent charge. A few months afterward I learned, however, that Mr. Carroll had been taken suddenly ill and died in a few hours afterward; but to this day there is not a man, woman, or child in Chestnutville, outside of the lodge, bold enough to go after nightfall within trumpet-sound of the *haunted lodge.*

The conclusion of this story disgusted everybody in the fog. Old Billy Davids, whose hair had been in an electrified condition during the first part of it, loudly ejaculated his dissatisfaction. The ex-Congressman called it a *fizzle.* Others hoped "we would n't feed them on any more such soft truck like that," and we learned from that hour *never* to give a rational explanation to a ghost story. The love of mystery is inherent in every breast, and a well-prepared yarn that selects its *dramatis personæ* from the other world, is a welcome gift to every one. But then no earthly element should be substituted for the ethereal, else there is a feeling in the minds of the auditory that their reasonable anticipations have been disappointed.

The recital of this incident, so ridiculously terminated, had the effect to turn the attention of the company to subjects of a horrible character, in which the young doctor was facetiously rich. His experiments on poisons, so fatal to the brute creation, afforded him a pure joy in the recital, which few of us, it is to be hoped, shared. His resurrection-exploits, as he related them, had almost depopulated the graveyard, and, if his statements could be believed, he would something rather have a corpse in his bed-room at night, than a live body of either sex. We soon got tired of this, however, and then old Billy Davids had his turn. He had once gone through a scene calculated to turn a man's very wig gray, having in a lonely place, and late at night, found an open coffin strangely occupying the middle of the road he was traversing. Others pitched in with stories more or less unreasonable and ghostly, and then, after we got our breath, we changed the subject to that of dreams. We had gone to sleep one night, after reading Preston's Illustrations, and dreamed that we were in King Solomon's presence, just at the opportune moment when he was delivering his final charge to the craftsmen who had done such faithful service at his command. This was a fortunate occurrence for us, for we had often exercised our ingenuity in guessing what sort of a legacy the king gave them at parting, and were never quite satisfied upon the subject. We therefore listened with both ears while the Royal Philosopher descanted upon the merits of those who had earned distinction, enlarged upon the honors and rewards that would inure to them as temple builders, and warned them against the errors of disobedience and pride.

The whole was too good to be lost, and so, when we awoke and arose next day, we took to our "rhyming ware," and embalmed the whole as nearly in the Egyptian style as we knew how:

KING SOLOMON TO HIS BUILDERS.

King Solomon sat in his mystic chair,
His chair on a platform high;
And his words addressed
Through the listening West,
To a band of Brothers nigh;

Through the West and South,
These words of truth,
To a band of Brothers nigh:

"Ye builders, go! ye have done your work,
The capestone standeth sure;
From the lowermost rock
To the loftiest block,
The fabric is secure.
From the Arches' swell,
To the Pinnacle,
The fabric is secure.

"Go, crowned with fame! old time will pass,
And many changes bring;
But the Deed you've done,
The circling sun,
Through every land will sing:
The moon and stars,
While earth endures,
Through every land will sing.

"Go, build like *this!* from the Quarries vast,
The precious stones reveal;
There's many a block,
In the matrice-rock,
Will honor your fabrics well:
There's many a beam,
By the mountain-stream,
Will honor your fabric well.

"Go, build like *this!* divest with skill
Each superfluity:
With critic eye,
Each fault espy,
Be zealous, fervent, free!
By the perfect Square,
Your work prepare;
Be zealous, fervent, free!

"Go, build like *this!* to a fitting place,
Raise up the Ashlars true;
On the Trestle-board,
Of your Master's Lord,
The GRAND INTENTION view!
In each mystic line,
Of the vast design,
The GRAND INTENTION view!

"Go, build like *this!* and when exact
The Joinings scarce appear;
With the Trowel's aid,
Such cement spread,
As time can never wear!
Lay thickly round,
Such wise compound,
As time can never wear.

"Go, Brothers; thus enjoined, farewell!
Spread o'er the darkened West!
Illume each clime,
With art sublime,
The noblest truths attest!
Be MASTERS now,
And as you go,
The noblest truths attest!"

These sentiments aroused the ex-Congressman, who, we apprehended, had been slightly dozing on his bench. He begged leave, in his heavy, parliamentary way, to agree with us in our views as to what King Solomon's bequest was likely to be, and slightly tickled our approbativeness as to the smoothness of the verse, etc. Say what you will, compliments from a Congressman are several shades more highly valued by us sensitive gentlemen, than those from ordinary quarters. Yet who would be a Congressman?

A loud crow from an adjoining hen-roost called out our inquiry as to the time of night, which we found, upon examination, to be verging upon day-break. The weather, too, was clearing up. The rain had ceased, and there was a prospect of a fair sky. We, therefore, took a drink of coffee all round —at least, the writer did, and, judging from the noises, the other twenty-seven imitated so worthy an example—and announced that we had but one more story to tell ere daylight would separate us. This roused up the crowd. Free calls for tobacco implied that the supply was running short, a last stock of pipes was manufactured, and, when perfect stillness was restored, we began

Our Sixth Story,

OF THE MASTER ELECT.

DURING the pleasant night now ending, I have said little or nothing, my Brethren, of official duties, cases of discipline, or the means of awakening and sustaining a band of Craftsmen in the performance of duty. These topics have formed the staple, as you know, of many a lecture delivered you in times gone by, whose memories, mingling with the memories of this happy night, will alleviate many a moment of sorrow, many a burden of toil and pain in the pilgrimage T G A O T U shall allot to us ere we reach T C L A. It was not well, I thought, to propose topics too serious or contemplative for your seven hours' entertainment in the *Night in the Lodge-Room*, just now ending.

But now, in closing, I would speak to you yet in the same pleasant story-telling strain, of the relationship which exists, according to the oldest regulations known to this oldest of associations, between the Master of the lodge and the membership. In illustration of which, I will instance a circumstance that occurred in Lux Fuit Lodge, and the occasion shall be the annual election of its officers on the natal day of St. John the Evangelist.

No election held in this lodge for many years had excited so much interest, or so general an attendance, as the one in question. The old Master, Brother Campbell, Scotch by birth, as his name indicates, and strongly Scotch in his views of government, his piety, his industry of research, and aptness of application, after twelve years of consecutive service under the letter G of that lodge, had claimed the exemption due to age, infirmities, and faithful labor, to decline a re-election. The query as to who should take his place was one calculated to interest the members of the lodge in a peculiar manner.

In point of fact, it is about as difficult to supply the place of such a Master as Brother Donald Campbell, without detriment to the lodge, as it is to afford the sorrowing widow a second husband, who will prove a proper substitute for the one she has lost. There is so much difference in men that one can never learn the secret of the success of his predecessor so as to follow it. Each must, to a considerable extent, work by his own views of right and wrong; and so the loss of such a Master as Brother Campbell is well-nigh irreparable.

To illustrate this matter further, it was the practice of the old Scotchman to read and expound a brief passage of Scripture at every meeting of the lodge; to offer up his own prayers at the opening; to lead in the musical portions invariably introduced at every turn in the Masonic ceremonial; to give an elaborate lecture upon some historical or philosophical point in Masonry; to read such correspondence as his busy pen had secured from other lodges or intelligent Masons; to confer his own degrees with accuracy and impressiveness; to repeat catechetically the whole of the accompanying lectures; to visit surrounding lodges in person for the furtherance of good feeling and mutual advantage; to represent his lodge at every Communication of the Grand Lodge; in brief, to do, say, and plan all that appertained to the weal of the Craft in general, and his own lodge in particular. How could the place of such a man be supplied?

The answer was, *by Brother Benton.* This man was a pupil and protégé of Brother Campbell's, having received initiation at his hands, and sat at his feet metaphorically ever since the hour he was brought to light. He was his son-in-law, and dwelt in the same neighborhood. In all Masonic missions to surrounding lodges, and in the annual journey to Grand Lodge, they were companions. Brother Benton had served the lodge in every capacity, save the posts of Tyler and Treasurer, having begun his official career as Junior Deacon; acted as Master's proxy, as Senior Deacon; kept the books two years as Secretary; governed the Craft while at refreshment for a twelvemonth, and while at labor for two; and knew, if any man did, the ways and designs of the long-time Master. The answer, therefore, was *Brother Benton;* and the general attendance of the members that day was to secure, if possible, by unanimous vote, his election.

The meeting was solemnized by the farewell remarks of Brother Campbell. Few present had ever heard anything in Masonry so affecting. He recounted his services, and asked if he had not earned an honorable dismissal? He cited the members present and absent, naming each by his name, and demanded to know if there was aught against him, in his official character, during all the twelve years he had wielded that emblem of authority at their request? He summoned the dead, who lay in the Masonic portion of the graveyard, in plain view from the windows of the lodge; he called each by his name (for the name of each was printed on the Memorial Board in the south-east corner of the lodge), and demanded whether any, who had gone to his last rest, had borne with him one remembrance of unkindness for anything that he, his Master, had done or said to him while living? And to every appeal, whether to the living or dead, there was a marked and flattering silence.

Then he said: "Never let the breath of scandal

assail me. As I sit by my fireside in my pain and decrepitude, wearing out the few hours yet allotted to me, let me feel assured that when the tongues of my Brethren are in any way busying themselves concerning me, it will be in love, honor, and respect. To my heart there will come a secret pang, sharp and torturing, if ever thoughtless or ungrateful Masons speak lightly of my services, or my instructions, during the long years I have presided over this lodge; and when I go to rest (it can not be long), I ask that every member of this lodge shall accompany me on that journey, and that, in the hearing of my friends and neighbors, and the Brethren of surrounding lodges, and the strangers who, peradventure, may be present that day, a declaration shall be made by the then acting Master of *Lux Fuit Lodge*, that the departed Brother Campbell did honest service to his Brethren in his day and generation, and defies any man to gainsay it."

Then the venerable Brother took his diploma, old and worn, and bearing the signature of one of Scotland's noblest lords, and asked that it be preserved forever in the archives of that lodge in his memory. He took his watch, heavy and golden, by which the time of opening and closing the lodge had been so long and so accurately measured, and laid it upon the pedestal in the East, as his donation for the use and guidance of their Masters elect, so long as the lodge should live. This was followed up by the presentation to the lodge of the hall and the lot of ground on which it stood, both of which were his property, and which he now presented to his Brethren as a clear gift, for the consideration of love and respect, and then he directed that the annual election of Lux Fuit Lodge should be proceeded with.

Brother Benton was, of course, elected, and unanimously. It was a tribute due alike to his past services and his promising merits. For his Wardens, two were selected who were known to entertain the same views upon Masonic government and moral principles as himself; for it is a poor compliment to a young Master to checkmate his plans with Wardens who differ from his views; and the South-east was filled, as heretofore, by an excellent Mason of an intellectual cast. Each officer received an unanimous vote to his respective position.

It had been understood and agreed beforehand that the installation of officers this year should be, as usual, public, and the next day, which was Saturday, had been set apart for that ceremony. The neighboring lodges had acceded to an invitation to come and assist in installing Brother Campbell's successor, and preparations for a festival had been made upon a large scale. Brother Campbell announced that he should be prepared to deliver an address, as his last legacy to *Lux Fuit Lodge*, and appointed a reverend Brother to follow it with a short discourse upon "the religious element in Masonry,"

These arrangements being settled, and but a short hour remaining before night, the old Master gave his usual lecture at parting, in which he adapted the words of DeWitt Clinton, who had said as early as 1793, that

> "A Mason is bound to consult the happiness and to promote the interests of his Brother; to avoid everything offensive to his feelings; to abstain from reproach, censure, and unjust suspicions; to warn him of the machinations of his enemies; to advise him of his errors; to advance the reputation and welfare of his family; to protect the chastity of his house; to defend his life, his property, and, what is dearer to a man of honor, his character against unjust attacks; to relieve his wants and his distress; to instill into his mind proper ideas of conduct in the department of life which he is called to fill; and let me add, to foster his schemes of interest and promotion, if compatible with the paramount duties a man owes to the community."

Brother Campbell indorsed all this as the ancient Scotch theory of Masonic duty, and enlarged upon each of its inculcations. Then, with a friendly word to each, and an exhortation to stand to and abide by these ancient doctrines in their daily intercourse with each other, he closed the lodge and departed. Brother Benton, who remained a little longer, was accompanied by a group of friends on horseback to the ford, where, it being quite dark, he took leave of them, waved his hand and dashed into the stream. He was heard to shout, in a cheerful tone, Good-night, was seen once more to wave his arm, and then the darkness enveloped him.

Great was the gathering upon the following day. Popular as old Mr. Campbell was, it was felt by his neighbors—Masons and non-Masons—that a general turn-out upon such an occasion as this, would be esteemed by him as a personal compliment; and there were but few settlers within three miles but what mounted something in quadrupedal form and "came to the celebration." The neighboring lodges appeared in full force. From each direction a long cavalcade of Masons, well mounted, and displaying the aprons and scarfs of their Craft, wound over the hilly country, and met at the door of *Lux Fuit Lodge*. To the gratification of all, the Grand Master himself did honor both to his own standing and to the occasion, and came down more than one hundred miles to unite with his Brethren in so interesting an event. This was the crowning point of the general joy.

Eleven o'clock arrived, and Brother Campbell, the Grand Master upon his right, opened the lodge. His short explication of Scripture, his strongly-accented Scotch prayer, the Masonic opening ode, were all performed as usual, and his lecture exhibiting the three-twist cable tow of a Mason, was even better than usual. The preliminaries of the procession were arranged, the Marshal of the day being one who had served as colonel in his country's cause, in more than one bloody fight. All was in readiness to march, but still—and the matter began to be whispered about as somewhat strange—Brother Benton had not arrived! A messenger was sent to the church hard by, where the ladies were assembled, to inquire of his wife if anything was the matter with him, and brought back for answer, "that Mr. Benton had not returned home the preceding night, but was engaged, she supposed, in the lodge until it was too late!"

And now a messenger knocked at the door, who brought tidings from Brother Benton. He was admitted; but his scared face and trembling limbs were for awhile the only story he could tell. Looking toward the East, and observing the genial, expectant countenance of Brother Campbell, he covered his face with his hands and wept aloud.

The messenger had been one of those who accompanied Brother Benton to the ferry the evening before, had shaken his parting hand, had answered his cheerful hail, had seen him disappear in the darkness. Alas! it was the darkness of death! His horse, it is supposed, stumbled and threw him into the water. Some sharp point in the rocky ford had met his forehead, and the waters had ingulfed him; for the next morning his body was found lying a mile below upon the banks, at the very gateway of the Brother who now essayed to tell this fearful tale!

Down, like an aged tree, fell the venerable Master from his station in the East, and ere high twelve was announced in the South that day, his spirit, for years but loosely occupying the clay tenement of his body, had flown to unite with that of his son-in-law, in whatever regions of space the souls of good men occupy.

The festival was postponed until the morrow, and then it was made a funeral. The Grand Master and the delegations remained in the vicinity, and held that night a *Sorrow Lodge*, which will never be forgotten by those who formed it. On the following day they took possession of their own, the Master and the Master elect, and bore them to an honorable interment in the Masonic portion of the necropolis hard by. There the Grand Master (few could have done it better), raised his voice until the voices of the mighty pines overhead were hushed in silence, and demanded, as the old Scotchman had but two days before requested, "if any man there, whether living or dead, had been wronged in word or act by this man now lying with uncovered face, prepared for his last sleep?" And the dead and the living were equally silent!

Thus closed our story of "the Master elect," and now it was broad daylight and time to depart. We formed a circle and sung in unison a farewell ode. Being requested to do so by the ex-Congressman, we repeated the lines which follow:

THE LEVEL AND THE SQUARE.

We meet upon *the Level* and we part upon *the Square*;—
What words of precious meaning those words Masonic are!
Come, let us contemplate them, they are worthy of a thought,
With the highest, and the lowest, and the rarest they are fraught.

We meet upon *the Level*, though from every station come;
The rich man from his mansion, and the poor man from his home;
For the one must leave his wealth and state outside the Mason's door,
And the other find his true respect upon the checkered floor.

We part upon *the Square*, for the world must have its due;
We mingle with the multitude, a cold, unfriendly crew,
But the influence of our gatherings in memory is green,
And we long upon *the Level* to renew the happy scene.

* * * * * * * *

There's a world where all are equal—we are hurrying toward it fast;
We shall meet upon *the Level* there, when the gates of death are past;
We shall stand before the Orient, and our Master will be there
To try the blocks we offer by his own unerring *Square.*

We shall meet upon *the Level* there, but never thence depart
There's a *Mansion*—'tis all ready for each trusting, faithful heart—
There's a *Mansion* and a welcome—and a multitude is there,
Who have met upon *the Level*, and been tried upon *the Square.*

Let us meet upon *the Level* then, while laboring patient here;
Let us meet and let us labor, though the labor be severe;
Already in the Western Sky the signs bid us prepare,
To gather up our Working tools, and part upon *the Square.*

Hands round, ye faithful Masons, form the bright, fraternal chain,
We part upon *the Square* below, to meet in heaven again.
O! what words of precious meaning those words Masonic are—
We meet upon the Level and we part upon the Square!

Then we took those good fellows, one by one by the hand, and said "good-by." It was hard to look into those kind faces—ah, shall we see them again in the world to come?—and say it. Old Billy

Davids was deeply affected, and laying his hand upon our head he prayed in words divine, "The Lord bless thee and keep thee. The Lord make his face to shine upon thee and be gracious unto thee. The Lord lift up his countenance upon thee and give thee peace!" Brother Coldstreet, quoting from the Ancient Charges which he knew and loved so well, exhorted us to continue our mission for the good of the Craft, teaching Masons "to cultivate Brotherly love, the foundation and capestone, the element and glory of the ancient fraternity; to avoid all wrangling and quarreling, all slander and back-biting; not permitting others to slander any honest Brother, but defending his character, and doing him all good offices as far as is consistent with their honor and safety." The ex Congressman was eloquent in the expression of his good wishes—and an old Brother present who had n't said a word the livelong night, clapped us fearfully upon the back, and declared that "though we mought n't make money or get rich in this business, yet, at the judgment day he was sure we would bring up as many *skelps* as any of 'em!"

And so that good night became of the past. By a little help from the outside, the whole of us descended to the earth, and each pursued his several way. We have never been there since. But we have learned from time to time how the little band prospers; how they have dropped off, one by one, accepting the friendly invitation of death; how one by one they have added to their members of the rising generation, until they number on the Grand Lodge books thrice the tale of those who faced us that night; and how all, both old and young, treasure up in loving hearts the memory of him who spent his "NIGHT IN THE LODGE-ROOM!"

THE END.

BOOKS

FOR

FREEMASONS.

UNDER this title we have commenced a series of Masonic works, to be extended to about twenty or twenty-five volumes, of which the

Tales of Masonic Life

is the first. They will be of the size of this, and uniformity of binding, colors of cloth, etc., will be adopted. Their contents will be, like the present volume, entirely original and practical in their character, and full of animated and sparkling life. Price for each volume, post-paid, $1.

The second volume is now in press. It is

THE MASONIC MARTYR,

being the biography of Eli Bruce, Sheriff of Niagara County, N. Y., who, for his fidelity to Masonic principles, was incarcerated for thirty months in the Canandaigua jail. This is a volume of startling interest, and develops the most stirring events of the anti-Masonic warfare. Price, post-paid, $1.

The other numbers of the series will be continued at intervals of three months, and the whole will form an elegant practical set of twenty Masonic works, suitable for all classes of readers, both Masons and non-Masons.

MORRIS & MONSARRAT,
LOUISVILLE, KY.

THE

Freemason's Monitor,

BY THOMAS SMITH WEBB,

With Annotations, and an Appendix,

BY ROB MORRIS.

This Monitor, first published in 1797, and since issued in some thirty editions, is the source from which all the Charts, Craftsmen, Manuals, Trestle Boards, etc., etc., have been taken, with which the country has been flooded, and is far superior to any of them. There is a general disposition manifested, among the more intelligent class of Masons, to discard the imitations and return to the original.

Morris's edition is a literal copy of the work as Brother Webb left it, enriched with a great number of practical notes and remarks, such as he is so well able to give, and enlarged with an Appendix, which, in the space of about one hundred pages, presents a complete synopsis of Masonic Law. This renders it an invaluable hand-book to every Mason.

To those who are so zealously pursuing plans tending to general *uniformity of Work*, this Monitor is an essential aid.

Price, post-paid, per mail, $1 25.

MORRIS & MONSARRAT,
LOUISVILLE, KY.

www.ingramcontent.com/pod-product-compliance
Lightning Source LLC
LaVergne TN
LVHW010141110826
845151LV00002B/393

* 9 7 8 1 4 2 5 5 3 8 5 2 1 *